An excerpt from *More Than Rivals*...

"Who are you, Anna Stratford?"

Anna shivered at Ian's low growl in her ear.

The best way to figure that out was to be direct and honest about what she wanted. Starting tonight.

She raised her head. "Who am I? I'm someone who finds you very attractive. And I'm wondering if the reason you approached me on the terrace was because you find me attractive. And if so, perhaps we should do something about it. Tonight."

She held her breath as amber flames flared to life in his brown eyes.

"Fairy wings and glitter caught my attention. But I'm finding the woman who wore them to be far more intriguing." He lifted his right hand, the back of his fingers caressing her cheek, trailing sparks in their wake. "Is this why you came to my room?"

"True. I wanted—" her breath caught, leaving just enough air to exhale one word "—*you*."

Declan leaned in.

Mara's breath caught. This close, despite the dim early evening light, she could still see the fleck of bullion that radiated around his pupils. His eyes had always fascinated her, the way they faded from a crystalline blue to burnished gold. His head tilted, as if preparing to slant his mouth over hers. "Thank you for considering about the offer."

"Of course," Mara breathed back.

Declan bent his head to hers. Then his mouth missed hers and traveled past her cheek, stopping above her right ear. "Say yes," he rasped.

Sparks raced along her nervous system from the tips of her fingers to the soles of her feet, quickly followed by chagrin at having even entertained the thought that he might kiss her.

"I'll let you know," she managed to force out.

"I look forward to it." Then he straightened and smiled at her. "We made a great team. We will again."

SUSANNAH ERWIN

MORE THAN RIVALS...
&
SEVEN YEARS OF SECRETS

HARLEQUIN
DESIRE

DESIRE

Recycling programs for this product may not exist in your area.

ISBN-13: 978-1-335-45762-2

More Than Rivals... & Seven Years of Secrets

Copyright © 2023 by Harlequin Enterprises ULC

More Than Rivals...
Copyright © 2023 by Susannah Erwin

Seven Years of Secrets
Copyright © 2023 by Susannah Erwin

Harlequin Enterprises ULC
22 Adelaide St. West, 41st Floor
Toronto, Ontario M5H 4E3, Canada
www.Harlequin.com

Printed in U.S.A.

CONTENTS

MORE THAN RIVALS... 9

SEVEN YEARS OF SECRETS 233

A former Hollywood studio executive who gladly traded in her high heels and corner office for yoga pants and the local coffee shop, **Susannah Erwin** loves writing about ambitious, strong-willed people who can't help falling in love—whether they want to or not. Her first novel won the Golden Heart® Award from Romance Writers of America and she is hard at work in her Northern California home on her next. She would be over the moon if you signed up for her newsletter via www.susannaherwin.com.

Books by Susannah Erwin

Harlequin Desire

Titans of Tech

Wanted: Billionaire's Wife
Cinderella Unmasked
Who's the Boss Now?
Ever After Exes

Heirs of Lochlainn

More Than Rivals...
Seven Years of Secrets

Visit the Author Profile page
at Harlequin.com for more titles.

You can also find Susannah Erwin on Facebook,
along with other Harlequin Desire authors,
at Facebook.com/HarlequinDesireAuthors!

Dear Reader,

Welcome to the secrets and scandals of the Lochlainn family! This new two-part series begins with media mogul Keith Lochlainn, who has recently been given a terminal diagnosis. He decides to hold a contest to determine which of his newly discovered grandchildren should inherit his empire by giving them each a business objective to complete. This is a tale that has been percolating in my head for a long time, and I'm so thrilled to finally share it with you.

More Than Rivals... is the story of the first grandchild, Anna, and the setting is very dear to my heart: a theme park! I had so much fun creating my own tourist destination—after years of spending my vacations at theme parks in California and Florida—and I hope you have fun, too! And what theme park is complete without a nighttime spectacular? But the real fireworks take place between Anna and her rival to control the theme park, the enigmatic—and oh so sexy—Ian Blackburn. Anna finds herself forced to choose between pleasing her recently found grandfather and her heart...while Ian has his own family secrets to contend with that might stand in the way of a fairy-tale happily-ever-after.

Please enjoy Anna and Ian's story, and please also feel free to contact me! I'd love to know your thoughts. You can find me on Twitter, @susannaherwin; on Facebook at susannaherwinauthor; on BookBub, @susannaherwin; or at my website, www.susannaherwin.com.

Happy reading!

xoxo

Susannah

MORE THAN RIVALS...

For Charlotte,
but not until you're old enough to read this

Prologue

Six months ago

Keith Lochlainn could no longer deny reality.

He was dying.

Oh, not today. Probably not even this year.

But the doctor's report clutched in his hand—the fifth doctor he had consulted—confirmed what he had already been told: his heart had a looming expiration date and he was out of options to push the day back. No medical procedure would save him from the inevitable.

And it was inevitable, wasn't it? This wasn't news to him. All living things had a finite amount of time.

But he'd thought he would have more time to put his affairs in order. More opportunities to arrange who would succeed him at the helm of the Lochlainn Company, the multinational media conglomerate started by his father, Archibald. Control of the company still stayed within the family, with most of the shares still held by Keith. After he died, however...

Keith crumpled the sheets of paper into a ball. This was why he preferred paper to computer files; paper was far easier to destroy. Easier to pretend he'd never read the contents in the first place.

He'd planned to leave the company to his only child, Jamie. The regret of his life was that he hadn't sired more children, followed by the regret that his desire to do so had driven Jamie away as a teenager when Keith had divorced his mother, Diana, to marry a younger woman. For decades, Keith had feared he would have no heir, as wife number two through wife number five produced no offspring and Jamie rebuffed all attempts at contact, refusing any and all financial support offered by Keith.

Then, seven years ago, his son had returned to him. Smart, driven, and ambitious, Jamie had built a famed name for himself as an investigative journalist, using an old family name on his mother's side to avoid being connected to his father. But then Jamie had met someone and, although the relationship fizzled, he'd decided the globe-trotting life wasn't conducive to eventually raising a family. He'd contacted Keith about working for the Lochlainn Company and was welcomed back with open arms, any past grievances forgiven and forgotten.

But their reconciliation had been too good to be true.

Keith sighed, his shoulders slumping. He still had energy. He could and did run rings around the arrogant MBAs who ran the various divisions of the Lochlainn Company, who believed they could steer the organization better than he could. He'd be damned if he allowed his family's legacy to pass to that bunch of hyenas after his death.

A knock at the door caused Keith to snap his head up. His current wife, Catalina, entered the library, carrying a tray heaped with plates and glasses. Didn't see a coffee mug on the tray, damn it. No more caffeine for him. He stared at a generous arrangement of imported cheeses. She intercepted his look and brought him a salad.

"Chef made this for you." She placed a bowl filled with leafy greens on the table in front of his wing chair. "The rest of the food is for your one o'clock meeting."

Keith nodded and took a bite, chewing the spinach leaves methodically. Catalina settled into the chair next to him and fixed him with her dark gaze. "You're thinking about Jamie again," she said softly.

"You think you can read me so well? Bah." Keith stabbed a cherry tomato with his fork.

"I know what today is. It's hard to believe it's been seven years since...well. Since."

Keith put his fork down. If his wife wanted to poke the bear, he would oblige. "Seven years of idiotic bureaucratic tangling with the French authorities. Seven years of wasted investigations." He pointed at her. "I didn't want him declared dead. You pushed me into it."

She smiled sadly at him. "Keith, he was gone immediately. He couldn't have survived the explosion. The yacht was nothing but matchsticks. And even if he did, he would have drowned in the aftermath. Everyone agrees."

"You want to move on," Keith muttered. "You wanted Jamie declared dead, so you have unfettered claim to my money when I'm gone."

"You know that's not true. I'm not entitled to anything from you. Nor do I want your money." She placed a glass of water on the table and portioned out three pills from a plastic box, handing the first one to him. "But it was fun playing this game with you. Never gets old."

"Bah," Keith said again, and swallowed the pill. "Where's Bingham?"

Another knock sounded. Catalina rose and opened the door, and then turned back to Keith. "He's right on time."

Bingham Lockwood brushed past Catalina and planted himself in front of Keith, remaining standing.

Keith looked up at him. "Well?" he barked.

Bingham slid his gaze over to Catalina, who had followed him back into the library, and raised his eyebrows. She shook her head slightly.

"Speak," Keith snapped. "I can handle it. Don't pay attention to her."

After another exchange of glances with Catalina, Bingham handed a manila folder thick with printouts to Keith. He took it with trembling hands and placed it on the table next to his abandoned lunch. He couldn't make himself open it. "Just give me the news."

"There are two confirmed living results," Bingham said. "We're searching for more, but the records indicate this might be all."

Two. Keith exhaled. "Names? Ages? Genders?"

"Wait." Catalina picked up the folder. "You're sure?"

Bingham nodded. "We received much cooperation from former staff at the fertility clinic. The Lochlainn name goes a long way."

"And the Lochlainn checkbook, no doubt," Catalina said under her breath. "Please tell me you didn't violate any privacy or HIPAA laws."

Bingham kept his gaze focused on Keith. "Per Jamie's college roommate, Jamie supplemented his ability to pay for his university tuition by making sperm deposits at the fertility clinic in exchange for payment. There were two successful pregnancies attached to his identity number. We have ascertained the names and locations of the resulting children."

"I don't think—" Catalina started, but Keith spoke over her.

"Tell me everything about them," he demanded. "Now."

Keith was dying, true. But now he had heirs. And he'd be damned if he died before seeing one of them succeed him at the helm of the Lochlainn Company.

The only question was which heir should he choose?

One

Ian Blackburn avoided three things.

One, large crowds of people. He preferred gatherings where one could easily converse—and easily escape the conversation, should it become necessary, which often it was. There were drawbacks to having one of the country's more recognizable surnames.

Two, holidays. In his estimation, they were trumped-up excuses to sell consumer goods and pressure people into celebrating whether they wanted to or not. Not that he begrudged the existence of greeting card companies and producers of holiday movies. Companies had to turn a profit, after all, and there was a lucrative audience for forced cheer and blatant heartstring tugging. Blackburn Amusements, his family's business better known as BBA, did its best business around federal holidays when people had extra time off work to enjoy the thrill rides and other forms of entertainment on offer. But Ian had learned all too early in his life to beware of emotional manipulation.

And third of his list of avoidances: Lakes of Wonder, the theme park owned by one of BBA's fiercest rivals, the Lochlainn Company.

Tonight boded to be a personal hell of epic proportions, considering the date on his smartwatch read October 31 and he stood amid a raucous crowd of costumed partygoers eager to celebrate Halloween, packed tightly into a hotel rooftop restaurant and adjoining terrace to celebrate the holiday. And not just any hotel: the Shelter Cove Hotel, which stood at the front gate of Lakes of Wonder.

In short, a perfect trifecta of Ian's worst nightmares.

But he was willing to overlook his aversion to all things saccharine and overly manufactured and to ignore the heavy press of attendees. If all went to plan, Ian would accomplish the goal that kept him going, day and night, despite the difficulty of the last several years. And only one thing stood in his way:

Anna Stratford. The newly appointed Lochlainn Company executive who held his future captive with a stroke of her signing pen.

If only he knew who she was.

Ian's gaze searched the other guests at the party. It was an interesting mixture. Most of the people had paid—and paid dearly—for the privilege of celebrating Halloween at tonight's party. The attendees wore elaborate getups, most of them inspired by the costumed characters who roamed the theme park during the day. While there were trick-or-treat stations set up around the terrace for the guests to help themselves to candy and soft drinks, the real draw of the event was the spectacular view of Lakes of Wonder, lit up below them and picture-perfect for selfies to be splashed across guests' social media accounts. People began staking out the perceived best place from which to watch the promised fireworks show almost as soon as the doors opened and refused to budge as the party grew more crowded, leading in one case to near fisticuffs.

Thankfully, Ian didn't have to contend with the worst of the crowds. He was in the section of the terrace cordoned off with velvet ropes for invited guests and other VIPs, the area guarded by a Lakes of Wonder executive wearing a headset and flanked by two imposing security guards. Here candy stations continued to be available but were joined by tables heaped with sugary desserts as well as several open bars. But most of the VIP guests shunned the food—although not the alcohol—choosing instead to gather in small groups, exchanging murmured conversation. Not a few turned to glance in his direction, their gazes darting away the moment he caught them looking. No doubt they were discussing why the CEO of rival amusement park company, BBA, was at a Lakes of Wonder party.

Let them look. The public would soon discover why he was there.

"You would not believe what I went through to get these." Tai Nguyen, the senior vice president of strategy and operations for BBA, appeared at Ian's side. He carried half-full glasses of neon-green liquid with light-up plastic ice cubes in the shape of Seamus Sea Serpent, the mascot of Lakes of Wonder, floating on top. The ice cube changed color as Ian stared at it, from neon yellow to fuchsia to aqua blue. A more unappetizing sight Ian would be hard-pressed to conceive of.

Tai tried to hand one of the glasses to Ian, but he refused to take it. Tai shrugged. "You're missing out," he warned.

"Humans aren't meant to consume beverages that glow in the dark. And that's without the fake ice cube." Ian turned his attention back to the theme park.

Tai shook his head. "This drink encapsulates the quintessential Lakes of Wonder experience," he said. "Whimsy. Colorful. Fantastical." He took a sip from the drink in his right hand and wrinkled his nose. "On the surface. Watered down and not as strong as it once was underneath."

"I'm impressed you got all that. Very appropriate metaphor. 'Watered down and not as strong as it once was' is an accurate description of this place." Ian's gaze was caught by the Lighthouse of Amazement; the towering icon of the park was lit in orange and purple spotlights for Halloween. The Lighthouse was once famous the world over as a symbol not only for Lakes of Wonder but as the main logo for the Lochlainn Company, the vast multimedia conglomerate that owned the theme park as well as a film studio, television networks, several news organizations and a publishing house, among other businesses. However, seven years ago, the Lochlainn Company changed its branding to be an interlocking "L" and "C," removing all trace of the Lighthouse.

And soon the Lochlainn Company wouldn't own Lakes of Wonder.

Tai followed his gaze. "It's a shame."

Ian shot him a look. "What is?"

"That the Lochlainn Company let Lakes of Wonder get so rundown in the last decade or so. To think that it was more popular than Disneyland back in the day."

"For a short day," Ian said. "The first amusement parks, like Coney Island, were more like carnivals with rides with iffy safety records and disreputable clientele. Lakes of Wonder was the first amusement park with immersive, themed areas. But then Walt Disney did it bigger and arguably better, and now everyone thinks Disneyland was the first to offer a family-friendly experience. And, of course, BBA came next, and our parks provide more thrills." His gaze traced the outline of the lighthouse. "Although the original design of Lakes of Wonder was revolutionary. The technology in some of the original rides is so advanced, it hasn't been improved." He knew that for a fact because Cooper Blackburn's name was on the patents. Ian's great-grandfather, who had been

Archibald Lochlainn's original partner in Lakes of Wonder before their partnership ended in acrimony and Cooper struck out on his own, founding BBA as Blackburn Amusements.

"To be honest, I prefer Lakes of Wonder to Disneyland. I know it's smaller and not as well-maintained. But there's something about taking that slow ferry between all the different lands that I really enjoy. It's...oddly relaxing."

"Not lands, ports," Ian corrected. "Each themed area is supposed to be a different port on a different lake. Buccaneer Bayou, Valhalla Fjord, Heroic Harbour, et cetera. The exception is the Lighthouse of Amazement, which is on an island at the center where all the lakes converge." Another design by his great-grandfather, who'd gown up on Mackinac Island in Michigan and used the Great Lakes as his inspiration. Of course, if one asked the Lochlainns, they'd point to their name—Gaelic for "land of lakes"—as the inspiration for the park, but Ian knew which story he believed.

"Well, I, for one, look forward to conquering the ports." Tai saluted Ian with his second drink. "Once the park is ours, that is,"

"It will be." Ian pulled his gaze away from the Lighthouse. He'd have all the time in the world to inspect Lakes of Wonder after the deal was signed. There was only one small possible wrinkle in his plans, and he was at the party to meet her ahead of time. "When you were getting the drinks, did you ask about Anna Stratford?"

Tai shook his head. "I barely escaped the crush at the bar alive. But earlier I ran into a few Lochlainn Company execs who were also looking for her. She must be from the New York headquarters. No one associated with the park or the LA office seems to know who she is."

Ian's stomach clenched. "Interesting."

Tai shrugged. "You think so? She's probably a business development exec or someone on their legal team who finagled a boondoggle trip to California to rubberstamp the sale of the park. We've both commented on how uninterested the big guys at the Lochlainn Company seem to be in the sale of Lakes of Wonder to BBA. Sending someone like Anna out here is more indication of their lack of interest."

"Maybe." Ian didn't buy Tai's speculation. He had too much experience dealing with the Lochlainns. Hell, his family had too much experience, going all the way back to Cooper and Archibald.

The crowd was growing thicker, even in the VIP area, as the time for the fireworks show drew closer. Ian searched the faces. One of them had to be Anna Stratford, but who? But he didn't spot anyone matching the appearance of a Lochlainn Compay executive he didn't already know.

One intriguing female guest held his attention. Too bad she was obviously a Lakes of Wonder fan who'd talked her way into the VIP area. That would also explain why she was alone and not working the crowd, hoping to build her network in case the rumors about Lakes of Wonder's future were true. She stood in the far corner of the balcony, her hands gripping the wrought-iron railing as she leaned over the waist-high barrier, her rapt expression tightly focused on the Lighthouse of Amazement.

Unlike the others in the VIP area who'd skipped wearing Halloween costumes in favor of suits of gray and black, she was dressed as a fairy in a strapless dress of shocking pink with shimmering wings attached to her shoulders. A crown of equally pink flowers sat on top of blond curls that cascaded past her shoulders. Her cheeks sparkled with glitter, her glowing skin illuminated by the strings of globe lights strung above the terrace.

She appeared utterly out of place.

She appeared delectable.

The costume suited her. The dress clung to her luscious, round breasts and full hips, the skirt flaring above her knees and revealing curvaceous calves. His gaze traveled the length of her long legs, to her metallic high-heeled sandals and up again, past the bend in her waist and the slope of her shoulders to the top of her rosy floral headpiece. He was unable to pull his gaze from her, vivid and vivacious in a sea of monotonous monotones.

Ian didn't have a "type." He thought the concept was sophomoric and not a little bit pedestrian. Love at first sight was even more laughable, a concept wholly foreign to him in its sheer ridiculousness. But he had to admit if he did have a type, then she would fulfill his every visual requisite plus ones he didn't know he had.

"Spotted your quarry?" Tai broke him out of his revery.

Ian almost jumped before he realized Tai was referring to Anna Stratford and not the current object of Ian's interest. He admonished himself to cease staring at the fairy princess. Not only was he being impolite—or worse—but he had a time-sensitive mission. And it was not to hook up with a random Lakes of Wonder superfan, no matter how fascinating he found her. "Not yet."

"You sure? Seems like you might have a different type of quarry in your sights." Tai grinned and then finished off his second drink.

Ian regarded Tai. There were advantages and disadvantages to working with his closest friend. Tai was an excellent business development executive whose financial savvy was second to none. Asking him to join BBA had been a no-brainer. However, Tai also knew where all of Ian's buttons were located and how to light them up with nimble dexterity. "I have only one reason for being at this tedious event."

"If you say so." Tai wiped off the Seamus-shaped ice cubes with a napkin and pocketed them. "Linh is going to love these. Maybe my team should create financial projections for a series of afterhours events like this one at our parks."

"When three-year-olds like your daughter are our target audience, sure." Ian's gaze returned to the woman at the railing. Now she was talking on her phone, her face turned toward the crowd as she laughed at something being said on the other end. She threw her head back to expose a creamy length of neck, her curls tumbling around her shoulders as they shook with mirth. A real laugh, deep from within. Authentic.

Ian wasn't used to people revealing their inner emotions in such an unguarded way in public. He was aware his stare verged on rudeness but he was unable to glance away.

Tai's gaze followed his and he smirked. "I'm going to mingle. Do you want to meet later tonight or in the morning?"

"Tomorrow is fine. No need to pregame our strategy. We'll meet at the conference room."

Tai's smirk deepened and he nodded toward the woman in the fairy costume before turning to leave. "Enjoy your night.".

"My night would be more enjoyable if I could find Anna Stratford." Ian grabbed a champagne flute off a passing waiter's tray. It wasn't until he was about to take a sip that he realized the champagne was colored blue. He rolled his eyes and lowered the glass.

He meant what he'd said to Tai. Tomorrow should be a mere formality, a ceremonial signing of the deal. But the introduction of a mystery negotiator into the deal at the very last minute caused all his senses to go on high alert. His hand tightened on his plastic flute, causing the stem to crack off, and he flagged down another waiter to take the pieces away.

He was letting the Lochlainns get into his head, like he had all those years ago when he was straight out of business school and handling his first negotiation for BBA. The Lochlainn Company and BBA had been locked in bitter rivalry ever since Archibald and Cooper had abruptly ended their partnership. A younger and more naïve Ian had thought surely the old family rivalry would not stand in the way of an excellent business proposition to partner on a new ride technology that both BBA and the Lochlainn Company could then customize for their own individual needs.

He'd walked into the conference room to close the agreement to discover that Keith Lochlainn had swooped in at the last minute and locked up the new technology exclusively for Lakes of Wonder. Ian had been left embarrassed and, worse, the misstep had cost him trust with the BBA board of directors, who'd been willing to install Ian as CEO a few years later but then put Ian's stepfather, Harlan Bridges, in place over him as the chairman of the board.

If there was no love lost between the Blackburns and the Lochlainns, there was even less between Ian and Harlan. And to rub salt in the wound, the Lochlainn Company hadn't used the new technology. Ironically, by buying the Lakes of Wonder, Ian would finally be able to utilize the new system—only, ten years later, it wasn't so revolutionary.

Damn the Lochlainns. Anna Stratford might be their last-minute twist, but Ian was older and much wiser now. And after the deal was successfully concluded tomorrow, the Lochlainns would be out of the theme park business – and Ian would finally have a path to removing Harlan from BBA.

He checked the time on his smartwatch. The party would be over soon. He would make one more sweep of the VIP area to see if he could identify the mystery Lochlainn executive and then call it a night.

His gaze firmly avoiding the corner where the woman in pink was now swaying to the music being piped over the loudspeakers, he spotted a clump of newly arrived guests speaking to the woman guarding the velvet ropes. He recognized the tall brunette standing in the middle and smiled. Finally, the night was turning his way. Catalina Lochlainn was here.

He may have his issues with Keith Lochlainn and his lieutenants, but he had always liked Catalina. Besides, she wasn't a true Lochlainn, just one by marriage. And since she was the one who told him about tomorrow's new addition to the negotiations, Catalina should be able to point the elusive Anna out to him.

Catalina smiled as he approached and excused herself from her companions to greet him. "Ian! Good to see you. I thought this type of event wasn't your cup of tea."

"Doing my last bit of due diligence before tomorrow's acquisition closes."

"I'll miss being invited to these parties. And having free access to the park."

"You are a welcome guest at our theme parks whenever you like."

"Thank you, but that's not the same. But you didn't come over to talk to a Lochlainn for social chitchat."

"What makes you say that?"

"Perhaps the fact that Keith still has a dartboard

with your face on it after you hired away his favorite chef for your executive dining room."

He laughed. "That's minor. What about when the Lochlainn Company snatched the deal for Apex Comic characters to appear in theme parks out from under BBA? And then they never appeared at Lakes of Wonder. He did the deal to keep us from using them." That still smarted. Not as much as the first time the Lochlainns had double-crossed him, but the scar was there.

"Ah, but you disturbed Keith's stomach, and that is unforgivable. Still, I'm glad this deal is going through. So, how can I help you?"

"Anna Stratford."

Catalina's eyes widened, just for a second. "What about her?"

"What do you mean? You called to give me a heads-up yesterday."

She folded her arms and regarded him. "Is that why you are at the party? To meet Anna?"

"Due diligence," he reminded her. "Why else would I be here?"

Catalina sighed. "I'm not officially part of the Lochlainn Company. And I have nothing to do with the sale. But I don't like blindsides." There was that flicker in her expression again.

Blindside. Ian was right to be wary about the sudden addition of Anna to tomorrow's meeting. "Anna. Is she here?"

Catalina glanced around the terrace and then her

expression softened. "See the blonde standing alone in the far-left corner of the terrace?"

Ian followed her gaze then frowned. The woman in pink? *His* woman in pink? "You mean the Lakes of Wonder superfan who somehow talked her way into the VIP section?"

"What makes you think she's a superfan?" Catalina arched her eyebrows high.

"She's in costume. She's not networking. That says this is not a work function for her. She's barely taken her eyes off the Lighthouse of Amazement since she arrived. Conclusion—superfan."

Catalina bit back a smile, but not before Ian saw it. "Sounds like you didn't need me to point Anna out to you after all."

Wait. Catalina couldn't be serious. "The superfan wearing glitter is the Lochlainn Company's new shark?"

Catalina nodded, no longer keeping her smile contained. "She is the newest addition, yes."

He struggled to keep his expression intact. Anna Stratford looked as tough as the shot glasses of overly sticky butterscotch pudding now being passed around.

Then he remembered he was still dealing with the Lochlainn Company.

There had to be a catch.

Catalina regarded him, her smile fading. "I take full responsibility for my phone call, but I overstepped my place in telling you about Anna. Please don't make me regret my decision to tell you. Neither of us want to be on Keith's naughty list. Trust me."

Ian searched Catalina's gaze. There was something else. Something she wasn't saying. But then, that was the Lochlainn way. "Don't worry. The call stays between us."

"Good luck tomorrow." And with that, she was gone in a swirl of silken skirts.

Ian's gaze zeroed in on Anna. When she turned her head to accept a glass of blue-tinted champagne from a passing waiter, her beaming smile was almost bright enough to light the area all on its own.

He frowned. In his previous dealings with the Lochlainn Company, the executives had been as jaded and as cynical as Ian himself. No one else in the VIP section so much as batted an eyelash at the waiters serving food being passed.

And, may the theme park gods help him, he was more intrigued by her than before.

He straightened the cuffs of his shirt, smoothed his jacket, and prepared to unwrap the enigma Anna Stratford presented.

Two

Anna Stratford shivered, unsure whether the chill came from the evening breeze or the ghostly chorus chanting Halloween music over the loudspeakers. When she'd put on her favorite sundress in her hotel room earlier that day, the temperature had been in the high eighties, not too dissimilar from the weather back home in Ft. Lauderdale. But Southern California lacked Florida's humidity and, once the sun went down, the heat disappeared. Her glass of chilled champagne—she'd texted multiple photos of the blue-hued drink to her cousin Maritza, to share with Maritza's five-year-old daughter, Pepa—was delicious, but not warming.

"Are you cold? May I offer you a hot drink?" A man spoke from her right.

Anna jumped. She'd thought she was done with making small talk with Lakes of Wonder executives who obviously wished they were anywhere else but babysitting her for the evening. She was sure she had said good-night to her main handler a while ago, reassuring Teri McWilliams, the head of corporate communications, that she would be able to find her way back to her hotel room from the party on the terrace by herself without any problem.

She turned to address whoever had drawn the short straw and had to check up on her. "I'm fi—"

Her pulse skipped a beat. Then her heart rate sped up, the rapid thump drowning out all other sound.

The speaker had to be one of the most flawless specimens of male adulthood it had ever been her privilege to view—if on the stern and forbidding side. Broad shoulders in a charcoal wool jacket designed to display them to their best advantage, the silky black shirt underneath tailored perfectly to his form. Cheekbones that could slice the wind. Bottomless dark eyes that seemed to see right through her and into the next county. Tousled black hair that was neither straight nor wavy, a touch too long for the "forbidding captain of industry" look he pulled off elsewhere, but she liked the length—it made him seem a teeny bit accessible. Human, even.

Who was he? He certainly wasn't one of the Lochlainn Company executives she'd met, nor did he appear to be on staff at Lakes of Wonder. Maybe an actor? She was in Southern California, after all, although Hollywood was a two-hour drive north of Lakes of Wonder. Or a major league athlete of some kind?

He quirked an eyebrow in question and her brain stopped processing thoughts. She could only stare at his perfection, like a Roman statue come to life in all-too-vivid color. "Is that a yes?" he asked. "They're handing out cookies and hot chocolate." He indicated a tight knot of people surrounding a nearby concession cart.

"Um…" Her mouth opened and closed a few times. Try as hard as she could, she couldn't get her lips to form words, just sounds. People who looked like him were rare occurrences in her life. People who looked like him definitely didn't walk over to her and offer her drinks.

"If you're concerned, you can watch me go to the cart and come straight back. No funny business." He held out his hands, palms up, and all she could do was notice how…large…they were. Large and well formed, with long, thick fingers and…

She found her breath. With difficulty. "I, um…" His grin started to falter. "I mean, thank you. A drink would be nice. Thank you."

He smiled, and if she thought him handsome before—well, she was wrong. The smile transformed his face, turning foreboding to panty-melting sexy. And judging by the gleam in those knowing eyes, he was aware of his effect on her. "Don't move."

Now that she'd had time to adjust to his presence, her brain could start to process again. She glanced to her left and her right. More and more people were

discovering her corner of the terrace and filling in
any empty space. "I have a feeling this is a 'you move,
you lose' type of situation."

She was referring to the spot she had staked out
on the terrace to view the upcoming fireworks, but
he flashed that grin at her again, even more knowing than previously, before plunging into the cookie
and cocoa cart melee. She inhaled. Did he think she
was flirting?

Was she flirting?

She didn't have a lot of experience with which to
compare. Having had the same boyfriend for the last
six years until they'd broken up a month ago—even
if the relationship had been effectively over much
longer—meant she was woefully out of practice in
giving and receiving romantic signals. She shook her
head to clear it and grasped the wrought-iron railing
with both hands, allowing the solidness of the metal
to reassure her that this was indeed her life now. That
she was standing on a five-star resort's exclusive rooftop terrace as part of a VIP crowd about to watch
Lakes of Wonder's renowned Halloween firework
show, with movie-star-handsome men asking if they
could bring her treats.

She had to speak to Maritza, to ground herself in
reality – or least, the reality that had been hers until
that fateful knock on her office door. No one knew
Anna better than her cousin, who was also her best
friend and housemate. When Maritza had found herself suddenly single a month away from giving birth,
Anna had moved into her small bungalow to help with

newborn and never moved out. Although she had last spoken to her cousin not less than an hour ago, the purpose of that phone call had been to say good-night to Pepa. The five-year-old should be asleep by now, so she and Maritza could freely speak.

"So what's happening now?" Maritza answered. "Did you sell the theme park already? I thought that was tomorrow."

"Shh! You're not supposed to know why I'm here." But Anna had had to tell someone about the surreal turn of events that had led to her trip to Southern California, and she'd trusted Maritza with her deepest secrets her entire life. "And don't remind me about tomorrow. I haven't been told who I'm meeting or even allowed to go over the paperwork. The Lakes of Wonder people continue to brush me off, saying those are details I don't need to worry about. All I know is I sign the agreement, I shake hands, I pose for a photo, I walk out." Her gaze remained locked on the man who had offered her a drink. True to his word, he joined the back of the line at the concession cart.

"They sound awful."

"They're fine." They weren't—the managers she'd met were more condescending than any of Anna's wealthy interior design clients ever had been—but Maritza had enough stress in her life. She didn't need Anna's minor-by-comparison annoyances added to them. "The situation is…unusual."

"That's the understatement of the century. Who has someone with no prior experience or connection jump in and sign off on a massive sale? A sale that will be scrutinized by the media, and the IRS, and the Justice Department, and—"

"I guess Keith Lochlainn does," Anna interjected. "Who knows why billionaires do anything?" The man was third in line now. He wasn't really buying a beverage for her, was he? This had to be a prank. Perhaps a Lochlainn Company executive had put him up to it, as revenge for Anna being thrust into their carefully negotiated deal at the last second.

She wouldn't mention meeting him to Maritza, just in case.

Maritza sighed. "Sorry, I didn't mean to make you more apprehensive about the whole thing. You're still processing everything you learned and—"

"I'm great." Anna cut her cousin off. No need to go into how well she was dealing—or not dealing—with the major life changes that had been thrust upon her. "And tonight's party is fun." She failed to mention she was the only guest in the VIP section wearing a costume and that the other guests had no problem staring at her with visible smirks. "The desserts are amazing and the view…there are no words for how spectacular this view is. I can see the entire theme park, with the Lighthouse smack-dab in the center. But, hey, the show will start soon, so I wanted to quickly check in without little ears listening. How is Pepa?"

"She's better now that we finally have a diagnosis, although she keeps asking where you are. She wants to show you how she can make her own lunch now and not feel 'icky.'"

"I'm sorry for leaving. I wish I could be there to help as you figure out how to work with her diabetes."

"Stop apologizing. Nothing is your fault." Anna could picture Maritza's narrowed eyes and free hand on her hip as she said it. "My mom and dad are here. I've got support."

"Right. Your parents," Anna repeated through suddenly numb lips. She forced moisture back into her mouth and attempted a smile. Aren't people supposed to hear your smile even when they can't see it? Not that she could fool Maritza. "That's good."

Maritza exhaled. "I saw your dad today—"

Out of the corner of her eye, Anna spied the man walking toward her, his hands laden with mugs. If this was a prank, at least she would get a hot cocoa out of it. "I need to get off the phone."

"You need to talk to your parents. They're worried—"

"I know." Anna screwed her eyes shut. When she opened them, the man was closer. "Let them know I'm fine.

"Anna—"

"Gotta run. Love you." Anna hung up as the man reached her side. "You returned much faster than I thought you would."

"I have sharp elbows," he said dryly, handing her a sealed plastic mug and a see-through bag containing a frosted jack-o'-lantern sugar cookie larger than Anna's hand.

"Halloween marks the start of the holiday season. I'm pretty sure elbowing small children out of the way for cookies and cocoa puts you on Santa's naughty list." She opened the mug's lid and breathed in the chocolate scent before sipping. Delicious. So far, not a prank.

Here came his smile again, even more devastating than before. "You're the second person tonight who suggested I could be put on that list," he said.

"Oh?" Anna raised her eyebrow. "Why? Do you regularly elbow small children? Fleece widows out of their inheritance?"

His warm expression fled, replaced by an assessing stare. She resisted the urge to hide behind her mug the best she could. "Is that what you expect from me? A fleecing?"

"Expect? Am I supposed to expect something from you? I'm sorry, do we know each other? Or perhaps you have me confused with someone else." That would explain why he had approached her. This had to be a case of mistaken identity. He was too... well, too *everything* to be interested in her.

His stare turned quizzical then his brow smoothed out. "You're right. We haven't been formally introduced." He held out his right hand for a handshake, which she accepted. "Ian."

His touch was warm and firm, his fingers enveloping hers with their strength. Her father—well, Glenn—always said one could tell the nature of a person based on their handshake. Ian's grip said he was powerful and used to getting his own way. He was in control of how long their hands remained connected. But he was also careful not to overwhelm her with his strength.

"Anna," she responded. He released her hand, triggering a wave of disappointment that took her by surprise. "Pleasure to meet you."

Ian continued to regard her, his eyebrows raised as if in expectation. She cleared her throat. "Is it not a pleasure? I'm sorry, I'm from Florida. Do people say something different after an introduction in Southern California? This is my first time here."

He laughed. His laugh was deep and rich and sent frissons of electricity from her fingers to her toes. "Oh, the pleasure is definitely mine."

Her stomach squeezed at the light of appreciation in his gaze, while her face was hot enough to warm everyone standing on the terrace. Thankfully, the lights overhead winked out as the announcer told the guests to relax and enjoy the evening's show, sparing the entire party from seeing her blush brighter than a stoplight. In the ensuing darkness, she put her cocoa on a nearby cocktail table and hugged her arms tight across her chest, trying to appear calm and sophisticated. As if being in the VIP section and talking to men whose grin could make every panty within eyesight spontaneously combust was another day ending in "y" for her.

Her actions didn't have the intended effect. Instead, he frowned. "Still cold?"

She shook her head. Cold was the last word to describe the awareness lighting her nerves, causing the little hairs on her arms to rise to attention. He had her literally quaking in her sandals. "I'm good," she choked out.

He shook his head. "You're shivering." Before she could object, he'd taken off his charcoal-gray suit jacket and draped it around her shoulders, easily covered her costume wings. "Your dress might be perfect for a Florida evening, but it doesn't stand a chance against our cool California nights."

His jacket enveloped her like a warm hug. Her fingertips skimmed the surface of the fabric, ran along the seams. Working with textiles was one of the joys of her job as the in-house interior designer for her family's furniture store, and the fine wool outer layer and smooth silk lining were very fine textiles indeed. She inhaled, breathing his scent, redolent of pine and musk. So delicious, if the scent could somehow be bottled, he would put most perfume companies out of business within a month.

She should give the jacket back to him. Instead, she snuggled deeper into its luxurious embrace. "Thank you."

"Can't have you freeze to death, after all. His tone was light but his mouth wore a sideways twist. "Wouldn't be hospitable. Certainly not before you finish everything on your agenda."

"My agenda?" She did have an agenda—as in meetings she was expected to attend in the following days—but he made it sound as if she had an ulterior motive. And she also had one of those—but how would someone she just met know that? The Lochlainn Company attorney had assured her the reason she was at Lakes of Wonder was known only to a handful of trusted family insiders. Not even the theme park executives she'd been dealing with knew. It certainly wasn't public knowledge.

Or maybe the events of the last month were causing her to question even the most innocent of statements, and the only thing he meant was her agenda as a tourist. Maritza would tell her to relax and enjoy his company, after all—

A glorious burst of gold and silver sparks exploded over the Lighthouse of Amazement and chased her thoughts away. "Oh!" was all she could manage to exhale.

Music poured over the loudspeakers, orchestral and stirring, the fireworks timed perfectly to the beat and tonal shifts as the soundtrack shifted from stirring chants of heroic action to melodic love ballads to comedic set pieces. Anna even sang along, if under her breath, to some of the more popular songs she remembered from her childhood. She oohed as the fireworks created spinning discs of fire in the sky, and aahed when the sparking lights revealed entwined hearts. Then the soundtrack shifted to spooky Halloween music, the fireworks blazing orange and purple. Ghostly figures over the Lighthouse as the music built to a crescendo and then stopped.

The crowd on the terrace clapped. Anna turned to Ian. "That was fun—"

Out of the corner of her eye, flames streaked upward from the Lighthouse. She jumped and grabbed Ian's arm, firm and strong and warm under the silky cotton of his shirt. She dropped her hands when she realized what she was doing. He merely smiled and directed her attention back to the Lighthouse. "Don't miss the big finale."

The flames—controlled, and part of the show, Anna could see now—leaped in time to the music. The Lighthouse appeared to be on fire, but that was an illusion created by realistic projections on the building's outer walls. Then Seamus Sea Serpent appeared out of the lake. He dove back down and, when he emerged again, the magic of special effects made it look as if he expelled streams of water to douse the flames. The music started again, more triumphant than before, as more fireworks than Anna could count lit the sky brighter than daylight, one giant circular burst of color after another.

The applause was thundering this time. Anna waited a few beats before joining in. "Now that's the end," she deadpanned.

"That's the end," Ian agreed. "Impressive, although they grossly overspent on the effects and the return on investment is nonexistent. By the time the show pays for itself, the technology will be outdated, and even more money will need to be spent." The lights came up on the terrace as he turned to her. His gaze swept over her expression. "I take it you don't agree?" he asked.

"There's more to investment than dollars and cents." To some people, Anna's parents might just sell furniture. But Anna knew better. Stratford's Fine Furniture sold comfort, home, a place to form and nurture a family—

Family. Her mind stuttered on the word. Maritza knew she had to talk to her parents. But she was still processing the news that the solid foundation upon which she had relied her entire life was…well. Her parents were still her parents. Her solid foundation still stood. The Knock did not change that. Her heart knew that truth, implicitly.

Her brain, on the other hand, needed more time. And that was the real reason why she was in California.

"What about joy? Delight? The show creates memories, and those are priceless." She swept a hand, indicating the rapt crowd on the other side of the velvet ropes, chatting animatedly as knots of people began to move away from the railing and back toward the tables laden with sweets and alcohol. "See the kids? They'll still be talking about tonight when they are twice my age."

Ian regarded her as if she had grown a unicorn horn in the middle of her forehead. "Interesting argument."

"What?" Anna picked up her hot chocolate. "Are you trying to tell me you've never thought of theme parks as places of happiness?"

"Now I know you're kidding. That's the marketing. But we know that's not the reality."

She laughed. "I don't think—"

A small child rammed into Anna's legs. Her knees buckled and she fell forward, the perpetrator bouncing off her and running away. Before she could even exclaim, Ian's large hands were there, grasping her elbows, keeping her upright. Her arms wound around his shoulders and she sank against him.

He smelled even better that his jacket. The notes were deeper, richer. Warmer.

She pulled back, suddenly aware this was the second time she had clung to him in less than a half hour. And without so much as asking for his consent. Her gaze locked onto Ian's. Was he angry? Or worse, amused that she was literally throwing herself at him—multiple times? But instead, his eyes were dark with concern. "Are you okay?" he asked.

She nodded, her breathing coming back under control. "I'm fine—"

No. Wait. She wasn't fine. She was...she sniffed and looked down.

When the child had hit her, Anna's cocoa mug had tipped before falling out of her hand. Now she wore most of its contents. Ian's beautiful jacket was splattered and wet.

"Oh, no!" She grabbed a stack of napkins from a nearby table and started to dab at the cocoa. "Don't worry. I'll have this dry-cleaned and returned to you."

He shook his head. "I'm checking out early in the morning. My morning is packed, and then I'm flying to a conference in Hong Kong. My assistant can take it to the cleaners when I return next week."

"Next week? You can't let a stain like this sit. Chocolate and milk are a recipe for destroyed fibers. I can mail it to you after it's cleaned."

He shrugged. "It's just a jacket. No need to go to so much bother."

Just a jacket? She smoothed her fingers over the wool. The silk lining slid against her skin, causing voluptuous shivers. If she owned this jacket, she wouldn't wear anything underneath so the lining could caress her like the world's most tender lover. "You said you were checking out tomorrow—are you a guest at this hotel?"

His eyes crinkled at the corners. "I am."

"So am I. I travel with a stain removal stick. It's so miraculous, it practically walks on water. Can I at least try to get the worst of the spill out and then return the jacket to your room?" She ran her fingers across the fine weave. "It would be a shame if this were ruined. Merino wool, I'm guessing. Italian milled."

She looked up. He was gazing at her as if the unicorn horn had regrown out of her forehead.

"What?" she asked.

"You're not—" He stopped. Then he nodded, a slight one, as if he were agreeing with an unspoken thought. "Right. So. You're proposing you remove the stain tonight."

"At least, I hope I can. It shouldn't take long."

"And bring the jacket by my room?"

Her stomach flipped at the way he lingered on the last word. "I can leave it at the front desk if you prefer. But I'd feel better if I made sure you received it before you leave."

He smiled then, a halfway smile that slightly

dented his cheeks. "My room is fine. I was planning on being up, anyway. To prep for tomorrow," he clarified, his eyebrow raised.

"Right." He had mentioned he had a packed morning. "Sure, I'll bring it by."

"I'm in 3140. The Wonder Suite. Why don't we say in one hour? That should give both of us enough time." He held up an index finger in the universal sign for "one minute" at an Asian man approaching them, his hands full of jack-o'-lantern cookies. Then Ian turned back to her. "Until then."

She swallowed, trying to work more moisture into her mouth. "See you later."

Ian nodded and left, finding the other man. The two talked for a minute then they walked together toward the exit. Anna watched them until the crowd hid them from view, and then held her chilled palms to her overheated cheeks. Ian's voice had deepened and lingered on the word "then," rolling the word on his tongue like a promise of more fireworks to come—only this time, the pyrotechnics would involve only the two of them.

Unless that had been her imagination.

Anna wished she had dated more in college. Or in high school. Or any time, really. Then she would have more experience with reading people and whether they were interested in her or merely flirting to flirt or if she was making the whole thing up because she found Ian attractive. Her fingers could still feel the strength of his arm as she'd clutched him, the breadth of his shoulders. She'd practically climbed him as if he were her own personal gym equipment.

She didn't act this way with people she didn't know. She didn't act this way with people she *did* know.

She wanted to continue to act this way with Ian.

Her last relationship had been fine if predictable. Monotonous. She couldn't blame her boyfriend for breaking up with her, either. *She* was monotonous. Anna, the good student, the obedient daughter, the dutiful girlfriend.

Her life had stretched out before her in easily measurable chunks: earn a scholarship to Florida State, meet a nice man, earn her degree. Work at her parents' furniture store as the in-house interior designer, learn the clientele and their wants and dislikes. Take over the business after her parents decide to retire. Spend two weeks' vacation every summer at the Stratford family compound of lakeside cabins in the Smoky Mountains. *Noche Buena* at *Tía* Belen's house, Passover Seder with Uncle Simon and his husband. Marry the nice man and when children came along, introduce them to same cycle of holidays and family get-togethers.

She had a good life. A great life. She was lucky and privileged, in so many ways.

Then came the Knock. And everything that she thought she knew—everything that she thought she was, down to the marrow in her bones—was called into question. Leaving her confused and, yes, still angry the life that had been hers until the lawyer had showed up on her doorstep had been based on a lie, leaving her with no idea of who or what she was meant to be.

Maybe she was someone who saw someone to whom she was attracted and went for it, potential embarrassment and social strictures to "be a good girl" be damned.

And maybe someone like Ian—someone who exuded success and command and was so devilishly handsome he made movie superheroes appear lackluster and pedestrian—could be interested in a furniture store "client customer success manager" as her business cards read.

The party was starting to dissolve around her. People streamed toward the wall of glass doors that led to the hotel's signature restaurant and, beyond it, the elevators. The cookie and cocoa cart had been wheeled away. Wait staff were dissembling the towers of sweets. The bar was still doing brisk business, but it was evident the event was over.

She pulled Ian's jacket tighter around her, reveling anew in the soft silk of the lining and his spicy male scent—albeit now mixed with chocolate—and went to her hotel room. She was at the most Wonderous Place on the Planet, as the ads for Lakes of Wonder proclaimed. Perhaps her stain removal stick would not be the end of the magic the night had in store for her.

Three

Ian rolled his neck. The desk and office chair in his suite were more ergonomic than expected for hotel furniture, especially considering most guests would be spending their time in the theme parks on vacation instead of in the room working, but he couldn't seem to release the tension making a knotty home for itself between his shoulder blades.

His laptop was open on the desk, the contract in vivid black and white on the screen. He should be going through the sales agreement to see if there any loopholes he had missed. "Be prepared" wasn't just a scouting motto or a song from a Disney movie; it was the code by which he conducted his life, to the point of taking over the preparations for his twenty-first birthday surprise party. Leaving outcomes to chance was for amateurs.

But, try as he might, he couldn't focus on the page in front of him. His thoughts were otherwise occupied by the enigmatic-and oh-so-appealing Anna Stratford.

She was not what he'd expected. At all. Nor had she batted an eyelash when he'd introduced himself. To anyone else, it would appear as if she hadn't known who he was. But that was impossible. Of course, she'd know who her opponent would be in the boardroom tomorrow.

She must be a good actress, he decided. So good, she was almost impossible for him to read. Perhaps that was the twist. Present him with a last-minute opponent so unexpected he would be taken off guard, miss a step. Pay more to acquire Lakes of Wonder or cause him to make unwise concessions.

Or maybe he had Anna all wrong. Maybe she was as guileless and transparent as she'd seemed on the terrace. After all, he'd approached her...although Catalina Lochlainn had all but pushed him in her direction.

He supposed he would find out which version of Anna was correct if she made good on her promise and came by his room. He looked forward to seeing if she would offer anything beyond his cleaned jacket. His cock grew heavy at the memory of how her lush breasts had pressed against him, her soft gasps in his ear as her hands gripped his shoulder. The hot cocoa spill had been an accident, but Ian admired people who took advantage of serendipity to press their advantage. He did the same.

But whatever happened—if indeed, she showed up—he had no illusions that Anna Stratford was anything but the latest in a long line of Lochlainn tricks and feints.

His phone rang. Tai. "Did you find anything?" he answered.

"My team has been over the supporting documents and schedules twice," Tai responded. "They're airtight."

Ian rose from the office chair and began to pace on the carpeted floor. "Have them read it again."

"Let's save time. Go ahead and tell me what the issue is," Tai suggested.

"I…don't know. Yet."

"Then why are you so sure one exists?"

"Because there is always an issue with the Lochlainns." He reached the opposite end of the room far too soon and turned around.

"Can I persuade you to stop overthinking this?" Ice cubes rattled in Ian's ear as Tai took a sip of whatever he was drinking. "I've gone over the terms so many times, I have them memorized. The agreement to buy Lakes of Wonder is straightforward."

Ian shook his head. "There's something the Lochlainns aren't telling us." A vision of Anna's eyes, shining with unfettered joy as she'd watched the fireworks, almost stopped him in his tracks. Her generous full mouth curved into a smile so broad she couldn't be faking her enjoyment—could she?

Who offered to get stains out of jackets in the first place?

Or maybe it was part of a Lochlainn ruse to spring an unsuspecting trap on him at the last minute.

Tai's sigh echoed through the phone. "Look, I wasn't raised on castle intrigue the way you were—"

"Castle intrigue. Nice. Another good use of metaphor."

"I wasn't referring to amusement parks." Tai snorted. "Although it does fit, seeing as how you were born into an amusement park dynasty."

"I wasn't raised on castle intrigue."

"No, only to look for ambushes around every corner."

"I'm thorough and prepared. That's why BBA is the number two amusement park operator in the world." Although allowing Anna Stratford to walk off with his jacket—an obvious pretense to contact him again this evening—was not exactly erring on the side of caution. Would she come to his room in her fairy costume? He hoped so. He wondered if her skin would turn the same color as her dress when she—

Too late, he realized Tai was speaking.

"—not saying you aren't justified. You were brought up by Harlan, after all."

Ian's hand ached. He released his tight grip on his phone. "What's your point?"

"My point is your stepfather is a jackass. Since he consolidated his control over BBA's board, you've been under attack as CEO. And this is the first major deal as CEO you get to put your imprint on. So, I understand why you are kicking the tires a few more times than necessary. But maybe stop kicking them into oblivion. You can't go anywhere if the tires are shredded."

Ian made a dismissive gesture. "Forget everything I said about your metaphors. That one is tortured."

"I'm not wrong about Harlan."

"Harlan is a nonentity. Or he will be once we close this deal. Preston and Olive have promised to vote with me to kick him off the board." And out of the family for good, he thought grimly. His mother had suffered enough.

"And that's another reason why you're spinning your wheels. Pun intended." Tai fell silent for a moment. "You know, speaking of Preston and Olive, I never asked why your uncle and cousin are joining you now when you've been trying to get rid of Harlan since I joined the company."

Ian exhaled. "We don't talk of this publicly. But my great-grandfather, Cooper, was Archibald's original partner on Lakes of Wonder. Family legend says Cooper even designed the Lighthouse, only for Archibald to kick him to the curb before the park's opening. Cooper went on to found Blackburn Amusements, so no one should cry for him. But Preston and Olive have been obsessed with Lakes of Wonder as long as I've known them. I've agreed Preston will be charge of Lakes of Wonder once the sale goes through, hands off."

"Aha!" Tai said. "I get it now. This acquisition is a family honor thing and that's why you expect the

Lochlainns to screw BBA over. I knew your mother's Sicilian influence was involved somehow."

Ian smirked. "This isn't a vendetta."

"You sure? Do I need to start shopping for a horse's head to slip into Keith Lochlainn's bed?"

"This is a business deal, not *The Godfather*. The Lochlainn Company has a well-earned reputation for underhanded tricks that I'm staying ahead of. Besides, the horse's head would be for Harlan."

Tai snorted. "Can I give you advice?"

"No, but you will anyway."

"Stop borrowing trouble and get some sleep." Ice rattled again on the other end of the line. "I have an early breakfast about the San Diego expansion. See you at the meeting?"

"Nine a.m. at the Lakes of Wonder admin building. Sixth floor conference room."

Tai said his goodbyes and Ian turned to his previously ignored laptop screen. Maybe his friend was right. Maybe there wasn't a twist. Perhaps Anna didn't have a strategy up her nonexistent sleeves that would filet the sale like trout being prepared for dinner. After all, Tai was correct that Ian had learned early and often with Harlan as a stepfather—and later as chairman of BBA's board—to be wary and to watch his own back at every turn.

But to paraphrase the old saying, was it paranoia when the conspiracies turned out to be real? When Ian's mother, Guilia, divorced Harlan, Harlan had exploited a loophole in their prenuptial agreement that gave him ownership of Guilia's BBA shares and secured his seat on the board. So far, Ian had managed to sidestep the knives and arrows aimed at his back—and often, his front—but he was more than ready to remove Harlan for good. If Preston and Olive held to their end of the bargain and voted their shares with Ian at the next board meeting, he would finally have the power to do so.

A knock came at his hotel room. Finally.

He threw the door open. "I was wondering when you would come—"

A bellman blinked back at him. "Sorry for your wait." He held out an ice bucket. Condensation frosted the sides and the corks of three bottles poked over the top edge. "Compliments of the Lochlainn Company. Welcome to Shelter Cove Hotel."

Ian swallowed his disappointment and took the bucket, placing it on the table in the sitting area. He returned with a generous cash tip, which he handed to the bellman. "Thank you."

"Enjoy your stay, sir." The bellman left and Ian examined one of the bottles. Champagne. Pricey stuff, too. Well, apparently the Lochlainn Company expected him to celebrate, one way or another.

Another knock at his door, the same staccato rhythm as before. Did the bellman forget something? He wrenched the door open. "Yes?"

The person on his threshold wasn't from bell services.

"Anna," he breathed.

"Hi," she said, her smile as genuine, if a bit more tentative, than it had been on the restaurant terrace.

She held up his jacket. "I'm so sorry I took so long. The cocoa was a bit more stubborn than anticipated, and I didn't want to harm the fibers. I also had to be careful of the silk lining—I didn't want to leave a water mark. But I think it's mostly as good as new?"

Her words tumbled in a torrent, but Ian barely heard them, fascinated by the vision in front of him. Anna had changed out of her bright pink dress and towering sandals into light pink joggers topped by a matching hoodie. Her hair had lost its flower crown and her blond curls flowed freely across her shoulders. The fairy-dust glitter was sadly gone from her cheeks, but a dash of fresh lipstick outlined her lips.

There was even a tiny water droplet on the tip of her nose, no doubt left from washing her face. A rather delectable nose, he noted, and then wondered when he had ever paid attention to that portion of someone's anatomy before. But in way, Anna Stratford's nose was the encapsulation of everything he found intriguing about this mystery woman: a perfectly ordinary physical feature that, by virtue of belonging to her, was made extraordinary by her animated energy.

Her rush of words had ceased. She was waiting, her eyes wide and questioning, for him to respond. "Sorry, you lost me somewhere around 'fibers.'" He held the door open wider. "Come in. I don't have hot cocoa, but the hotel supplied champagne. It's a better vintage than whatever that was served at the party."

She shook her head and continued to hold out the jacket. "I don't want to impose. You said you were checking out early and I was about to go to bed. I only wanted to make sure I returned your—" Her gaze sharpened as she focused on something over his right shoulder. "Wait. Is that...? No way. You can see Lakes of Wonder from your room?"

He stepped to the side and indicated she should enter. "I've been told this room offers the best view. Even better than the view from the rooftop terrace earlier."

She hesitated, but only for a second. Then she walked past him and crossed the room until she was almost pressed flat against the floor-to-ceiling windows that made up the far wall. "Whoever said that wasn't wrong. Look, from this angle you can see Mythic Springs and Buccaneer Bayou as well as the Lighthouse of Amazement."

He joined her at the window, stopping briefly by the suite's wet bar to pour two flutes of champagne. He handed one to her and kept the other for himself. "It's not as centered of a view as the terrace for the firework show, but I appreciate the bird's-eye perspective. You get a better idea of the park's layout." With his free hand, he indicated a brightly lit silver flag discernable in the distance. "There's Black Hole Bay."

Her left index finger traced the spot on the glass. "It's closer to Olympic Cay than I thought. It felt like I walked forever to get between them when I was in the park earlier today."

"Illusion," he said. "The original designer created winding paths that double back on themselves to give the appearance of distance. So guests would feel as if they'd traveled through time to reach the next destination." He shrugged. "And the more time guests spend walking, the happier they are to sit and watch one of the live entertainment shows. And if guests are watching a show, then they aren't standing in line for a ride, thus decreasing the wait times for other guests."

"Really?" She turned shining eyes to him. "That's clever."

Clever? He shrugged. "It's standard operations. Create ways to keep crowds dispersed and traffic flowing." He drank from his flute, his gaze focused on Anna. "But that's theme park 101, as you know."

Anna opened her mouth then snapped it shut. Her lips made a perfect bow shape when they were closed, Ian noted, and wondered again at his apparent obsession with cataloging human features—an obsession that began when he'd opened the door. "Let's pretend I know nothing. Teach me?" she asked, her gaze focused on his.

Four

Coming to Ian Blackburn's room was a mistake. Anna was sure of it. She should have trusted her first instinct and asked bell services to deliver the jacket to him. But lately, she didn't have a great track record of being right about...well, anything.

Interacting with Ian was like was staring at an enormous open box of jigsaw puzzle pieces, but the cover was missing so she had no idea what picture she was supposed to form.

Like now. She had no idea how to read him. His gaze was narrowed, but a faint smile played on his lips. "Are you quizzing me on how well I know the attractions industry?"

"Just picking your brain," she demurred. Earlier, while trying to remove the stain, she'd been racking her brain why Ian approached her. Now, she decided, perhaps fate was the reason. She needed a crash course on how Lakes of Wonder operated, since the Lochlainn Company executives had decided not to educate her in advance of the meeting tomorrow, and the universe had provided an instructor. "I'm all ears. What else do I need to know?"

He regarded her, a speculative light in his eye, then he smiled. "Okay. I'll bite." His left arm brushed hers as he raised his hand to indicate a point in the distance. "Theme park 101 it is. Let's start with...see the tall structure in the center of the park? You know what that is, right?"

She scoffed. "That's easy. That's the Lighthouse of Amazement."

"That's the name. But do you know what it is?"

"A tall lighthouse?"

He turned to face her, leaning his left shoulder against the window. A smirk played on his lips as he bent his mouth close to her ear. She shivered. "That's the weenie," he said, and straightened.

His breath was warm and her nerves were on red alert, simultaneously craving him to come nearer yet apprehensive he would—because if did, she would have to be honest with herself about what she hoped would happen by coming to his room. She had to blink a few times before she fully processed his words. "You have to be kidding. Weenie? As in..." She indicated the Lighthouse, lit up in the distance. "It is rather phallic, I suppose."

A bark of laughter escaped him. He glanced down

at her, the gleam in his eyes intensifying. She wanted to bask in his heat, like a cat finding a sunbeam. "As in the treat used to train dogs," he corrected.

"Oh." She hoped the warmth flooding from her checks to her chest wasn't visible in the room's dim light. "It doesn't look like kibble."

He gave her the same assessing stare as he had earlier on the terrace. She resisted the urge to check if a unicorn horn truly had sprung out of her forehead. Then his smirk deepened. "It's named that because dog trainers use weenies to draw dogs' attention. Park weenies are designed to draw guests' attention. Weenies at the center, like the Lighthouse, keep people moving further into the park so the entrances don't become crowded."

His eyes reflected the neon glow of the park, the pinpoints of light beckoning her closer. She immediately understood the concept. "Ah. That's how the park gets guests to move from one place to another?"

"Testing me on techniques used to capture guests' attention?" He indicated her hoodie. "There are several ways. Bright colors, for example. People are drawn to them." His gaze dipped to her mouth, his dark eyes becoming pools of black. "As you know. Your pink lipstick makes it difficult to focus on anything else."

His rough-edged words caused an instant rush of heat between her legs. She couldn't look at him for fear of betraying how much he was affecting her. No doubt he would laugh if he knew. He probably entertained late-night guests in his hotel room all the time, beautiful, sophisticated guests who knew how to banter and lightly joke. People unlike her. Or, at least unlike her before the Knock.

She drank deeply from her flute despite knowing better. Champagne shut off her critical thinking centers. But the cool liquid was welcome as the room's temperature seemed to be increasing. "Is that why you wear monotones?"

His eyebrows rose. "Me?"

She drained her glass and set it down, turning to face him. "If people wear bright colors to draw attention, then those who wear dark colors—like you—must be dressing to avoid it. Right? I mean, Batman doesn't hunt criminals dressed in neon yellow."

He snorted. "I suppose dark clothes would be better at night. If one were a stealthy superhero, that is."

She looked down. Her flute was full again. "Considering my glass was empty fifteen seconds ago, I'd say stealth is something you excel at." She raised her gaze to him. "So? Is that why you dress the way do? To avoid detection?"

"Are you asking if I fight crime in my time off?" he said, topping off his own glass. "Sorry, no."

She looked at him from over the top of her flute. "I think I'm right. Not that you have a secret identity that fights crime, but you want to avoid attention."

"Really." His tone was dismissive, but for the first time his gaze wouldn't fully meet hers. "Why would I do that?"

She shook her head. "I don't know. Maybe it's because you know bright colors would alert your prey and you wouldn't be able to get close enough to them otherwise."

He didn't respond, but his fingers tightened on the stem of his glass.

Anna's success at work relied on reading her customers' body language. Often, a client would outwardly express delight or enthusiasm, but there would be something in their stance—feet braced as if preparing for impact, shoulders a half inch higher than normal—that told her their internal reaction was something quite different. Ian continued to lean against the window, no change discernable in his position, but his gaze now studiously contemplated the brightly colored lights of the theme park below.

Maybe she was learning how to read him after all. She smiled as she held out her half-empty glass. "Is there more? This is the best champagne I've had in…ever."

The sharp light returning to his expression, he poured what was left of the bottle into her glass. "There is. And you're incorrect."

"No, I'm sure this is the best champagne I've tasted."

His half-smile dented his left cheek. "No. About colors. Theme parks use shades of green or blue to cover buildings and objects they want guests to ignore. The colors blend into the vegetation or the sky. The guests' eyes slide over them."

"Hmm." She considered his words as her limbs turned heavy, the stress that had kept her shoulders rigid and her jaw tight for the last several weeks now dissipating. The alcohol, she knew. Considering her dinner had consisted of nothing but desserts containing enough sugar to keep a bakery in business for a week, it was a miracle she wasn't drunk. But she wasn't, not yet, just warm and relaxed and slightly fuzzy around the edges. "Blues and greens might redirect guests' eyes, but only during daylight. After sundown…one needs dark colors to go unnoticed." She widened her eyes in mock horror. "Until it is too late for the unsuspecting."

His smile deepened as he opened a new bottle of champagne. "You make me sound like a vampire."

"So far, I've only seen you after sundown. Maybe you wear green and blue during the day. Or maybe you really are a vampire and can't go out in the sun." She looked up at him from under her eyelashes. She wasn't sure if she had the flirting thing down pat, but she would prattle on about any subject if it meant his gaze stayed riveted on her. "Are you?"

He topped off her newly empty glass. "Interesting question. What do you think?"

She took a sip. The new bottle was different. The champagne was brighter, more acidic. Bolder. Like she should be perhaps? Maybe this was where she truly belonged, drinking champagne with a man who exuded danger—not to her physical well-being, but to her mental equilibrium. As it was, he was already occupying far more of her brain space than someone she just met should be. Or rather, that was how she would have reacted before the Knock. Now? She caught his gaze. "I think whoever you bite would enjoy it very much. Even if they regret it in the morning."

His hand froze, his flute halfway to his mouth. He recovered almost instantaneously, but she knew she hadn't imagined it. "But perhaps your partner objects to you going around biting people," she continued.

He drank deeply from his glass then set it down on the side table. He took another step toward her. This close, she could see his eyes weren't a dark brown, as she'd initially thought, but a mix of amber and gold and bronzed umber. "They would. If I had one."

He was very imposing. His shoulders were broad, his black shirt slightly straining across his chest. The sleeves were rolled up, revealing muscular forearms. Forearms that looked more than up to the task of supporting her weight, holding her steady as she moved above him…

She had no idea where that image came from but now that it had found a home on the main screen of her mind's cineplex, she couldn't get rid of it. She swallowed. "I don't have anyone in my life who would object. Not that I'm a vampire. Obviously."

Here came that look of scrutiny again. She lifted her chin and met his gaze until a smile dented the left side of his face. "No. But you aren't what I'd expected, either. I'm beginning to suspect you wear bright colors to distract and disarm."

"Or maybe I just like pink," she countered.

"No one likes pink that much."

"No one likes nothing but moody monotones, either, yet here you are." Their breaths comingled. She could almost taste the champagne in the air.

He bent his head, the space between them dissolving to scant millimeters. "I wonder. Who are you, Anna?"

She shivered at the low growl in her ear, goose bumps rising almost painfully along her arms. Who was she? She had no idea how to answer him. How could she when the answer eluded her own grasp?

But maybe she could find the answer. And the best way to start was to be direct and honest about what she wanted. Starting tonight.

She raised her head, her gaze catching his. "I'm someone who finds you very attractive. And I'm wondering if the reason why you approached me on the terrace was because you find me attractive. And if so, perhaps we should do something about it. Tonight."

She held her breath, scarcely believing she'd said the words out loud. Then her breath exhaled in a shaky swoosh as amber flames flared to life in his brown eyes.

"Fairy wings and glitter caught my attention. But I'm finding the woman who wore them to be far more intriguing." He lifted his right hand, the back of his fingers caressing her cheek, trailing sparks in their wake. "Is this why you came to my room?"

She swallowed. "I didn't spill the hot chocolate on purpose."

"Bell services could have delivered my jacket."

"True. I wanted…" Her mind spun. There were so many ways to finish the sentence. So many things she wanted, from a clean bill of health for Pepa to discovering how she fit in the world after the Knock. Then his thumb traced a path over her lower lip and all else burned away. Her breath caught, leaving enough air to exhale one word. "You."

His smile couldn't be more devilish if he were wearing a horned costume and carrying a pitchfork. "Glad to hear it."

"I leave tomorrow."

"So do I. After the meeting, of course."

Right. He'd mentioned he had a packed morning. Of course, she had a meeting of her own to attend. She nodded. "One night only. No questions, no regrets."

His left hand came up to join his right, cupping her face in his warm, generous grasp. "I guarantee regret is the last word you'll use."

She didn't doubt it. And she wasn't lying. She wanted him. So much, her knees were soft with it. So badly, she might expire from shivery anticipation alone, craving his touch on her breasts, between her legs. Still, there was something in his tone—a hint of self-satisfaction, or perhaps conquest?—that caused her to hold her chin high and stare him down. "Prove it."

The embers in his gaze flared into flames, the amber flecks gleaming in the reflected glow of the Lakes of Wonder neon lights. Then his mouth crashed down on hers and she couldn't see, couldn't think, could only feel.

She dissolved into a molten pool of desire. Somehow her legs functioned enough to walk backward toward the large bed, their mouths never losing contact, his hands knowing exactly where she needed to be touched for the flames to leap higher. Somewhere along the way she lost her joggers, then her hoodie, revealing the lacy bra she put on in the hopes that was happening would indeed happen before it, too, was discarded. Her knees finally gave out as the backs met the cool, crisp sheets and she fell onto the bed, only for Ian to pull her toward him until she was half on the bed, half off, her legs held open in his sure grasp.

She used her elbows to prop herself up and met his half-lidded gaze with a smile. "Well?" she said. She kicked off her slip-on shoe—very glad she was no longer wearing her sandals with their multiple buckles—used her right foot to caress his calf through the fabric of his trousers. "We only have one night. Are you going to stand there and look? Or are you going to put those hands to a better use?"

She'd never talked that way to a partner before. She always let her boyfriends take the lead. But Ian seemed to enjoy her words. His wicked mouth twisted with a promise that scored a direct hit to her core, causing an answering rush of wetness between her legs. His hands played with the bare skin of her legs, raising goose bumps that had nothing to do with the room's temperature. Not that she knew if the room was cool or warm, as she was burning up from inside. If his fingers brushed a centimeter higher, she might spontaneously combust into flames from how much she wanted him.

Then his fingers did go higher, pulling aside the damp silk of her panties. He smiled up at her. "So beautiful," he murmured, and she flushed at the pleasure in his tone. He brushed the pad of his thumb over what he saw and she bucked, hard, unable to control her movements. She was going to come, just from a slight touch.

She'd always had a hard time orgasming with her previous boyfriends. Unable to relax, perhaps. Too worried about pleasing them to be able to take her own pleasure.

But with Ian...

Then his mouth replaced his fingers, his tongue drawing her in and finding her most sensitive spot, and the fireworks that erupted behind her eyelids were brighter and more brilliant than anything Lake of Wonder had to offer.

When she calmed, his hand on her stomach keeping her anchored to this world, she opened her eyes and found him lying next to her, still fully clothed, his gaze focused on her. "Wow," she breathed.

He laughed. "I'll take it."

She rolled onto her stomach and started to undo the buttons of his shirt. "That was...wow." She got his shirt open and began to play with the treasure she uncovered. Gorgeously defined pecs above a firm abdomen, flat, coppery nipples and a happy trail of crisp, dark hair leading to one of the most impressive erections it had ever been her privilege to handle once she freed him from his trousers and briefs. He growled at her touch, a deep groan that caused her insides to clench and demand his attention anew.

This was relatively new to her, to take her time, to explore and wander. Her last partner had always been so eager to get to what he called "the main event" that she'd forgotten how much fun it could be to just touch and taste, discovering what caused him to squeeze his eyes shut and his skin to shudder. She couldn't get enough of his erection, drawing him into her mouth, her tongue swirling and lapping, her hands experimenting until she found the right rhythm and pressure to make him lose control.

When he came, she reveled in the knowledge she'd caused that. She, Anna Stratford, had made this glorious human being, this accomplished, smart man far out of her usual league, fall apart. She grinned up at him. "Want to go again before the night is over? Might as well make our time count."

She shivered at the gleam in his eyes as he pulled her up and over him, his hands coming up to cup her breasts before his fingers found her tightly furled nipples. "We're going to run out the clock," he promised before kissing her into oblivion.

Five

Anna giggled then clapped her hand to her mouth and glanced around to ensure no one overheard her decidedly unprofessional laughter. The hallway of the Team Lakes of Wonder stretched out in front of Anna for an infinite distance. Or maybe that was just how it appeared to her to senses, addled by a night of truly amazing sex. Did everyone feel this…well, alive, after a one-night stand? Anna was aghast at what she had been missing all her adult life. Or maybe last night had been the perfect confluence of setting, partner and timing.

Her head pounded despite the two pain relievers she'd taken after sneaking back to her hotel room that morning while Ian showered. She needed a vat of coffee followed by an ocean of water. Her gait was unsteady and she slowed her pace despite running late. But her legs still reminded her with almost every step of her activities the night before, her thighs deliciously tender where Ian had grasped them. Her muscles ached from wrapping around Ian's solid torso, pressing into him as he pumped into her, his gaze never leaving hers, ensuring everything happening between them was with her full consent and resulted in her pleasure. Her hand flew out to brace herself against the wall as her memories triggered a rush of wetness between her legs, her nipples hardening to painful points as her knees threatened to give out.

Thank goodness she and Ian had agreed it was only night, because Anna wasn't certain she would survive many more. She certainly wouldn't have a productive life. She wanted nothing more than to return to her hotel room and relieve the pressure building fast and hot deep inside her. If only she'd brought her vibrator with her on this trip, but who knew it would have been necessary?

She took a deep breath. She had the rest of her life to draw upon last night for her wildest fantasies. She needed to pull herself together and get through today. And another side benefit of Ian occupying all five of her senses so fully? She hadn't had the time nor energy to stress about this morning's meeting. Until now.

She glanced at the numbers on the doors as she passed them. While part of her was glad she'd turned down an escort from the hotel to the meeting—she wouldn't have had the mental focus to make small talk with whomever had been assigned to babysit her—it might have been nice to be sure she was heading in the right direction. Finally, she came to a large glassed-in conference room. Several people had arrived before her and were standing in small conversational groups or availing themselves of the table laden with bagels, donuts and baskets of leftover Halloween candy. Ian would have fit right in with their tailored black and gray suits. She, on the other hand… she smoothed the skirt of her lemon-yellow dress and pushed the door of the conference room open, her pulse beating fast as her throat suddenly went dry.

Wherever Ian was, she hoped his meeting was going well. Not that she knew why her apprehension was at DEFCON levels. As had been explained to her ad nauseam the day before, her role in today's meeting was mostly ceremonial. Sign, shake hands, skedaddle.

People's heads turned as if one when she opened the door. Anna beelined toward the first Lakes of Wonder executive she recognized, her hand held out for a handshake greeting. "Hi, Teri. Good to see you again. Hope I'm not late."

Teri shook her head. "Right on time. We're still waiting for the BBA team to arrive. Can I get you anything?

"Coffee. A swimming pool of it."

Teri smiled. "Will a large cup do?"

"If I must. I can have seconds, right?"

Teri laughed and made a motion at a young man standing nearby. Before Anna knew it, a steaming

mug of coffee had materialized in her right hand and
Teri was directing her to a seat at one end of the very
long and wide table. Anna sank into the oversized
black-leather chair, the seat back looming high behind
her, feeling like a kid who had been invited to sit at
the grown-ups' table for a holiday dinner.

She glanced at the documents that had been placed
on the table in front of her chair. She'd seen them before, but the amounts of money involved in the sale
still took her breath away. Previously, Anna had never
been involved in any business negotiation larger than
helping a family pick out a house full of furniture.
That, granted, could be a hefty bill—for a family.
But nothing compared to selling a theme park worth
billions.

Family. Anna squeezed her eyes tight and then
opened them to look around the room. No one was
paying attention to her, per the usual whenever she
interacted with the Lochlainn Company executives.
No one caught her gaze. And no one else sat down at
the conference table as they continued their conversations in scattered groups around the room. Phrases
foreign to her such as "four quadrant release" and
"value added loyalty program" were tossed around.

The message that she was an interloper and had
no real place in today's discussion couldn't be clearer
than if they had hired the Lakes of Wonder Marching
Band to play "Hit the Road."

She took out her phone and saw she had a string
of texts from Maritza, asking if she was okay, and
groaned. She missed her usual call to say good morn-

ing to Pepa before kindergarten. In her defense, she had been otherwise occupied. Rising from the table, she found a corner that was mercifully free of people using jargon and called her cousin.

"You're alive, after all," Maritza answered.

"Is Pepa upset?"

"No. She's fine. She was excited to get to school to show off her Halloween toy haul to her friends."

"Careful, she might start a trend of swapping candy for toys." Anna laughed then sobered. "I'm sorry about missing the call."

"Yeah, that's not like you. So, I'm hoping the reason is really good one. As in *really* good." Maritza dropped her tone to low and breathy, the vocal equivalent of a wink wink nudge nudge.

"Um…" Anna hoped her blush would subside by the time she had to return to the conference table.

"Tell me everything!"

"I will, but not now. I'm in the meeting room. But the people from BBA haven't showed up yet." Her gaze swept around the conference room. Yesterday's meetings had been on a lower floor, in a windowless space. That was not the case here. Once again, she was overlooking Lakes of Wonder, although this view was not one meant for guests. She could see the service road that circled the park's backstage areas, and the rear of the buildings that housed the Buccaneer Bayou attractions. The Lighthouse still stood proud in the background, however, drawing her focus. Like a good weenie should, she thought, and smiled at the rush of warmth lighting her from within.

She wrenched her gaze—and her thoughts—away from the vista with difficulty. Only then did she notice the three framed photos hanging on the opposite wall.

She approached the nearest framed work for a closer look. The black-and-white photo depicted a half-built Lighthouse of Amazement in a field of mud, with a crane off in the distance. In front of the building site, both wearing hardhats, were a beaming Archibald Lochlainn, the founder of the Lochlainn Company and its subsequent empire—she recognized him from the Wikipedia article she'd read—holding a baby she could only assume was his only child, Keith.

Keith. Her biological grandfather.

"Anna? You still there?"

Anna wrenched her thoughts back to her phone call. "Yeah, I'm here."

"You zoned out. Again."

"I know. I just…it's weird, being here, you know?"

"It's been weird ever since that lawyer showed up." Maritza paused. "Are you mad at me?"

"Why would I be mad at you?"

"For asking you to send in your DNA to that company. I thought it would be fun. I had no idea—"

"*You* had no idea?" Anna laughed. The laugh sounded angry to her ears and she winced. She tried again, softening her voice. "You had no idea? That's an understatement.

Not for the first time, she wished she had never answered the Knock. But how could she have known that the pleasant-appearing man in his Brooks Brothers' suit was there to erode the solid ground upon which she had built her life?

Her parents had kept the truth of her conception from her. Her biological father was not Glenn Stratford. She did not inherit from him her blonde curly hair or her tendency to freckle, as she had assumed all her life. Instead, her parents had used an anonymous sperm donor to conceive her.

And the donor's identity turned out to be Jamie Lochlainn, the now-deceased son of Keith, who had sold his sperm to a top fertility clinic to pay for college when he had been estranged from his father and refused to touch his family's money.

"But it's okay," Anna hurried to reassure Maritza. "I mean, look where I am. Free, all-expenses-paid trip to California."

"Yeah, that's part of the problem. You ran off without speaking to your parents. And you're still not speaking to them." Martiza's tone softened. "They miss you. Please call them."

Anna sighed. "I will. I just… Not now. Let me get through today's ceremonial signing first." When she'd answered the Knock, the lawyer—whose name she would never forget, Bingham Lockwood—had not only told her the truth of her parentage but offered her a once-in-a-lifetime opportunity: finalize the sale of Lakes of Wonder to the BBA Group. If she completed the transaction by the end of the year, she would earn a place in Keith Lochlainn's will.

Her grandfather's will.

The grandfather she'd never known existed.

She never did receive a satisfactory answer as to why Keith was insisting on such a complicated hoop for her to jump through. To her, it was simple. Either he accepted she was conceived from Jamie's sperm, or he didn't. Perhaps asking her to oversee a complicated business deal indicated he thought something else had been passed down to Anna aside from twenty-three chromosomes. Something intangible that made her a Lochlainn.

"Okay," Maritza said. "Break a leg or whatever people say in business meetings. I'm here if you need me."

"Thanks, although I should be the one there for you and Pepa."

"Hey, you earn a spot in Keith Lochlainn's will, you will be," Maritza joked. Then she turned serious. "But I know that's not the reason you accepted that lawyer's challenge. Just…" She sighed. "We all love you, you know. The Lochlainn thing, it doesn't matter. Not to us. You're still our Anna."

"I know." Anna's nose tingled and she blinked back the tears before they could form. "But it matters to me." She said her goodbyes, her gaze returning to the photo of Archibald and baby Keith, before turning her attention to the other images.

Centered on the wall was a photo in yellow-tinted saturated color. The Lighthouse was complete, soaring high into the cloudless blue sky. Looming next to it was the iconic mechanical Seamus parade float, several stories tall and rumored to have breathed real fire in its heyday, which had long ago been mothballed. In the foreground of the photo stood a much older Archibald, his back hunched but his gaze direct. Next to him she recognized Keith, perhaps in his thirties or early forties. And Keith was holding…

A toddler Jamie. Who grinned for the camera as if he knew this kingdom would all be his someday.

Before Anna knew what she was doing, her right hand reached out to trace the curve of Jamie's cheeks. She recognized the mischievous glint in his eyes. She'd seen it often enough in photos of herself as a baby and small child.

The third photo on the wall had been taken recently. The image was in high definition, the banners on the Lighthouse vivid and vibrant for Lakes of Wonder's seventieth anniversary. But no one stood in front of the Lighthouse. No Keith, no Jamie. Just the tall white tower, the surrounding grounds empty and deserted. No doubt the photo had been taken before the theme park's opening, judging by the silvery morning sunlight, but the empty landscape still made Anna shiver.

What happened? How had the Lochlainn family gone from being the proud possessors of Lakes of Wonder to selling it off? She squinted, willing the two-dimensional Keith to impart his secrets.

The photo remained silent.

The room started to buzz with conversation. "Anna?" Teri materialized next to her. "The BBA team has arrived. We're ready to get started, if you are?"

"Of course." Anna put on her brightest smile and

turned around to greet the newcomers. She held out her right hand for a handshake to the nearest BBA executive, a tall, beautifully dressed Black woman. "Hello, I'm—"

"Sorry we're late. My fault."

Anna froze. She knew that voice. She'd last heard it that morning. In bed.

Ian's bed.

It couldn't be him. She must have heard wrong. Her subconscious, which was still playing erotic images from last night whenever her mind wandered, must have conjured his voice.

She peered around the woman shaking her hand. Her stomach dropped to the floor. No, she wasn't hallucinating.

Ian filled the doorway of the conference room, the last of the group to arrive. "Hi. Ian Blackburn, BBA's CEO. Good to meet everyone in person, finally."

His darkly amused gaze caught and held hers in the seconds before he was rushed by several Lochlainn Company executives eager to greet him.

"Anna." She forced her name through numb lips and then finally remembered to let go of the woman's hand she was shaking. "I'm Anna Stratford."

"Shall we take a few minutes to grab coffees?" Teri asked. The Lochlainn and the BBA factions began to drift toward the table of food, making small talk along the way.

Anna somehow found her chair at the conference table, the room out-of-focus and spinning around her. A fresh cup of coffee appeared in front of her, giving her something to focus on. She looked up to thank whoever had delivered the mug to her.

Ian was leaning over her chair. His smirk was even more pronounced as he bent down and spoke for her ears only.

"Hello again. Let's hope today's signing is as equally...pleasurable...as last night. I have to say, that was the most fun I've had dealing with a representative of the Lochlainn Company.

He was amused. No, more than amused. He was *smug*. His lips may be incredibly talented, but she wanted nothing more than to wipe that expression off them. "Did you know?"

"Know what?"

"We would be on opposite sides of the table today."

His smirk didn't falter. "Of course. The Lochlainn Company informed us last week that you would be joining today's signing."

Oh, *of course*. Her pulse sped up even as her heart sank past her stomach. "That's why you approached me on the terrace."

"I wanted to meet you before this morning's meeting." His smirk turned knowing. "And I have no regrets. As promised."

His voice seemed to come from far way. She screwed her eyes shut, hoping when she opened them again, she would be on the hotel's terrace waiting for the fireworks and this would all be a very bad, awful nightmare brought on by too much blue champagne.

How could she be so...blind? And naïve. Categorically naïve.

She had only herself to blame. Maybe if she'd taken the time to become more acquainted with the theme park industry, she would know all the players and their names, but everything had happened so fast. And she'd been so hurt by her parents keeping the truth of her parentage from her, she'd barely kept herself together to put on a brave face for Martiza and Pepa while ensuring her design clients would be taken care of in her absence before getting on the plane at the required time. Besides, Bingham Lockwood had told her she only needed to show up. Make her mark—literally—as a Lochlainn by signing the deal, and she would fulfill the challenge Keith had set her.

She suppressed her groan.

Once again, she had gone with the flow, doing exactly what others had expected of her without questioning or stopping to think the situation through. And the one time she'd thought she was breaking free from the rules by which she'd lived until now—a no-strings-attached, one-night stand with a stranger—it turned out he wasn't really a stranger. Or rather, she wasn't a stranger to him.

And yet his scent caused her breath to stutter, the heat of his arm across the back of her chair making her pulse jump in erratic leaps.

She closed her eyes to stop the room from spinning around her. When she opened them, she found Ian regarding her, his expression unreadable. She raised her eyebrows. "What?"

"You didn't know."

"That covers a lot of things," she said. "As I'm discovering."

"You didn't know I would be here today," he clarified. "As part of the BBA team."

"Of course, I knew." Her chest burned. It was one thing to realize how badly she'd screwed up by blithely going along and not paying more attention. It was another to know Ian Blackburn had deliberately played her. That last night had been…calculated, and not the result of an attraction that, damn it, even now caused heat to pool deep in her belly as her skin yearned for his touch.

She put on her most professional expression, the one she brought out for clients who insisted on ordering sofas too big for their spaces despite her counseling against it and then demanded the ensuing unworkable result was Anna's fault for not warning them. "I'm merely surprised you were told I would be here."

That wasn't much of a lie. She was a very recent addition to the proceedings.

His gaze narrowed. "We never did establish what position you hold at the Lochlainn Company. Business development, I assume?"

She inhaled deeply, hoping the oxygen would clear her brain. "Interesting question. But—"

Teri dropped into the seat on the other side of Anna. "Good! I see you've met."

Ian didn't remove his gaze from Anna. "Yes. In fact, we were discussing what Anna does at the Lochlainn Company."

Teri made a sweeping motion with her hand. "What doesn't she do?"

"Doesn't do," Anna said. "That covers it—"

"Anna is a special liaison to Keith Lochlainn." Teri spoke over Anna. "She's been sent by New York specifically to oversee today's closing. And we're honored to have her for today's signing. Isn't that right, Anna?"

Teri held Anna's gaze. Her "don't screw this up" warning was clearer than if she had spray-painted the words on the boardroom's walls. Anna nodded, avoiding looking in Ian's direction. "I am here at the request of Keith Lochlainn, yes."

"Then let's get to it." Teri opened the file folder in front of her. Everyone else at the table followed suit. "Shall we start?"

Six

"Agreed. And…done." Ian signed the last page with a flourish then stacked the documents neatly together before sliding them across the table to Anna. "Your turn," he said, the words coming out a bit rougher than he'd intended.

Last night, "your turn" had had a different meaning. She shifted in her chair, rearranging her legs. He smiled. It seemed he was not the only one having a harder time than normal concentrating without being interrupted by memories of their recent activities in vivid detail.

His smile deepened. This meeting had gone better than expected. Not only had he needlessly worried about a last-minute negotiation twist, but he was able to spend the morning gazing at his companion of the night before.

He preferred the Anna that had been in his bed, all tousled curls and flushed skin and swollen lips begging to be kissed again and again. But the woman across the table from him was a delightful vision, today dressed in a yellow dress with a high waistline, emphasizing those heavy, glorious breasts. To his surprise, she didn't speak much during the meeting, allowing the Lochlainn Company executives to do the bulk of the talking. Instead, her focus appeared to be caught by the photos lining the wall opposite her. Whenever she did catch his gaze, her expression remained carefully schooled in a mask of calm, reminding him she was an excellent actress—except when they were in bed. That hadn't been an act, he was positive. Too bad they were currently sitting in a boardroom. Once they finished the meeting...

They'd agreed last night was a one-and-done. And he was scheduled to leave for Hong Kong tonight. But perhaps she might be amenable to a repeat in the near future. To see if they could make lightning strike twice.

Her gaze flicked over and caught his. He smiled at her, a smile informed by the delightful images in his head of her sprawled against his pillows, limbs akimbo and skin flushed hot. As if she had read his mind, a warm pink washed over her cheeks as she pulled the papers to her. She flipped to the first page and her pen hovered over the paper. Then she put the writing instrument down and crossed her arms on the table. "Why do you want to buy Lakes of Wonder?"

He furrowed his brow. "We spent the last two hours discussing that."

"No, you spent the last two hours going over the financials and determining the price was fair. You never expressed why you want to buy the park."

The chatter in the room slowed, trickling to a stop. All eyes in the room were focused on them. He kept his expression neutral. "It's a good business decision," he said.

She shook her head. "Not answering my question."

"BBA owns amusement parks. Lakes of Wonder fits into our portfolio. Therefore, we made you a fair offer. Theme park 101," he offered, his gaze falling to linger on her mouth. Were her lips still swollen, or had they always been that delectably pillowy? The terrace and his room had both been dimly lit, after all.

She threw him a sharp glance and thinned her lips into a tight line, much to his disappointment. "But does Lakes of Wonder truly fit? It's a theme park for families. BBA's properties offer thrills for teens and other adrenaline seekers. I do know it's difficult to market to two different audiences. Like, for example…um." She hesitated and then her words tumbled out. "Like a business that sells furniture to families with large houses and a business that sells furniture to single people who live in smaller apartments. The first sells big, heavy pieces, so they need a spacious showroom. The second can sell multipurpose items that take up less room. You don't get—what's the word?—advantages from combining the two."

His smirk grew smaller the longer she talked. She was right, of course, even if her examples lacked the finesse he would expect from a Lochlainn Company executive. But what game was she playing? Why bring this up at the last minute?

"The word you're looking for is 'synergies.' But any costs associated with bringing Lakes of Wonder into BBA's operations are our problems, not yours. Another reason why this deal is very advantageous to the Lochlainns."

Her gaze focused on the large photos of Lakes of Wonder on the opposite wall. "When we last spoke," she said, and he noticed she was careful to avoid referring to when that was, "you said theme parks don't bring joy. That happy families are just a marketing gimmick. Do you really believe that?"

Yes. He did. Because he'd grown up in amusement parks and he knew from experience they didn't bring families closer. Didn't create fond memories, and certainly not ones he wanted lasting a lifetime. They did create infighting and backstabbing and heart attacks at an early age, however. "Does what I believe matter to today's negotiation? We've agreed on the terms. The financing has been approved. Unless you have a deal point we haven't covered, what I personally think isn't germane to the discussion. I leave marketing up to my marketing team." He glanced around the table at the other Lochlainn Company executives. "Any other questions? No?" He glanced at his smartwatch and then turned back to Anna. "We're scheduled to take photos commemorating the deal signing in fifteen minutes, so…"

Anna stared him down. She really did have gorgeous eyes. He could lose himself in their blue depths if he wasn't careful.

But he was always careful.

He smiled at her and indicated her abandoned pen. Her gaze narrowed. Then she reached for it—

No. She reached past the pen. Her hands instead pulled all the pages together in one neat pile, aligning them with a tap of the edges on the boardroom table. Leaving the papers in a neat pile, she pushed her chair back, pulling the strap of her purse over her shoulder as she rose and made her way to the exit. "I'm so sorry to have wasted everyone's time, but there will be no signing today."

The door slammed behind her and the room erupted into chaos. Ian could scarcely keep track of who was shouting what. Several Lochlainn Company executives jumped up, their intent to go after Anna and drag her back to finish the meeting clearly written on their expressions, but Ian cut them off with a loud, low, "No. I'll handle this."

He was almost out the door when Tai appeared at his elbow. "You sure? We have a potential breach lawsuit in the making. We should leave instead."

"No, it's my…" Ian stopped. "This might be payback."

Tai opened his mouth then snapped his lips shut. "I don't want to know, do I?"

"Can you calm things down here? Let them know we still want to go through with the acquisition."

"Sure," Tai said, but Ian was racing down the hallway before Tai finished uttering the syllable.

He spotted her waiting for the elevator. He ran, ignoring the shocked gasps from the people he passed. "Anna, wait!"

She ignored him, tapping her foot as she waited. The elevator doors opened and she scurried inside. The doors started to close. With a burst of speed, Ian managed to insert his foot into the decreasing gap between the doors, and then slid the rest of his body into the elevator cab.

Anna stared at him, her mouth slightly open.

"What was that about?" His lungs burned and he gulped air.

She huffed and tore her gaze away, staring straight ahead. "I decided not to sign."

"You can't do that. BBA and the Lochlainn Company have an agreement."

"I can, and I did."

"You've given us grounds to sue on breach of promise. We will take action."

"I didn't say I wasn't selling you Lakes of Wonder. I said I wasn't signing today."

The elevator ground to a halt. Anna flung out her arms and braced herself against the walls. "What the...what happened?"

"I pushed the stop button."

"You did—why isn't the alarm ringing?"

He pointed to a red button marked Alarm. "Separate system. It's an old elevator. This building dates to the construction of Lakes of Wonder."

She lunged for the control panel but he easily blocked her access. "You're safe."

"Trapped with you?" She scoffed.

"You didn't seem to mind being in an enclosed space with me last night."

Red flooded her cheeks. "People need this elevator, you know. What if someone with mobility issues is waiting to use it right now?"

"There are three other elevators." He unfolded his arms and closed half the space between them. "You realize today was the culmination of months of negotiating. Of time-consuming back-and-forth emails and conference calls, research, pulling numbers together…"

"I'm aware. And I'm sorry. But I…can't."

She truly was a damn good actress. He almost bought that was regret making her eyes widen, causing her to bite those plump lips. Almost. Because he also remembered those lips giving as good as they got, biting and sucking and whispering wicked words. She might play the sweet princess in her summer-colored dresses, but he'd had a taste of what Anna Stratford was capable of last night and it was far from innocent.

He was so close. So. Damn. Close. To ridding BBA of Harlan's disastrous, poisonous leadership. To freeing not only his company but his family from his former stepfather for once and for all. All he needed was

Lakes of Wonder to secure his uncle's and cousin's votes on the board of directors.

This deal had to happen. And he would not let the Lochlainn Company pull the rug out from underneath him again, no matter how attractive the woman doing the pulling.

"Can't. That's an interesting choice of words." Before he knew it, he'd closed the remaining space between them. The elevator light yellowed and flecked with dust gathered over the years, but it was bright enough to illuminate the freckles bridging her nose and spilling over her cheeks. Freckles that still stood out despite the crimson still blooming in her cheeks. "Seems to me all you needed to do was pick up a pen. And as I recall, your hands are in excellent working condition. You had no problem with grasping—"

"Stop right there. Yes. I can physically sign. But I can't..." She inhaled, the curves of her breasts pushing against the flimsy yellow fabric of her dress. Breasts that had overfilled his hands, warm and satiny with dark rose tips that—

He shook his head to clear it. Reconciling the woman who stood before him with the temptress tangled in his sheets the night before would have to wait. "Why, damn it? What is wrong with the deal?"

"You are!" The words burst out of her.

"Me?" He stared at her. "What the hell...look, if this is about last night, I have a very good memory and you were a consenting participant. But this is a multibillion-dollar deal you're deciding on a whim—"

"This isn't about last night. I mean, I'm not thrilled to learn you had ulterior motives—"

"Ulterior? What are you accusing me of—" He stopped. "Wait. You really didn't know I'd be in the meeting today, did you? Do you think last night—"

She exhaled, a loud puff of breath. "Never mind. Let's not talk about last night. Ever. It happened and will never happen again."

"Then why—"

"If Lakes of Wonder must be sold, it should be to someone who cares about its history and its legacy." She rested her balled-up fists on her hips. "Not to someone who sees it as only dollars and cents."

"You can't—" He took a deep breath. He'd known the Lochlainns would throw a twist into the deal. His mistake was believing Anna, despite her fairy costume and predilection for pink, would be honor-bound to play by the normal rules of cut-and-dried dealmaking. He had to give the Lochlainns credit, however, for taking him so off guard. "If you read the deal paperwork, you'd see that BBA has laid out a very prudent offer that considers Lakes of Wonder's past and present-day goodwill—"

She shook her head. "You're babbling more MBA buzz speak. Why do you want to acquire the park? Tell me. Or better, teach me. I want to be convinced you are the right buyer."

Oh, he could teach her so many things. Things he'd wanted to teach her the night before but they'd run out of time. And theme parks had little to do with the lessons he had in mind.

He had to give the Lochlainns credit for this latest gambit, however. He'd been right. Anna wasn't the usual Lochlainn shark. She used earnestness instead of cynicism, enthusiasm instead of jaded weariness. That made her even more dangerous.

But perhaps he could make the delay in signing the deal work to his advantage. He could use the time to consolidate his position with the other directors on the board who weren't in Harlan's pocket, gain more votes to make his victory over his stepfather secure.

He smiled and placed his hand on the slick metal of the elevator wall above her right shoulder, resting his weight as he leaned toward her. "I'm happy to show you anything you want. Anytime."

Her breathing stuttered. She smelled of lemon and mint, of summer breezes and fresh air despite being trapped in an elevator on a gray November morning, and he suddenly wanted nothing more than to forget BBA, forget the Lochlainn Company, and whisk her off to a secluded bungalow with a large bed and no other furniture.

Then her gaze narrowed into daggers of dangerous light, and he was back to standing in an airless elevator cab stopped between floors in an ancient office building. "I've already experienced what you're suggesting and there will be no repeat. Unless you want me to add 'reneges on his word' to the reasons why I'm hesitant to sign."

He straightened and held up his hands, palms out. "I'm referring to Lakes of Wonder only, of course."

Her gaze searched his. What she was looking for,

he didn't know, and from the frown lines appearing on her forehead, she wasn't successful at finding it. "Okay. We have our first deal."

"Second," he reminded her. "Last night. Remember?"

Her gaze flashed. "Fine, second. Here. Shake." She held out her right hand.

"Not so fast."

Her hand lowered. "Now what?"

"I can't wait around forever for you to make up your capricious mind about whether you feel like selling or not. There needs to be a time limit."

"Fair enough. How about…by New Year's Eve?"

"December first. The deal must be closed by the end of BBA's fiscal year, which is December thirty-first." And by the next board meeting.

She pursed her lips. "Fine. But you better be prepared for a full demonstration of why I should sell to BBA."

This time he was the one who offered a handshake. "I plan to be very thorough."

Her gaze narrowed at his insinuating tone but she took his hand, her palm sliding against his. The resulting electric spark didn't take him by surprise. He already knew when they came together, lightning struck.

"Let's hope you are. I plan to be satisfied. Before I sell the park." She released his hand, but red still flew high on her cheekbones.

Oh, he'd satisfy her. He had the utmost faith in his ability to charm even a chameleon like Anna into going along with his wishes. Exhibit A, his hotel room. He pushed the stop button, releasing the elevator, and the cab began to move again. "What's your phone number?"

"What? Why—"

"We're going to be spending a lot of time together at Lakes of Wonder. It would be helpful to have a way to reach you."

The elevator reached the bottom floor and dinged open. They exited to an empty lobby. "Give me your phone," she said. When he acquiesced, she typed furiously before handing it back to him. "There. Now you have it."

He looked at his screen. "Make me believe" read the name on his contact list. He laughed. "I have meetings I can't rearrange in Hong Kong. Shall we say a week from today? We can meet a half hour before the park opens at the VIP entrance."

She shook her head. "No. Meet at the main entrance gate. The ticket booth furthest to the left."

He frowned. "It's faster to use the VIP entrance."

"But it's not the experience most parkgoers have." She raised her eyebrows. "Have you ever visited just as a regular guest?"

He...no. Not even as a child. As a member of the Blackburn family, he'd had VIP guest privileges at most amusement parks around the world. "If you insist. Main entrance gate."

She smiled. It turned the grim lighting in the lobby into a bright summer's day. "Don't be late."

Oh, he wouldn't. He needed this deal to be done.

He wanted Anna Stratford.

He saw no reason why he couldn't be successful at attaining them both. Woo Anna, and the theme park would also fall into his hands.

He would beat the Lochlainns at their own game. Twice over.

Seven

Anna checked the time on her phone, sighed, and then returned the device to her ear. "He'll be here," she insisted to Maritza, on the other end of the call. Her foot tapped a staccato rhythm on the pavement. She wasn't nervous about seeing Ian Blackburn again…was she?

She was. Nervous. And scared. She'd blown up the big deal between the Lochlainn Company and BBA. She'd risked billions of dollars on a whim, driven by seeing the photos of Archibald, Keith and Jamie, wanting to know more about this place that brought generations of Lochlainns together, only for Keith to let it fall into disrepair and to be sold.

Nervous and scared…and excited. Her stomach fluttered like it had every time she had thought of Ian in the last week. He hadn't been exactly forthcoming about his identity. On the other hand, she wasn't about to tell him she was a Lochlainn. She couldn't, per the terms of the Knock, or she would risk her place in Keith's will. But every time she tried to stir up a bout of righteous indignation at sleeping with Ian under false—no, not false, just not fully honest—pretenses, she only stirred up memories of how amazing his body had felt against hers. Hot, vivid memories causing her breath to catch and her pulse to race.

"Yes, he'll show up," her cousin agreed. "With a lawsuit. I still don't know what you were thinking."

"I was thinking…" Anna screwed her eyes shut. "Ugh. I wasn't thinking. I was reacting."

"Have the Lochlainn Company people said anything to you yet?"

"No." Anna's phone and email had been very quiet about the unsigned paperwork. Too quiet. The only item that could be termed a response was a mass email sent to all the Lochlainn Company executives who had been in the meeting, reiterating Anna was calling the shots in the negotiation and to follow her lead. "They seem to be leaving everything up to me."

"We're talking billions of dollars. That's weird."

"I know."

"And unsettling."

"I also know." Anna sighed. "But there might be a method in their madness. I think there is more going on, both with Keith Lochlainn and with Ian Blackburn. This deal isn't as clear-cut as it was presented to me."

"What makes you say that?"

Anna hesitated. "A feeling..." She winced and took the phone away from her ear. She put it back up in time for the tail end of Maritza's long-suffering sigh.

"Anna..."

"Have my feelings ever steered me wrong?" She bit her lip. Damn it, Maritza was not the person to ask.

"Do you seriously want me to answer that?"

"If that's a reference to my parents lying to me—"

"What? No!" Maritza huffed. "It's a reference to you pretending you can continue to ignore your parents. You said you'd call them."

"I know, and I—" Anna sighed. "You know what I find the most hurtful about the Knock? It's not that my dad—Glenn—it's not that he and my mom lied. Or rather, didn't tell me. It's that a family, whose only connection to me is a DNA test, is trusting me with one of their major businesses, while the people who raised me barely trust me to talk to clients on my own."

"I know you feel that way." Martiza inhaled. "But you're not playing with someone's suite of living room furniture—"

"Playing with? Now you're doing it, too."

"I didn't mean it that way. You yourself call it playing."

"Because designing interiors is fun!" Anna rubbed her forehead with her free hand. "I know you and my parents have only my best interests at heart. But I need to see this Lochlainn thing through. And I need more time before I can talk to them."

Maritza clicked her tongue, a sign that she was willing to drop the discussion. "Okay. Just remember you're making a decision about an icon of people's childhoods."

"Even more reason for me to dig deeper and understand what is going on."

Maritza snorted. "Are you sure you're not doing this because you want to dig deeper into Ian Blackburn? Like 'dig your fingernails into his back' deeper?"

To be fair, the thought had crossed Anna's mind. More than once. It might have been the starring act in her dreams the last six nights. "I was given a task to do, and I want to do it properly."

"If you say so." Maritza did not sound convinced. "I have to run. Call me after your date."

"It's not a date—" But Maritza had hung up.

"Ugh." Anna squeezed her eyes shut.

"It's not a date? Guess I shaved for nothing."

Her eyes flew open. Ian stood in front of her, his amused grin lighting the air around him, brighter than the still-rising sun.

Any stress from her phone call with Maritza fled, replaced by a new tension. The taut strumming started low in her belly and then flew along her nervous system, her heartbeat a loud timpani drum solo in her ears. Really, it should be illegal for any human being to look as good as he did, especially considering the early morning. If she thought Ian in his sharply tailored business suits and pressed suits were enough to take her breath way, that was nothing compared to Ian in black jeans that appeared to have made precisely to hug his muscled thighs and well-defined ass, topped with a dark gray Henley pullover with the sleeves pushed up to reveal his forearms. Tensed forearms that had held him suspended above her before their bodies came together in—

She blinked, the vision disappearing. Sure, that night had been fun. More than fun. But there would be no replay of that scene. She resolutely dragged her gaze from the exposed skin below the pushed-up fabric and turned to look over at the crowds starting to form. "Sorry to have caused you to waste your time. I prefer stubble to clean-shaven, anyway."

"Noted." His grin caused her stomach to jump in interesting patterns.

She rolled her eyes and looked away, hoping to appear as unaffected as possible. "I see you're still in your camouflage."

He looked down at his outfit. "I'm dressed for a day in the parks."

"Wearing an absence of color," she pointed out.

"Black is the result when all colors are mixed. I contain multitudes."

She laughed. "Shall we go in? I have a pass that allows guests."

He pulled a card out of his wallet and waved it at her. "Your pass or mine? It's amazing what perks you receive when you are prepared to spend billions of dollars, only for the rug to be pulled out from under the deal at the last minute." His tone was deadpan, but amusement gleamed deep in his dark gaze.

"The rug isn't gone for good, just…rolled up for now." They entered the park and strolled through Seamus's Seaport, then crossed the bridge that marked the boundary between the seaport and the six lakeshore ports that comprised the park. The bridge was themed to resemble the Pont Neuf in Paris but was much wider than the original to accommodate throngs of guests. However, Anna and Ian could easily meander as the crowd was sparse, mostly consisting of mothers with children too young for school strapped into strollers.

"Not a huge turnout this morning," he noted.

"It's a Friday," Anna rejoined. "During the school year. People have work, you know."

"Precisely. Fridays are a day people take off work for an extended weekend. It's one of our busiest days at BBA parks."

"It's also the start of the holiday season. People have more commitments than normal."

"And that's why the park should be more crowded than normal, with people eager to see the decorations." He looked over at her. "Point one for selling. Lakes of Wonder isn't attracting the guests necessary to stay financially afloat. BBA parks are."

"This is just one day, in the early morning. The place could be packed by this afternoon."

"Agreed. Today is only one data point. But we have the historical attendance figures. They're in the deal paperwork."

Anna pressed her lips tightly together. She couldn't blame the weather for the lack of guests. It was a gorgeous Southern California morning. The air was crisp, a reminder that colder days were coming, but also promised a warm afternoon, a reminder that autumn still brought high temperatures. Sunlight lit the faux French storefronts lining the bridge and the Lighthouse of Amazement in the distance, throwing the buildings into sharp relief, a contrast to Florida's softer, more golden glow. Not even the hint of a cloud lingered on the horizon.

She'd always thought California was desert-dry, dusty and filled with car exhaust. Now she understood why people clamored to live here.

"Let's sit on that bench." She pointed to a wooden bench festooned with intricate wrought-iron curlicues.

Ian shot her a quizzical glance. "Tired already?"

"No. But we're here to observe, right? So, let's observe."

Ian's expression was skeptical, but he followed her lead as she beelined to the bench. It provided the perfect view of both the people entering the park looking left and the Lighthouse of Amazement looking right. "So now what?" he asked once he had arranged his long legs next to Anna's.

"Now we watch."

"For how long?"

Anna turned to him. "Do you have a problem with sitting still?"

"You make me sound like a kindergartener refusing naptime."

"Well?"

"I don't know how you do things at the Lochlainn Company, but at BBA, we belong to the 'time is money' philosophy."

She rolled her eyes. "In my line of work, it's always wise to observe the customer in their setting before making sweeping changes."

"Right. Your work. What is it that you do at the Lochlainn Company again? We never established that." He leaned back against the wooden slats of the bench, stretching his arms out across the top of the bench. If she leaned back, her shoulder would fit neatly into the loose grip of his hand. His hand, so warm, so sure, so knowing...

She kept herself perched on the forward edge of the bench. "What don't I do?" She echoed Teri's words at the meeting. They weren't a lie. She literally did nothing.

His gaze narrowed. "You aren't on the business development team. I checked. There isn't an Anna Stratford matching your description registered to the California or New York bar, so you aren't a lawyer. You—"

"Look!" Anna indicated a toddler dressed in a "Lad of Wonder" T-shirt running down the wide paved road, a woman who appeared to be his mother judging by their shared bright auburn curls in hot pursuit. "He's heading straight for the Seamus balloons," she predicted.

Sure enough, the toddler came to a dead stop in front of the balloon vendor, his gaze fixed on the bright green helium-filled balloons bearing the smiling image of Seamus bobbing in the morning breeze. The mother caught up, visibly winded, and with a smile for the vendor and a frown for her son, picked him up and began to carry him away. The toddler burst into loud, angry sobs, attempting to throw himself out of his mother's grasp, his hands opening and closing in the direction of the balloons.

"Poor thing." Anna got up from the bench. Ian put his hand on her arm. His touch was warm. And electrifying. Her toes and fingertips crackled with the heat. "What?"

"She has her reasons for not buying the kid a balloon. And she's trying to bribe him with carrots she took out of her bag instead of buying snacks from a Lakes of Wonder concession cart. You need guests who will spend money at the park. Concentrate on them."

Anna couldn't keep her mouth closed. Her jaw insisted on hanging open, wider with each word Ian uttered. "She's looking after a toddler. Of course, she brought snacks for him. For all you know, he has a food allergy."

"The park sells prepackaged carrots." He shrugged.

"For ten times the cost of cutting up your own carrots at home."

"Lake of Wonder's profits in the snack category are abysmal. Guests who use Lakes of Wonder as a substitute for the city park are not profitable." He gave her a lopsided grin, the rakish angle of his lips making him seem even sexier. "You want a lesson in business? Revenues need to exceed expenses to equal profits."

And to think she'd found Ian Blackburn attractive. Still did, damn it. "Thank you for explaining basic arithmetic. I'm going to see if she needs help. Perhaps *she*—" Anna stressed the word—"would appreciate a random act of kindness." She shook off his light grasp, her skin still bearing his impression, and approached the mother struggling to get her son back in his stroller.

"A random what?" Ian called after her, but if she heard him, she didn't give any indication. He watched her go through narrowed eyes. Looked like he would need to change his tactics even more if he wanted to successfully woo her into selling the park. This was unlike any other business negotiation he had conducted and, for the twentieth time that morning, he wondered what, precisely, was her angle. Or rather, the Lochlainn Company's angle.

Still, he couldn't help admitting the view was delightful. Anna had foregone the country-club dress she'd worn to the meeting for what he could only assume was her idea of blending in with the parkgoers—because she certainly wasn't dressed as a theme park executive. Colorful leggings in shades of green outlined the curves of her legs and clung to the round globes of her ass. On top, she wore a lime green T-shirt, topped with a turquoise hoodie. Her blond hair was pulled back in a braid interwoven with green and turquoise ribbon. She literally sparkled, and it took him a second to realize she once more wore glitter on her cheeks.

Anna finished her conversation with the mother and, after a brief exchange with the balloon vendor, came back and handed the toddler the object of his desire. The toddler beamed, the mother beamed, and Anna—

Ian realized he was wrong. She didn't glow because she wore glitter. Her joy at making the small family happy lit her from within.

Anna was almost back to the bench before he belatedly understood the reason for her colorful outfit— she was dressed to remind people of Seamus, from the abstract sea-serpent-scale print on her leggings to the beribboned braid that resembled the plates on Seamus's neck.

"You really are a Lakes of Wonder superfan," he commented when she sat down. A little closer to him this time. He smiled.

"I read up on what people wear when they come to the park. I wanted to fit in for my first time." She swiveled her head at the sound of drumbeats. "Hey, there's a drum corps approaching!"

"The park used to feature a marching band, but budget cuts eliminated it. How can this be your first time at Lakes of Wonder?"

"What?" Her eyes widened. "Oh. I mean, first time wearing a Seamus-inspired outfit. Let's go see the musicians." She rose from the bench and didn't wait for him to join her.

Ian stared after her. While he didn't doubt this

was her first time wearing her outfit, he was pretty sure that wasn't the original intention of her words. He took out his silenced phone and glanced at the notifications filling the screen. Harlan's assistant sent an urgent message that Harlan was looking for him. Ian hit Delete. Simonetta Igwe, the COO, needed his attention. He texted back with a time to speak that evening. He scrolled through tens of other urgent messages, and then put the phone back into his rear jeans' pocket.

He hadn't planned on spending the whole day in the park. He'd cleared his schedule for two hours, at most, and that included a meal. But solving the ever-evolving mystery of Anna Stratford had shot to the top of his very extensive to-do list—because he needed to close the sale to remove Harlan from BBA, of course. Not for any other reason.

Certainly not because when he'd been wide awake with jetlag in Hong Kong, he'd tried reading the most boring prospectus he'd brought with him only for his thoughts to linger on Anna, the fireworks in the sky reflected in her rapt gaze. Anna, those gorgeous eyes blinking heavily after their first kiss then closing as she'd reached for him, her mouth open beneath his and her tongue playfully teasing his until the time for teasing was over. Anna, shuddering above him…

Anna, her shocked expression when she saw him in the boardroom.

His conscience twinged and not for the first time. Perhaps he should have been more straightforward when they'd first met, but she'd literally knocked him sideways with her glitter and fairy wings. He didn't like the implication Anna thought he had been trying to play dirty, even though playing dirty was the Lochlainn Company's preferred modus operandi.

At least the postponement of the sale had had one silver lining: he had time to prove to her that while he intended to drive a hard bargain for Lakes of Wonder, the offer was a fair one and he, at least, intended to play with honor.

He rose from the bench to join Anna where she watched the drum corps when his phone rang with the ringtone assigned to Tai's personal cell phone. He sighed. He could ignore everyone else, but Tai never called unless it was critical. "Where's the fire?" he answered.

"Harlan," Tai responded. His voice echoed, as if he were standing in a stairwell or some other place where he could have privacy and not be overheard.

"Now he's using you as his messenger? His assistant already sent me a message."

"No, the fire *is* Harlan. I found out he's calling for a vote of no-confidence in you as CEO at the next board meeting. It's supposed to be hush-hush but my assistant is friends with—"

"Harlan knows." Ian wondered where the day's heat went. Then he realized the sun was still blazing overhead. He was the only one chilled. "He's going on the counteroffensive. Someone must have told him about my upcoming vote to oust him."

"He's going to use the failed acquisition of Lakes of Wonder as the pretense for the vote. Something about how it was vital to securing BBA's future, et cetera."

"The acquisition didn't fail. It's not closed. There's a difference."

"Do you have the votes for the ouster?"

"Not fully secured," Ian admitted. "Olive and Preston will only vote with me if they're given Lakes of Wonder to run."

"Does Harlan have the votes to get you out?"

"If he wins Olive and Preston to his side, yes."

"So, you need the acquisition either way."

Ian's gaze sought out Anna, standing on the outer edges of the small crowd gathered to listen to the drum corps. She was bouncing on the balls of her feet in time to the music, her blond braid swinging. When a young child bumped into her, she whirled around. But instead of scolding him for running into her legs, she stepped back and let the child, along with the apologetic adults accompanying him, step in front of her, the better to see the musicians.

He almost didn't want to join her. He was enjoying the view far too much from where he was. The leggings she wore should be declared illegal for how they clung to her legs and ass.

"Don't worry, I'll be successful. The acquisition may be delayed, but it shouldn't take much longer to close it. When's the vote?"

"He tried to strong-arm people into a special meeting of the board, but no-go. So, next scheduled meeting in December."

"More than enough time to ensure the only one

getting voted out is him." Ian ended the call and made his way to Anna's side, who moved over to make room for him with a broad smile.

Lakes of Wonder must be his. If wooing Anna Stratford into selling the park to him was what he needed to do to ensure he could oust Harlan from BBA, then that was what he would do. And if, as a result, Anna Stratford found her way back into his bed, that would be an extra—and very pleasurable— bonus.

Eight

Wooing Anna was taking longer than Ian had expected.

Not because the time they spent together was wasted, but because he didn't have enough time to be with her. BBA had twenty-three parks in the United States and seven overseas, with active plans to expand into additional countries. Even without the battle lines with Harlan being clearly marked, Ian would be working sixty-hour weeks across ten time zones.

He had managed to carve out a few days over the two weeks since their first meeting in the park to walk around Lakes of Wonder with her. Wandering the theme park in her company was crucial to securing the deal and therefore spending as much time with her as possible was vital to the future of BBA, or so he'd told himself. So what if he cancelled his standing meetings and his assistant now automatically said no even to urgent requests so Ian wouldn't miss his scheduled time with Anna? He only had the best interests of his company in mind.

His presence in the park today had nothing to do with the way she made him laugh. Or how her observations, which seemed to come out of left field, always contained a pithy kernel of truth he had never considered.

No. He had no other motive than to get her signature on those documents, and maybe entice her to sealing their deal over a repeat bout in his hotel room. The sex truly had been too good not to repeat. But that was all.

Or so he knowingly lied to himself.

Anna was sitting at a small round white table outside Space Alien Al's Savory Snacks. Her elbows rested on the plastic surface, her hands providing a cup for her chin. A soft smile played on her lips as she watched the crowd—still light, in Ian's professional opinion—and her gaze was warm and relaxed.

She'd looked at him that way that night. After the fireworks had dissipated and their bodies were cooling. She'd turned to him, that exact same air of contentment wrapped around her.

Wrapped around both of them.

He approached, catching her gaze, which snapped back to her usual expression when they were together: cool, professional, guarded. He shouldn't be disappointed she automatically injected distance into their interactions; he was still in the early stages of winning her over.

But he was.

He handed her a plastic cup heaped high with berry-flavored frozen custard and decorated on top with a Seamus-shaped cookie. "Here. This is the best thing served at Lakes of Wonder. We tried to get the exclusive rights for our parks, but…it didn't work out."

Because the Lochlainns came in with a higher bid at the eleventh hour. Of course.

Anna took a bite and then another, closing her eyes as she licked the spoon, and then she stuck the spoon back in the cup for another taste. Her pink tongue swirled as she lapped up every trace of custard.

He had to look away. Otherwise, it would be apparent to everyone within eyeshot what an immediate, potent effect she had on him. Next time, he would wear his baggiest jeans. And maybe a long shirt that fell halfway to his knees.

Her sigh of satisfaction didn't help his situation. "This is delicious. Whatever Lakes of Wonder is paying for the rights, it's not enough."

He agreed. Anything that made her moan with pleasure like that was priceless. "I have the Pieces of Eight coaster next on the schedule. Ready?"

"I have a better idea. Since you said I need a bird's-eye view of the business, then why don't you provide one literally?" She rose from the table to throw the empty cup away, then grabbed his left wrist with her free hand and began tugging him toward a brightly painted sign that read "Skyroute to Valhalla."

He planted his feet on the purple brick walkway. "No."

"No, I don't need a high-level view of the business?" She tugged harder. He didn't budge.

"No, you don't need a literal one." He removed her hand gently and indicated the adjacent path that led to Buccaneer Bayou. "Next stop, the scurvy septet of scurrilous scoundrels, or so they keep singing. And singing."

She crossed her arms over her chest and propped herself against the edge of the table. "We've already spent a lot of time in Buccaneer Bayou."

"But you haven't been on the coaster," he pointed out. "I wanted to show you—"

"I know. You've said and I quote, 'The Pieces of Eight coaster has a fast-loading capacity, making it one of the better investments in the park,'" she recited. "I get it. Instead, I'd like to visit Valhalla Fjord. Since it's one of the original and therefore most outdated sections of Lakes of Wonder, I'd like to hear your thoughts on its future should BBA purchase the park."

"Certainly." He turned to his right. "This way to the Valkyrie Bridge. We'll need to walk through Heroes Harbor first."

"Or…" She pointed overhead to a rickety bucket suspended from a thin wire. It looked barely capable of holding two kittens, much less two grown adults. "We take the Skyroute."

No. He was not going to go on the Skyroute. But then Anna shifted, and that's when he noticed she was leaning on the table, not for effect, but to take her weight off her feet. Feet that appeared red and raw where her sandals' straps met her skin.

He bit back his exclamation. When Anna had showed up in her flimsy footwear, he'd warned her they might not be appropriate for walking several miles on the park's concrete walkways. But the sandals looked great on her, showing off her curvy calves to great effect, so he hadn't argued his point too hard. "Trouble walking?"

She started to shake her head and then she sighed. "Yes. These shoes weren't as broken in as I thought they were."

Something inside him twinged. Mostly anger at himself for not noticing she was in pain earlier. "Do you want to take the Skyroute?"

She smiled. "I thought you'd never ask."

Their flimsy metal pail—Ian couldn't think of a better way to describe the Skyroute vehicles and wished he didn't have to think about this mode of transportation at all—shuddered as it left the loading station and ascended at what had to be an unsafe speed into the sky. He didn't look ahead, because he would be reminded they were suspended several hundred feet in the air, traveling on what appeared to be a rather thin and insubstantial wire. He didn't look down, as the theme park guests below them had shrunk to the size of carpenter ants. He didn't look to the right, where death contraptions like the one he was in whizzed past, traveling in the opposite direction. That left looking to his left.

Looking at Anna.

She had no trouble taking in their surroundings, her head swiveling as she identified as many landmarks as possible. "There's Heroic Harbor—so that ugly square building must be the Supervillain's Revenge ride." She paused. "I see what you mean about the lack of three-hundred-and-sixty-degree theming." She took out her phone and started to make notes. "There should be a budget to theme the entire building so guests on the Skyroute are still immersed— Oh, look! The Lighthouse! I bet this would be a great place from which to view the fireworks."

"The Skyroute is shut down at night."

"What? Why?"

The real question was why it wasn't shut down 24/7, he wanted to respond. "Smoke from the fireworks."

"Right." She typed another note. "Still, I wonder if there is some way we can take advantage of the view from up here? Maybe reopen after the fireworks are over so people can see the park's lights from this angle? Or maybe as a special event on nights when there aren't any fireworks?" She scooted on the bench so she could look over the side, making the bucket rock slightly. Ian gritted his teeth, bile sloshing as his stomach flopped. "This is spectacular."

Focus on Anna. Focus on Anna. Focus on Anna.

But keeping his gaze locked on her only made his stomach flip harder, although in a much more welcome manner. The sunlight, when it wasn't playing hide-and-seek with clouds, turned her locks to gold and created a corona around her. Her cheeks were flushed pink, her eyes sparkling as she pointed out new items of interest.

He was counting the freckles on her right cheek, the one most visible to him—a task that required much concentration and took his mind off where and how far up he was—when he noticed two things.

One, the gondola was swaying side to side far more than usual.

Two, the gondola was no longer moving forward. They were stopped, suspended in midair. There wasn't even a gondola stopped in the other direction with which to commiserate with its passengers across the distance. He could see the back wall of the gondola ahead of them, but that was the only indication they weren't just…dangling. He swallowed, his mouth in dire need of moisture. Damn it, he'd known better than to take the Skyroute. He should have insisted Anna go by herself, and he should have traveled on foot to meet her.

Anna turned to him. "Wonder why we stopped? Maybe there's a guest needing assistance at one of the landing stations."

He nodded, a small, jerky movement. He didn't trust himself to speak.

The wind picked up. What would have been a welcome breeze on the ground was a nerve-plucking gust that caused Ian to tighten his grip on the edges of the bench. He closed his eyes for what he could have sworn was only a nanosecond. But when he opened them, he found Anna staring at him, concern spilling from her gaze.

"Everything okay?"

He nodded again.

Her gaze narrowed. "Why don't I believe you?"

He shrugged. To avoid her perceptive stare, he took out his phone. Perhaps Park Operations would know how long the Skyroute shutdown would last.

There weren't any cell signal bars on his phone.

His throat tightened, making it hard to swallow even as his mouth dried out and required moisture. His palms were clammy, causing his grip on the bench to slide. The gondola was open to the elements and the air was brisk and cool, but his lungs couldn't take in enough oxygen.

A slight breeze shook the gondola and he squeezed his eyes shut, hoping to stave off the vertigo he could feel building. He did not want to show weakness in front of Anna. Because she was a representative of the Lochlainn Company, he insisted to himself, and she would exploit any weakness against him. That's what Lochlainn loyalists did. She would find a way to use his soft spots against him in the negotiation.

But as her concerned gaze met his, he felt some of his dizziness recede. He grabbed onto the comfort of her presence and held on for dear life.

Anna regarded Ian. If she wasn't mistaken—and she wasn't—his complexion was several shades lighter than it had been earlier that day. She didn't miss his white-knuckled grip on the bench, either. She scooted along the seat until her left leg brushed his right one, letting her knee press against his, while ignoring the thrill that left her feeling somewhat light-headed at being so close to him. It would not do for both of them to pass out. "Is it the height or the type of ride vehicle or both?" she asked.

Ian's head whipped up. "What do you mean?"

"You're not having a good time."

"I—" He pressed his lips together and stayed silent. She waited, keeping her knee where it was, letting him know she was there. After a few beats, his leg relaxed, falling against hers. "I dislike being suspended in midair."

He may not be enjoying their time in the sky, but she was enjoying the press of his thigh, the brush of his shoulder as he leaned toward her and away from the edges of the gondola. "I appreciate you indulging me despite your obvious aversion to traveling in this manner."

"Your feet hurt."

"Yes, but you did warn me. You could have said 'I told you so' and continued our march across the park." She whistled a few bars of "Seventy-Six Trombones" from *The Music Man* while mimicking a marching band drum major keeping time with a baton.

The ghost of a smile appeared. "Hopefully I'm not being that regimented."

"No. But I did feel like I had to keep up or else. I'm enjoying our current enforced break, but I'm sorry this isn't enjoyable for you."

"I'll be fine."

The breeze picked up, turning into a strong wind. The gondola wobbled, just a slight swing, but enough movement to ensure Ian's expression returned to blank stone.

"I'm sure we'll start moving any second now," she offered.

Ian nodded, a short, curt bob of his head.

Anna stared at her sandals. Stupid footwear. She knew they weren't practical. But they made her legs look incredible.

A burst of static from the speaker overhead caused Anna to jump, shaking the gondola further. "Sorry!" she gasped.

"Please stay seated and keep your arms and legs inside your vehicle," a voice said from the speaker. "We are experiencing technical difficulties. Our attraction will resume shortly."

She turned to Ian. "We should be moving soon."

Ian shook his head. "No."

"Why not?"

"The message said they need more time to fix whatever is wrong."

"How do you know that?"

"The use of 'technical difficulties.' If this were a quick blip, the recording would say 'momentary stop.' It's code so the ride operators will know how to manage guest expectations without causing alarm."

Anna blinked. "That's clever."

Ian shrugged, a small, economical movement. "All parks use something similar."

Another gust of wind, stronger than the previous one, blew through the open vehicle. The sky, which had been a clear robin's-egg blue earlier that day, was now full of jagged clouds piled high. "I think a storm is coming," she said, and immediately wished she hadn't.

He glanced at the sky. His expression turned as gray as the bottom of the cloud directly above them.

Anna didn't mind the movement of the gondola—the way it shimmied in the air was rather thrilling—but the more the wind picked up in speed, the lower the air fell in temperature. Her T-shirt and shorts provided little in the way of protection. She crossed her arms over her chest, hugging them to her for warmth.

Ian glanced over. For the first time since the gondola had taken to the sky, a spark of interest flared in his gaze. "Cold?" he asked.

She was about to protest she was fine, keeping up the pretense she'd been engaged in all day, but she liked seeing a hint of the Ian she knew return to the stoic statue currently sitting next to her. "A bit," she acknowledged. "Guess my sandals weren't the only bad choice I made getting dressed."

Ian relaxed his grip on the bench, lifting his left arm in a silent invitation to move closer and share in his warmth. She knew she should keep her distance. Knew that if she allowed Ian to embrace her—even if only to ensure she wasn't chilled and numb from the wind—she would forget to be angry at him.

Forget he had lied. Well, okay, he hadn't told a bald-faced falsehood, but he also hadn't told her who

he was. A lie by omission was still a lie. And thanks
to the Knock, Anna had had her fill of lies of omission—but Ian's paled in comparison to her parents'.

Forget that a deal worth billions of dollars was
on the line.

Instead, she would remember. Remember the heat
of his mouth and the fire of his touch. Remember how
he felt inside her, filling her, pressing deep, insistent,
demanding...

Remember that she, too, was not who he thought
she was.

So really, who was she to hold that night against
him?

"Anna?" Yes, there was life back in his gaze now.
"Come here. No need for us to suffer separately."

He was right. Why be a martyr? She scooted closer
to him, keeping her movements small so as not to
cause the vehicle to move, and allowed his left arm
to gather her close.

She realized her mistake as soon as his warm hand
closed over her shoulder. His touch seared her skin
as if her thin T-shirt didn't exist. She inhaled, hoping fresh air would break the spell his presence was
beginning to weave over her, a spell of softening resolve and building desire, and quickly realized that
was a mistake when his scent filled her senses. She
was instantly taken back to that night in his room,
her nose buried deep in his neck, surrounded by his
addictive essence that was difficult to describe in
words but made her blood heat.

Like now.

Her nipples were hard and aching and the cool breeze was not the culprit. Thankfully, her bra would hide the evidence of Ian's effect on her, and her goose bumps—the tiny hairs on her arms quivering with awareness—could be attributed to the temperature. But she didn't dare look at him, for there was no disguising the want that must be naked on her face.

The breeze picked up and gondola shook again. Ian's hand tightened on her shoulder and she patted his thigh, keeping her touch light and as impersonal as possible. He only wanted the comfort of another person next to him. A golden retriever could take her place. In fact, maybe he might prefer the unconditional attention of a pet to her awkward movements right now—

"Anna." He breathed her name as if uttering a prayer. "Thank you."

On reflex, she lifted her head to respond. "Of course—"

Their gazes met with an almost audible clash. She swallowed the rest of her words, the fire in his dark eyes lighting the embers kindling deep in her belly. Licks of flame raced through her veins, until every nerve ending popped and sizzled.

She had to move away from him. Or she would do something she would regret.

She rose halfway up from her position on the bench, intending to scoot back to her original position. But the wind changed position and rocked the gondola sideways. Anna lost her balance and fell, half landing on Ian. Their legs entwined as Ian's arms came up to hold her waist while her arms instinctively circled his shoulders, seeking a secure hold as the gondola continued to sway.

Too late, Anna realized she was sitting sideways on Ian's lap. Her cheeks radiated fierce heat as she rocked herself forward to untangle her limbs from his. But Ian held fast and she gave in to her desire to relax into him. His thighs were hard and solid and they scorched her legs below her shorts.

"Anna," he repeated, and her name was no longer a prayer but a statement full of need. Their gazes continued to tangle as his right hand left her waist to stroke her hot cheek, his thumb trailing sparks as he brushed her lower lip.

He wanted her.

And she wanted him. She may not know who she really was. She may be an ocean's depth over her head with the theme park negotiations. But she knew one thing with an eternal certainty. She craved Ian Blackburn. As a friend, as a business rival, as her teacher in theme park negotiations—she'd take him any way she could have him, even temporarily, even for a stolen moment in a stalled gondola.

"Ian," she responded, marveling she could still form words when all the air had escaped her lungs. "I'm no longer cold."

"Good." His other hand began to explore the curve of her waist, discovering the sliver of bare flesh between her waistband and the hem of her shirt. She gasped. "But perhaps I should ensure this area does not become chilled."

"In fact, I'm rather warm."

"Then my efforts are working." His fingers traced abstract designs on her skin, leaving lightning bolts in their wake.

She swallowed, hard. "I propose an addendum to our deal. The first deal."

His touch slowed then stopped. She hurriedly added, "We shook hands on land. So, if we're in the air…the deal is null."

She would regret this. But up here, alone, the two of them suspended in the air on the slimmest of wires, no one to see them save for pigeons and the occasional seagull, she could pretend nothing else mattered. No Lakes of Wonder sale. No Lochlainn heritage to claim. No questions about where she belonged. Just her and him and the chemistry bubbling between them, threatening to ignite into an inferno.

He didn't answer her in words, but his left hand came up to join in right in framing her face. Then his lips were on hers and she forgot to think.

His mouth was warm and welcoming. She sank into his embrace, seeking and answering, their tongues exploring and tangling as if this was their first kiss. And in a way, it was. When they had kissed in Ian's room, the promise of sex had been thick in the air, the kiss a mere prelude—a hastily-blown-past checkpoint, in fact—on their hurried way to the main event.

But here in the gondola, with sex not even a remote possibility, they were free to focus on kissing. To learn each other's likes and preferred methods.

Anna learned Ian enjoyed a gentle tug of his lower lip, shuddering as her teeth lightly grazed him. He made a sound of triumph in his throat when she moaned as he kissed her jawline and found the sensitive skin below her ear. Their mouths came together again as he pulled her to him, his hands tangled in her hair, her fingers holding on to his shoulders for support as otherwise she would be a melted puddle on the floor, nothing remaining but her treacherous sandals. They experimented with pressure and speed, learning each other's rhythm and discovering, in the end, they could ignite the other with a simple brush of lip against lip.

Making out with Ian Blackburn was a transcendent experience, turning her veins into lava and her nerves into pure electricity. The ground was literally shaking underneath her—no.

The gondola was moving.

She pulled back from Ian, keeping her eyes squeezed shut, afraid to see what might be in his gaze. Would she see triumph, for getting her to break her vow of not becoming involved physically with him again—even if it was just a kiss?

But it wasn't just a kiss. Anna was sure of that.

She opened one eye, then the other.

Ian's gaze was focused on the gondola station where they would disembark, coming steadily closer. "We're almost on the ground," he said, his tone neutral. "There's a gift shop next to the station. We can find you a pair of walking shoes and a sweatshirt before we continue with our tour."

His tone was brisk and professional, acting like

a bucket of cold water on the desire still swirling in her veins.

This had been just a kiss after all. To him.

"Right. The ground." Anna swallowed. "About our deal. I, um, I…enjoyed the kiss. A lot." Her words built in speed, coming faster and faster until they tumbled one right after the other. "But it doesn't change anything. I still haven't decided what I'm going to do. About Lakes of Wonder, I mean. I don't want you to think I kissed you to lead you on or to otherwise manipulate you, because I didn't. And I know I should pretend the kiss didn't happen, but I can't pretend something didn't happened when it obviously just did happen, so—"

"Anna."

She looked up. Ian's gaze was steady and constant, his focus on her a flame without a hint of flicker. Her breath caught. "You kissed me as a distraction. I appreciate it. Nothing has changed."

She sat back on the bench, his words having an oddly deflating effect on her mood. "You think that's what happened?"

A half-smile dented his left cheek. "You wear your emotions embroidered not on only your sleeve, but your entire outfit."

"So. We're back on. You'll continue to show me why you are the best owner for Lakes of Wonder."

"Until December first." He smiled at her. "Unless you have all the information you need now and want to call an end to our bargain sooner."

No. That was the last thing she wanted. She

thought spending time with Ian would buy her time
to learn more about the Lochlainn family. Instead,
she only grew more confused about who she was—
and who was starting to matter to her, very much, in
a way that did not bode well for the future stability
of her heart.

Their gondola was slowing down, the station looming closer. The guests in the vehicle ahead of them
were disembarking, the park staff ensuring they
safely exited their gondolas. "I still have some open
questions. For instance, our destination of Valhalla
Fjord. I heard the Viking Longboat has dry rot?"

"Parts of the boat have been closed to guests, yes."
Their gondola settled into place next to a revolving
walkway. Ian jumped out and turned to give Anna
a hand. She tried not to wince when her shredded
feet met solid ground again. "But it's been that way
for years."

"Why didn't the Lakes of Wonder management
fix it?" Anna clung to the railing as they descended
the embarkation station's stairs, allowing the metal
balustrade to support her weight. Too late, she looked
up to see Ian's speculative stare.

"I was hoping you could tell me," he said. "You're
the one who works for the Lochlainn Company."

She swallowed, hoping to work moisture into her
mouth. "I want to hear your theory. About why re-
pairs haven't been done, that is."

Her heart pounded furiously against her chest
walls. The terms of the challenge required her relationship to Keith Lochlainn to be kept out of the press.

If the public found out Jamie was her biological father before Keith decided to reveal all, she would be cut out of the Lochlainn estate.

She wanted to trust Ian. She was enjoying his company far too much than she should. And that kiss… she was proud of how well she appeared to have recovered. She wasn't stuttering. She was controlling her breathing. Any stumbling in her gait could be put down to her uncomfortable shoes and not to the real reason: her knees turned to liquid whenever he caught her gaze. And she liked him. He was smart—his quick observations about the theme park business opened new perspectives for her—and he made her laugh.

But something held her back from telling him the real reason why she was in charge of the sale. After all, the fate of Lakes of Wonder was still in her hands. And he wanted the park.

He regarded her for a moment, his eyes searching hers. Then he shrugged as he guided her to the entrance of the nearest gift shop.

Anna headed for the clothing section, Ian following close behind. "My theory is Lakes of Wonder was the crown jewel of the Lochlainn empire when Archibald ran the company. There was talk of building more theme parks, but Archibald was exacting and the plans were never to his satisfaction. After he died, Lakes of Wonder fared well under Keith, but then he seemed to lose interest…maybe thirty years ago? He stopped investing in the park in favor of spending time and money on the Lochlainn Company's other businesses. But he also wouldn't sell the park." He slid her a sideways glance. "Until now."

Thirty years ago. Anna was twenty-seven. That meant Jamie's and Keith's estrangement must have occurred around the same time Keith decided to stop putting new money into Lakes of Wonder. "Hmm," she murmured, not willing to share the direction of her thoughts with Ian. Not yet. Maybe not ever. "Look, slip-on shoes!" She grabbed a pair in her size, uncaring they were decorated with garish cartoons of Seamus Sea Serpent's face. In fact, that was a point in their favor. "And...here's a hoodie."

"You would pick the pink one," he said.

"Of course. I'm not the one who wears camouflage 24/7. There's a matching one in dark gray if you like. It should go with everything in your wardrobe." She tossed the sweatshirt to him.

He caught it. "I think you know that shade of pink matches your cheeks. That's why you picked that one."

"I wasn't aware you paid attention to my cheeks."

"I've paid attention to every inch of you. If you recall."

"That was weeks ago. You can't expect to recall every last detail." She did, of course.

"Refresher courses are free, you just have to ask."

She turned to grin at him. Then her smile slipped.

She was used to seeing Ian smirk at her as he delivered his cheesy comebacks. Or contemplate her silently with his eyebrows quirked as he digested something she blurted. She even knew the weight of his stare when it was hot with desire.

But an Ian who lightly teased her, his expression open and relaxed? That, she was not used to. Her pulse thumped against her eardrums, drowning out the cheerful music being pumped into the store.

She liked this carefree Ian. Very much.

Too much.

But falling in deep "like"—her mind refused to consider the word "love"—with Ian Blackburn was firmly off her agenda.

For now.

Nine

A week later, all Anna had accomplished was to muddy the already murky waters passing for her thoughts. She wasn't ready to sell Lakes of Wonder and return home to Ft. Lauderdale – or as Martiza put it, she was continuing to avoid her parents. And after a trip up the coast to Los Angeles, where Anna paid for a tour of Lochlainn Studios and visited the small museum on the film lot dedicated to the family's rise to prominence, she was even more conflicted about where she fit into the powerful dynasty—or if she was even meant to fit in. After all, the only thing she had in common with them was half her chromosomes. Blood may be thicker than water, but that was a low bar to pass. Blood was still pretty thin.

The one area where her conflicts seemed to be resolving was her feelings for Ian. Ever since the kiss in the gondola, he seemed to have taken up permanent residence in her subconscious. She could go about her day perfectly fine, with only the occasional stray thought—like now, and she pressed her legs tightly together in a vain effort to relieve the pressure that seemed to build every time his name even whisked across her brain. But at night, he starred in her dreams, leaving her restless and empty when she woke up and he was not physically present.

She doubted she took up nearly as much space in his subconscious. He gave no indication he felt anything for her except willingness to repeat their night together. Yet she checked the time on her phone with her breath held in anticipation for the fifth time in ten minutes. She should be seeing him in person for the first time since the day they kissed in the gondola right about—

Now. She smiled when she spotted him.

She'd asked him to meet at sunset, an hour before the park closed. It was a Friday, which meant fireworks would signal the end of the park's operating hours; Anna had learned they were too costly to set off every night. Still, crowds of people were streaming toward the exit, especially families with small children who were too tired to wait for the evening spectacular. But the packed walkways didn't slow down Ian, who was swimming against the tide with ease. He deftly dodged a double stroller holding twins while capturing an errant balloon just before the string disappeared into the atmosphere. He handed the balloon back to a small child who stopped, midcry, with an astonished look on her face. He didn't wait for the parents' gushed thanks, choosing to wave them off as he continued his forward progression without missing a step.

She applauded as he reached her side. "That was a flawless grab. Eleven out of ten."

He shrugged. "I happened to see the kid untie the string weight and release the balloon at the right time."

"You can accept a compliment, you know. Say, 'Thank you, Anna, for appreciating my chivalrous act.'"

His smirk was lopsided. "Nothing chivalrous about it. I was saving my eardrums from the kid's shrieks. I should have let the balloon go so the kid could learn actions have consequences."

Anna returned his smirk. "Right. You were being purely selfish."

"Chivalry is dead." But his smirk turned into a smile. "So. You wanted to meet? And it had to be now?"

She took a deep breath. Although they had returned to their state of professional détente after the kiss, being near him was half pleasure, half pain as every moment brought their time together closer to an end. "Yes. You've been very generous with your time these last few weeks, and I appreciate it. But we haven't spent time at the park after dark."

He raised his eyebrows. "I have no objections to

spending time with you after dark. But I thought we took those activities off the table."

She laughed, even as she repressed the shiver caused by his low tone. She knew he was just teasing. Their usual harmless flirtation that meant nothing. At least to him. "Not in that way, and you know it. But the park is a different place after sundown. The lights, the mood—everything changes."

He looked around. The area in which they were standing was starting to fill with knots of people staking their space to watch the fireworks in an hour. "Yes. It becomes a crowded mess here, while the rest of the park remains open but few guests are utilizing the rides and restaurants. A waste of resources."

She frowned at him. "Or people are thrilled to watch the nighttime entertainment and the park provides them with twenty minutes of spectacle they will remember for a long time."

"Not when they're too busy filming it to put on their social media—and impeding the view of the people behind them—to make actual memories."

"You're hopeless."

"Are you just now figuring that out? I thought you were a quicker study than that."

"I dare you to watch the faces of the kids tonight and tell me they aren't enthralled by the fireworks."

"I don't need to observe them. They will be. But they're kids. Kids are thrilled to find a stash of stale candy three months after Halloween."

"How did you get to be so cynical?'

"If by cynical you mean practical as well as profitable…" He shrugged, his gaze turning flat and cold. "Experience. A lot of it."

She turned away. He'd scored a direct hit on the one target for which she had no protection. She had no experience. Not with theme parks, and not even with running a business. Her parents rarely shared decisions about the operations of the store with her. She decided not to dwell on how shut out that made her feel—on how shut out she'd always felt. She'd untangle her emotions later, although a small part of her brain wondered if, again, this was why she refused to let Lakes of Wonder go. Despite never meeting Keith or Jamie, at least the Lochlainns were allowing her to participate in major decisions about the direction of their family legacy.

Her parents, who'd raised her from birth, did not.

For the one thousand, three hundred and forty-second time that week, she wondered at what the Lochlainns expected of her. And why their expectations seemed so unattainably high even if she had been born and bred a Lochlainn, while the family who raised her had such low ones of her.

"Well, Mr. Experienced—"

"Thank you. A bit late, but I'll take the compliment." He mock-puffed his chest.

"Ha. Ha," she deadpanned. "You may know a lot about spreadsheets and profit and loss columns. But what do you know about how people feel?"

He stepped closer to her. The teasing glint deepened, accompanied by something far more primal.

"I'm very good at making people feel. As you should know."

He scored another direct hit, affecting her low and deep, a rush of warmth making her knees soft. "Not that kind of feelings. Emotions. Happiness, joy, comfort—evoking those in others."

"I've been known to create happy endings. Come with back to the hotel and I will remind you." He waggled his eyebrows and she laughed.

"You're incorrigible. And you know..." She held up a finger. "One, we have our deal, and two—" a second finger joined her first one "—not what I meant. Again."

The crowd began to build in the plaza. Parents placed small children on their shoulders. The crowd's chatter began to crescendo, drowning out the background music loop coming from hidden speakers in the bushes and building walls. The air vibrated with anticipation as the lights lining the walkways began to dim. The hairs on Anna's arms rose as she shivered. She held her right arm out to Ian, pointing out the goose bumps. "See? This is what I mean. The feeling that something magical is about to happen."

He traced a finger, slow and deliberate, down the delicate skin at the center of her inner forearm. Her blood caught fire, the flames catching instantaneously. She snatched her arm back. He merely smiled and let his hand drop. "I am aware of how to create that feeling, yes."

She was saved from having to answer when the lights winked out and a warm male voice announced over the loudspeaker that the show was about to begin. But the impression of his touch lingered far longer than it should have. Her skin ached for more of his feathery-light strokes. Who knew it was possible to become addicted to Ian Blackburn in a few short weeks? She didn't think it was possible to crave the feel of someone's skin on hers this much. To ache with want—not just desire, the demanding urge to find sexual completion—but want. Wanting his fingers to casually tangle with hers. Wanting his shoulder to brush hers as he leaned down to whisper something in her ear. Wanting the heat of his gaze concentrated on her so much she could taste it, a metallic tang equal parts hope for the future and part despair her want would never be fulfilled.

For when it came to what Ian Blackburn desired... oh, she had no doubt he would agree to a repeat of their night in his hotel room. Perhaps even a third or fourth repeat. The sex had been that good. But she was clear on what he truly wanted.

He wanted her park.

Not her.

They watched the fireworks in silence, Ian's gaze focused on the sky while hers wandered over the faces closest to her. Couples leaning on each other, their arms entwined as they lifted their faces to the bright explosions overhead. Children who'd been perpetual energy machines minutes before the show began were now still with awe, exhilaration shining in their eyes. Parents, faces taut with harried exhaustion, the lines relaxing as they oohed and aahed and held phones up, recording the night to be relived at home.

This was why Lakes of Wonder mattered. Not the thrill of the rides or the amount of profit made in the gift shops and at the concession stands: this. A communal making of memories, a fifteen-minute respite from daily annoyances and chores and even bigger issues. A chance to be dazzled by music and lights and colorful explosions and believe, if only for a split second, and then deny it forever more, that magic really could exist.

Ian remained impassive beside her, his expression never changing during the show. Not even during the grand finale, when the eruptions built and built until the night's darkness had been banished and the world was lit by purple and green and gold and red, brighter than a summer morning. Not even when the music evoked childhood wishes and dreams in a blatantly manipulative maneuver to jerk tears from the listener's eyes—and Anna obliged, her cheeks wet as the chorus sang of familial love and believing in oneself.

The lights came back up in the park and the crowd starting to move toward the exit as if one large organism. It was all Anna could do to keep her feet planted and not be swept up in the tidal wave surging for the gates.

Ian wrapped his arm over her shoulders, keeping her close. To protect her from the crush of people? No doubt. But she leaned into his strength, reveling in the feeling of his protection even though she could fight the crowds on her own. "Let's get out of here," he said low in her ear.

He guided her into a nearby gift shop, past the displays of toys and souvenirs that were being raked over by parkgoers eager for one last purchase, and to a door in the back, almost indistinguishable from the wall. They slipped through and Anna found herself in a utilitarian hallway, white and plain and distinguished mostly by the running lights that lit the walkway.

"Service corridor?" she guessed. She'd read that Lakes of Wonder had almost an entire city built behind and underneath the theme park, allowing custodial staff, repair technicians, and staff who didn't want to be seen wearing the wrong costume in the wrong part town to move freely about the park without guests seeing them.

"Yes," Ian answered. "But they are rarely used. Some of the foundations have been compromised. This corridor is no longer in use, to avoid any potential safety issues."

"But they can be made safe again, right?"

Ian ran a hand through his hair. "I know what you want me to say. Anything is possible—"

"If you dream it, you can do it," she interjected. "Is that what Walt Disney said?"

"That quote is attributed to him, but he didn't say it. However, Disney probably would've agreed anything is possible if you throw enough money at it. Do you think Keith will pump the necessary funds into Lakes of Wonder if you don't sell the park?"

She stayed silent.

"I didn't think so. So—"

She placed her right index finger on his lips and shook her head, not ready to let the lingering magic of the nighttime show be dissipated by another discussion on the practical aspects of the theme park business.

He frowned at her and spoke around her finger. "What? Are you ready to leave?"

No. That was the last thing she wanted to do. Every time she exited Lakes of Wonder, she was one step closer to selling it. And one step closer to returning to the mess she'd made of her life in Ft. Lauderdale. She shook off the clammy hand clenching her stomach at the thought of seeing her parents again. She knew she owed them an explanation for running off to California the way she had, without so much as a goodbye text. Yet the longer she put off the long, in-depth and no doubt emotional conversation they needed to have, the more hurt would be built up and the harder the discussion would be. And yet...

She pointed at the tunnel ahead of them with her chin. "Where does this corridor go?"

Ian followed her gaze. The safety lights were on, illuminating the passage. The tunnel was surprisingly free of dust, and he supposed the Lakes of Wonder custodial team maintained the underground passageways despite their disuse. The sound of people chatting and laughing as the cash register beeped with transactions came faintly through the closed door leading back to the gift shop. The crowds would still be thick in the park for at least another hour.

Truthfully, he wasn't ready for his time with Anna to be over. Their original deal had dwindled down to one week, and his calendar held only one more scheduled meeting. And being with Anna meant his shoulders stood their best chance of losing the knot that had held them stiff around his ears for the last week. He'd had to muster up every ounce of self-control he had to put behind him the video call with Olive and Preston that had made him late this evening.

If he shut his eyes, he could still see his uncle's and cousin's smug faces. Hear their voices.

"Harlan came to us yesterday with a very interesting proposition," Olive had begun, steepling her fingers under her chin as if she were a James Bond villain. *"You know he's calling for a vote of no confidence in your leadership at the next board meeting, right?"*

When they were kids, Olive had stolen his favorite Star Wars action figure and thrown it into a roaring fireplace. He had the feeling his Han Solo toy got off easy compared to what she'd wanted to extract from him now.

"I'm aware," he said.

"Right, Tai runs and tells you everything," she said with a sniff. *"Anyway, Dad and I still back you. Right, Dad?"*

Preston nodded.

"But!" Olive held up her index finger. "We want... guarantees...in return."

"You'll get Lakes of Wonder." Ian shuffled papers on his desk as if he were bored. "There was a due diligence issue impacting the sale that I'm taking care of, but the park should be ours soon. Once we integrate operations into BBA, it's yours to run, as we discussed."

"That's the thing." Olive examined her blood-red fingernails. "Dad and I talked it over and we don't want to run the park after all. Too much math involved. Right Dad?"

"Don't like numbers," Preston rumbled.

"Okay." This was turning out better than Ian anticipated. "BBA will run Lakes of Wonder. So what guarantees do you want? Profit sharing? Control of the entertainment?"

"See, that's the problem." Olive cocked her head to the side. "We still want all of Lakes of Wonder, only we don't want BBA to run it."

Here came the migraine, right on time. "You're not making sense."

Olive frowned. "I'm as smart as you are, Ian. I'm tired of people saying I'm not."

"You're very intelligent, Olive," Ian agreed through his teeth. "Please tell me what you want."

"To shut down Lakes of Wonder."

"What?" Ian's gaze ping-ponged between Olivia and Preston. "Why? It's still a moneymaking proposition. Under BBA, the park would turn a tidy profit."

"And Dad and I have an opportunity to develop

the land into a live/work/retail opportunity." She shrugged. "I'm tired of theme parks. And Lakes of Wonder is perfectly situated to be retail destination."

"You said you don't like numbers," Ian said slowly. It was the only argument that sprung to mind.

"Oh, we'll hire people to do that. Right, Daddy?"

"Right," Preston said.

"Preston." Ian appealed to his uncle. "You know what Lakes of Wonder means to our family. Surely you don't want to destroy—"

"That's our deal," Preston said. "We get Lakes of Wonder, no questions asked. You get our votes. Or we vote with Harlan and get what we want from him anyway, he doesn't give one flying damn about the theme park biz and you know it. I like you, son. But I've waited long enough for my slice of Blackburn pie with nothing to show for it. So I'm going to take my slice now and start my own thing. No one will miss Lakes of Wonder. It's not part of the BBA portfolio."

"It has legions of fans," Ian protested. "It's a landmark."

"It's a theme park. And now it will be a retail destination." Preston's gaze darted off camera. "We have to go now. You can have a few days to think about it. But then we vote with Harlan. Be seeing you, Ian."

"Ian?" Anna's voice brought him back to the dimly lit tunnel.

If they left the park now, he would have nothing but a tension-filled night ahead as he negotiated his uncle's and cousin's demands. Demands that would change Lakes of Wonder forever, should Ian be successful in acquiring the park for BBA. And he would be. He had no other choice.

He turned to her. "Up for an adventure?"

Her gaze narrowed. "What kind of an adventure?"

Ian indicated the door. "This tunnel exists because the gift shop was originally a private lounge for the original investors in Lakes of Wonder."

Anna's brow creased. "I thought the private lounge is located in Heroes Harbor, on the second level of Mount Stupendous."

"That was built shortly after the park opened, when the original lounge proved to be too small. And too easily seen by guests as they enter and exit the park."

"Okay, the shop was originally a lounge. Where does the adventure part come in?"

Ian motioned for Anna to follow him as he walked to the far wall where a simple schematic carved in metal was still in place. She traced the bas relief symbols with her fingers. "This tunnel leads to..." Her index finger followed the map's path and she turned to Ian. "The Lighthouse?"

He nodded. "So guests of the private lounge could easily visit the even more exclusive residence inside the Lighthouse."

"Wait. You can go inside the Lighthouse? I thought it was a façade. Like a Hollywood prop, only three-dimensional and bigger."

"Real building. With real plumbing and electricity, even."

"Have you been inside the Lighthouse?"

"Never had the chance." And might not ever have the chance again, even if he successfully purchased the park. Not if Preston and Olive had their way.

"How do you know about it? I've read everything I could on Lakes of Wonder. Even read all the legal paperwork. There's no mention of the Lighthouse as a functional structure. It's just a...landmark." She smiled. "A weenie."

The warmth of her expression broke over him and he grinned back at her, to his chagrin. He didn't want to smile back at her. He didn't want to be friends with her. He was happy to flirt to get what he wanted and, sure, he'd be more than happy to repeat that night in his bed, but that was sex. He didn't need the sudden rush of...something, this inexplicable urge to bask in her light while building more in-jokes between them, more transparent lines of connection.

He cleared his throat, shoving the ball of something that felt very much like emotion back down, hopefully to dissolve for good. "Want to find out if I'm right?"

Her smile deepened, damn it, a pickax smashing holes in the thick walls he'd long ago built to ensure he only relied on his head, never his heart. Whenever he allowed his heart to lead, he always ended up looking like a fool.

"Let's go," she said.

They walked mostly in silence, Anna breaking it only to note where they were in relation to the theme park above them. Then the tunnel starting to slope upward, and they climbed until the passage came to an end at a heavy metal door.

Anna tried to turn the doorknob. "It's locked." She sighed. "Well, this was fun, anyway. I wonder when the last person walked this tunnel before us? But we should turn back. The park is going to close soon."

Ian dug into his pants' pocket and brought out a key. "I was once told this key could open all the doors in Lakes of Wonder."

She stared at him. "Where did you get that?"

He didn't answer. It had been a whim to pick up that key, all those years ago in his grandfather's home, and even more of a whim to carry it on him still. But Ian had grown used to its shape and weight. Some people carried lucky pennies; others bought charms. Ian didn't believe good fortune could be embodied in an item—you had to make your own luck—but whenever he left his house without the slight weight of the small metal object in his pocket, the world felt wrong, somehow. And once he knew Lakes of Wonder was in play and available for sale, he ensured he carried the key with him.

His grandfather had laughed when Ian had showed him his find, telling him the tale of how Archibald Lochlainn and Ian's great-grandfather, Cooper Blackburn, had had a falling out. The last item Cooper had taken from his office was the master key to Lakes of Wonder. Then his grandfather had chuckled and said it was no doubt useless now, so Ian was free to take it.

He found himself holding his breath as the key went into the lock. At first the lock wouldn't turn, which disappointed him more than he'd anticipated. He hadn't really expected his grandfather's story to be real, had he? Or, even if it had been a true story, for the locks to never have been changed in all the ensuing years? But then something gave, deep inside the tumbler, and the key turned with a loud click. The door fell ajar.

Anna's eyes widened. "Whoa…"

He took her elbow with his right hand to ensure she wouldn't stumble and, with his left, pushed the door further open. They encountered nothing but darkness. Fumbling with his free hand, he patted the wall until he located what felt like a light switch. Mentally crossing his fingers that the power hadn't been disconnected, he flipped it on.

She gasped from beside him.

An overhead light revealed they stood in the living area of an apartment that appeared as if it had been summoned directly from the set of a 1960's television series. In the middle of the room was a sofa, covered in a cheerful floral brocade. Oak bookcases contained porcelain knickknacks and ornately curlicued silver picture frames. A burled walnut coffee table held pastel-colored candy dishes—empty, thankfully— while the matching side tables were laden with jar-shaped lamps with fringed shades. Beyond, an open door provided a glimpse of a small kitchenette, complete with two-burner white range. Another door was closed—no doubt to the hallway that led to the bedrooms. Three of the walls were covered with ornate floral wallpaper, while the fourth wall was draped in floor-to-ceiling velvet curtains.

Anna slipped from his grip on her arm and began to explore, her smile broadening with each item she examined. "The chair—that's an original Eames. Oh! And this table is signed by Stickley." She turned to Ian. "This place is every antique hunter's dream. Where are we?"

Ian had remained still. Now that he was in the apartment, now that he had confirmation that it was real and not just a vague suspicion, he didn't know what to do next. Where to look next. It didn't help that the photos he'd seen had been in two-dimension black-and-white. Experiencing the apartment in three dimensions and in living color overwhelmed his senses. "This place? It was the apartment built by the creators of Lakes of Wonder for their families."

"So m—Archibald Lochlainn built this? For Keith?"

Ian nodded and then cleared his throat. "You could say that."

Her gaze flashed and she turned back to perusing the items on the bookshelves. He decided to explore what was behind the closed door and found a bathroom—luckily with running water—and two rooms emptied of furniture, although the mural of stylized planes, trains and cars that occupied the wall of one of the rooms suggested it had been meant as a young boy's bedroom. The other room had faded gilt-striped wallpaper where squares of bright color revealed where pictures had once hung.

He returned to the living area. Anna was where he had left her, still intent on picking up and examining the bookshelves' occupants. "Someone has been taking care of this place," she said without looking at him. "There's not much dust. It's been looked after."

"I agree." But who? he wondered. She was right that the apartment had been maintained, but it was also obvious no one had used it in a long time. Not only because the bedrooms were bare, but because the appliances were some fifty years out of date. Case in point, the television. It was a museum piece, a heavy hunk of furniture with a small, curved screen in the middle. He bet if the television did work—and could by some miracle receive an over-the-air broadcast signal—the picture would be in black-and-white.

Anna sniffed, breaking into his thoughts.

"You okay?" he asked.

"Must be the dust."

Ian frowned. "We just discussed how well-kept this room is."

"I guess I found what little still exists." She sniffed again.

That didn't sound like a suppressed sneeze. It sounded like...she was about to cry. He frowned. "You sure you're okay? You didn't hurt yourself while we were in the tunnel?"

Another sharp inhalation through her nose as she kept her face turned away from him, her eyes focused on an object in her hands. "I'm fine."

His gaze narrowed and he crossed the room to stand next to her, leaning over her shoulder to see what kept her so enraptured. A piece of memorabilia from the opening of Lakes of Wonder? But it was a photo of Keith Lochlainn with a small infant in his arms. "Oh. Do you always cry at photos of babies?" he teased.

She jumped. The photo slipped from her grasp and bounced on the carpet, landing facedown. Ian bent to pick it up before she could react.

It wasn't a particularly artful photo. The subjects were posed in front of the Lighthouse, and whoever had taken the photo hadn't accounted for the sun that day, as Keith was obviously squinting into bright light. But the sheer happiness on his face...

Ian began to understand why she'd found the photograph so compelling. This was not a side of Keith Lochlainn the public got to see often, if ever. Keith's public image was that of a taciturn, serious man who wore either scowls or amused smirks in his official photos. He would never appear so unguarded. So, well...joyful. It was the only word Ian could think of to describe the emotion pouring from Keith's two-dimensional expression.

Too bad he kept this side of himself under wraps in public, because Keith had a nice smile. It softened his square chin and the hard angles of his cheekbones. He appeared more approachable, more like someone who would lend you their umbrella instead of raising an eyebrow and asking why you hadn't thought ahead and been prepared. Someone who might care about one's well-being instead of silently calculating how much money they could take from you without it being called outright robbery. Someone like…

Anna.

She had the same smile as the Keith Lochlainn in the photography.

Ten

Ian peered closer at the photo, mentally flipping through every image of Keith he could dredge up from his memory. Now that he saw the resemblance, it was all he could do to not unsee it. Anna not only had Keith's smile, she had his eyebrows: straight but with the slightest bend as they narrowed toward the outer edges of her eyes. She had his jaw, sharp and square.

Did she also have his killer instinct? His determination to find his opponent's jugular vein and slash it open at the precise time when the slice of the blade would hurt the most? Had the past several weeks been nothing but a setup?

Had that night been only a ploy?

Ian thought he had the upper hand. He was the game master. The pieces were falling into place at his instigation. He was in control and he dictated the moves.

The knowledge that he had been played from the start crushed him, closing off his windpipe, caving in his chest, his breath coming in short pants as he guarded against the pain.

"May I have the photo back?" she asked.

With supreme effort, he dragged his gaze away from the framed image to meet hers. The room was still and dark, and so was she, hidden in the shadows. A perfect metaphor, he thought. What else was she concealing in those dim corners with her?

"It took me a while. But I figured it out."

"Figured what out?" She held out her hand.

He went to give the photo to her, but when she moved to take the frame from him, he found he couldn't let go. "Who you really are."

Her brow furrowed. "What are you talking about?"

"You. The Lochlainns. You're one of them. That's why you came in at the last minute to stop the Lakes of Wonder sale." He shook his head, his pulse ringing in his ears with the movement. "Now everything makes sense. I can't believe I didn't see it before, but then the family has kept your existence very quiet. The perfect stealth operative."

The only question was how she was related to the Lochlainns. Archibald had only one child, Keith. And Keith's only child, Jamie, had died without producing children. A distant cousin? The result of a hush-hush affair?

Anna didn't move, her eyes wide, her mouth open

in shock. Then her chest started to rise and fall in rapid motion. "What…how did you—"

"The photo." He finally released his grip on the frame. "The family resemblance is clear."

She grabbed the photo before it could hit the ground again. "It is?"

"The smile. Keith is rarely seen with one. You, on the other hand…" His stomach squeezed, harsh and painful, as memories of her smile flooded in. Anna gazing up at the fireworks, delight on her face. Anna laughing at him on the gondola then taking his hand in hers when she realized he wasn't faking his reaction to heights. Anna, pushing her hair off her face, her chest rising and falling against him, smiling with pure joy and delight after she came in his arms.

Anna traced Keith's frozen image with her index finger. "I haven't seen this photo before."

"I doubt many people have. Keith is particular about his public image. But then, you already know that. Since you're a Lochlainn." He folded his arms across his chest. It was either that or howl with the knowledge of just how much the Lochlainns had taken him for a ride. Had she been laughing at him with her family after their park excursions? Using their time together to probe for the chinks in his armor? Chinks, he had to admit, she'd caused to appear. "Were you going to tell me?"

"I…maybe. I guess. I don't know." She sank onto the sofa, under the floor lamp. The light lit her golden hair, almost as if she wore a halo. An angel of perfidy, perhaps.

"You don't know?" He crossed his arms and leaned against the bookcase. "Or you do know, but you're figuring out what to say next because your cover has been blown."

Her head snapped up. "Cover? What cover? May I remind you, *you* slept with *me* under false pretenses."

"False? I wasn't hiding who I am."

"Neither am I!" she shot back. "I've never pretended to be anyone but who I am." Then her shoulders fell. "Of course, how can I be who I am when I don't know who that is?" she mumbled under her breath.

The room wasn't large but the walls were thick and well-insulated from the noise of the theme park outside, so he heard her perfectly well. "You don't know who you are? Are you claiming amnesia now? What's next, the Lochlainns found you under a cabbage leaf and that's why no one has heard of you?"

She glared at him. "You wouldn't understand. How can you, when you've known all along who you are and where you belong? What is it like, being born a Blackburn, knowing you have a place in the family business?"

He stared at her. "What are talking about? The Lochlainns inserted you into the sale of Lakes of Wonder. You seem to have a place. The Stratford name, though, that's a nice touch."

Her head shook rapidly. "My name *is* Stratford. At least, that's the name I was born with. And I can't believe you would call me a, how did you put it, 'stealth operative.' I think it's been clear I am hopeless when it comes to understanding theme parks. Or billion-dollar negotiations."

She sounded sad. Exhausted. Frustrated. Not the emotions he expected from someone who had been beating him at his own game.

And she was right.

Not that she was hopeless at understanding the attractions industry – on the contrary, her insights were smart and incisive, even when he didn't agree with her – but that he was wrong to accuse her of operating in bad faith. Anna had been nothing but genuine with him, he realized. From the start.

From the night they shared together.

"I apologize," he said. "You've done nothing to earn doubts of your intentions. On the contrary. And you've made me look at theme parks in whole new ways."

"Thank you." She kept her gaze averted and he sat next to her on the sofa, almost but not quite touching.

"But you are a Lochlainn," he said.

She nodded, then shook her head. "Yes. No. It's complicated."

"Did Keith refuse to acknowledge he was your father until recently?" It was the only explanation that came to mind.

She laughed, but there was a frantic undertone to the sound. "Keith didn't refuse. He didn't know."

"Your mother never told him you were his daughter?"

Her laughter came harder. "You mean am I a secret baby kept from him? No. And Keith is my grandfather...well, biological grandfather. Jamie is my father. No, strike that, my sperm donor."

"What?"

Ian had been surprised before in his life. Shocked, even. Usually by something Harlan said or did in the name of BBA. But of all the things he'd expected to hear over the course of his lifetime, this didn't make the top ten thousand. "Jamie Lochlainn...is your father."

"My parents used a sperm donor to conceive me, yes. The donor was anonymous. They had no idea he was Jamie Lochlainn."

He blinked. "And how did you find out?"

She pushed a lock of hair behind her ear. "The Knock."

"Excuse me?"

"That's how I think of it. The Knock. With a capital *K*." She sighed, falling back against the sofa cushions. "Ever have one of those events that divide your life into before and after? Like, you were one person before the event happened and a different person after? And there's no going back to before?"

"Yes. I lost my father when I was twelve."

She sat up, her body twisting to face his. Her gaze, soft with empathy, locked onto his. "I'm so sorry."

He started to shrug, his usual response to expressions of sympathy. But there was something about the dark, still room, a now-secret shrine to lost family relationships, that caused him to rethink. Or maybe it was Anna and the fact she obviously had a complicated relationship with her parents, too.

"Thank you," he said simply. "It was a long time ago. But I know that feeling. That something immeasurable has changed and you can't return to being the same person as before, even if you want to."

"Precisely. Although, in my case, I didn't lose anyone. I guess you could say you I gained people." She bit her lower lip. "Thanks for putting it into perspective."

He shook his head. "If your life was impacted, it was impacted. That matters."

She picked up the photo of Keith and a baby Jamie from where she had placed it on the coffee table, running her fingers once more over their smiling faces before putting the framed picture back down. "And perhaps I did lose someone. I lost me. Or rather, who I thought I was." She glanced at him, her mouth twisting into a rueful smile. "I'm being so melodramatic. I apologize. Should we leave? The park must be shooing the last guests out of the gates right now."

He stayed where he was, stretching one arm out along the back edge of the sofa. "You haven't told me about the Knock."

"There's nothing to tell." When she could no longer hold his stare, she sighed. "It was a Monday morning. I was in my office—wait, I never told you what I do. I work for my family's furniture store as the in-house interior designer. The family that raised me, I mean. Not the Lochlainns, obviously."

"Now the excitement over the Eames chair makes sense. But I'm interrupting. Please, continue."

"At first I thought the person at the door was my

mother. We were planning a trip to North Carolina for a furniture show. But when I answered the Knock, it was a man I'd never seen before. He asked if he could come into my office to speak in private. Over his shoulder, I could see both my parents. Their expressions... I'd never seen them appear so terrified."

She closed her eyes and leaned back against the cushions. He pulled her to him and she willingly went, his arms encircling her, lending her as much of his support as she wanted to take. "And they were afraid because?"

"Because they had to tell me the truth. My dad was not my father. Not my biological one."

"You learned this from a stranger?"

"No, my parents jumped in to tell me. But I wasn't given time to let it sink in. The man was from the Lochlainn Company, and he had a proposition for me." She lifted her head from his shoulder. "I'm not supposed to tell anyone the next part. If it gets out to the press, I'll lose."

"Lose?"

She sighed. "It's public knowledge Keith and Jamie were estranged for many years. When Jamie left as a teenager, Keith cut him off without a cent. But what people don't know is Jamie...well, he apparently earned money by..."

"Selling his sperm. I knew some guys in college who did the same thing."

She nodded and her head fell onto his shoulder again. He could smell her vanilla-scented shampoo, feel the warmth of her cheek where she lay against him. He shifted so he could take on more of her weight. "And I was the result." She lifted her head again. "Or one of the results. I haven't even thought about..." She swallowed.

He stroked her hair. The golden strands were silky-soft, the ends gently curling around his fingers. His chest walls ached, as if something deep inside was expanding and pushing against his limits. "That's an issue to figure out later. What happened when he told you? What's not supposed to get out? That Jamie sold his sperm, or you are his child?" He turned to look at her. "How did the lawyer know you are Jamie's child in the first place? Through the clinic?"

"The records are supposed to be sealed. My parents didn't know. They were shocked when the representative showed up."

"So how...?"

She sighed. "I took one of those DNA tests. I'd forgotten about it, until the Knock."

"And the Lochlainns found your results."

"Or they had the clinic's records unsealed. They wouldn't say."

"Trust Keith to make a mockery of privacy rules. And then the Lochlainns gave you Lakes of Wonder." He grunted. "Not a bad welcome-to-the-family gift."

"Oh, they didn't give it to me. I'm still proving myself."

What? "You're Keith's flesh and blood. You must prove yourself to him?"

"But that's the thing. We're related—I was required to take a more extensive paternity test—but he didn't raise me. He doesn't know me from a... hole in the wall."

"You carry his genes."

"So? Look at how often kids disappoint their parental figures."

"Or vice versa," Ian muttered.

Anna snorted. "True. But just because you're someone's child doesn't mean you grow up to be like them."

"Because you are raised by someone doesn't mean you'll be like them."

She glanced up at him. "You sound like you're speaking from experience."

He didn't want to think about his stepfather and his own tangled family issues. He tugged her head back onto his shoulder. "We're talking about you. Go on."

"Long story short, Keith gave me the sale of the theme park to oversee, to prove I have what it takes to be a Lochlainn. If I succeed to his standards—and who the hell knows what they are—then I will earn a place in his will. If I don't, I guess I go back to being some stranger he's never heard of." She laughed, but there was little humor in her expression. "I mean, who does that? Who decides if someone is worthy of being a relation based on a wholly arbitrary task?"

"A Lochlainn."

"Y'know, you've made several similar comments about the Lochlain family over our time together. Care to explain why you feel so strongly about them?" She straightened up to catch his gaze. Some of the despair that had been clouding her expression was starting to clear. Good.

"I suppose it's only fair I tell you my family story in return. So here's the Blackburns' secret—" He paused for dramatic effect. "Lakes of Wonder wasn't developed by Archibald Lochlainn. It was the creation of Cooper Blackburn—my great-grandfather."

She laughed. "C'mon. I've read as many books as I could find on Lakes of Wonder and—"

"History is written by the winners. And Archibald made it very clear that Cooper was to be exorcised from the history of Lakes of Wonder."

"That seems like something that would be difficult to cover up."

"I repeat, history is written by the winners. How did you think I knew about the Lighthouse? And the key?"

She pursed her lips into the most delectable shape. "I don't... I guess I think of you as the theme park guru who knows everything. Even to the point of magicking up a key. Rather silly, now that I think of it."

"I found the key in my grandfather's things. But my larger point is you're romanticizing something that isn't romantic. The Lochlainns don't care about people. They only care about profit. And they are ruthless about getting what they want."

Her gaze narrowed. "Then why did they come looking for me when they learned about my existence?"

"If I were a gambler, I'd bet Keith approached you

as a form of proactive defense against you discovering the truth about your parentage. By approaching you first, he controls the narrative. He controls your place in the family." Too late, he realized he'd growled his words, his tone harsh and fierce. But Anna needed to know what she was up against. He had experience with the den of vipers a family-run conglomerate could be. She didn't.

"I don't..." She squeezed her eyes shut. "Okay. Fine. Maybe." She rose from the sofa, her movements jerky. "We should go. It's long past closing time. I don't want to explain to security why we are running around after the gates are shut."

The bright light that seemed to always illuminate her from within was extinguished. "Anna, I didn't mean to upset you—"

"You didn't." Her hunched shoulders and arms wrapped tightly around her chest said otherwise.

"I don't want you to get hurt. I've seen it happen too many times in families when there is a large company at stake. Believe me, the only ties that bind when it comes to business are contracts. Blood may be thicker than water, but paper is thicker than blood."

"Got it." She kept her eyes focused on the floor.

"The more knowledge you have, the better you can protect yourself. Did you sign anything? A non-disclosure agreement, perhaps? Have you to talked to lawyers?"

She shook her head, the movement small but shaky.

"I know some very good ones who would love to

get their hands on anything regarding the Lochlainns. I can recommend—"

"No." The word reverberated in the small room. "No lawyers."

He stared at her. "Anna, you're not thinking clearly. There's a lot of money at stake and the Lochlainns threw you into the deep end without a net. You need to talk to—"

She scoffed. He'd never heard such a bitter sound from her. "I need. Yes, everyone is an expert on what I need. Or what I can or can't do. You know what I really need? To stop talking about this and to get out of here."

"Okay." He'd meant it when he'd said he didn't want to upset her. But on the other hand, the sooner she understood the truth about her birth family, the better life would be for her in the long run. He was doing her a favor, damn it. He stood. "Let's go. I know a shortcut to the park's exit."

She didn't answer, choosing instead to march to the door. She placed her hand on the doorknob and then turned to him, her gaze wide.

"The knob won't turn. The door is stuck."

Eleven

Ian motioned for Anna to step aside. "Let me try."

She was right. The doorknob was frozen. He tried again, throwing his right shoulder against the thick door in the hope of jarring it loose. The only result was a sore shoulder.

"Use your key," she urged.

"I would if there were a keyhole on this side." And if he had the key. Too late, he remembered he'd left it in the lock on the other side of the door.

"I guess we'll have to call someone—" She brought out her cell phone and then groaned. "I don't have service. You?"

He looked at his screen. No bars appeared. "Lakes of Wonder's weak cell network and even weaker WiFi strike again."

"It's the twenty-first century. How can there be no signal?"

"I've told you. Keith has refused to invest in the park. It's falling down around your ears."

She narrowed her gaze. "Right. Convenient of this situation to remind me. I don't suppose this was your plan, to lock me up in this Lighthouse tower and feed me stories of my terrible family and their terrible custodianship of this park until I agree to sell?"

Ian had to laugh, despite their predicament. "No, Rapunzel, I did not plan this. I didn't know you were a Lochlainn until we arrived here."

She smirked. "I had to ask, in case I could persuade you to let me go early."

"Now you're telling me. If I knew all I had to do to get you to sell was to lock you in a lighthouse—" At her mock glare, he stopped. "Too soon?"

"Let's find another way out of here first, then the jokes. The park has security. And custodial staff. We just need to get their attention." She went to the curtains on the far wall and drew them back, revealing the large round window spanning from floor to ceiling that overlooked Seamus's Seaport.

He joined her. The view over the park was spectacular, especially with holiday lights outlining the buildings. And empty. Not a person could be seen. The pavement around the Lighthouse was wet, indicating the street sweeper had already made its rounds.

Anna pointed to a figure in the distance. "Look!" A man wearing the distinctive purple-and-gold uniform that marked the Lakes of Wonder private security force came into view. She waved furiously. "Hey! Up here!"

The man kept his gaze roving, but only on the storefronts at his eye level.

The window was not meant to be opened. She banged on the glass anyway. "Hey!" she shouted again.

"He's not going to hear you." Ian felt it was necessary to point out the obvious before his hearing was damaged. "The glass is thick, meant to withstand heavy storms and earthquakes. We're several stories above him. And all security guards wear a headpiece. You're going to hurt your hands."

"The balcony." She indicated the narrow walkway circling the exterior of the Lighthouse. "Is there a way to get to the balcony?"

"Right. Of course." He should have thought of that sooner. After some searching, they found the door, covered with the same wallpaper as the living area. The handle turned but the door only opened an inch.

"Hurry," she urged. "The security guard is about to finish his round of the plaza."

"I'm trying," he gritted. "Something is blocking—" Then the door suddenly gave way and he almost fell. Anna pushed past him and he stumbled onto the balcony after her.

"Hey! Help!" She grabbed onto the metal railing as she yelled. "Up here— No! Wait! Come back!"

The guard turned onto the path for Heroes Harbor and was soon out of view. Ian strained his vision, but he couldn't spot anyone else in the park.

"Looks like they cut the security budget," he murmured to Anna. "Another indication the park is in financial trouble."

If looks could incinerate, he would be a pile of smoking ash. "What are we going to do?" she asked.

She sounded as if she had learned an asteroid was on direct collision course with the planet and they had fifteen minutes to live. He touched her arm. "It's going to be okay. Worst-case scenario, we spend the night here. I'm supposed to be in a BBA executive committee meeting in Los Angeles in the morning. Tai will send out a search party when I don't show up. They'll find us."

"Not until the morning?" She started to shiver. "Locked in here?"

He peered at her. Her pupils were dilated, and not because the evening sky was dark Her freckles stood out as dark smudges, her skin pale even for moonlight. The sharp rasp of her quickened breathing filled the air. This was not anger at the situation, nor frustration at being locked up with him. This was something deeper, more personal.

"We'll be fine. The plumbing works. There's even a couch for you to sleep on." He dug into his pockets. He'd worn these jeans on the plane earlier and hadn't had time to change before he'd met Anna. "And if we get hungry, I have a bag of airline snacks."

She took three gulping breaths. "You have your thing with gondolas. I…have a thing about locked rooms."

He reached out and took her hands in his. They

were colder than if she had plunged them into a snow-bank. "We'll be out of here in a matter of hours."

She started shaking her head even before he finished speaking, her eyes becoming unfocused. Her legs trembled as if they were about to give out.

He steered her toward the sofa, guiding her to a seated position. "Don't faint until you feel the cushions."

That got a glare from her. Not a very strong one, but he was glad to see a spark in her gaze. "You don't need to coddle me. I'll be fine. I just need to get… accustomed."

"You don't look like you're getting over it."

"I'll be fine," she repeated. A faint sheen of perspiration appeared on her brow.

Something inside Ian's chest twisted, hard. He swallowed and pushed the pain down. He sat next to her. "Tell me something about your childhood."

"What?" But her head came up, her gaze catching his.

"Your childhood." He faked a yawn. "I'm bored and I doubt the TV works. Entertain me,"

"Entertain you?" She laughed. "I doubt you'd find my life entertaining. I'm very boring. Well, except for the whole sperm donor thing, and you already know that."

He smiled, his gaze lingering on her blond curls, her flushed cheeks, her perfectly normal nose, which shouldn't be as fascinating as it was and yet he couldn't take his eyes off how her features all came together in a compelling package. "Nothing about you is boring."

"You're only saying that because you want my theme park." She took several gulping breaths. "I'm merely an interior designer who works for her family's furniture store. The most interesting thing that happened to me before the Knock was winning a vacation in the Bahamas thanks to a charity raffle. But when my cousin and I went on the trip, the hotel was undergoing renovations and not only was the restaurant closed, but our window was covered by scaffolding, so we couldn't see the beach. See? Boring."

"You practice random acts of kindness. You whistle Broadway tunes. You bring a fresh perspective to Lakes of Wonder daily." She surprised and amazed him at every turn. He never tired of listening to her thoughts on the goings-on in the park. He found himself looking forward to the fresh ways she would challenge his long-held opinions. No one else made him laugh as much.

Being with her made him happy.

The realization took his breath way like a solid punch to his solar plexus.

"That's considerate of you to say—" She looked at him then did a double take. "Are you okay? Is saying nice things really that painful for you?"

"No, I—" He cleared his throat, hoping to buy time to restore the flow of oxygen to his brain. "I meant every word."

"Uh-huh." She snorted. "Your face looks like you bit into an entire crate of lemons."

"Are you accusing me of lying?" He wasn't. It shocked him how much he wasn't.

"It's fine. You don't need to butter me up to get what you want."

"Despite the phrase 'butter you up' creating very intriguing images—"

She laughed. "Are you never not flirting?"

"There was no buttering intended. Sadly." Her head was turned away from him and he couldn't see her expression. "Hey. Are you okay? How can I help?"

"You are helping. The talking is helping." She shifted on the cushions, turning so her body was angled toward him. Her eyes glistened in the dim light, but otherwise her signs of panic had vanished. A sense of calm settled in his limbs. "I find *you* fascinating, you know," she continued.

And just like that, her nearness made his veins sing, his nerves taut with heat. "Really." He kept his tone light, but it was a struggle. "Go on."

"Why is closing the deal with Lakes of Wonder so important to you? Why not walk away? BBA is doing fine. The company has two theme parks in Southern California, you don't need a third."

"Ah. It's not me you find fascinating, but BBA." The disappointment was crushing. Too crushing.

"Aren't they one and the same?"

"No—" He stopped. Were they? He'd been focusing on getting Harlan out of BBA for so long. Fighting Harlan's irrational directives and underhanded attacks. Concentrating on removing Harlan's influence not only from the company, but from his family, so that the lines between them blurred.

"You asked why closing the deal is so important. BBA is a family business. There's been a Blackburn at the helm of the company since my great-grandfather started it. But as I mentioned, my dad died young and my mother, in her grief, married a family friend because she wanted a male role model for me. But my stepfather—Harlan—turned out to be anything but. She signed a very poorly written prenup that gave Harlan control of the shares she'd inherited from my father. And those shares got him on the board, where he consolidated power and became chairman. Long story somewhat shorter, I have the votes to force Harlan off the board, but only if I acquire Lakes of Wonder." That was the truth. Just not all of it.

"Then it comes down to family for you, as well."

"I suppose so. Yes." Not in the way she meant, but close enough. He was doing this to ensure Harlan stayed out of his family and his family's business. Stopped mentally torturing his mother at every company function.

"I always thought I knew where I belonged," she said softly. "Even as I went away to college, I knew I would come back home. Friends might come and go, even boyfriends, but my family…they're my rock. Were my rock." She blew out a puff of air. "Still are. But I used the Lakes of Wonder sale as an opportunity to run away. I…need space to figure out who I am."

He nodded. "My father worked long hours. Then he had a heart attack. But I knew I belonged to BBA."

"Shouldn't that be the other way around? BBA belongs to you?"

He shook his head. "No. You spoke about your family as your rock. That's what BBA is to me. The one constant in my life." Another reason why Harlan needed to be thrown out. He was destroying that foundation.

"I don't think I'll ever belong to the Lochlainn Company. Not in that way. I only wish I knew where I belonged," Anna murmured. She leaned over to pick up the photo of Keith and Jamie from the coffee table, but it eluded her fingertips. Ian reached for the frame, intending to slide it closer to her, but she had already scooted to the edge of the sofa to extend her grasp.

Their hands collided, their fingers meeting. The resulting spark nearly short-circuited his brain. Her head flew up, her gaze meeting his. In the dim light, her eyes were dark and wide.

The room grew very quiet. The only sounds were her soft breaths and his heartbeat, a painful and rapid thump against his eardrums.

Her fingers relaxed, tangling with his, her warm touch soft at first, but increasing in intensity until she held on to him as if he were her only hope of not getting swept up in the currents beginning to swirl around him.

But he was not her harbor of safety. Thanks to Olive's and Preston's new demands, he would be the unyielding rock upon which her ship would crash.

He moved to take his hand away, but her grasp only tightened. And, damn it, he didn't want her to let go. He wanted to continue holding her hand. Wanted to hold more of her, to press her soft length against him. Wanted to rest his lips in the hollow of her throat to feel her pulse leap, and then trace her shivers with kisses down her beautiful full breasts and the dip of her waist to her lusciously dimpled hips and thighs and the delicious damp triangle between her legs.

Anna's gaze met his. He saw his desire reflecting from the bottomless blue depths—or maybe it was hers. Theirs.

"Ian?" Her soft whisper reverberated in the stillness. "I know we said…that one night was…"

"Never to be repeated."

She nodded, her pink tongue briefly appearing to wet her lips. He was mesmerized by its appearance. "But I…tonight… I…" She swallowed. "I want to kiss you. May I?"

He brushed an errant curl away from the curve of her cheek. "Of course. I'm happy help you take your mind off the locked room." He grinned. "Turnabout is fair play, after the gondola."

She shook her head, tiny rapid tremors. "No. I want to kiss *you*. Because you're you. Not because of the situation."

Ian's heart twinged, a painful, sharp twang that pulled all the oxygen out of his lungs. The lack of air made speaking difficult. But he could still move. He cupped her face with his hands and brought her closer to him.

He intended the kiss to be a gentle one. A comforting one, meant to reassure her she was safe despite her fear of locked rooms. He whispered his lips over hers, barely touching, letting her know he was there for her, however she needed him.

Then she moaned against his mouth, her own hot and warm and insistent, her tongue demanding he open to her. "I want you, Ian," she whispered. "Tonight. One more night."

Twelve

Ian knew how good sex with Anna could be. That night in his hotel room would live in bright, unfading color in his memory until his deathbed. Being with her the last few weeks had been a supreme test of his self-control as he'd literally willed himself not to respond physically whenever her hand brushed his by accident. It was not an accident that he gave up his more tailored trousers for causal, loose pants or jeans when they were in the park, the better to hide when his self-control inevitably wasn't up for the challenge.

Anna's touch trailed streams of fire, her hands finding the hem of his shirt and tugging it over his head. He pushed her T-shirt up and off, making short work of her bra immediately after, and groaned when her breasts once more overflowed his hands, where they belonged. Her nipples were long and hard and he needed them in his mouth, now. He steered her toward the high-backed sofa, bending her backward until he could suit action to desire and finally claimed those tight buds, sucking and lathing while inhaling the clean, fresh scent that was uniquely hers. She moaned, moving against him, but when she would wrap herself against his leg to push her core against his thigh to relieve her pressure, he held her off. Tonight was about her. And he was going to make every second last as long he could. He stripped off her jeans and her panties in one motion, and then paused to take in the glory that was a nude Anna, her gaze warm with want, her arms reaching for him.

The pressure in his own jeans was becoming painful but he ignored it. His life had been spent pursuing control and while he'd rarely needed to deny himself in the bedroom, he was going to put that vaunted control of his to good use for Anna's sake. Because she hated being in a locked room. Because she wanted him.

Because he wanted to please her. Because he wanted her to know she was worthy of being worshipped. And he wanted to be the one who worshipped her.

"Turn around," he whispered to her, guiding her to do so with his hands, helping her bend herself just so over the back of the sofa. Anna looked back at him as he dropped to his knees and she whimpered, her legs parting for him without needing to be asked.

God, she was beautiful, trembling for him, her

hips bucking at his slightest touch. He adjusted himself. Yes, he was known for wielding his control but he feared this would test him beyond his limits. He breathed her in, reveling in her most intimate scent, relishing the slick proof of how much she desired his touch.

He kept his mouth on her, bringing her as close to the heights as he dared and then changing his rhythm to bring her back down, then driving her up again to glimpse the peak as many times as he could, finally allowing her to come apart on his tongue and lips as she shuddered and gasped, catching her in his arms as her legs finally gave out and settling them both on the sofa. She blinked up at him, her blue eyes dark and unfocused. "I changed my mind," she said, and his heart skipped a beat.

"What about?" he asked, hoping her mind hadn't changed about them, about this night.

"About locked rooms," she sighed, her eyes closing. "This isn't so bad." Then her breathing slowed and he smiled. He'd achieved his goal. She was relaxed enough to sleep.

Then one of her eyes opened. "I haven't forgotten you." Her hand drifted between them and found his erection, still pushing painfully against his zipper. "Just give me a few minutes,"

He laughed and gathered her close. "I've had more than my share of fun, believe me." Watching Anna come apart, knowing she trusted him enough to let go of her fears, was all the release he needed.

* * *

The bright morning light, no match for his closed eyelids, woke Ian. He blinked, confused at first as to why the hotel forgot to give him his customary early wake-up call. If the sun was shining this hot, the hour was long past his usual time to rise. He reached out for the phone on his bedside table, intending to call the front desk and demand to know what went wrong, but his hand encountered nothing but empty air.

He came fully awake and realized where he was. And with whom.

Anna was curled next to him on the wide sofa, her blond hair a wild cumulus cloud framing her peaceful face. He propped himself up on one elbow, his gaze loath to leave the relaxed planes of her face. He'd always found Anna attractive, as much for her disarming charm as her lush curves. But sleeping in the sunlight, with dust motes dancing around them as if they really were in an enchanted castle filled with pixie magic, she was beyond beautiful.

She was precious. Precious to him.

The realization was both awe-inspiring and humbling.

She sighed softly, her head stirring slightly. She would be fully awake any minute now. He both anticipated and regretted the moment they would need to leave the hidden apartment. Part of him wanted nothing more than to stay here, locked away from the world and their responsibilities and the demands placed on them. Another part was anxious to leave and tackle those very same demands—because while they existed, Ian and Anna would never be fully free to move forward and live the lives they wanted. A life, he was starting to realize, that would not be complete unless she continued to be in it. But they wouldn't—couldn't—even be friendly acquaintances if the deal remained a sword of Damocles hovering above their heads, threatening to sever the growing connection between them.

Ian prided himself on his strategic skillset. He'd never met a cake he couldn't have and also eat—it was a matter of figuring out the right solution. There had to be a way to oust Harlan from Blackburn Amusements without harming the relationship he had built with Anna. A way to get Olive and Preston on his side without agreeing to their demands to dismantle Lakes of Wonder and turn it into a retail site. But even as his mind raced through options, he discarded them before the thoughts could be fully formed.

Anna yawned and stretched, bringing him back to the present. The very pleasurable present. Hell, she was gorgeous waking up, her hair tumbled across her shoulders, her cheeks flushed, her mouth relaxed and softly parted. She sat up, the blanket Ian had found midway through the night falling away to reveal her rose-tipped breasts, and his hands begged anew to cup their glory.

But they had to get out of the Lighthouse sooner or later. And if he didn't maintain his focus on that goal, sooner would be later would be never. "What time is it?" she asked, her voice redolent with sleepy satisfaction, and though he was no longer looking at her, his cock grew even harder.

"A little after eight," he answered. Anna squeaked with surprise and the sounds of a frantic search for discarded articles of clothing soon followed. "We have an hour before the park opens, but the early morning crews should be here. Hopefully, I can get someone's attention." He crossed to the balcony door, half buttoning his shirt as he went, and pulled it open.

Anna gasped. "Wait. It's Saturday morning. Don't—"

Too late. He'd stepped onto the balcony.

And hundreds of park guests dressed in yoga wear, spaced evenly apart on the concourse that surrounded the Lighthouse, their arms raised in unison to begin a sun salutation sequence, stared back at him. Or so it seemed. Perhaps a few had their eyes closed or were focused on their alignment. But enough shocked gazes met his—and not a few of the guests immediately held up camera phones to memorialize his appearance—to assure him that their presence in the Lighthouse was no longer a secret.

He slammed the door shut and turned to face Anna. "The morning yoga in the park special event is today."

She nodded. "I'm sad I'm missing it," she said with a straight face. "Do you think they'll refund my fee?"

"I'm sure you can talk to management if you run into problems. Speaking of, I'm guessing security will show up here in the near future.

"It's okay, I'm related to the park's owner." She

smiled, and the room was bathed in light brighter than the earlier morning sun. Then the brilliance faded. "So. About last night—"

He crossed to where she stood, taking her right hand in his. "I enjoyed every minute. I enjoy being with you."

"Same here. But—"

"Last night was same as the gondola. Nothing changed," he stated, wanting to give her the reassurance he assumed she needed. Even though his recent epiphany meant his mouth felt full of broken glass as he shaped the words. "The deal is back on."

She shook her head. "No! Last night changes everything."

Something blossomed in his chest. Something he had never experienced before. An ache, equal parts pleasure and pain. "What do you mean?" he asked, keeping his tone neutral, not sure how he wanted her to answer the question.

She kept her head down as she finished buckling the strap of her second sandal. Then she lifted her gaze to his. "You're the only person I've told about my connection to the Lochlainns. Why I'm here. Why I'm obviously out of your league when it comes to the negotiation."

He sat down beside her, ignoring the rumpled cushions that still bore witness to their activities of the night before. "I'm honored you trusted me. Especially since I'm—" *The enemy.* He stopped himself before he revealed too much. "The other party in the deal."

"But you're more than that, right?" Her clear blue gaze searched his.

He wanted to be. The realization nearly made him fall off the sofa. Damn it, he wanted to be more. He had no idea how he could be.

"I mean, Lakes of Wonder is as much part of your DNA as it is part of mine," she continued. "It's your legacy, also."

His breath returned, his lungs inflating as normal again. Of course. That's what she meant. She was focused on the theme park, not him. Not *them*.

Who knew disappointment tasted as bitter as the old cliché asserted?

"Yeah, sure." He rubbed his temples, hoping she would take any dimness in his glance for tiredness. It's not like they'd gotten much sleep, after all. In fact, it was a relief to focus on the deal and not on any implications for his personal life. He didn't need the distraction. On the other hand, seeing her hopeful gaze as she reminded him Lakes of Wonder had been as much a Blackburn creation as a Lochlainn one, only reminded him he would wipe that light away for good once she learned what Preston and Olive planned to do with the acquisition once it was completed. "But I've had much longer to process my family's involvement—or lack thereof, when it comes to this park. I understand this is much newer to you."

"Right. And that's why we need to talk about the sale. Now that I know—"

A hard and insistent knock drowned out whatever she was about to say.

"Ian! You in there?" came a gruff shout.

Thirteen

"Ian?" A louder knock on the door. "I hope you're in there."

Tai. Ian couldn't decide if he had never been happier or more frustrated to hear his friend's voice. "We're here," he called back.

"We?" said Tai, and then he was opening the door. He smiled when he saw Ian and Anna sitting quietly on the sofa, the apartment in almost perfect order aside from a few cushions still on the floor. "Of course. Hello, Anna. Nice to see you again. We met at the closing—or rather, what wasn't the closing—"

Ian rose off the sofa. "Good to see you, too. We found ourselves locked in."

"Thought as much. The key was in the outer lock. Guess you discovered your lucky charm had a practical purpose after all." He tossed the slender item into the air and Anna caught it.

"How did you know we were here?" she asked. "We can't get a cell signal and there's no WiFi."

Tai tried to hold back his smirk, but Ian saw it. "Seems there was a half-naked intruder at the Lighthouse. It's all over the internet. There are some very clever reactions on TikTok—"

Ian pinched the bridge of his nose. "Great."

"Hey, can't tell it was you in the video. But you didn't show up for our breakfast. And Maeve—that's my assistant," he said to Anna, "heard from friends at the Lochlainn Company that you didn't show up for the yoga event." He turned back to Ian. "And you know me. I'm a numbers guy. I knew you were meeting at the park last night and I know how to add two and two together. Or, in this case, one missing exec and another missing exec. Don't worry, we called off security. Your secret is safe."

"It's not what—" Ian paused. He didn't owe Tai an explanation. He and Anna were consenting adults. And Lakes of Wonder was hers…well, her grandfather's. They weren't theme park aficionados trying to pull one over on the park's security. She had every right to be there. And so did he, in a manner of speaking.

He spoke over Tai's knowing chuckle. "Let's get out of here. I can still make the rest of the exec com meeting."

Tai's laughter died. "Yeah, about that." He threw a sideways glance at Anna, who was pretending to examine the contents of the bookshelf so Tai and Ian could have a semblance of privacy. "The meeting was canceled."

"What? But I didn't—"

"The conversations are happening above my pay level, which was made very clear to me every time I try to dig for more information. But I think you should return to Denver immediately. From what I gather, Harlan is planning a board coup. He got Russell to join his side, or so the rumor mill says."

"Russell?" The sun disappeared and Ian wondered if there had been an eclipse before he realized it was his vision turning blackly dark. "He's in the Caymans, counting his yachts or some similar nonsense."

"He showed up at the Denver office yesterday, according to Maeve. Look, I don't know Russell nearly as well as you do—"

"He's my second cousin and that's too close for comfort," Ian muttered.

"And I know swarm is Russell's default setting," Tai continued. "But Maeve said this wasn't his usual oily slither around the Blackburn executive suites. He was on a mission."

"Why would Russell..." Ian stopped when the answer hit him, hard. "Preston. Or Olive."

"Which one?" Tai asked.

"Both. Russell is looking for the best way to leverage the board's loyalties for his own gain. He's shopping for the best deal."

"Is there anything I can do?"

"Have Maeve book the BBA jet as soon as you can. I need to be in Denver ASAP."

Ian's gaze lingered on Anna. There was still so much for him to process, for him to sort through the emotions that threatened to swamp his usual excellent and coolly discerning strategic thought centers. So much to say. So much to discuss, like the future of Lakes of Wonder. The future of whatever they would be to each other—

No. *Stick to the plan*, he told himself. This was nothing but a speed bump. A very pleasurable one, but a minor inconvenience on his way to getting what he needed. Nothing positive ever came of allowing hormones to have a say in business relationships. It was a recipe for disaster, and he refused to be the main course in the banquet of humiliation that Harlan would throw should Ian fail to remove him from the board of BBA.

And he was close. So close.

Anna looked over and caught his gaze, her smile so warm and bright, his jaw ached at having to leave her light behind. "You two all caught up? Are we ready to leave?"

"Yes. In more ways than one. Listen, I need to go to Denver."

The light in her expression dimmed, a mere cast of a shadow, but it was perceptible to him. "Of course. I was hoping we could have some of those Seamus-shaped waffles for breakfast, but business waits for no stomach."

"Something like that. I'm sorry."

She crossed to his side and picked up his hand, entwining her fingers with his. "Is there anything I can do to help?"

He blinked. People offering their assistance was new to him. "No," he responded, his mind already ninety-five percent occupied with his upcoming confrontation with Russell, Olive and Preston. If he lost their support, he was dead in the water. "This is a BBA issue. Nothing you have any insight into. I don't need anything."

Too late, he realized how his words sounded when she dropped his hand as if he had burned her. "Insight. Right. Of course, you don't need my help. I don't have the requisite experience. Nor, apparently, do you need any support from me, moral or otherwise." Her tone was ice-cold.

"That's not what I—"

"Ian, we need to go." Tai was staring at his phone.

"Wait, you have service?"

"Just a bar but enough to get text messages. Told you to switch providers."

"What is it?" Ian gritted.

"Harlan is having a hard time reaching Johnson Miller for the emergency board meeting. Probably on purpose. Johnson doesn't like being dictated to. He'll keep Harlan dangling for at least another half day, to show he's independent."

"But then he'll dance to Harlan's tune. As always."

"Tigers don't change their stripes," Tai agreed. "But he's buying us time, so don't look a gift jungle cat in the mouth."

"Right." Ian strode toward the door. But as he was about to cross the threshold, he realized Anna wasn't following him. "Aren't you coming?" he asked her. "I'd thought you be happy to get out of here."

Anna's gaze was distant. "You're obviously in a hurry. You go. I'll find my own way out. Don't worry, I'll have Teri from the Lochlainn Company set up the next meeting for this coming Friday."

"The next meeting? You and I can schedule that, you don't need Teri—"

"The last meeting," she clarified. "The sale."

"Ian, we need to go—" Tai started to say.

Ian cut him off with a shake of his head and turned to Anna. "We still have several weeks left. I thought we could—"

She shook her head. "I have all the information I need. And there's no need to extend my trip past Thanksgiving. Might as well put us both out of our misery, waiting for the inevitable." She smiled, but there was no brightness to it. "Thank you for bringing me to the Lighthouse. It sounds like a bad pun but being here put a lot of things in a new light."

"Ian." Tai's voice was firm. A tone he rarely took, considering Ian was formally his boss.

"It's okay," Anna said. "I'm okay. You have to leave. I understand." She tucked a curl behind her ear. "See you soon."

"You need to read the texts I received," Tai said, and there was a clear warning in his words.

Ian held up his left hand in acknowledgment of

Tai but kept his gaze focused on Anna. "I'll call you from the road."

"You need to concentrate on whatever is going on at BBA," she said. "I'll see you soon." As if on impulse, she rose on her toes and brushed a kiss against his lips. "Good luck." Then she waved at Tai before walking back to peruse the dusty tomes on the bookshelf.

He couldn't be more dismissed if he were in a classroom and the bell rang. "Thanks," he said. "We'll talk. Soon."

He followed Tai out of the Lighthouse apartment. He couldn't stop himself from turning back for one last look at her. The sun streaming in from the window turned her hair to living gold before outlining her figure, her shoulders ramrod-straight and her chin held high.

He wanted nothing more than to reverse his steps and take her in his arms, lead her back to the sofa where they could once again shut out the world and lose themselves in each other. But one glance at Tai's set jaw and he knew that was an impossibility.

He would make it up to Anna. Once Lakes of Wonder was his, he and Anna could figure out what they wanted to do about the crazy chemistry that ignited between them.

But if he didn't neutralize Harlan's threat, he would have no future to explore, with or without her.

Anna kept her gaze firmly fixed on the photo in her hands as Ian disappeared. Not for good—he would no doubt show up for the final meeting and the transfer of Lakes to Wonder to BBA—but his departure had an air of finality about it all the same. After last night, she thought…

Well. It didn't matter what she thought, did it? No doubt Ian viewed last night the same way he did the first time they slept together. A fun interlude, devoid of any meaning and certainly lacking any deeper emotion.

She sighed and carefully placed the photo back on its spot on the shelf. Unlike Ian, she didn't have urgent matters of multinational corporate concern to which to attend. She was just…someone who had a connection to Lakes of Wonder solely due to an accident of birth. She had no real role at the theme park, no corner office in which to ensconce herself. What she did have, in fact, was literally one job. And that job was to sign the papers selling the park to BBA.

She traced her way back through the tunnels and was soon slipping into the gift shop. No one noticed her entrance and she was quickly swept up in the crowd of guests eagerly rummaging around the new holiday-themed merchandise. She pushed her way through the shoppers and emerged onto Seamus's Seaport, blinking at the warm rays of sun on her face. Her phone was buzzing with missed calls, texts and alerts but she ignored them all in favor of hitting the button to video call Maritza. Voice wasn't enough. She needed to see the face of someone she knew loved her.

"Hey!" her cousin answered right away. "How's

sunny California?" Behind Maritza, Anna could see Pepa playing with her dolls—who were currently attempting to ride on the back of a plush toy version of Seamus Sea Serpent.

"Fine," Anna said. "How's sunny Florida?"

"The same," Maritza said. She turned to Pepa and held the phone so Anna and Pepa could see each other. "Want to talk to Anna? Look, she's at Lakes of Wonder! You can see the Lighthouse of Amazement behind her."

Anna glanced over her shoulder and silently cursed her choice of position. "*Hola, niñita*," she called.

"Don't wanna talk to Anna!" Pepa turned her back to the phone screen, her tiny shoulders rigid.

Maritza came back into view. "Sorry," she said. "It's been a morning. She's really leaning into her drama queen phase."

"That's okay—"

Something crashed in the background. Her cousin disappeared, to be replaced by blurry movement and then a view of the kitchen's tiled floor as Maritza ran to the source of the noise. Anna glimpsed a spreading sea of cloudy white before her cousin reappeared. "Sorry, need to go. Milk emergency."

"Talk to you later—" But Maritza was gone.

Anna found an empty park bench and sat, the cool metal pressing into her legs. She should go back to the hotel, take a shower, maybe even a nap to catch up on the sleep she'd missed. But then what would she do? She'd explored most of Lakes of Wonder— and thanks to last night, even seen areas that weren't on the maps. She could continue to check out rival amusement parks in the area, but she'd seen enough to know that Ian was correct. Lakes of Wonder was special thanks to its history, but it lacked the well-honed whimsy and tightly maintained machinery of a Disney theme park. Or the stomach-flipping chills of a thirty-story roller coaster drop at a thrill park, like those owned by BBA. Or the crowd-pleasing ability to get up close with land and marine animals of the local zoos and aquatic parks.

Lakes of Wonder had nostalgia on its side and little more—and no investment from the Lochlainns, who obviously didn't care if the park thrived or died.

Why did she care so much? Was her pursuit of Lakes of Wonder because she was chasing a connection to the man whose DNA she shared? Or was her insistence on learning more about the park before selling it just a pretense to spend time with Ian? She could tell herself all she wanted that she was a sophisticated citizen of the world; one who indulged in one-night stands for fun and to assuage her curiosity about people she found sexually tempting. But if this trip had taught her one thing about herself, it was that she'd slept with Ian the first time because she not only found him attractive, but because she liked him. She'd slept with him last night because she…oh, she might as well acknowledge the truth her heart knew several weeks ago. She was falling in love with him.

And he couldn't get away from her faster if he were an Olympic gold medal sprinter.

She sighed, a long, loud exhale. She'd tried being

someone other than who she was. She'd zigged where she would normally zag. She'd turned left instead of right. Yet she'd ended up making the same mistakes. Worse, she'd caused needless hurt and pain. She'd even made Pepa mad at her, although she knew Maritza was right and the five-year-old was milking—no pun intended—the drama for all she could. Yet Anna had ended up right back at the same square where she'd started, making the exact same mistakes.

Or worse ones. Because now she knew she could fall hard and fast for someone like Ian. Someone who made her laugh. Someone who made her legs weak with overwhelming desire, someone who took her breath away with a flash of his grin, someone who made her heart beat faster than a hummingbird's wings with one brush of his pinkie finger against hers.

Someone upon whose confidence and quietly commanding presence she'd grown to rely on, without realizing how much she'd come to accept him as a daily and much-looked-forward-to constant in her life. But that life, the one in which she and Ian had bantered as business rivals on the same equal footing, was not hers. Not really. She was borrowing it from the Lochlainns. Her actual life was in Florida.

In pieces.

She watched a family gather to take photos in front of the Lighthouse. The older daughter pouted, not wanting to waste time stopping. The younger daughter, around Pepa's age, refused to stand still and kept dancing out of the frame and having to be coaxed back by her father. The son had a Seamus-shaped bubble wand and wouldn't stop blowing cascades of bubbles in his older sister's face, irritating her more.

The parents looked hot and frustrated, despite the early hour. And yet, when the photos were finally taken, everyone broke into happy smiles. Their excitement at being at the park could be felt from where Anna sat.

Anna thought the park was magic. But watching the family walk off, the younger daughter still dancing, the older daughter now excitedly pointing out the sights to her brother, Anna finally understood: the real magic came from being with people you love. Family, whether by blood or by choice.

The photograph of Keith and Jamie in the Lighthouse floated in front of her vision. She had no way of knowing if she was right. But something—call it a Lochlainn intuition, perhaps the one thing she had inherited—told her the reason why Keith had let Lakes of Wonder fall into disrepair and that finally selling it was not because he'd fallen out of love with the park but because he'd lost the family he loved with whom to share it.

She still had no idea why Keith wanted her to handle the sale. But regardless of what happened between her and Ian personally, at least now she knew Lakes of Wonder would go to someone who also had a family tie to the park.

There was only one thing left for her to do.

Pick up the pieces.

She took out her phone again and searched her

contacts. Her finger hovered over the screen. Finally, she pushed Call and listened to the phone ring on the other end, her hand trembling but successfully fighting the urge to hang up and pretend she'd dialed the number by accident.

After enough rings to make her wonder if she had left it too late—if they'd looked at the caller ID and refused to answer because she was now persona non grata—she heard the line connect.

"Anna?" her mother said. "Anna, honey, is that you?"

"Mom," Anna choked out before tears threatened to close her throat for good. "Mom, I've made so many mistakes. I'm so sorry. For running off to California without telling you directly, for refusing to talk to Dad when he tried. I don't know if you'll ever forgive me, but I'm coming home for Thanksgiving and I want to talk if you want—"

"Shh," her mom said, the same soft sound of comfort used to soothe Anna since she was a fractious toddler. "We love you, Anna bear. We know you're dealing with a lot. And we're sorry you've been so affected by our choices. We're so sorry. We only want you to be happy and healthy."

"I'm healthy." Anna sniffed and then she poured out most of the story of her time at Lakes of Wonder, keeping only the most private, treasured moments to herself.

She'd come to California hoping to discover who she was. Only to learn she couldn't continue to run from her past. Now it was time to determine who she wanted to be in the future.

And if that future could contain Ian Blackburn.

Fourteen

The morning was crisp and cool, but the sharp bright sunlight outside his window promised a warm Southern Californian day ahead. Ian paced in his hotel suite, his gaze drawn more than he cared to the panoramic view of Lakes of Wonder below. He tried one last time to reach Anna before the meeting, but his call went immediately to voice mail. Damn it, now he was "it" in their game of phone tag. He could text, of course, but where would he start? How could he start?

A knock came at his door. He crossed to answer it, only realizing once he saw Tai that he had irrationally hoped Anna might be on his threshold instead. He nodded at his friend. "Hey."

"Hey back." Tai entered the suite, holding a paper

bag in one hand and a tray of coffees in his other. "I brought bagels. Time to carbo load."

"You make it sound like we're about to run a marathon." Ian took one of the coffees.

Tai sat down on the sofa and starting to spread cream cheese on his bagel. "Well, it's the end of a very long chase. Sustenance is required."

Ian grunted, sipping his beverage.

Tai shot him a glance. "You sound more like a man going to his execution rather attaining his long-held desire. Great job with Russell, by the way. He's so on your side, I got an invite to join him on his yacht in Sardinia. Might even take him up on it. He said I can bring Linh."

Ian put down his coffee. His stomach roiled, hard, and the acidic beverage was making it worse. "Am I doing the right thing?"

Tai raised his eyebrows. "Do you think you're doing the right thing?"

"I love her, you know." He did. He'd realized it late one night, sitting in front of computer screen trying to make sense of numbers that refused to stay put, jumping around until all he saw was her face, flushed and relaxed, and her blue eyes staring into his.

He was an idiot for leaving her in the Lighthouse. For choosing BBA over her.

And, God help him, he was about to make the same mistake again.

"I know," Tai said. "So I'll ask again. Do you think you're doing the right thing?"

Ian didn't answer, choosing instead to dial Anna's

number again. "C'mon, pick up," he said under his breath. But once again, only her voice mail answered.

"You're doing the right thing." Catalina Lochlainn poured more tea into the cup in front of Anna. "It's time for the Lochlainns to let go of Lakes of Wonder." She put the teapot down and smiled. "Thank you, again, for asking to meet. And for agreeing to have breakfast at this bistro. It's one of my favorite places."

"Of course. I know contacting you is against the terms of the Kno—the terms given to me by Bingham Lockwood when he discussed Keith's wishes." Anna picked up her cup. "But I couldn't leave California without at least trying to meet my new relatives. I'm only disappointed Keith didn't come with you. I would like to meet him."

"In time." Catalina's gaze warned Anna not to probe further. "But he wants you to know the sale remains wholly in your hands."

Anna placed her tea back on the table. "To be truthful, there's not much of an alternative if I didn't sign the sale documents, right? Like you said, the Lochlainn Company wants to be rid of the park."

"I wouldn't say 'rid,' exactly." Catalina cocked her head to the side. "More like it's been purposefully forgotten and needs to be rescued by someone else. And BBA is the only alternative to keep the park going. Otherwise, we've received many offers from developers to turn it into a golf course or shopping mall, something of that nature."

"And it's been forgotten because of Jamie. Because he cut off Keith, and then he died. And Lakes of Wonder is about families, but Keith no longer has one. Or at least, he no longer has his child."

The older woman maintained her pleasant expression, but a muscle jumped in her jaw. "You are very perceptive."

"I've learned a lot over these last weeks." Including that her heart was infinitely malleable and exponentially expandable. She'd had several long conversations with both her parents, full of tears and smiles and deep abiding love. No matter how they'd conceived her, the fact was she belonged to them and always would. But there was room for her Lochlainn relations, which was why she'd reached out to Catalina. She may never know if a certain trait was inherited from Jamie or instilled by her upbringing, but she was choosing the person she wanted to be.

And that person was in love with Ian.

She glanced at the clock on the bistro's wall. "Speaking of the sale, I should get going."

Catalina laid her hand over Anna's, stilling Anna's movements. "No matter what happens, I want you to know you have conducted yourself in this strange, unusual matter with grace. I am proud to call you my step-granddaughter."

"Thank you. And don't worry, the sale will go through. I'm sure of it."

Catalina shook her head. "Of course it will. I'm referring to the inheritance contest."

"The what? Contest?" Anna stared at Catalina,

who for the very first time seemed to lose some of her equanimity.

"Oh, dear." Catalina swallowed. "You were not told by Bingham? You are in a contest. With Declan."

"Who is Declan?" Anna heard her voice as if coming from a faraway distance.

"Your half-brother. Also fathered by Jamie via donation. You honestly did not know?"

With supreme will, Anna managed to shake her head, tiny movements from side to side.

"Oh, dear," Catalina repeated. She took Anna's hands in hers, but Anna couldn't feel the older woman's grip. Her fingers were numb. "We have much to discuss."

Ian strode down the hallway of the Lakes of Wonder executive building, retracing his journey of...was it only four weeks ago? So little time, from one point of view. An entire lifetime from another.

His steps slowed as he approached the door, and he smoothed his hair before he knew what he was doing. The thud-thud-thud of his pulse drowned out any other noise that might be present.

He pushed the door open.

Ten heads swiveled in unison to watch him cross the threshold. He only cared about one. Anna. His gaze zeroed in on her like a person trapped in a desert who spotted a well. He smiled at her, but the smile faded as he took in her appearance.

Anna was wearing black. A tailored black-wool pantsuit, unadorned save for discreet silver buttons.

Even the shoes peeking out from below her trousers were black. And the blouse underneath the trim jacket was stark white. There wasn't a splash of Anna-characteristic color anywhere. Her smile—her lovely, bright, irrepressible smile—was absent, while her blond curls were neatly combed back into a low ponytail. Worse, the light that usually suffused her from within, rendering her incandescent no matter the time of day or weather, was dim. Almost extinguished.

His pulse beat painfully against his eardrums. She nodded at him, once, then turned back to her discussion with Teri.

"Morning." He said hello to Tai, who had preceded him to the meeting, and nodded at the Lochlainn Company representatives. But his gaze never once left her. Every time he tried to take a step toward her, however, he was intercepted by one person after another. He adopted a close-lipped smile and listened patiently as they made small talk, the usual chitchat that precedes a much-longed-for but often-in-doubt closure of a business deal. Normally, he would revel in this moment, the calm after the storm, when both parties know the hard work of negotiation is over and the only thing standing between them and a celebratory cocktail or two are a few signatures.

But he was anything but relaxed. He tried again to catch Anna's gaze. But she evaded his grasp in every sense of the word until time ran out and he found himself ushered to the chair next to hers. The déjà vu was strong as he sat down in the exact same spot as the first meeting, only so much had changed. Everything had changed.

"What's going on? Are you okay?" he whispered to her out of the side of his mouth.

She shook her head, a sharp movement almost too small to discern. "Later," she whispered back, but then she shot him a quick glance and he realized this was another one of her masks—one he hadn't seen before and hoped to never again—but the real Anna, his Anna, was still there. He smiled at her, a fast upturn of his lips meant as a reassurance, before she turned to the rest of the group now seated around the board table.

"Shall we begin?" she asked.

Ian moved through the next half hour as if in a repeated dream. This time, Anna signed the papers first. He watched her hand sign her name in bold, confident letters on the various documents. Then the documents were picked up, straightened, and placed in front of him.

Anna sat back in her chair and regarded him. Some of the tension had left her shoulders but her gaze remained wary and watchful.

This was it. The culmination of everything he had been working toward. The end of the Lochlainn/Blackburn feud, with victory firmly in the Blackburn camp. Preston, Olive and Russell would vote with him to remove Harlan. BBA would remain firmly in his hands, in Blackburn hands, as it was always meant to be.

And all he had to do was sign.

And Lakes of Wonder would go to Preston and Olive, who would destroy the park forever.

He turned to Anna. "We need to talk."

Her gaze darted around the room as she noted the avid stares of executives from both companies. "Now? Can't we talk after you sign?"

He shook his head. "No. It will be too late."

She licked her lips. "Okay. Where?"

He rose from the boardroom table and strode to the door, pausing only for her to catch up with him before he swept her out of the room and into the hallway. She ran-walked to keep up with him, taking two steps to his one. "Ian? Where are we going?"

He didn't answer, leading her down the corridor until they reached the elevator lobby. When a cab arrived, he ushered her inside—and pulled the stop button.

"Sorry. This was the only place I could think of where we would have privacy and no one would think to look for us," he said.

"What's going on?" Her gaze searched his expression. "Are you okay? Are you ill? Is something wrong at BBA?"

"Yes. No. Yes," he answered, drinking in the nearness of her presence. He'd missed her. Being close to her again, even if she remained on the other side of the elevator cab, was a restorative tonic for his soul. He could breathe easier, think clearer, now she was near. And now he knew what he had to do. What, really, was his only course of action. "BBA can't buy Lakes of Wonder."

She remained still, an Anna-shaped statue in the corner of the elevator. "Why?" she finally asked, her lips the only muscles she moved. "Lakes of Wonder is as much a Blackburn creation as a Lochlainn one. You're the perfect buyer. You're the only buyer."

"Remember I told you about my stepfather?"

Some color came back into her face. "Yes. Your awful stepfather."

"He is." Ian felt the tension of the last month—maybe even the last twenty years since his father had died—begin to leave his shoulders. "And he wants to remove me as CEO. I want to remove him as chairman of the board. We've been fighting for board votes this past week, with the vote next month. I have enough votes if the acquisition of Lakes of Wonder goes through. He has enough votes if it doesn't."

"I don't understand." Anna moved closer to him, her slender fingers coming to rest on his arm. Warmth radiated from her touch. "Then buy Lakes of Wonder. Why did you say BBA can't?"

"Because I only have enough votes if I give Lakes of Wonder to my cousin and uncle. And they have a deal to raze the park to the ground and build a live-work-retail complex. One of those shopping centers that looks like a fake Italian town." He raked a hand through his hair. "I know how much you love Lakes of Wonder. I can't let that happen."

Her hand dropped from his arm. "But your stepfather will win."

He closed his eyes. "Yes. And I'll lose my position. But BBA will survive Harlan. I'll fight my way back to the top again."

"But why?" She stared at him, her blue eyes dark and unreadable in the elevator's dim light. "You can save your job. Save BBA from your stepfather. I don't understand."

He swallowed. Hard. "Because I love you, Anna. And I can't destroy something you love." He cupped her face with his hands. "I've loved you since I saw you dancing to Halloween music wearing pink fairy wings. My only regret is I took too long to realize it."

"Ian, I—"

He kissed her, because he couldn't put off kissing her one second later. She made a sound deep in her throat and then she was kissing him back, her arms entwining around his neck as his hands molded her waist, her hips, pulling her to him so her soft curves met his hard planes, fitting together perfectly as they always had. He could have remained in the elevator forever, kissing his perfect partner, but she pulled back first.

He loved seeing her lips swollen, her gaze wide and wild. He burned the image on his memory. "So, we'll go back to the conference room and tell them the sale is off—"

"No." Anna smoothed her hair, restoring order. "You have to buy the park."

"Did you hear me? If BBA buys it—"

"Yes, I heard you!" Anger flashed in Anna's eyes. "And if BBA doesn't buy Lakes of Wonder, the park will be bought by golf course developers. Or residential developers. Or commercial developers. You know the Lochlainn Company won't spend the money needed to keep Lakes of Wonder running. You know Lakes of Wonder needs a buyer." She laughed, but there was no mirth in it. "You know it will take months, if not longer, to find another buyer while the park falls further into disrepair." She crossed her arms over chest, her gaze turning sharp and emotionless, like a shark seeking prey. "Is this a gambit to get Lakes of Wonder for an even lower price a year from now?"

What? "No, I'm not—" Not that he blamed her. That would be a trick worthy of BBA. Or a Lochlainn. "Where is this coming from?"

She sighed, her shoulders falling. "I had breakfast with Catalina Lochlainn this morning. And she told me… It doesn't matter what she told me, I don't want it anyway. But she also explained the history between BBA and the Lochlainn Company. From the Lochlainn perspective." She caught his gaze. "I don't blame you for playing games, including the night we met. I know you must to survive your world. But I'm tired, Ian. I'm not built to be a corporate player. I don't jump through hoops well. I'm terrible at machinations and intrigues."

"What did Catalina say to you?" He caressed her cheek and she leaned into his touch before straightening and putting distance between them.

He let his hand drop.

Anna smiled. There was no warmth in it. "The sale of Lakes of Wonder? Is an audition to be Keith

Lochlainn's sole heir. He's pitted me against my half-brother—yes, I have a half-brother I didn't know about but Keith did, isn't that awesome?—and whoever performs the best at the task given to them will inherit the Lochlainn Company." She threw out her hands to the sides. "So, if you don't buy Lakes of Wonder, I am taken out of the running."

Ian inhaled. "Okay. We can figure this out."

She was shaking her head before he finished speaking. "I came to California because I didn't know who I was after the Knock. I thought I could reinvent myself, make myself into someone who was born a Lochlainn, not a Stratford." Her right hand traced the line of Ian's jaw. "The type of person who meets an incredibly handsome and charismatic man and has amazing one-night stand sex."

He pressed a kiss into her palm. "You are that person. And more than a one-night stand."

"But I'm also still the same me who fled her friends and family in Florida. And that me is homesick—not for humidity and bugs the size of dinner plates, California has been a pleasant surprise on those fronts." She tried to smile, a real smile, but Ian could see the effort it cost her. "But I miss my family. I miss the me when I'm with my family. I could belong to the Lochlainn world. To the Blackburn world. But I choose not to."

"Anna, I love you." His heart beat a warning rhythm. He was losing control of the situation.

"And I love you. I've loved you since you put your jacket on my shoulders." Her blue eyes shone with unshed tears in the elevator's dim light. "But BBA is your world. Your legacy. Your family. And I can't ask you to leave it. I won't. Because I know how painful it is to cut yourself off. Just look at Lakes of Wonder. It's dying because Jamie cut himself off from Keith and his legacy."

"But if you love me..." His mind seized on the few words that still gave him hope, that provided a path that would allow him to maneuver. "If you love me, we can solve this."

"Oh, Ian." This time she kissed him. He gathered her closer, deepening the kiss, begging the seam of her lips to open to him, to acknowledge the truth between them, to stop denying the inevitable reality. She sighed, their bodies melting together as she responded, her mouth welcoming his, her tongue seeking and asking for a response he was all too happy to give. She tasted of sunlight and joy and hope. She tasted of Anna, of home and future and promise.

Too late, he realized the elevator was moving. The doors opened, depositing them in the ground-floor lobby. She stepped out of the circle of his arms, her regard steady but resolute. "Love isn't a problem to be solved. It just...is," she said. "A part of me will always love you, no matter what the future brings. But if I stay with you, I won't be me. I'll be a game pawn, to be used by you or the Lochlainns.

"No. You're wrong. You—"

"Ian." Her smile turned sad. "Who did you think I was the night we met? What did you think I was?"

He couldn't hold her gaze.

She nodded. "I wish you nothing but happiness from now to eternity. Buy Lakes of Wonder. Save your company." She brushed her lips on his right cheek.

By the time his stunned limbs could respond to his brain's commands to go after her and make her stay, she was gone.

Fifteen

One month later

Lakes of Wonder had never looked prettier. Ian had
seen photos of the theme park's opening day when everything was new and fresh, and, even so, the theme
park outshone its previous self. The buildings were
draped in green-and-purple bunting, disguising the
patchy paint and sun damage over the years. Flowers were everywhere—hanging from baskets in the
Port of Entry, overflowing from planters that lined
the walkway, peeking from vines twined together to
decorate the signs and way posts. The staff—Seamus's attendants, in the vernacular of the park—was
smiling and waving at guests, their costumes freshly
washed and pressed. Even the weather cooperated,

a dark blue California sky dotted with marshmallow clouds, appearing like a painted backdrop made to order.

"You okay?" Tai materialized next to where Ian stood on the main thoroughfare, munching on caramel popcorn from a Seamus-shaped plastic bucket.

"Never better."

Tai regarded him then nodded. "Yeah, I agree. You know how I know?"

"How?"

"You're not asking me if you're doing the right thing."

Ian chuckled. "No. I'm not. I have faith this time." Faith, and not much less. But he was good with that.

"I have to say, I'm going to miss this," Tai said, sweeping his hand to indicate the picture-perfect vista in front of them.

"You can take your pick of parks operated by BBA."

"Yeah, but none of them have a snack this good." Tai threw a piece of popcorn into the air and caught it in his mouth.

"It's the same vendor." Ian checked his smartwatch.

"Really?" Tai ate another piece. "Must be the Seamus bucket that makes it so tasty. And the time is five minutes past the last time you looked."

"Don't want to be late."

"Right. Late. That's the only reason why you're acting like a frog."

"A frog?" Ian turned to look at his friend.

"Jumpy." Tai threw another piece of popcorn in the air.

Ian shook his head and lifted his left wrist, only to put it back down when Tai shot him an amused look. "I'll see you later. Teri is looking for me. Last-minute changes."

"You've done everything you could that's in your power. It's out of your hands now, Kermit." Tai grinned at him.

"No one knows that better than me." Ian tossed Tai a quick salute and left to go find Teri. Tai was right, in some respects. The New Year's Eve party, which was doubling as the closing event for Lakes of Wonder was already a hit. The journalists handpicked to be there were thrilled with their access, the invited guests full of joy to be included. Oh, there were protests when they'd announced the park was going to shut down, and public sentiment was running very much against the decision, but if all went to plan, that would be the least of his concerns.

He took a deep breath. The future might be out of his control, but that didn't mean he couldn't attempt to tip the odds in his favor as much as possible.

Nothing brought Anna more joy than seeing Pepa's eyes widen when the five-year-old caught her first glimpse of the Lighthouse of Amazement in the distance. "Wow," Pepa gasped, her always-in-motion feet glued to the ground for once.

"Pretty cool, huh?" Anna smiled at her and then exchanged glances with Maritza before kneeling to address Pepa directly. "So, I have a few errands I need to run. You're going to hang with your mom and then I'll meet you in front of the Lighthouse to watch the parade. Deal?"

"Deal!" Pepa gave Anna a high-five then turned to her mother. "I wanna go on the Skyroute!"

"Hold on!" Maritza grabbed Pepa's hand when she would dart off into the crowd. "You'll be okay?" she asked Anna. "You sure you don't want us to go with you?"

"I'll be fine." Anna hugged her cousin. "Thank you for asking, though. It's a quick trip in and out and then I'll join you, Pepa, and my parents. Just save me a place in case the crowd makes it difficult to get to you on time."

"Got it." Maritza hugged Anna back tightly. Almost too tightly.

Anna drew back and regarded her cousin with her brows drawn. "Everything all right? Sure you don't want me to stay and help you corral Pepa?"

Maritza blinked. "No. Don't you dare not go to the Lighthouse. Right now. In fact, you should hurry. Get going, you!"

"O...kay." Anna drew out the word. Were Maritza's cheeks flushed? Was she coming down with something? "You sure you're all right?"

"Yes. I am." Maritza nodded rapidly. "I'm great. Since I'm here at the park. You know, a place I never thought I'd visit. Now go." She playfully shoved Anna. "See you later."

"All right. Have fun." Anna took a deep breath

and then plunged into the gift shop, making her way to the hidden door without any difficulty. Before she knew it, she was in the tunnel and heading toward the Lighthouse.

Her heart stung more than she'd anticipated to be back at Lakes of Wonder, for the very last time. Everywhere she looked, she saw Ian. Even here in the tunnel, all she could see was Ian walking next to her, shortening his long strides to match hers, sneaking glances at her when she wasn't sneaking glances at him. His smile, tinged with cynicism in public, but always one-hundred-percent sincere when they were alone. The gleam of excitement in his eyes when they'd discovered the mythical door to the Lighthouse was real.

The sale to BBA had closed quickly after that month-ago meeting. Although media reports had been vague about what would happen to the park after today, she had no doubt Preston and Olive were looking at retail-center renderings at that very moment. So when the VIP invitation to attend the closing party arrived in her mailbox, she'd thought long and hard about accepting it. But her experience in California had showed her there was no running from who she was. She was a Stratford and a Lochlainn— even if she had called Catalina and politely but firmly declined participating in Keith's contest for an heir. She was done with families whose bonds were transactional only.

Before she knew it, she stood before the heavy metal door that led to the Lighthouse apartment. She reached beneath the collar of her mint-green dress and drew out the key she had snagged the morning she and Ian were "rescued." The doorknob turned without a protest and she stood on the threshold of the owner's apartment, which looked like no one had been there since—

No. Someone had been there. The cushions were back on the sofa in their respective corners. The blanket was folded neatly. And there wasn't a mote of dust anywhere to be found. The cleaning crew was apparently still cleaning, despite the park's eminent closure.

She entered the room, taking her time so she could savor the moment, soak up every impression while the room was intact, and the Lighthouse still stood. She brushed her fingers over upholstery on the couch, the smooth leather cool to her touch. Her gaze traced the worn beams of the ceiling and counted the cracks in the rough plaster cast of the walls. With her sandals slipped off, her toes gripped the worn Persian rug.

How was it possible to miss a place when she was presently standing in it?

But then, how was it possible to miss one person so much her heart threatened to crack like an egg under the weight of so much yearning?

She was still convinced she couldn't live in Ian's world. She'd made the right decision. She and her parents were communicating even better than ever. They'd offered her a partnership in Stratford's, but she'd turned them down in favor of finishing her college degree, in business this time, with plans to start her own independent interior-design business. But, oh, how she ached for Ian. And the ache gave no indication of diminishing any time soon.

She shook her head to clear it. She needed to hurry. If she lingered too long, she would miss meeting her family to watch the parade. Part of the reason why she'd agreed to the invitation to attend the closing party was the opportunity to share her Lochlainn heritage with her parents and her closest relatives, and she wanted to be there to see Pepa's eyes light up as the floats passed by. But she had one last piece of business before she could let Lake of Wonder go for good.

She found the bookshelf where the Lochlainn family photos continued to sit in their previous positions and picked up the picture of Keith holding a small Jamie's hand. She couldn't let such a precious memento fall into the hands of people who would only value for it for its collectible value, or worse, be destroyed along with the park.

Her gaze fell on frame holding a photo of Archibald with another man who could only be Cooper Blackburn. He had the same square chin as Ian, the same high cheekbones, the same patrician nose that gave them the appearance of a stern emperor deciding who should sit next to him at the banquet and who was being sent to the coliseum to face off with wild animals. In fact, dress Cooper Blackstone in a well-tailored suit and photograph him in color and it would be hard to tell the difference between him and his great-grandson.

She scooped up all the photos she could find and

wrapped them in protective bubble wrap before placing them in her backpack, lingering on the photo of Jamie and Keith. Her biological grandfather still refused to meet her, leaving her to wonder why she had been chosen for the Lakes of Wonder task and not Declan. But maybe Keith had wanted one of his grandchildren to see the place Jamie had loved. Maybe that was all he'd wanted, to know one of Jamie's offspring had been there at the end.

She inhaled. This was it. Goodbye to Lakes of Wonder. But the park would live on in her memories. Memories that she was counting on to keep her warm for the rest of her life. Her relationship with Ian may have been brief, but was so intense, she knew she would be hard-pressed to find another partner with whom she fit so perfectly in so many ways—except when it came to what they wanted most out of life. Although her heart yearned to glimpse Ian while she was in the park, her brain told her it would be best to continue with the clean break that had started when she'd walked out of the elevator.

Her soul would always hurt for him.

She put her hand of the rough plaster of the wall next to the front door. "I'm sorry we're coming to end. But thank you for all you've given me—"

A loud bugle fanfare nearly caused her to jump out of her sandals. She checked the time on her phone. The parade wasn't supposed to start for another twenty minutes, according to the schedule of entertainment handed out at the gate when they'd entered the park. She should still have plenty of time to meet her family. Was there a special New Year's Eve event happening?

She made her way to the window and peered through the streaky glass. The plaza in front of the Lighthouse was packed with parkgoers, wearing the iconic lavender and mint hats decorated with Seamus's sea serpent scales. But she could see a path had been cleared from the Seaport entrance to the Lighthouse, the Lakes of Wonder staff doing its best to keep the crowd clear.

She squinted, trying to make out the activity in the far distance. There was a parade float, but not one she recognized from the parades she'd seen earlier. It looked like...a giant Seamus? A burst of flame erupted from the float and she jumped. It was Seamus! Had someone at Lakes of Wonder found the old parade vehicle? The sea serpent float was still a distance away but even from where she stood the float looked identical to the one in the photo that hung on the conference room wall—the float supposedly destroyed decades ago. What a fitting way to say goodbye to Lakes of Wonder, by bringing back its original iconic figure.

The music grew louder. She resisted the urge to step onto the balcony. Might was well find a comfy spot on the sofa—no matter that everywhere she looked she saw Ian. Couldn't run her hand along the leather whether remembering Ian's hands on her. Couldn't glance at the overstuffed decorative pillows without remembering how she'd fallen apart and flown with his mouth on her. How—

Loyal Readers
FREE BOOKS Voucher

We're giving away **THOUSANDS** of **FREE** **BOOKS**

See Details Inside

Get up to 4
FREE FABULOUS BOOKS
You Love!

To thank you for being a loyal reader we'd like to send you up to 4 FREE BOOKS, absolutely free when you try the Harlequin Reader Service.

Just write "YES" on the Loyal Reader Voucher and we'll send you 2 free books from each series you choose and a Free Mystery Gift, altogether worth over $20.

Try **Harlequin® Desire** and get 2 books featuring the worlds of the American elite with juicy plot twists, delicious sensuality and intriguin scandal.

Try **Harlequin Presents® Larger-Print** and get 2 books featuring the glamourous lives of royals and billionaires in a world of exotic locations, where passion knows no bounds.

Or **TRY BOTH** and get 2 books from each series!

Your free books are completely free, even the shipping! If you continue with your subscription, you can look forward to curated monthly shipments of brand-new books from your selected series, always at a discount off the cover price! Plus you can cancel any time.

So don't miss out, return your Loyal Readers Voucher today to get your Free books.

Pam Powers

LOYAL READER
FREE BOOKS VOUCHER

YES! I Love Reading, please send me up to 4 FREE BOOKS and a Free Mystery Gift from the series I select.

Just write in "YES" on the dotted line below then return this card today and we'll send your free books & gift asap!

➡ YES ⬅

Which do you prefer?

☐ **Harlequin Desire®**
225/326 HDL GRTA

☐ **Harlequin Presents® Larger-Print**
176/376 HDL GRTA

☐ **BOTH**
225/326 & 176/376
HDL GRTZ

FIRST NAME	LAST NAME

ADDRESS

APT.#	CITY

STATE/PROV.	ZIP/POSTAL CODE

EMAIL ☐ Please check this box if you would like to receive newsletters and promotional emails from Harlequin Enterprises ULC and its affiliates. You can unsubscribe anytime.

HD/HP-622-LR_MMM22

HARLEQUIN Reader Service —**Here's how it works:**

Accepting your 2 free books and free gift (gift valued at approximately $10.00 retail) places you under no obligation to buy anything. You may keep the books and gift and return the shipping statement marked "cancel." If you do not cancel, approximately one month later we'll send you more books from the series you have chosen, and bill you at our low, subscribers-only discount price. Harlequin Presents® Larger-Print books consist of 6 books each month and cost $6.30 each in the U.S. or $6.49 each in Canada, a savings of at least 10% off the cover price. Harlequin Desire® books consist of 3 books (2in1 editions) each month and cost just $7.83 each in the U.S. or $8.43 each in Canada, a savings of at least 12% off the cover price. It's quite a bargain! Shipping and handling is just 50¢ per book in the U.S. and $1.25 per book in Canada*. You may return any shipment at our expense and cancel at any time by contacting customer service — or you may continue to receive monthly shipments at our low, subscribers-only discount price plus shipping and handling.

▲ If offer card is missing write to: Harlequin Reader Service, P.O. Box 1341, Buffalo, NY 14240-8531 or visit www.ReaderService.com ▲

BUSINESS REPLY MAIL
FIRST-CLASS MAIL   PERMIT NO.717   BUFFALO, NY

POSTAGE WILL BE PAID BY ADDRESSEE

HARLEQUIN READER SERVICE
PO BOX 1341
BUFFALO NY 14240-8571

NO POSTAGE
NECESSARY
IF MAILED
IN THE
UNITED STATES

"Anna! Come to the balcony!"

Now she was even hearing his voice as well as re-living the glide of his skin against hers. She really wished the parade would go away—

"Anna! The balcony. Open the door and come out."

Her eyes flew open. She wasn't imagining Ian's voice. That really was him. What the…? She searched the wall and found the door, which opened easily—

And came face-to-face with Seamus, his mechanical head nodding and twisting from side to side in a slow rhythm. Her gaze traveled along Seamus's long neck to the sea serpent's back. And riding on Seamus…

She couldn't breathe. Her heart was in her throat.

She leaned over the balcony railing, ignoring the loud cheer that went up from the crowd when she made her appearance. "Do you have a death wish? What are you doing on Seamus—no, wait, where did you even get Seamus?—no, let's go back to the first question. That thing is breathing fire! And you're riding on it!"

"How else could I get your attention?" Ian flashed his grin.

"Maybe by saying hi? Buying me a frozen custard? Ways that don't include putting your life in danger? She couldn't take her gaze off him. He looked good. So good. She drank in his appearance, not realizing until she could look her fill how starved she'd been. "You definitely have my attention now. Will you please get down from there?"

Ian's smile grew. "I have a better idea." He fiddled

with something—controls of some kind, Anna surmised. Seamus's head stopped moving and froze into place. Then the sea serpent's neck started to elongate, until Seamus's massive head touched the wall of the lighthouse just below the balcony.

Surely, Ian didn't mean for her to hop over the railing and step onto a rickety mechanical sea serpent from the 1970s? She stared at him. "What are you... you're not expected me to..."

"Of course not." Ian scoffed. "I am."

He unbuckled himself from the seat at the back of Seamus's neck. Then he stood up and began to walk across Seamus's neck, his arms outstretched like a tightrope walker, his only concession to safety a thin guidewire attached to the mechanical serpent.

"Ian, stop! You hate heights!" Her heart beat hard and fast in her throat, almost choking her. Her eyes squeezed shut. She was not going to watch him. She would not be a witness if the worst happened. "Don't—this isn't worth it—you're several stories above the ground, if you fall—"

"If I what?" Ian said from close by. "You can open your eyes. Because you are indeed worth it."

She did. The first thing she saw was Ian's dark gaze, warm with humor and joy. Her knees nearly gave out, both from relief and from the effect he always seemed to have on her bones' ability to remain solid.

Ian stood on Seamus's head, with only the thin metal railing separating them. Then she laughed, exhilarated both by his nearness and by the ridiculous and over-the-top situation they were now in. She indicated the crowd below them, a sea of faces partially concealed by the phones being used to record their meeting, with a sweep of her hand. No doubt they were being live-streamed around the world on multiple social media platforms. "What happened to keeping this room a secret?"

"No more secrets. You were right. I wasn't upfront and honest when we met. And that caused you to doubt my intentions throughout our relationship. So..."

Her head shook on its own. Her brain was still processing he was there, in front of her, and— "What are you wearing?"

"What?" He glanced down and a half-smile appeared on his face. "This old thing? I mean that literally. This costume is the same vintage as Seamus."

Ian's princely outfit glittered in the sunlight. The jacket and pants were a blinding white, with a crimson sash falling across Ian's chest from his right shoulder to end his left hip. A bright blue cape trimmed with gold braid was thrown over his left shoulder. Brass-plated medals set with large paste jewels in bold colors decorated almost every inch of the jacket's chest. He winked at her and pulled a red cap adorned with three fluffy white feather plumes out from under his jacket, perching the hat rakishly over his right eyebrow. "There. I didn't want it to fall off before you saw it.

"You're wearing colors. You're definitely not avoiding attention." She stated the obvious, simply because Ian's costume was so ridiculous, she could scarcely believe the evidence of her eyes. "You won't be able to sneak up on your prey."

She was joking, of course, because if she were to take the event's happening seriously, she might cry. Big, ugly, red-nosed crying, the kind that would wash away her waterproof mascara in three seconds flat. Besides, she wasn't quite sure if she could take what was happening at face value. This might all be a waking dream, her subconscious creating a happy ending to assuage her guilt over not securing a more positive outcome for Lakes of Wonder.

"You asked me to make you believe." Ian doffed his cap and bowed, causing the crowd to cheer. "How else than to show you I finally understand theme park magic is real?" He flashed his smile again, the smile he always kept for her.

"I don't understand," she said, her synapses beginning to fire again after recovering from her shock. "Preston and Olive…want a retail destination. Why… how…" She continued to sputter, finally seizing on a coherent sentence. "Ian, it's not practical or good business to bring the Seamus float out of mothballs and get it operational again if the park is going to be plowed…under…" Her words trailed off as Ian's grin grew larger. "But…today is the closing party?"

Ian took her hands in his gloved ones. "Lakes of Wonder is closing. But only so I can get all the rides and experiences updated and up to code. Then it will reopen, better than before. I hope it will be a true Blackburn/Lochlainn collaboration this time."

Anna never knew hope could be so painful. Her chest was tight, her lungs struggling to bring in air. "Your plan to oust Harlan—"

"Worked," he said simply. "BBA bought Lakes of Wonder. Preston and Olive and, as it turns out, most of the board, voted with me."

"But—"

"And then I sold my shares in BBA and used the proceeds to buy Lakes of Wonder." He smiled at her. "The park is mine and mine alone. Tai is the new CEO of BBA"

"What?" Anna searched his face. His beloved, wonderful face. "But BBA is your family. Your legacy. Your inheritance. You said there had always been a Blackburn at the helm and always will be."

"I was wrong." He caressed her cheek with his white-gloved hand, then pulled the glove off with an expression of disgust. Then his fingers were wiping away the tears that had decided to appear after all. "BBA is a company. But that conversation in the elevator… I've thought long and hard about it ever since. You showed me that being true to oneself is a choice. Belonging to someone else, being in their life, is a choice. And I chose you, Anna. I want to be part of your family. And create one of our own, together. On our own terms, no games, no machinations. If you want me."

"I do," she choked out. "I always have."

His grin could rival the brightest fireworks. Then he dropped to one knee, her hands tightly clutched in his, his gaze shining so bright not even the fireworks could compete.

"Anna Stratford, heir of the Lochlainns, will you be my Lady of the Lakes?"

She could barely see him, despite holding both her eyes as open as wide she could so she could take in as much as she could, to hold the vision close in her heart forever. "Ian of the Blackburns, I accept, forever and ever."

And then his lips were on hers, a kiss of fire and heat carrying the promise of forever.

* * * * *

A former Hollywood studio executive who gladly traded in her high heels and corner office for yoga pants and the local coffee shop, **Susannah Erwin** loves writing about ambitious, strong-willed people who can't help falling in love—whether they want to or not. Her first novel won the Golden Heart® Award from Romance Writers of America and she is hard at work in her Northern California home on her next. She would be over the moon if you signed up for her newsletter via www.susannaherwin.com.

Books by Susannah Erwin

Harlequin Desire

Titans of Tech

Wanted: Billionaire's Wife
Cinderella Unmasked
Who's the Boss Now?
Ever After Exes

Heirs of Lochlainn

More Than Rivals...
Seven Years of Secrets

Visit the Author Profile page
at Harlequin.com for more titles.

You can also find Susannah Erwin on Facebook,
along with other Harlequin Desire authors,
at Facebook.com/HarlequinDesireAuthors!

Dear Reader,

Welcome back to the secrets and scandals of the Lochlainn family! This two-part series kicks off when Keith Lochlainn, a media mogul whose doctors say he is dying, decides to hold a contest to determine which one of his newly discovered grandchildren should inherit his empire by giving them each a business objective to complete. The first book, *More Than Rivals...*, is the story of Keith's granddaughter Anna.

Now it's his grandson Declan's turn. Declan, already a renowned investigative journalist, isn't interested in taking over the Lochlainn empire. But he has been carrying secrets of his own for seven years—secrets pertaining to his journalism school rival turned brief lover, Mara Schuyler. When Declan is given a news streaming service to run to see if he is worthy to inherit, he jumps at the opportunity to give Mara a job as a news correspondent to help relieve his conscience.

Declan broke Mara's heart when he ghosted her after their one week of passion seven years ago. She wants nothing to do with him. But when he makes her a job offer she can't refuse, it doesn't take long for her former feelings to resurface. However, even as Mara pursues the lead that could make her career, she can't help but feel that Declan is hiding something from her.

And when the secrets come tumbling out, Mara must choose between following her story and following her heart.

I hope you enjoy *Seven Years of Secrets*! And please feel free to get in touch. You can find me on Twitter, @susannaherwin; on Facebook at susannaherwinauthor; on BookBub, @susannaherwin; or at my website, www.susannaherwin.com.

Happy reading!

xoxo

Susannah

SEVEN YEARS
OF SECRETS

For Lisa Lin,
for being the superstar that she is

One

The mid-October sky was bright and clear, the slight breeze still held a touch of warmth but promised brisker days ahead and the maple trees lining the sidewalk wore crowns of fiery leaves. Autumnal wreaths of sunflowers, wheat stalks and colorful gourds hung on streetlights, while the windows of the quaint mix of shops and restaurants that comprised the small town's commercial district were decorated with pumpkins and straw bales.

Mara Schuyler couldn't ask for a more picture-perfect site from which to report on a harvest festival than Roseville, New York, situated forty miles south of the Canadian border and an entire mindset away from New York City. This was one of the more photogenic assignments she'd received since joining the five o'clock news team of WRZT-TV—the "Voice of North County."

Photogenic, but not earthshaking. Not that Mara minded. Much. She'd given up on her ambitions to be the next household name in broadcast journalism and left far behind her desire to be the host of her own television news magazine show watched by billions around the globe. She knew now that was the dream of a small child who never missed the Sunday evening ritual of watching *60 Minutes* with her grandparents.

She was grown now. A realist. And she was damn lucky to have any paying job in journalism, much less an on-air role as a correspondent for a local news station. Even if WRZT was the third-highest rated newscast in the 189th largest media market in the US. Even if her assignments to date mostly involved stories like interviewing the winner of the annual soap box car race and covering the town hall meeting where the public debated if city funds should be used to convert an unused lot into a skateboard park. The stories might not be holding heads of state accountable for their inequitable actions or taking down a drug cartel from within as an undercover investigator, but they mattered to the community.

Well, at least they mattered to the three viewers who commented online on her soap box story—no one commented on the skateboard park piece. Although, one viewer berated her for not giving his son, the second place winner, more airtime, and the next offered his opinion that she should smile more. The third comment detailed how to double one's current salary at home through data entry, so Mara suspected whoever wrote it may not have watched the segment.

"We all set?" she asked her photographer, Hank Yi.

Hank looked around at the picturesque main street and shrugged. "One spot is as good as another. Want to do your run-through?"

She took a deep breath, plastered a smile on her face and started speaking. "This is Mara Schuyler, coming to you live from downtown Roseville where the local merchants are preparing for the sixty-sixth annual Pumpkin Festival. Who will have the most impressive pumpkin display? Will Abe Nagasaki finally lose his crown as the carving pump-*King*?" She widened her grin as she hit the last syllable. Mara was twenty-eight years old, but dad jokes were becoming her trademark. Whether she liked it or not. "I know I'm on the edge of my seat—Wait… That doesn't make sense. I'm standing, not sitting."

"It's a figure of speech." Hank lowered the Sony HDC-3500 camera that had been perched on his shoulder.

"But not accurate."

"So? No one's paying attention at five o'clock. They're doing homework or thinking about their workday."

She gave him an exaggerated eye roll. This was a familiar conversation. "We're reporting the news, Hank. Words matter. Precision matters."

"You'd think you were Declan Treharne, the way you obsess over every detail."

Her smile froze. Why did she ever tell Hank she

once knew Treharne, the hot rising star of print and broadcast journalism? Damn that bottle of tequila after the ambulance story fiasco.

Not that she'd had much of a past with Declan. Just almost four years of intense rivalry in journalism school, then a week of even more intense passion, followed by devastating betrayal. Now Declan was winning plaudits and fame on both coasts for his hard-hitting investigative stories that led to the toppling of empires, both corporate and political, and she was—

"—it's a story that serves as background noise," Hank continued, unaware she had tuned him out. "We're going live for the teaser in five minutes. pick something and go with it."

"You never stop underestimating me." Mara dug into her pocket and brought out a pen. She tried to scratch out the offending phrase on her notes, but the pen didn't function without something solid to write on. "Do you have a clipboard?"

"Do I—No. Four minutes and counting."

"I'm on the edge…no. I'm breathless with anticipation…nuh-uh. The suspense is killing me?" She wrinkled her nose. "That's not only cliché but I'm obviously not dying. Um…" She continued to ponder.

"Two minutes."

"Creativity can't be rushed." She scrawled words on her hand, then rubbed them off.

"And we're live in four, three, two—" Hank pointed at her.

"This is Mara Schuyler, coming to you live from

downtown Roseville where the local merchants are preparing for the sixty-sixth annual Pumpkin Festival. Who will have the most impressive harvest display? Will Abe Nagasaki finally lose his crown as the carving pump-King? The suspense is thicker than a slice of three-time blue ribbon winner Betsy Goldstein's pumpkin pie! This year's festival will be held Thursday through Sunday. Don't forget to pick up your free tickets at your local Buy and Save supermarkets while supplies last. You don't want to miss this guaranteed *gourd* time!" She held her smile until Hank lowered his camera, indicating the signal had been cut and they were off the air.

Mara let her shoulders fall. She and Hank had twenty-eight minutes before interviewing the chairman of this year's festival for a short piece that would close out that day's half hour five o'clock news broadcast. She dug into her tote bag, searching for her phone and her electronic tablet so she could check messages and then review her notes.

"Angling for a piece of that pie? Is it really that 'gourd'?"

"Yeah, well, it never hurts to curry favor with the Roseville mayor in case we need access to her later. And she does bake a good pie." Mara scrolled through her phone, only half paying attention to Hank—

Wait.

Hank was already down the block, scouting for the best place to interview the chairman.

And she knew that voice. Seven years may have passed since she last heard him speak in person, but she'd had plenty of opportunities to listen to him expand on various topics of national importance over that time.

She kept her gaze on her phone, hoping against hope she was wrong, and the voice was a trick of her imagination brought on by Hank's mention earlier. But when he cleared his throat, she looked up and her hopes were dashed.

"Hello, Treharne."

Declan smiled and took off his mirrored aviator sunglasses. "Hey, Schuyler. You look great."

So did he. Damn, damn and double damn. Declan Treharne looked even better in the flesh than he did on television. The TV didn't bring out the highlights in his dark blond hair, cropped short these days with the barest hint of the tousle she remembered. The camera didn't capture the intense blueness of his eyes, the color fading inward from dark navy bands around the rims of his irises to a cerulean spring sky to the starburst of golden flecks surrounding his pupils. And no small screen could convey his sheer physicality. Declan wasn't the tallest man Mara had known— far from it—but he was certainly the most comfortable in his body. His leather jacket moved with him like a second skin. He appeared both wholly at home on Roseville's main street and yet completely otherworldly—a herald from a life Mara once dreamed of but had long given up on achieving.

And just like that, she was rocked back on her heels by his radiating charisma, as if she'd stepped through a rip in the space-time continuum and had sat down in the first row on the first day of Introduction to Journalism, confident she was going to rock the class hard—only for Declan to come through the door and all her concentration to go flying out of it.

She realized she was staring at Declan, her mouth opening and closing like a fish impaled on a hook but still eager to reach the worm, when his smile faded. "Everything okay?"

"Everything…" she repeated. Then she blinked, and then blushed, and then hated herself for doing both. "Everything is fine," she said, after taking a few beats to work moisture into her mouth.

"Good. Do you have a minute to talk? Can I take you out for coffee?" Declan motioned to a vehicle parked at the curb. She followed his gaze to a futuristic-looking two-seater sports coupé, sunlight bouncing off the silver metallic paint. She blinked several more times.

"You want me…to get in a car that costs more than the balance on my sizable student loans…with you?" Finally, her thoughts were slowing enough that she could form—well, almost form—complete sentences. Unfortunately, the next sentence that came out of her mouth was: "What the hell?"

"Is that a no on the coffee?"

"That's a 'what the hell!' As in 'what the hell are you doing here, Treharne?' And how did you know where to find me in the first place? In Roseville, I mean?"

"I looked you up in the alumni directory and then

I called your station manager." Declan scratched the back of his neck. "I'm here to invite you to coffee."

She squeezed her eyes shut, not only to give her some space to make sense of the situation, but also because she forgot that looking at Declan for an extended period was like staring at the sun; his brilliance threatened to burn her retinas. "I can't get coffee. I'm working. I'm going on air with an interview in…" She opened her eyes to glance at her smart watch. "Twenty-two minutes. And I need to review my notes beforehand."

"Coffee after your interview?"

At least one thing hadn't changed about Declan, despite his overwhelming success. He was still persistent. Probably why he was such a good journalist. "I'm going back to the television studio after I finish. To get notes and prep for tomorrow." She held up a hand when his mouth opened. "And I have plans tonight." She didn't, unless one counted watching *Jeopardy* and then binging the latest episodes of her favorite true crime documentary series, but he didn't need to know that.

"Breakfast tomorrow, then." It was his turn to shake his head when she tried to object. "You have to eat. You might as well eat with me." His grin was that of someone who rarely heard the word "no," especially not from people with whom he once shared a torrid week exploring their combustible chemistry. Just touching on the memory caused a rush of wetness between her legs. She'd had her share of dates since that lost week of debauchery—even had a boyfriend for nine months when she worked for the local paper in Hightown, some sixty miles away, until she got the call to join WRZT-TV and they both agreed the relationship was at best treading water—but while the sex had been good it hadn't been—

She was doing it again. She was letting Declan occupy her frontal lobe rent free. She spent months evicting thoughts of him from her brain. All he had to do was show up and boom! It was if he'd never left that comfy suite she'd created for him in her skull. "I'm not having breakfast, or coffee or any beverage or food substance with you. Not today, nor tomorrow nor any day for eternity until you tell me why you are here, at my shoot. And it's not because you have a hankering for Roseville's finest coffee, because it's mostly burnt water."

"Burnt water? How does that—" He stopped joking when she intensified her glare. "I'd like to explain, but perhaps our discussion should wait until you're less stressed—"

"Stressed? You think I'm stressed? Why? Because you deigned to show up in my life seven years after...?"

No. She would not let him know how much she cared. Not now, not with other memories flooding back, like how Declan always told her she worried too much and worked too hard on trivial details, leaving the bigger story untouched.

She shoved her tablet and phone back into her tote bag and began to march toward Hank, who was several blocks away chatting up the festival chairman in front of the Roseville city hall, draped in orange, brown and sunflower gold bunting for the festival. "I have work to do," she threw back at Declan over her shoulder. "You can vanish back to wherever you apparated from. We have nothing to discuss."

She left him standing on the sidewalk. And when she didn't hear footsteps pounding behind her and Declan's voice demanding she stop and talk to him, she lied to herself that was the outcome she wanted.

Two

The two-minute live interview with the chairman went smoothly. If Mara's hand holding the microphone shook, the viewers at home were none the wiser thanks to Hank's careful framing of the shot. She said her thank yous and goodbyes and refused Hank's offer to ride with him in the news van back to the studio. The viewers may not have noticed how affected she was by Declan's arrival out of the blue, but Hank could tell she was off her usual game and she was not in the mood to be interrogated on the drive. She told him she wanted to walk around Roseville and note any local color that might come in handy for the inevitable assignment to cover the Monarch of the Pumpkin Festival coronation next week. She'd

call a rideshare service when she was ready to return
to the station.

She sighed and walked toward the closest bridge,
intending to cross the river that ran through the center of the town for lack of a better destination, kicking at the fallen russet and yellow leaves as she went.
She loved her job. She did. She just wished, perhaps,
Declan Treharne didn't have to show up and rub her
nose in the fact that he was a famous investigative
journalist while she was…making bad puns about
squash. Delicious squash, especially when made into
pie, but she wasn't risking her life taking down a
multinational organized crime ring from the inside,
like Declan's latest exclusive story for *The New York
Globe*. He even turned his story into an award–winning podcast. Of course.

She turned onto the side street that was her favorite shortcut to the river. At least she worked in a
lovely part of the country. She set her smartwatch's
meditation app to five minutes. Maybe if she stood
here and breathed in the beauty, she would breathe
out the frustration and, fine, the envy Declan's sudden arrival brought. She closed her eyes and inhaled,
then exhaled. Inhaled, exhaled. Inhaled—

"How about that coffee now? Or something stronger? It's past five o'clock, after all."

Damn it. Even when she was meditating, her brain
conjured him up.

"Your news director said you were done for the
day, so you can't use work as an excuse this time."

Her eyes flew open. Declan's car, its motor a low

purr, was parked at the curb next to her. She leaned down and peered through the rolled down passenger side window at him. "Isn't this the same model of car Tony Stark drove in the first *Iron Man* film?"

He grinned at her. "You know your cars. And your films."

She narrowed her gaze at him. "I knew you, and you haven't changed. Not interested, superhero. Go stalk someone else."

"Hear me out. I promise I'll disappear and leave you alone after we talk. If that's what you want."

"Let's pretend we did talk, and now is after. Guess I won't see you around." Mara straightened up and strode down the street.

Declan's car kept pace with her. "I'm sorry," he shouted through the open window.

She stopped, whirled and put her hands on her hips. "Sorry about *what*?"

She could think of many ways he could answer that. Sorry about letting her do all the heavy lifting on their joint project in sophomore year because he was being feted by the university's trustees for uncovering a ring of thieves who were stealing materials—and secrets—from the engineering research center. Sorry about scooping her on the story she worked so long and so hard on—the story that won him the IJAW fellowship that included an internship with a tech incubator focused on the next generation of journalism, which made him independently wealthy thanks to the app they devised now being used in newsrooms around the world. Although, to be fair, his scoop had been her fault. She let the story get away.

Sorry about dumping her and never looking back. That one was definitely on him.

Declan put the car in park and exited the driver's side. "Sorry I didn't get in touch sooner. I got your email about the class reunion. I kept meaning to respond, but—"

Her eyes would not stop blinking. "That's what you're sorry for? Not answering a mass mailing about our five year reunion? The reunion that was held over two years ago?"

Unbelievable.

He shrugged and gave her an apologetic smile. "I still should have responded. Because the email came from you. We…we were friends. And our friendship meant something."

She was used to the confident Declan, the brash Declan, the take-no-prisoners Declan. She liked to believe herself finally immune to his charms. But a sheepish Declan, looking at her at her with…could that be regret in his eyes? Was Declan Treharne even capable of regret? That was new.

She was not immune to the charms of a Declan who apologized to her.

"That was a long time ago. As for the reunion, no one else wanted to be class secretary," she murmured. "It's not like I emailed you specifically. And we knew you weren't coming. You were in Kyrgyzstan covering postelection protests."

"You follow my stories?" A light flared in his gaze.

"Oh, please. You have the number one podcast in the country. You're on a different cable news show nightly. I am a journalist, too, y'know. I keep up."

Even as the words left her mouth, she realized how inane she sounded. And not a little jealous. She should leave before she dug her hole any deeper, which was a tremendous accomplishment considering she already had both her feet in her mouth. "Well, it's been nice catching up. Bye."

"Schuyler, wait." He placed his hand lightly on her arm. His touch burned through the layers of her blazer and button-down shirt. "I have a proposition for you I think you'll like."

He flashed his golden boy grin at her. She knew from experience how skilled he was at using that grin to get whatever he wanted. "Proposition? I'm not sleeping with you again," she blurted out.

His smile disappeared. "I wasn't…that's not the proposition. Although, I meant what I said. You look great."

"Good. I mean, good on the not propositioning thing." No, it was not so good. She'd only just then realized how much she'd held on to a fantasy that he would indeed appear out of the blue and confess that week had made as much of an impression on him as it did on her, haunting his dreams and his waking thoughts until he could no longer stand it, and so he had to find her so he could carry her off to his bed where they would stay—

Too late, she tuned into what he was saying. "—ork with me."

She held up a hand. "Wait. Maybe covering traffic accidents has done a number on my hearing, standing next to ambulances with their sirens on full blast, but did you say, 'work with you'?"

"Yes. Come work at LNT."

The events of the day must have done a number on her synapses because she could have sworn he said LNT.

"LNT? As in Lochlainn News Television?"

"The same."

"I thought you worked for *The New York Globe*."

Declan scratched the back of his neck—one of the two nervous tells she knew he possessed. "I do. But I'm on a leave of absence to pull together LNT's launch of its streaming news service. They want original programming for streaming only. And they've put together an extensive budget. I'm hiring journalists with unique points of views to create documentary specials and series. You can pursue whatever story you want. LNT has the resources for research, travel, you name it."

The world spun around her in a blur of red and green and gold. "You want me—" she pointed to herself "—to work with you—" she pointed at him "—at LNT?"

"The LNT streaming service," he corrected. "Which is even better. We get to shape the future of news, Mara. You'll be a pioneer."

A pioneer. She always dreamed of being on the forefront of journalism, of blazing a trail for others to follow, especially for those who traditionally were shut out from receiving resources and advantages. But something about his offer didn't add up. "I don't understand. Why did LNT hire you? You're an investigative journalist. You're not a suit."

"What can I say? They told me they wanted a fresh perspective, so they looked outside the usual LNT suspects." Declan shrugged, but his gaze slid up to the left—his second tell: the one that said he wasn't being wholly truthful. Mara narrowed her gaze. That was interesting. "What do you say? I would need you in New York City by next week. The service is scheduled to launch in the beginning of January."

"January is three months away. And one of those months is December, when everybody is distracted by winter holidays. That's not very long. At all."

"Which is why I need an answer. Are you in?"

"I have a job here." That was the first thing that popped into her head. "I would have to give notice… I would have to move… Oh! And I would need to quit as the high school newspaper advisor…"

"Is that a yes?"

"No! Besides, you haven't told me the basics. Will I be paid? What about benefits?"

Declan named an annual starting salary number so stratospheric, Mara thought at first that he'd misspoke. Then he repeated it. When he said the amount for the fourth time, the numbers finally started to sink into her consciousness.

She could do a lot with that income. Like sponsor scholarships and grants for journalism students. Provide funding for outlets in underserved communities. Help underwrite a struggling local newspaper. So many possibilities.

"Why me?" she asked. "With that salary, you could have your pick of seasoned journalists with built-in national audiences."

He grinned. "LNT has their own stable of stars. But for the streaming service, we want new voices. Originality. That's you."

This was too good to be true. No matter that she was eating up the compliments Declan was dishing her way. She'd had fantasies over the past years of what would happen when she saw Declan in person again—some more sexually graphic than others, she had to admit—but even when she pushed the limits of imagination, she never dreamed Declan would show up to hand her the keys to her very own documentary series.

There had to be a catch. Or an ulterior motive. Hidden agenda. Her journalistic nose could smell it.

"I cover harvest festivals and the high school team winning the state diving championship. Sure, sometimes I report on the occasional house fire or traffic accident when the senior reporters aren't available, and occasionally city council meetings can be a bit raucous—you should have been there when changing the Fourth of July parade route was discussed—but that's as hard-hitting as my stories get." She searched Declan's crystal blue gaze, as bottomless and clear as a mountain lake fed by newly melted pristine snow. "So, don't feed me a line about being impressed with my reporting. I'm not an inexperienced college freshman anymore. If you haven't noticed."

"I've noticed," he said, his tone low and suggestive, and that's when she realized his hand was still on her arm.

She shrugged off his touch. "Still not sleeping with you."

"Still haven't propositioned you in that way," he responded.

"Still waiting to hear why me for the LNT gig, after no word from you all these years," she retorted back. "I'm not buying you feel bad about not going to a reunion you weren't going to attend in the first place."

Declan scratched the back of his neck again. His smile faded, and his blue gaze turned up the intensity to eleven. "I'll be honest with you. There's a lot riding on the success of the streaming launch. And while I'm honored to be asked and can't turn the opportunity down, this is fresh territory for me." He reached out his hand and before she even knew her muscles were moving, she had entwined her fingers with his. "I could use a friend. Someone whose story instincts I trust. Someone who would want this to be a success as much as I do."

Her mind seized on one word. "Friend?"

"We were friends. Good friends."

"We *were*." She stressed the last word. "We're nothing now. And that's because of you. You left. We graduated and you left and you never looked back. You didn't call, you didn't text or email and you outsourced your social media. Why should I accept your offer when, for all I know, you will walk out the door and disappear the next day?" Now it was her turn to cut him off when he would respond. "And no, this isn't about the fact we slept together right before graduation. That's on me. That was my mistake. But you leaving? That's on you."

His gaze was regretful, the expression on his face chagrined. She took a mental snapshot and filed it away in the easily accessible memories drawer. She doubted she would ever witness a regretful Declan again.

"I know," he said. "I am sorry. Sorrier than you can imagine. I thought—it doesn't matter what I thought."

"It does. It definitely matters."

He inhaled. "Cam Brower said you were taking the *Financial Times* postgrad internship. In London. For a year."

"Cam said…" She stared at him. "Why did you take Cam's word? Why didn't you ask me?"

"I saw the plane tickets to London on your computer. Cam was your roommate, so I figured he knew." He shrugged. "Graduation was nearing. You knew I was moving to New York City. You were entitled to go to the UK and start your own career. I knew I didn't have any say in the matter. And I didn't want to come across as if I presumed I did. So, I didn't ask. I figured you would tell me if you wanted me to know."

"I…" How Cam got that wrong was a mystery, but then Cam never did pay much attention to what his roommates said. Or what most people said. He had not been the most reliable source of school gossip. Or news reporting, for that matter. No wonder Cam was now working for *The National Inquisitor*, a tabloid known for its fake scurrilous rumors.

Declan was right. She didn't tell him a group of her high school friends had been planning a backpacking tour of Europe that summer. She bought the steeply discounted plane tickets just in case, but she wasn't sure if she would use them. Because she'd thought she might have a future with Declan. Or at least a relationship that would last beyond graduation.

As it turned out, neither the trip nor the future materialized.

"You still should have asked and not assumed. And you could have called. You could have stayed in touch."

"So could you," he pointed out with impeccable logic. "Communication works both ways."

He was right. "I…you…" She opened and closed her mouth a few times. "I didn't think you…"

He put her out of his misery. "Let's relegate the past to the past. Please come to LNT."

She took a deep breath. Normally, the air would be filled with the sounds of the river rushing under the footbridge, birds calling to each other, the rustling of squirrels as they prepare for the coming winter and the occasional distant shouts of kids or the faint rumble of cars on the adjoining roads. But the only noise she heard was her heartbeat, a steady, loud thumping.

Was she going to accept his offer, no matter how

incredulous she still found his reasons for asking her? Give up her job, her cozy apartment, her volunteer work with the high school newspaper?

"I need some time," she said.

"Of course. I'm still free for breakfast tomorrow morning if you want to discuss the opportunity more." His grin returned.

"Not necessary. I'll give you an answer tonight." She needed to check her contract with the station. And maybe see if one of the other reporters would take over advising the students.

"Take what time you need." He closed the distance between them.

She was very aware they were alone on the bridge. The sun's last streaks had turned the sky deep pink and purple, a few stars valiantly making their presence known. Her mouth was dry. Her palms were not. Despite her stern admonishment to ignore his magnetism for once, she couldn't help but sway in his direction.

He leaned in. Her breath caught. This close, despite the dim early evening light, she could still see the flecks of bullion that radiated around his pupils. His eyes had always fascinated her, the way they faded from a crystalline blue to burnished gold.

He tilted his head, as if preparing to slant his mouth over hers. "Thank you for considering the offer."

"Of course," she breathed back. Oh, she'd missed his mouth. His mouth was the stuff of fantasies at 3:00 a.m., when the world was silent and dark and her mind could run rampant over the most arousing images she could conjure. Something about the way his lips fit with hers, just the right pressure, just the right firmness. His tongue…oh, his tongue. Her nipples contracted into aching hard points of need, making her grateful for the multiple layers she wore.

Declan bent his head. She inhaled, her eyes falling closed.

Then his mouth missed hers and traveled past her cheek. It stopped above her right ear. "Say yes," he rasped in her ear.

Sparks raced along her nervous system from the tips of her fingers to the soles of her feet, followed by chagrin at having even entertained the thought he might kiss her.

"I'll let you know," she managed to force out.

"I look forward to it." Then he straightened and smiled at her. "We made a great team. We will again." He turned and began walking back to the side of the road where he had parked his car.

"I could turn you down," she called after him.

"You won't," he called back. And then he disappeared into the lengthening evening shadows.

No, she wouldn't. She already knew she would accept.

But perhaps not for the reasons Declan suspected.

There was more to the LTN offer than what he told her. Something he wasn't telling her.

She would uncover the truth, whether he wanted her to or not. She let him scoop her once; she wouldn't back down from a story again.

Three

Seeing Mara again after seven years had been a gut punch in all the worst—and best—ways.

College-aged Mara had been pretty, all bouncy red hair and questioning green eyes and pale skin dusted with constellations of freckles. But adult Mara nearly brought him to his knees—her formerly coltish angles now lush curves, her sharp gaze filled with a confidence she'd been still developing as a student.

Not for the first time since a chance encounter with Mara's former roommate Cam had opened his eyes, he kicked himself, hard, for the choices he had made that last week of school. At the time, he'd seen no other path forward to attain his goals. But he knew now he had been selfish, prioritizing his own hurt and ambition over everything else, including her—

He sighed. Fine. He knew he'd been selfish then, too. He supposed he could blame his youth and general life inexperience, but Declan's late mother had always accused him of being an old soul and he'd certainly seen some of the worst the world had to offer by the time he started college.

So, instead of focusing on the past—and on the hurt and anger visible on Mara's face when she saw him—he would focus on the present. And on the challenge presented to him: successfully launch LNT's foray into streaming news so he would earn a place in Keith Lochlainn's will.

Declan had no affinity for video news. Sure, he did the occasional interview on air and lent his opinion to various network news programs, but he loved the freedom and creativity of using words to paint vivid pictures for his readers. He specialized in long-form journalism, his well-researched pieces running as features in *The New York Globe*'s Sunday magazine, and he loved nothing more than digging in deep and uncovering people's motives and dreams, focusing on the voices of those who were usually voiceless. And if he exposed the powerful and corrupt who would keep them voiceless, even better. He had yet to win a Pulitzer but he had a drawer stuffed with other prizes and besides, his career was still young.

He didn't want or need Keith's money. He only wanted one thing from the Lochlainn patriarch, and that was acknowledgment he was Jamie's flesh and blood. But he'd accepted Keith's challenge to launch

LNT because the position would give him the power to right some of his past wrongs.

Like Mara.

Four weeks later, Declan wasn't sure if his plan had been a stroke of genius or irrational in the extreme.

He walked into his glass-walled office on the thirty-second floor of LNT's corporate headquarters, a steel and glass skyscraper that dominated its section of Seventh Avenue despite being surrounded by other imposing buildings. The ground floors held the studios for the morning news and chat series aired on the Lochlainn Company's broadcast network, *Wake Up USA*. The top floors—with their expansive views across Manhattan—contained the executive offices with a Michelin-starred restaurant occupying the roof and adjoining terrace, and the cable news operation took up the middle floors. It was a longer elevator ride than those visiting the broadcast network, but when a fire drill occurred, it wasn't too taxing to walk down the emergency stairs.

The new LNT streaming app—there had been a debate about what to name the service but finally the execs landed on LNT Plus, following the naming convention of every other streaming service despite Declan arguing for something more distinctive—had been given the less desirable floors above the cable news operation. Longer elevator ride to get to the office, the fire drills were hell and they didn't have the views to compensate. Declan's office looked right into the office opposite him. He could predict the comings and goings of the woman who occupied the space with a ninety-seven percent accuracy rate.

This was why he shouldn't have a desk job. He didn't do well with predictability. Predictability made his skin itch. Predictability made him irritable with boredom, snappish with lack of new stimulation. He didn't fault those who sought a secure nine-to-six job, where the goal was to minimize how many fires one had to put out; he wished he'd been built that way. But he was an on-the-move kind of person, jumping from crisis to crisis.

As if the universe heard his thoughts, his phone rang. Declan smiled when he saw the name on his screen. "Hi, Bobbi. No, I'm not ready to come back. Yet."

Bobbi James, the legendary editor of *The New York Globe* for the past thirty years, Declan's mentor since he won the IJAW fellowship seven years ago and his boss at the paper for the last four, sighed over the phone. "When will you be ready?"

"January 15. Launch day."

"I'm holding you to that. Still can't believe I lost my best reporter to broadcast."

"Not broadcast. Streaming."

"Does it matter? People watch pictures on a screen. Instead of reading words on a page, which is how the great deity in the sky designed news to be consumed."

He laughed. "If you say so. Listen, thanks for the check-in. I've got to run to a meeting."

"Wait." Bobbi's voice was oddly tentative. He

frowned. "I'm hearing rumblings that all is not well with Keith Lochlainn's health. Serious rumblings. You okay?"

Declan took his phone away from his ear, his feet rooted to the ground. He didn't know what to say. He wasn't sure what he could say.

Bobbi was one of two people who knew of Declan's connection to Keith Lochlainn. Well, he supposed, more must know now. There was the Lochlainn Company representative who came to his door with the offer to work at LNT. And Keith's current wife, Catalina, undoubtedly knew. But as far as people in whom Declan confided, there was his grandmother and Bobbi.

He held the phone back up. "I hear he's not in any immediate danger," he said, choosing his words carefully.

"I don't want to pry, kid," Bobbi said. "I know, I know. Funny thing for someone like me, infamous for snooping around, to say. But my concern is you. You okay?"

"Why would I be otherwise? I work for him. It's not like we have a relationship." The representative had been very clear. There was to be no contact between Declan and Keith until after Declan had completed the task set by the mogul.

He must have sounded more bitter than he intended, for Bobbi's tone shifted to gentle. And Bobbi James did not do gentle. "I'm sorry. Keith should have accepted you were his grandchild years ago when you first confronted him."

He closed his eyes. He hated to be reminded of how naive he had been. But he had been so excited when he put all the pieces of the puzzle together and contacted Keith's office. Only to be run off and threatened by a phalanx of lawyers who promised to bury his "charlatan fortune-seeking ghoulish ass for good" if he persisted in his efforts to meet the Lochlainn patriarch.

"My timing wasn't the best," he said. "I couldn't have known it at the time, but Jamie had just disappeared. And here I come, with the barest of circumstantial evidence Jamie was my biological father."

"But Keith is willing to acknowledge you now if you do this work at LNT? That's the part I'm unclear on."

"No. Only that Keith will grant me some sort of bequest when he passes on." Declan rubbed his forehead.

"That's bullshit," Bobbi huffed.

Declan agreed, yet hearing the sentiment from Bobbi made him oddly defensive of Keith. "I could see admitting that I'm the result of his son's hatred of him and the family legacy—since Jamie sold his sperm to help pay for college rather than accept any money from Keith—might not be something Keith wants to do publicly."

"He could still acknowledge you privately. You're his only grandchild. You're a good kid, kid. But if you tell anyone I said that I will have your head for my door decoration."

"I wouldn't be so quick to say I'm his only. When I

spoke to the representative from the Lochlainn Company, I got the impression I'm in some sort of competition, although he didn't say in so many words."

Basic science and math dictated that if Declan had resulted from Jamie's sperm donation at a reputable fertility clinic, there was bound to be at least one other successful pregnancy out there. Not that Declan thought much about his possible half siblings. The mere fact that Jamie, who had been his journalistic idol long before Declan started to investigate the identity of his sperm donor, was his biological father was enough to occupy his mind.

"What does Louise have to say about all this?" Bobbi asked, who had met Declan's grandmother on several occasions.

"The clinic kept the sperm donor anonymous. My grandmother is glad my mom never knew I'm one-half Lochlainn, as people like Keith Lochlainn—who believed they owned the world and other people were placed on this planet to serve them—were the bane of her existence in the diplomatic corps." Declan chuckled, even as the wave of sadness at the loss of his mother when he was high school broke over him. The crest was smaller now but would never fully dissipate.

"Your mother would still be proud of you," Bobbi said.

"She would have told me to tell the Lochlainns to go to hell."

"So why didn't you when they came to you with the LNT assignment? Not going to lie, I could use you back."

Declan glanced at the glass wall of his office. People were gathering for the creative meeting. Mara's red waves were among the heads seated around the large conference table. "I have my reasons. Now I need to run."

"Fine, I know when I've been told that's enough prying for one day. Go to your meeting," she commanded.

"It's as if you still think you're my boss," he joked.

"Because I am. You're on loan. Don't forget it."

Declan ended the call as he walked into the conference room and took his seat at the head, aware he'd arrived two minutes early and thus, by his own standards, was late. Mara's gaze bore into him from her position several seats away, but he didn't turn to face her. A thick haze seemed to envelop his cognitive thinking center whenever she was near and that was not conducive to a productive meeting.

"Thanks, everyone, for coming. T minus eight weeks—less if we include the winter holidays—and counting to launch week. Let's run down what we have so far." He pointed at Mads Jefferson, the popular TikTok star he convinced to join LNT Plus as the inside expert on pop culture, and their producer, Adanna Obi. "You're up first."

Mads and Adanna detailed the stories confirmed for Mads's series on how Gen Z was changing entertainment. The hooks were solid, Mads's takes were well-founded and the guests lined up were stellar. One potential headache to strike off his list.

Next came Bryan Winner, a news anchor with over

forty years of experience on the number one evening news broadcast. He'd been lured to LNT Plus with an unlimited budget to investigate anything he was interested in, which ended up being space exploration and the limits of earthly physics. At first, Declan was worried he'd made a mistake, especially when Bryan started to go deep into the math, but when he saw the final video Bryan had put together, he relaxed. The material was easily understood. And who knew Bryan was funny?

Declan continued to go around the table. Everyone was excited to be part of something with the potential to be groundbreaking and they were all bringing their A game to LNT Plus. With each report, Declan's shoulders fell another half inch. The launch would be a success. And Keith Lochlainn could go pound sand.

Declan didn't accept the LNT Plus assignment to win Keith's approval. He'd decided long ago, when Keith sicced his lawyers on him, that he would be a success without any Lochlainn help. He took the position for one reason.

And that reason was sitting by herself, the chairs on either side of her empty. His gaze narrowed. Mara returned his stare with equanimity. "By yourself today, Schuyler?"

"Yes." Still with the same calm expression.

"Was Tobey not able to make the meeting?" He'd paired Mara with Tobey Haulfield as her producer. Tobey was an old hand at producing news documentaries, having worked at NBC News on their prime-time news specials. While Declan had faith in Mara's ability to nail an on-air story, he'd thought Tobey's experience would offer additional value.

"Tobey…decided to seek opportunities elsewhere. The role might not have been the best use of his skills." She smiled at him.

The conference room, which had hummed with energy, went still. No one looked directly at him or Mara, but there were plenty of sideways glances and lifted eyebrows.

Declan's gaze battled with Mara's, neither of them giving an inch. "Tobey decided."

"Well, we decided. It was mutual."

"And were either of you going to fill me in?"

Mara lifted one shoulder with a delicate gesture. "You're being told now. I would have told you before the meeting, but you were late."

The room was so quiet, if a feather fell to the floor, the sound of its landing would echo like thunder. People were going to turn blue and pass out if they didn't start breathing soon. He stood up. "Good work, everyone. Meeting adjourned. I'll speak with the teams individually as needed, but for now, keep doing what you're doing."

The sounds of chairs being scraped back from the table filled the air, along with muted chatter. Declan kept his gaze focused on one person as she started to exit the room. "Schuyler, stay behind."

She froze where she was, her back stiff. Then she turned and faced him, her smile still plastered on her lips. "Anything wrong?"

"Please, sit." He sat and indicated the chair next to him.

"I assume this is about Tobey." She took her seat. "We had creative differences. This is for the best. My stories will be stronger, and the show will benefit as a result."

"What the hell is going on?"

That put a crack in her polite veneer. "What do you mean?"

"Tobey was your third producer. I get why the first two didn't work out. They were too inexperienced, and the chemistry wasn't there. But I paired you with Tobey because he complimented your strengths and weaknesses—"

Her smile disappeared. "How do you know what my strengths and weaknesses are?"

"C'mon. I know you—"

"No, you knew a college student, and it's evident you still think I'm one because you assigned Tobey to me. But just because you and I slept together doesn't mean you knew me then, and you don't know me now."

He'd always appreciated the way her green eyes flashed when she was amused or angry. She was the definitely the latter. "Is that what this is about? The past? If you can't put that behind you and make the most of the opportunity I'm handing you—"

"Handing me?" Too late, he realized he had gone too far. Much too far. Storms of lightning filled her gaze as she nodded, her head a blur. "Yes. Yes, that's what this about." She gathered up her laptop computer. "This is about me being unable to put a week of mostly mediocre sex seven years ago—"

He stared at her. Mediocre sex? What?

"—out of my head and unable to be oh so appreciative of—what did you call it?—an opportunity you're handing me." She snorted. "Handing me. So much for being impressed by my work at WRZT. I knew you had some sort of ulterior motive—"

He snapped out of his shock. "Wait. No. That's not what I meant. Bad choice of words—"

"You don't do bad choice of words," Mara pointed out with cold precision. "You are an excellent word chooser."

"Not in this case, apparently," he muttered. "That's not—"

She stood up. "Do you want a formal resignation letter? Better we call this to an end before more time passes and we find ourselves too mired in a situation that becomes too difficult or painful to extricate ourselves from—"

He knew that speech. He blinked at her. "Are you throwing my words from the night before graduation at me?"

She held her arms out, palms to the ceiling. "Well, yes. I mean, you weren't wrong then. And I should've known better than to accept a job working with you. You and I are not able to—"

"I said that because you were going to London. I was saving you the trouble." And he had just opened the first of many letters from Keith Lochlainn's lawyers, his sense of self-worth pounded flatter than a paper towel. He hadn't been in any shape to be with anyone. Especially not Mara, who deserved more than he could give her at the time.

"Oh, so you were being chivalrous, breaking up with me." She threw her gaze to the ceiling. "Except I wasn't going to London."

"Regardless. When you didn't show up for the party that night or the traditional breakfast after graduation, that sent a clear message—"

"So now I'm the one who ghosted you? No. You always forgot. Not all of us had full ride scholarships that included room and board. Some of us had jobs." She stressed the last word. "I had to work early that morning. The rent didn't care I'd recently graduated." Her gaze met his, frank and not a little disappointed. "You could have called if you were so concerned. Communication goes both ways," she reminded him.

Touché. But that was the night the IJAW fellowship had been announced. When she didn't call *him* to congratulate his win, *he* had been miffed. He'd known she'd been up for the prize as well, but they had competed before and they'd always been happy for whoever came out on top.

Now he realized they'd not only parted less than amicably, but the story that won him the fellowship had originally been hers. He didn't know why she didn't publish what she had. She never said a word to him at the time, even though when she read his piece she must have known they had been pursuing the same leads. But the result was the result. "You're right. I'm sorry. I should have remembered that you had a job and couldn't join us. I should've called you."

She blinked at him. "Wait. I'm right? You're sorry?" She looked around the conference room. "Are there hidden cameras in here?"

He laughed. "I can admit when I'm wrong."

"Really. I seem to recall someone who refused to admit he ate the last cookie at our study sessions even when he had crumbs all over his shirt."

He shrugged. "What can I say? I'm a bigger person now."

She smirked. "You were pretty big then." Then she clapped her hand over her mouth. "Sorry. That flew out. I've missed arguing with you, Treharne."

"I've missed this, too," he said, and he wasn't sure if he was referring to trading words with her, or the way warmth spread through him when she was near, or both. "But," he warned, bringing his mind back to the present, "you can't keep forcing your producers to quit. You'll get a reputation as being impossible to work with. And I know you're not."

"Right. About that." She sat in her chair again. "I should have said something sooner about Tobey and shouldn't have let it get to the point where one of us quit. I thought I could turn our relationship around, but this morning was the last straw."

"What happened?"

"Let's just say Tobey was patronizing."

He frowned. "Tobey has lots of experience, yes, but—"

"I have lots of experience, too. Only it was at a

small team in a minor market, so obviously I must be treated as if I'd never seen a camera before. Then this morning, I saw his rough edit of our first story and…" Anger sparked back to life in her gaze. "He used nothing but outtakes. He made me look foolish. And incompetent. The other producers were laughing."

"What? That's—"

"Dishonest? Sexist? Condescending? Take your pick." She shook her head. "He didn't want to work with me. He took the job because he wanted to work with you. He shot all my pitches down and treated me like a puppet—just sit in the chair and ask the interview subjects the questions he came up with and nod my pretty little head as they answer. Do I look like I have strings?"

"Never." He caught her gaze. "I'm sorry Tobey was an ass. I should have vetted him better."

Their gazes held, tangled. The room faded away, reduced to the sound of his own heartbeat as he stared into her forest green eyes. She always did have the most expressive eyes. He didn't realize until now how much he had missed watching her thoughts tumble and churn.

Then she averted her gaze. "Don't worry about it. On paper he was great. I was looking forward to working with him, until I wasn't. However…"

Her voice trailed off in a very uncharacteristic manner. He threw a sharp glance at her. "However, what?"

She inhaled, then blew out a long stream of air. "Tobey and I filmed footage for three pieces. Like I said, there's a rough cut of the first one, although it needs reediting. But the stories themselves…" She waved her right hand in the air as if shooing something away. "Boring. Old hat. Don't add a fresh perspective. I know we're under a time crunch until launch…"

There was an unspoken "but" hovering in the air. He leaned toward her. "What stories did Tobey shoot down?"

"Well." She pondered, pursuing her lips. The shape was imminently kissable. "Tobey told me I was insane for wanting to pursue this story—and I didn't appreciate him being a mental health ableist—but here goes. I'm not sure if you remember my brother Tim, but he married Lavinia Palmas."

Declan sat back in his chair. "Lavinia Palmas? As in Palmas Chicken? Tim married the poultry princess?"

Mara rolled her eyes. "She hates that nickname. A paparazzo called her that one night and it stuck."

"Wasn't there a scandal?" He rarely paid attention to the society pages—not his beat—but he couldn't help but overhear newsroom gossip.

"Her parents weren't happy she was marrying an environmental scientist whose work centers on how agribusiness is contributing to increased greenhouse gases, considering their major source of income—"

"Right. They cut her off."

Mara shook her head. "No. Lavinia cut them off. They live on Tim's salary. Lavinia was a management consultant, but she's pregnant and on bed rest now."

"You want to do a story on children who turn their backs on their wealthy families?" That might be cutting too close for comfort, considering Jamie Lochlainn had been one of the best known scions of a billionaire to disavow his father's riches.

"That could be another story down the road, sure." She stopped, tilting her head to the side. "Hmm. Kids who say no to their tainted inheritance because their family fortunes were built on the broken backs of workers? Lavinia is very vocal about how exploited laborers are responsible for her family's wealth—she's donated much of her trust to farm worker unions and cooperatives. Could be a great story. If we could find more examples—which is a very big if, but there must be others—"

"If Lavinia isn't your story, what is?"

"Right." She snapped back to the topic. "I brought up Lavinia so you know where I got the story tip. She really has given away most of her trust but she hangs on to one thing from her former life and that's the various fashion weeks—"

"Ah. So, a story about couture fashion."

"No. And if you would stop interrupting, I'd get to my point."

"Sorry."

"At the last New York Fashion Week, Lavinia went to a party at Keith Lochlainn's penthouse apartment—"

"Keith Lochlainn?" Judging by the look Mara shot him, Declan had spoken far too loudly. He lowered his voice. "I'm surprised Lochlainn has an interest in fashion."

"His wife Catalina, is a brand ambassador for House of Logan, so she hosted cocktails…" Mara stopped, her eyes lighting up. "You know who would also work for the kids who give up their inheritance story? Jamie Lochlainn. He was recently declared legally dead, but I wonder—"

"Your story," Declan bit out.

"So. Lavinia had been an art history major in college, and one of her favorite artists is Alain Robaire—"

"Like most people."

"Right. Well, she mentioned it to Catalina and this man that she described as, 'like, totally sketch' overheard her and they started talking about Keith Lochlainn's most recent acquisition, which Lavinia had never seen before and Lavinia likes art as much as she likes couture. She wrangles invites to private collections all the time. And this person—"

"The 'sketch' person?"

"Yes. He said the piece—a fifteen million dollar Robaire—came from a very private collector in Portugal and that's why the piece wasn't listed in any accounts of Robaire's paintings. They started arguing about it and he got very huffy. He said Keith Lochlainn is not the only Manhattan one percenter who is displaying art that was previously unknown and suddenly popped up. But then someone else entered the room and Lavinia said he turned white and he left the party. So, I did some deep digging. And there's a rumor—"

"This isn't already a rumor?"

"—there's a ring of people selling art with suspicious provenance as a money laundering scheme. And there's additional whispers the laundered money is then funneled into dark money campaigns, to buy judges and politicians." She stopped speaking, folding her arms across her chest and looking at him as if waiting for his reaction.

He frowned. "And?"

"That's the story I want to tell."

"You want to reveal that the wealthiest people in Manhattan—"

"And not just Manhattan. Lavinia said—"

"Including Keith Lochlainn. The owner of LNT." And his grandfather. Biologically speaking.

Keith was many things, not all of them nice. Most, in fact, were on the ruthless and callous side. But hiding in the shadows to pull strings was not among them. Keith made his power moves in the open. "I don't think Keith would—"

"See, that's why Tobey shot it down. He thought you'd balk at—"

"—knowingly own counterfeit art that is a cover for laundering dark money."

Mara folded her arms and gave him a considering look. He knew that look. Her brain was making calculations. And he needed to head her off before she managed to add him and Keith Lochlainn together.

"This is based on your sister-in-law arguing with

someone who is, and I quote, 'like, totally sketch'? The sketchy part is where I'm balking, not the involvement of Keith Lochlainn." Not completely.

"Lavinia thought he seemed totally sketch. But it turns out he's an art dealer. Alan Skacel. Owns a well-regarded gallery on the Upper East Side."

"Will Skacel go on record?"

She shook his head. "He disappeared. After the Lochlainn party. The gallery is closed, with a padlock on the door. Phone number goes to voice mail, which is full. He hasn't been home in weeks but his neighbors say he travels frequently and for long periods of time so they aren't concerned. No one seems to have seen him since the night at the Lochlainn penthouse."

"You want to do a story on his disappearance?" Audiences loved a true crime story. And this one had ties to the glittering masses of Manhattan's one percent. "Great," he continued. "We'll look for a new producer—"

"You agree? I should pursue the story?"

"When we find you a new producer—"

"No time. I need to go to the Poets and Artists Ball. This Friday. And I need you to get me an invite."

"The Poets and Artists Ball? Why?" The ball was one of the main events on the New York City social calendar. The event raised money to provide fellowships for promising young writers and artists, and everyone who was anyone clamored for a ticket and a chance to show off their finest couture for the cameras. "That's a hefty ask."

Mara bit her bottom lip, the first sign of uncertainty he'd seen since she entered the conference room. "I know. But Freja and Niels Hansen are the chairpeople of the ball this year, and guess who also recently bought a Robaire from Alan Skacel?"

Declan leaned back in his chair and regarded her. His palms itched, a sign of his instinct telling him she had a story worth pursuing. There wasn't much to go on, but he'd broken stories that had less to begin. And if she could prove a conspiracy among the upper crust of Manhattan....Mara would have her pick of offers with which to build a spectacular career. Print, television, radio, long-form: the world would be her very comfortable oyster.

The involvement of the über wealthy Hansen twins sealed his approval, though they were far from Declan's favorite people. "Okay. But on one condition."

"Don't worry, I can provide an outfit. Lavinia has been begging me to borrow her fancy dresses since she won't be able to wear them for a while."

"Not the condition. But good to know because your expense account does not cover clothing."

She narrowed her gaze. "If you're going to continue to tell me I need a producer and I can't start to put the story together on my own until I have one—"

He shook his head. "No. Although we'll start interviewing tomorrow."

She crossed her arms over her chest. "Fine. What's the condition?"

He grinned. "The company isn't buying you a ticket to the Poets and Artists Ball. Seats start at fifteen thousand dollars even if there were tickets available, which there aren't." Getting her access to the event would be nearly impossible for most…but he wasn't most people. He raised his hand, cutting off the thunderclouds building on her expression. "Instead, you'll go as my plus one."

Four

Mara glanced up from the note she was entering on her phone as the town car hired for the night glided to a stop at the curb. The door to where she sat in the backseat opened to reveal not the driver but Declan, holding his right hand out to help her exit. She eyed his hand with a slight frown.

Not for the first time, she wondered if she had made the right decision. Tobey hadn't been the only one who doubted if the story was real or merely a fun piece of scurrilous gossip told to her by Lavinia, although Alan Skacel's disappearance was an intriguing angle. But after that infuriating edit, Mara had no choice but to prove Tobey—and everyone else at LNT Plus who wondered out loud in her hearing why Declan had hired her—wrong.

One lesson was learned. She should have gone to Declan sooner. She let her pride trip her up. If she'd told him sooner about her issues with Tobey, then perhaps there would have been time to purchase her own ticket to the Poets and Artists Ball. There was no way being Declan's plus one for tonight would be beneficial for her focus.

Take now, for example. Instead of concentrating on her notes and mentally reviewing everything she wanted to accomplish tonight, she could only stare at the hand he offered, remembering how it felt to twine her fingers with his, their palms fitting perfectly together, his grasp warm and sure and offering strength. She had other memories of those fingers, too: tracing patterns on the sensitive skin of her stomach, whispering over the tops of her thighs, parting her slick folds and pressing and pulling until she screamed his name…

"Mara?" Declan bent down and looked at her. "You coming?"

Heat rose in her cheeks. Good thing he couldn't read her thoughts.

Enough with strolling down memory lane. Tonight was about showing Tobey and anyone else who'd doubted her that she was a force to be reckoned with. She put her hand in Declan's, ignoring the electrical charge when his skin met hers, and allowed him to assist her out of the car.

His eyes widened when she straightened, revealing the transformation her appearance had undergone for tonight's event. While she wore makeup and took pains with her hair whenever she was on camera, tonight took worrying about how she looked to a whole 'nother level. Attending business luncheons and charity galas were one thing but attending a fundraising ball where the tickets started at fifteen thousand dollars a seat was a new experience. She'd spent valuable hours earlier that day, sitting in a salon chair being primped and polished, her friend Amaranth Thomas—one of the few new friends Mara had made since moving to the city—keeping her company and her nerves under control with jokes and banter. Amaranth had pronounced the result more than gala-worthy, fanning herself as she took in how the makeup artist made Mara's eyes seem wider and her lips fuller.

But when Declan remained still and silent, Mara wondered if perhaps Amaranth had been wrong in her assessment and Mara did not look as sophisticatedly glamorous as she'd intended. She patted her hair, ensuring the complicated updo was still intact, and then touched her ears to reassure herself that the diamond and opal earrings her parents had given her for her last birthday were still in place.

"Everything okay?" she asked. Maybe it was her dress. She checked the straps of the beaded emerald green chiffon gown Lavinia had overnighted to her. Nope, still on her shoulders. Lavinia had a larger bust than Mara and the thin straps holding up the loosely draped bodice had a bad habit of slipping. But if Mara remembered to hold her posture upright all evening, she should escape without any embarrassing wardrobe malfunctions.

Declan blinked, then his expression relaxed into his usual grin. "Everything's great," he said, offering his right arm to Mara. "But you're not wearing a coat. We better get you inside before you freeze."

She inhaled, hoping to breathe in courage along with the cold Manhattan evening air, and snaked her arm through his, giving herself a moment to balance on her precariously high stiletto heels. "Let's go."

Once inside the hotel, they joined the crowd ascending the wide, long stairs leading to the ballroom. Mara tried not to keep her head on constant swivel but she eventually gave up. Over there, wasn't that the actor from the television series about dragons? To her immediate right, she spotted a pop singer who recently made her smash debut on Broadway. And many more faces, recognized from studying the list of clients who bought art from Skacel.

Nor did Declan's presence go unnoticed. The paparazzi lining the lobby hoping for photos didn't call his name as loudly or as often as they did the other celebrities, but he was stopped to wave and pose for the occasional photo. Mara hung back in those moments. She wasn't Declan's date, as in a romantic connection. This was a work event. And Declan was her boss—technically—so she didn't want people, especially the stringers for the gossip websites, to get the wrong idea. Still, she couldn't help but feel proud of how well Declan handled the requests for his attention.

And how unbelievably handsome he appeared.

His dark blond hair was more closely cropped than six years ago, the deep grooves in his cheeks worn by his ever-present smile more pronounced. But his eyes were still the crystal blue of a spring-fed mountain lake, with similar depths in his gaze. Formal wear suited Declan, although, if she were honest, all forms of attire suited him. But there was something about the way his well-tailored jacket clung to his shoulders, then narrowed to fall over his slim waist. Beneath, trousers of the same silky black wool as his jacket hinted at the muscular legs underneath—he'd played tennis for fun in college and she'd spotted a racket in his office. She had no doubt the cut calves and hard, strong thighs she remembered were still present, and then shook a mental, chastising finger at herself. *Concentrate on getting the story.* She wrenched her gaze away from Declan and tried to find something else to focus on as a distraction.

But the crowd was growing thicker and each face that crossed her vision was more famous than the last. Her palms grew hot and she resisted the urge to wipe them on Lavinia's dress as her treacherous shoes started to slide on the polished marble floor. Declan tucked her hand firmly into the crook of his arm, ensuring she had enough support to stay upright. The crush of people kept her glued to his side.

She didn't mind. She took full advantage of the opportunity to catalog all the details she was curious about but didn't dare question. His bicep was warm and firm under the fine wool of his jacket, which

rubbed like silk against her fingertips. He smelled…
He smelled like Declan. She had to squeeze her eyes
shut. He smelled like one of the best times of her life,
of late night study sessions and early morning presen-
tation rehearsals, like laughing in the library stacks
despite the sign calling for "quiet," and like sneaking into the journalism school's video editing bays to
make last minute changes to their stories for that day's
school news broadcast. One inhale brought her back
to the senior year apartment she'd shared with Cam,
ordering pizza at eleven o'clock for the study session
that turned into an all-night conversation she and Declan only ended when her alarm clock reminded her
of her morning class.

The tall heavy doors to the ballroom opened and
the crowd pressed forward, causing her to slip on the
floor anew. Declan steadied her, his hand sure and
strong, and kept a grip on her shoulders as they entered the cavernous space and began to search for the
table to which they were assigned. The ballroom was
carpeted, which Mara thought would be an improve-
ment until her heels began to catch on the carpet's fibers. Thankfully, they didn't have far to walk. Declan
had scored again; their table was in a prime location
at the center of the room with a clear eyeline to tonight's speakers without being too close for comfort
to the stage. She eyed her chair with yearning, eager
to sit down and no longer worry about the torture instruments strapped to her feet. But the dinner was an
hour away, which meant she would be wasting prime
networking time. She sighed.

"Take off your shoes," Declan suggested. "Wear those flat slippers you have stashed in that purse."

She stared at him. How did he...? "You remember?"

"You hate high heels but insist on wearing them, so you carry backup shoes for when your feet hurt?" He grinned. "How could I forget? Freshman orientation. You changed shoes in the middle of questioning the health center representative about undergraduates' rights to free naloxone. Even I didn't know what naloxone was, that's how new it was."

"It helps to prevent death from fentanyl overdose, I thought the campus should make it available to students," Mara mumbled, her mind still marveling at the fact Declan recalled her habit of carrying spare slippers.

"And the campus eventually did. But that's when I knew."

The buzz of people chatting faded away, the whirl of brightly colored gowns and dark tuxedos replaced by utter stillness. The only sound she could discern was the bass thump of her heartbeat, reverberating against her eardrums. "Knew what?" she breathed.

Their gazes met and she drank in his clear blue depths. She wasn't sure how long they stood there—an hour? An eternity?—before he threw her his patented dazzling grin, the one that warned never to take him too seriously. The room spun to life around her as she dropped her gaze. Must have been only a minute after all.

"Knew I was going to sit next to you in class so I

could crib from your notes," he said. "I thought, now there's someone who is not only prepared with a second set of shoes, but she's on top of current events that matter to students. She knows her audience." He nodded at her purse. "So do you have them?"

She opened the bag and showed him her foldable ballet slippers. His grin widened. "Go ahead. Put them on."

"Here?" Mara smiled at the couple who took the chairs across the large round table from them, then turned to Declan. "With everyone looking?" she hissed.

"No one is looking."

"Well, yeah, I know I'm a nobody compared to you. But still—"

"That's not why no one is looking. Everyone here is concerned with how they look to the people they want to impress. So, they are not thinking about how you look to them. Take them off. If you want."

She bit her lip. He was right, no one was looking in their direction. Not even at Declan, and he was well-known. And her feet hated her footwear. Served her right for picking them out of Lavinia's closet during a video call based solely on the shoes' appearance. "I do want, but…"

"Here." He knelt. "Allow me to help."

Declan unbuckled the delicate strap around her left ankle. She steadied herself with a hand on the back of her chair and allowed him to slip her shoe off. The sense of relief was immediate, but the feeling warred with the awareness that had built as Declan's fingers brushed her skin. Who knew ankles were erogenous zones? Her nerves burned. He followed with her right shoe, and was it her imagination that his touch moved a tad higher than necessary, lingering a few seconds longer? She glanced down and the sight of Declan kneeling before her was superimposed on earlier memories, but his hands then were on her thighs, not her ankles. And his mouth was—

"There." He straightened and her memories fell away, although the wet warmth between her legs remained. "Shoes are under the table." His gaze flashed, focusing on a point over her shoulder, and he waved his hand in recognition before turning his attention back to her. "That's someone I need to talk to. See you back here for the dinner?"

"Of course. Happy hunting."

"More like 'happy keeping a source warm,' but same to you." He gave her a two-fingered salute and strode off.

He didn't seem hot and bothered at all, not even the smallest iota. She, on the other hand, needed a drink. Didn't matter what kind of drink, as long as it was ice cold and could counteract the heat still pumping through her veins. She swiveled her head, looking for the nearest bar—

Wait. Was that Freja Hansen standing near the stage? Mara knew better than to stare, so she used her peripheral vision to confirm. The elegant blonde in the beaded champagne-colored gown had to be her. Mara had never met the billionaire heiress to a Danish retail empire, but she'd seen many photos online. And Freja and Lavinia used to run in the same general social circles, although they weren't close. Mara took a deep breath, rehearsing in her head how to introduce herself to the dinner's chairwoman. Did she lead with being a journalist working on a story? Or ease into it?

Freja was deep in discussion with a distinguished Black gentleman Mara recognized as the chairman of the board of trustees for the society that awarded the Poets and Artists fellowships. Good. That gave her time to prepare, to ensure she would make a calm, sophisticated impression. She planted herself in Freja's vicinity, waiting for her to finish her conversation. A waiter carrying a tray full of drinks passed by and Mara grabbed the first glass that came to hand, keeping her gaze on Freja and her companion. The two appeared to be wrapping up and Mara's mouth suddenly went dry. She took a large sip.

And she sputtered, choking as the strong alcohol burned the back of her throat while the overly sugary taste caused her to gag. She dabbed at her mouth with the cocktail napkin, hoping the neon aqua liquid hadn't dribbled and spilled on Lavinia's dress.

She glanced up, hoping no one saw her, only to discover a now alone Freja smiling at her. Mara tried not to grimace. Great. Busted. So much for making a good impression.

Still, she smiled back and walked over to join Freja. One good piece of luck—Lavinia was a few inches shorter than Mara so removing her heels meant the gown was now floor length and would hide her decidedly not fancy footwear. She held out her hand for a handshake. "Hi. I'm Mara Schuyler. Overly sweet cocktails and I do not get along."

The woman took Mara's hand, her grip cool and firm. "Freja Hansen. You communicated how I felt about the taste quite expressively."

"But I bet you didn't do a spit take in public."

"True. But I will have sharp words with the food and beverage committee tomorrow." She eyed Mara's gown. "Is your dress from Sadie Soho's fall collection? It's quite lovely."

Mara looked down and smoothed out imaginary wrinkles in the skirt. "I think so?" She smiled at Freja. "May I be frank? I borrowed the gown from Lavinia Palmas. Well, Lavinia Schuyler now. My sister-in-law."

"Lavinia!" Freja's expression shifted from obligatory politeness to sharpened awareness. "She sat next to me at Gary Habit's last show. Is she here?"

"No. She's on bed rest at the moment."

"I'd heard she was pregnant. Has she hired her plastic surgeon yet?"

Mara tried hard not to blink at the non sequitur. "Plastic surgeon?"

"For when she delivers." Freja's tone carried an implied "of course." When Mara continued to wear her puzzled expression, Freja added, "For the tummy tuck. Otherwise, as you know, she might as well say farewell to couture."

"Right," Mara said slowly. "I don't know if she's found a plastic surgeon yet. I'll ask her. But I'm glad we had a chance to speak tonight. I was wondering if I could ask you about—"

"Freja! Finally. There you are." A man who shared Freja's stunning ice blue eyes and sharp cheekbones joined Mara and her companion. "Before you say anything, the wine is as abysmal as the cocktails, hence I am empty handed," he said to Freja, and then turned to Mara. "Hello, I'm Niels. The brother of that one." He jerked his thumb at Freja.

"Mara Schuyler. Pleasure to meet you." Niels really was attractive, but in the way she found a piece of artwork attractive. She could admire how the various planes and angles came together to form an aesthetically pleasing picture on an intellectual level, but physically? Inside her, nothing happened. "I see you share my taste—or rather, distaste—for overly sweet cocktails."

Niels's expression lit up, his eyes flaring to sharp, appreciative life. Nope, still did nothing for her. "The blue drink is a crime against taste buds." He turned to Freja. "Shall we find our table? Simon wants to talk to you before the inevitable rubber chicken is served."

"Mara is Lavinia Palmas's sister-in-law," Freja said, her eyebrows arching high.

Niels's back straightened and he turned to Mara. "Lavinia! I was talking about her earlier today. We miss seeing her around town. Is she here at the dinner?"

"I was telling your sister she's currently on bed rest."

"I see." He and Freja exchanged a glance. "Nothing too serious, I hope?"

"Her doctor is being cautious. She's doing well."

"Good. But it's unforgivable she failed to tell me she has such a charming sister-in-law." His smile appeared, the wattage nearly blinding. If he had been dazzling before, now he was outright stunning. She could see why he had been named one of Europe's sexiest men by a leading London tabloid several years in a row. "Tell her I am deeply disappointed in her."

Mara laughed. "I will, although charming is not often a word applied to me. Thank you, however."

"I refuse to believe that." Niels's forehead creased. "You must not be traveling in the right circles."

"Or perhaps I am, and you don't know me well enough."

He waved off her comment. "Nonsense. I am an excellent judge of three things—wine, art and people. Especially enchanting women."

Mara ducked her head. She'd had her share of flirtatious conversations in her adult dating life, but never from someone whose photograph was featured on gossip websites from Paris to Shanghai. "I trust your taste when it comes to cocktails, so I accept your word when it comes to wine," she said. "I would love to hear more about your taste in art. I understand you recently purchased a Robaire?"

His eyebrows rose. "I didn't think that was common knowledge. Are you a connoisseur of Robaire's work?"

"I wouldn't say a connoisseur. But you acquired a

previously unknown painting of his? Recently discovered when a very private Portuguese collector needed to sell his estate?"

Niels regarded her. "Charming and an art aficionado who knows the market well."

"Isn't that why we're all here? To support the arts?" Mara smiled at him. "I would love to hear more—"

Freja cut short the conversation she was having and turned to Niels. "The meal is about to be served. We should take our seats." She nodded at Mara. "Pleasure to meet you. If you would excuse us?"

"Of course—" Mara started to say, but Niels interrupted her, bowing over her hand.

"Please, come join us at our table." He exchanged glances with Freja, who held his stare until she finally gave him a nod as she left. Niels continued, "One of our guests couldn't make it at the last minute and we have an extra seat." His warm gaze ran over Mara, lingering perhaps a little too long over the bodice of her dress. She straightened up, and a shadow of disappointment passed over his expression. "We can become better acquainted between courses. And not to worry about the shameful wine on offer. I've arranged with the hotel staff to provide better alternatives for the meal."

"Thank you, but—"

He bent his head toward her ear. His warm breath wafted across her cheek, his low voice a husky timbre in her ear. "I won't take no for an answer."

Won't take no for an answer? That put his escapades with various women in the tabloids in a different perspective. Still, he was the lead she was here to pursue. "Well, I—"

She jumped as the heavy weight of a warm arm was slung across her shoulders. "Can't, because Mara is at my table tonight," Declan declared.

Niels blinked, and the connection between him and Mara was broken. She glared at Declan and tried to shrug his arm off, but he only tightened his grip on her shoulder in response. "I see," Niels said. "Treharne. Good to see you."

"You, too, Hansen. It's been a while since St. Alexander."

Mara's gaze ping-ponged between the two men, whose own gazes appeared to be locked in a battle for domination. St. Alexander was a prestigious boarding school in Switzerland. She knew Declan had been a student there, but that's about all she knew. He'd kept quiet when their friend group shared high school experiences. "You were at school together?"

"We overlapped." Declan's words were clipped.

Niels dropped contact first, and then turned to Mara. "I was a few forms ahead of Dec. And busy with sports and other social activities I'm afraid Dec didn't…partake in."

"He means I was there on scholarship," Declan explained to her.

"Well." Niels spread his hands in an apologetic gesture, although his expression was anything but. "Bygones and all that." He smiled, but his eyes stayed ice blue. "Good to see you, old chap. And how do you two know each other?"

"We're journali—" Mara began, but Declan's words drowned her out.

"We were college classmates." His tone left no room for questioning. "And we've been close ever since, right, Mara?" His hip bumped hers, just a little, but enough to let her know he was asking her to play along.

She shot Declan a warning glare before smiling at Niels. "Yes, Declan and I met our freshman year. But I wouldn't say—"

"Looks like they are rounding people up to take their seats so dinner can be served. Mara, we should get back to our table. See you later, Hansen."

"But of course." Niels took Mara's hand and bowed low over it. No one had ever offered such a courtly gesture to her. She had to admit she found it a bit thrilling, even as Declan turned to stone next to her. "To furthering our acquaintance later," Niels said.

"I look forward to it." Mara said. She waited until he was safely across the room before shrugging off Declan's arm and whirling around to face him. "What the hell was that all about? You knew the Hansen siblings were at the top of my list of potential sources for the art forgery story—"

"You're going to thank me." Declan turned on his heels and started to beeline toward their table.

Mara ran after him as best she could in her flat slippers, muttering "excuse me" and "coming through" as she darted around the celebrities and politicians wearing their finest. "What does that mean?"

"It means Hansen is spoiled and petty. I upped his interest in talking to you threefold."

She managed to get around Declan and plant herself directly in his way by darting in front of a film director well known for his blockbuster summer action flicks and almost causing him to spill his glass of red wine down the front of his suit. She ignored the scowl the director threw at her in favor of staring Declan down. "Wait. That chest thumping display back there... You think you were helping me? Look, superhero, I don't need you to fly in—"

Declan easily swerved around her and reached their table. "I don't think I was helping you. I know."

She rolled her eyes, made her way to her assigned seat and gripped the back of her chair so Declan couldn't pull it out for her. "I was doing fine without you. I was invited to sit at the Hansens' table before you showed up."

"Hansen likes to momentarily collect pretty things. But now he'll see you as someone to take seriously. Not as a piece of tissue."

"A piece of what?" Her hands dropped to her sides as she stored his use of the word "pretty" in the back of her mind, to be tossed around and examined from all sides when she was alone.

He pulled her chair out with ease. "Tissue. Something to be used and discarded."

"I'm a piece of trash?" She narrowed her gaze at Declan. "Tell me again why I'm supposed to thank you when the only person who has objectified me is you."

He sighed. "Look, I've seen Hansen in action quite a bit over the years. You want to talk to him about your art forgery story, fine. This will ensure he looks you in the eye and not—" His gaze dropped momentarily, his eyes widening before he returned his gaze to meet hers. "Lower."

She glanced down. What had caused his reaction—oh. The straps had shifted—the bodice falling precipitously low—and while there were young Hollywood up-and-comers at the party whose outfits were intentionally far more revealing, she was displaying far more of her upper body than she'd intended. Heat crept up her cheeks, but she tossed her head and held her chin high. "Oh, for heaven's sake, they're just breasts," she said. "I'm sure Niels has seen plenty of them. You, too. Half the world's population possesses mammary glands, you'll recall."

"Oh, I recall," he said, his tone low and rough, and she was transported to that week before graduation—that week when Declan had been particularly enthralled with her breasts, palming them with his large, sure hands, rubbing her nipples between his fingers and thumb, drawing the stone hard tips into his mouth, his tongue curling and swirling, his—

She blinked. She would not let Declan get into her head. And judging by the faint smile on his face as he watched her, he knew how his words affected her. How he meant for them to affect her.

Two could play at his game. She shrugged, and the straps fell farther down. She still technically wasn't breaking any decency laws, but Declan's gaze fell. And stayed.

"I'm parched. Aren't you?" She ran her left fingers lightly over her throat, allowing them to rest at the top of the shadowy valley between her breasts.

His Adam's apple bobbed as he swallowed. "Parched. That's a good word for it."

She knew what he meant as she struggled to work moisture into her own mouth. She let her fingers drift lower. Her nipples hardened, pushing against the thin fabric. He struggled to raise his gaze to lock on hers, but he finally gave up the battle.

She was teasing him. Flirting for fun. They both knew it. But she was enjoying his reaction. Enough to take the guardrails off and move closer to him, until her mouth found his ear. "And how do you propose we slack our thirst?" she whispered.

Declan's gaze snapped to a point over her shoulder. "If you want something to drink, there's a bottle of white wine in front of you. Excuse me. I see Bobbi James. I need to talk to her."

He left without helping her into her seat. Mara stared after him, her eyebrows raised high.

Ouch.

Well, at least she knew he wasn't wholly immune to her charms, such as they were. Useful information to have.

She turned back to face the table, only to catch the distinguished-looking gentleman from earlier sitting opposite her, also staring in the general vicinity of her chest. She shot him a narrow-eyed glare while she tugged her straps up and he turned back to his dinner companion, who also glared at him.

The rest of the dinner passed without incident, although Mara was careful to keep her posture rigid to ensure there was no further bodice slippage. Not that Declan seemed to care; upon his return to the table, he spent the entire meal engrossed in conversation with the woman seated on his other side. The man on Mara's left sat down, sipped some wine and then received a phone call that took him out of the ballroom—or at least away from the table—until well after dessert was served.

She stewed in silence. Her gaze returned more than once to the Hansens' table, where Niels and Freja appeared to be holding quite the merry court among the top of the crème guests. Once she caught Niels's gaze returning her glance, feeling her skin flush at getting caught.

Finally, the dinner ended after the honorees read from their works. Bright lights came up to flood the ballroom, letting the guests know the night was now over. As the room started to empty out, Mara pushed her chair back from the table.

Declan placed his hand over hers, warm and heavy. "Don't," he said.

"Don't what?"

"Don't go over to Niels." He threw a glance at her. "You've been too obvious with your interest as it was, although the blush was a nice touch."

"How… I wasn't…" She glared at him. "You didn't say one word to me all evening. How do you even—"

"Good. Keep that up. We look like we're fighting. He'll like that."

"You want to fight? We can fight. Why did you ignore me all dinner?"

He shrugged. "It's bad etiquette to talk to one's date exclusively at a social event."

She counted silently to ten. "We're not on a date. This is work."

"Agreed. But we arrived together. The etiquette still stands." He flicked his gaze toward the Hansen table. "Especially for those who expect us to play by their world's rules."

"I play by my own rules, and those rules are called politeness." She started, again, to rise from her chair. "I'm going to go over to the Hansens, thank them for a lovely evening and try to finagle an interview."

Declan rose with her. His left hand grasped her forearm. "Don't," he repeated.

"You really do want this to look like a fight, don't you?" His grip was loose but sure, his hand warming her skin. She ignored the pops of electricity fizzing through her nerves and tried to surreptitiously shake herself free, careful not to cause anything resembling a scene. He did not take the hint. If anything, his grasp tightened, his fingers sliding along the sensitive skin below her elbow.

"I want you to get your story," he said in her ear, his breath hot on her cheek. Her pulse beat an answering staccato rhythm. "Niels does not like being pursued. He does the pursuing. I know him well. You will blow your chances if you approach him."

She stilled. "Okay. What do I do?"

"Give him a reason to come to you."

She gestured with her left hand, the one not attached to the arm he still held. "And how do I do that? Especially since you apparently aren't interested in letting me go."

He blinked hard. "What—oh. Sorry." His fingers relaxed. But she didn't move her arm. She told herself the ballroom was overly cool, especially now that most of the guests had left, and she appreciated the body heat he provided. That was all.

She was lying.

"So?" she asked. "What should I do?"

He scratched the back of his neck. "I have an idea. It's not the most professional. You won't like it. I'm not sure it's wise, myself. But it will cement Niels's interest."

Mara flicked her gaze toward the Hansens' table. Freja was kissing her table companions on both cheeks to say goodbye, while Niels was straightening his evening jacket as if preparing to leave. "What is it?" she hissed.

Declan's gaze was also focused on the Hansens. "We kiss."

"We what?" Mara whirled to face him, all thoughts of Niels and Freja flown from her head. "You can't be serious. That's going to bring Niels over here?"

"He likes to take things that belong to others," Declan said. "He especially likes my things. If he thinks we're together, it becomes a competition to see which one of us will be triumphant."

"Do we have to be together? What if we recently broke up?"

A steel shutter fell over Declan's expression. She'd never seen him so cold and still. Not even when he told her they were better off pursuing separate lives after graduation. "No. You'll be nothing but a plaything to be broken. He'll get even more joy out of destroying something that he thinks once belonged to me."

Mara narrowed her gaze. "That sounds very personal. You are going to have to fill me in on your history with Niels Hansen. Why didn't you say anything about him in college?"

"Why would I need to? I left St. Alexander. That was the past—" Declan grabbed her shoulders. "He's looking in our direction. Ready?"

"I am—" The rest of her words were swallowed as Declan's mouth closed over hers.

At first she was still, her lips shocked as overwhelming memories made it difficult to discern if the moment was real or a memory or just years of fantasies made viscerally real. Her synapses took a beat to catch up with her nerves, who were singing a sweet song of pure electricity. He was a polite kisser, not demanding, not trying to force a deeper connection, waiting for her to determine what was permissible and what was not. And for a second, she returned like for like, remaining passive and calm, a press of lips only. Then his right hand fell from her shoulder to her waist, resting there, not pulling her closer.

The hell with that. She was kissing Declan Treharne for the first time in seven years and she would be damned if she let this opportunity go by without exploring what she dreamed of, late at night at her most alone.

She melted into him, entwining her arms around his neck. Her tongue traced the seam of his lips, begging him to let her in. He went still, his hands splayed motionless on her waist, but she sighed into his mouth and his fingers tightened, drawing her closer until only her dress and his suit was between them. His lips parted and finally, finally she was tasting Declan again, at once familiar and foreign, everything she remembered but tempered by the passage of time and the gaining of experience. Declan at twenty-two had been sure of himself with a rumored swathe of conquests through the undergrad and graduated programs; Mara tried very hard not to listen to gossip about which woman in the program he was dating that week.

The young man with whom she'd had a torrid, brief affair was still there. He was still Declan, But now he was so much...more. More skilled, his tongue stroking hers and igniting nerve endings she didn't know existed. Stronger, more demanding, in control of what he liked and how to show her what he needed. But also more aware of her, of how she wanted to be kissed, learning her responses and how to coax them from her.

Then she stopped comparing, stopped thinking at all as the embers kindling low in her belly erupted into pure conflagration and she could only feel. This was not good, the tiny corner of her brain still able to engage in rational thought tried to flag. She and Declan didn't work the first time. There was no way it would a second time. She didn't even want a relationship right now! She was building a career and couldn't get sidetracked.

She was—

"Excuse me." The low, cultured voice came from behind. "I hate to interrupt but I'm heading out. I'm taking an overnight flight to Europe I must catch, but I was wondering if I could have a word?"

Mara froze and then her eyes flew open. Declan disengaged first, his hands dropping from her waist so he could thrust them into his pants pockets. "What do you want, Niels?"

Mara slowly turned around. She must look a mess. Tendrils of hair that had escaped from her updo grazed her back. No doubt her lipstick was gone, as she could see traces of it on Declan's mouth. Too late, she realized her left strap had fallen down her shoulder and she tugged it back into place, trying not to shiver as the silky fabric shifted over her still hard and sensitive nipple.

Niels smiled as he addressed her. "You mentioned an interest in Robaire. Freja and I are having a small cocktail party, nothing too formal, at our place when we return to New York two weeks from now—a sort of private unveiling of the piece for our friends, as it were. Would you like to attend?"

She blinked, her brain racing to keep up with her ears. "I… I would be honored."

"Good." May I have your contact information so an invitation may be issued?"

"Um…" Her new business cards had yet to be printed. "I can write it for you on—"

Declan handed Niels one of his cards. "You can send the invite to me. I'll make sure Mara gets the information."

Niels's gaze turned frigid ice blue. "Of course. You're welcome to come as well, Treharne. Perhaps some culture might do you some good."

"I'll be there if Mara is."

"Of course." Niels turned back to Mara and the ice thawed. "I very much look forward to our next encounter. Perhaps we can have a real conversation—" he briefly turned his gaze on Declan "—alone, at the party. Until then." He bowed over her hand, nodded at Declan, turned on his heels and left.

Mara watched him go. She could either do that or look at Declan, and right now she wasn't sure if she could ever look him straight in the eye again. Not after that kiss. Not after she practically climbed him like he was a pole at a state fair climbing competition and she was trying to reach the prize on top.

"Right. That's settled then. Mission accomplished." Declan knelt, but before Mara could ask him what he was doing, he popped back up with her discarded shoes in his hand. "Here you go. Keep them off until you reach your car. Your driver is waiting for you downstairs."

She reached out automatically to take the shoes from him, her mind still trying to strategize how to explain away her reaction to his kiss. "Thanks. But we should—"

He cut her off. "I'll see you at LNT for the check in meeting on Wednesday. Have a good rest of your evening."

And then he was gone, swallowed up by the brightly dressed crowd as the partygoers slowly made their way to the exits.

Well, at least she didn't have to figure out what to say to him. She inhaled deeply, hoping oxygen would bring clarity to her disordered thoughts. She couldn't believe he just…walked off. But he'd been affected by the kiss as much as she had. She did not imagine his erection, pressing hard and heavy through the thin layers of their clothes.

Yet he acted as if the kiss never happened. Like how he ended their torrid week with a calm, unemotional speech about needing to pursue their own lives. Why should she expect today be any different than what happened seven years ago?

Honestly, she should be relieved. She finally had her big break in sight. The last thing she needed was to fall into another tangle of emotions over Declan Treharne. Even worse, seven years ago they had been fellow students, on an equal footing. Now, Declan called the shots when it came to which stories would air during launch week at LNT Plus.

She would never be taken seriously if people thought she'd slept her way into getting her story on air. Thank all the career gods that the ballroom had been nearly empty and no one—well, except for Niels Hansen—seemed to be paying attention to them.

No, the best thing to do was to forget the kiss as fully as Declan apparently did.

She felt the pressure of his lips on hers throughout the rest of the night and into the weekend.

Five

Declan kept his gaze fixed out of the car window, keeping a close lookout for Mara, while attempting to also focus on his phone conversation with Bobbi. He wasn't doing a good job on either front.

"Could you repeat that?" he said, his attention momentarily diverted when the front door to Mara's apartment building opened, only for a man pushing a stroller to exit the building. He looked at his smart watch. The cocktail party at the Hansen twins' Upper East Side penthouse wasn't supposed to start for another half hour, and guests weren't supposed to arrive on time in the first place but were meant to be fashionably late. But he wanted to have a conversation with Mara—a good conversation, not the professional, stilted exchanges they'd had in meetings or in the hallways of LNT since the Poets and Artists Ball. He tried to find the right opportunity for a more personal discussion, but Mara was occupied getting up to speed with her new producer while Declan was needed to put out several urgent fires at the corporate level. But if Mara didn't get into the car he hired to drive them for the evening, there wouldn't be enough time to say the things he wanted to say.

To apologize.

Bobbi sighed over the phone. "That makes twice I've repeated myself. No more stalling. What's your answer?"

He blinked. "Answer?"

This time Bobbi's sigh was pure exasperation. "Answer to the assignment I'm offering you."

This was not good. He'd obviously blanked out on the main reason why Bobbi called him. And the one thing the famed and feared Bobbi James hated more than anything was to be ignored when she was speaking to one of her reporters. Maybe he could back into what he missed, ask enough questions to reconstruct the subject of their conversation. "What kind of time commitment do you think—"

"You weren't listening to me."

Declan tapped his fingers on the leather of the town car's rear passenger seat. He was alone in the vehicle. The driver was standing outside, at the ready to open the door for Mara who continued to be a no-show. "Sorry. You're right. I wasn't."

Bobbi snorted. "At least you admit it. What's going on with you, Dec? Did we not discuss you would be open to assignments from the *Globe* while you are at LNT? If I have that wrong, that's fine. But you need to let me know. I'm wasting time talking to you if you aren't available."

Declan pinched the bridge of his nose. "Yes, I'm open."

"Good. So—"

"But—" Declan hated to cut off Bobbi. He could see her now, pacing as she looked out over Midtown from the floor to ceiling window in her office, her favorite way to take phone calls. Her expression would be schooled not to show a single emotion in case some unknowing and unwise subordinate happened to look into her office through the glass walls, but a muscle jumping in her cheek would signify her displeasure. "—I'm not open now. And I'll be back in mid-January."

"I know." Bobbi was silent for a moment. "I'll hold the assignment as long as I can. It's mostly rumor anyway, although the sources are reliable. Maybe we can corroborate their information in the meantime. But if it heats up further, I'll have to get someone else."

He nodded. If tonight went well, Mara would be well on her way to having a story that could jumpstart her career and help put her on the path to superstardom that should have been hers to begin with, and he could leave LNT. "That's fair. But can you repeat the assignment? I promise I'm listening."

Bobbie sighed. "You really weren't listening, were you? Monte Carlo."

Declan sat up straight. Monte Carlo was the home of the story that got away. The story that ended in tragedy. The one that still haunted him when he closed his eyes, whether daytime or night. "What? But she's—"

"Not dead. Or, at least, that's what we've been told. Would help if I had my top investigative reporter back in the bullpen, of course, but—"

He worked to get moisture into his mouth. "Alice de la Vigny has resurfaced."

"So said our source. We're working on confirmation. I can give you some time. But it might not be able to wait until February."

"De la Vigny is my story," Declan ground out.

"She was." Bobbi disconnected, a series of beeps in his ear letting him know she was gone. Declan allowed his hand holding the phone to fall, his gaze focused on the back of the seat in front of him but his mind seeing the manicured gardens and well-kept stone building facades of Monte Carlo.

"Hey." Mara stuck her head in the car. "Do you want to move over, or should I go around to the other side?"

With supreme effort, he dragged his focus back to the present. He trusted the team at the *Globe*. If anyone could confirm the source's story about Alice, they could. Might as well let them do the legwork for now. "I'll—"

Wow. Mara was stunning. Gone was the fancy updo and dramatic makeup. Tonight she wore her hair loose and down around her shoulders while her freckles were on full display. Although there had been nothing wrong with the glamorous Mara who attended the Poets and Artists Ball, not at all. He'd especially appreciated the dress she wore that night, the silky fabric skimming over her curves, hiding just enough that his imagination went into overdrive to fill in the missing details. And when they kissed and he knew there was nothing between his hands and her but that flimsy layer—

He cleared his throat and slid to the other side of the car. "Come on in."

She sat down next to him and buckled her seatbelt. The driver sat in his front seat, started the car and sped away from the curb. Her scent hung in the air, a light combination of lemon and strawberry. Her shampoo, he suddenly remembered. She must be still using the same brand. His hands tightened on the leather seat.

Mara looked out the window on her side, her head turned away from him. The silence stretched out, broken only by the sound of the car's engine and street noise from outside. He inhaled. He didn't have the time he wanted, but better to say something before they faced the Hansens.

Say something to her, before he started chasing other memories of Mara in college. Like Mara throwing on his shirt to fetch them coffee from the kitchen he shared with his three housemates, and when she didn't return to his bed in what he thought was adequate time, he ventured into the kitchen himself only to find her sitting on the counter, holding court with his friends—three avowed bachelors who had recently sworn off women for various reasons—eating out of her hand. She was delectable in the morning light, her tousled red hair glowing and her eyes shining, her long legs swinging as she exchanged baseball scores from the night before with the roommate who played club ball.

After his roommates left for their classes, he and Mara put that counter to good use…

Enough memories of the past. That was a distant country he would never visit again. "So—"

She spoke at the same time. "I knew it. There's something wrong. Am I not dressed right?"

"What? No. You're fine."

She glanced down at her navy blue dress, simple but elegant. "I spoke to Lavinia and she said not to try too hard, that people like the Hansens can smell desperation and fear. And that they definitely smell when you want something from them."

"You look great." And she did. So great, he was having a hard time looking at her, the way it was hard to look at the sun because the light was so bright. Mara would eclipse everyone at the party, he was sure. "Listen. We need to—"

"Because you hesitated when I came to the car. Like something was wrong."

"I…no. Nothing's wrong. At least, not with you," he said. Bobbi's news about Alice, on the other hand, had thrown him for a loop. Elegant and well-connected, Alice procured young women—very young women—for wealthy men. But she went to ground six months ago and the rumor was she was murdered because someone powerful got word she was about to expose the ring for whom she worked. The news she had resurfaced made his soul feel a little lighter—he hated thinking she was killed for talking to him— but that meant she was probably still involved in the same line of work. And that needed to be stopped.

"So something is wrong!" She shifted in her seat to face him. "What is it? Did you learn something new about the Hansens?"

"No. Not about the Hansens. Or tonight." He tried to smile at her, only to remember that Alice might still be out there, somewhere. And that he was wasting precious minutes not clearing the air with Mara. Traffic was not on his side for once; they were moving across town at a decent clip. "But we should—"

"You can tell me, you know." She faced front once more, her gaze fixed on the taillights of the cars in front of them that were visible through the windshield. "If something is wrong. We were good friends, once." He opened his mouth, but she continued. "If you need an ear, that is. Or if there's a problem."

Declan waited a beat. "Anything else?" he finally asked.

She glanced at him. "What? No."

"Good. Because we should talk. About the kiss at the Poets and Artists Ball. I went to HR and—"

"You went to HR?" She kept her gaze forward, but he saw her shoulders straighten. "The kiss was a ruse. It got us an invite to tonight's party. Why did you go to HR?"

"Because…we kissed. In public. And people might—"

"We kissed because it was an attempt to draw Niels's attention. Which worked." Her head tilted. "Unless it wasn't a ruse and there was another motivation."

"I—no." That had been the intent, but the result had shaken his soul to its core. However, since there wouldn't be a repeat, no need to say anything. He would be leaving LNT and Mara very soon as it was. "Good. We're on the same page about the kiss. And HR is aware that we had a prior relationship. LNT doesn't forbid dating—"

"We're not dating—"

"I know. But I want everything to be aboveboard. Workwise." Was it hot in the car? He should tell the driver to turn down the temperature setting. "But you and I should discuss—"

"Cliff!" she interjected. "Yes, we haven't talked much since Cliff came onboard to be my producer. He may not be as experienced as Tobey, but has a much better vision for the stories we can tell together. I think he's going to work out." She turned her head, giving him a brilliant smile that reflected the light from the streetlights flashing by outside the car windows. But her eyes remained shrouded in the shadows. "I appreciate your help. *Workwise*," she stressed.

Did the kiss leave her that unaffected? That was not the impression he got. She was pure flame in his arms, and he ignited right with her. "Glad Cliff will work out. But I want you to know that you are more than justified in going to HR yourself. If you wish to file a complaint over the kiss, I encourage you to do so. We work together and I control if your story will be on the air for launch week. There's a power imbalance—"

Mara snorted. "There's always been a power imbalance. At least this time the kiss was a means to an end that benefitted me as well." She waved a hand to indicate the car. "Like an invite to the Hansens'."

There had always been a power imbalance? "What do you mean—?"

"Oh, please." Mara turned a pitying eye on him. "You were the king of the castle, number one in the classroom and out of it. The golden boy. The kid who got all the prime slots. Being teamed with you on a project nearly always meant recognition by professors and school administrators. We all fought for you to pick us to be on your team, or more. Why do you think both Ahmed Shah and Julie Ting used to parade by your freshman dorm room on their way to the shower while wearing very little? They each hoped to catch your eye, and not because they admired your keen vision for stories."

"I thought they liked being clean," he mumbled. "I had a chance with Julie Ting?"

"You had a chance with Ahmed! I mean, you aren't exactly hard to look at, but Ahmed used to model in Italy. He was out of all our leagues. Anyway, my point is there has never been an equal playing field where you and I are concerned." The car began to slow, and Mara glanced out the window. "Looks like we're here."

Declan didn't move. "I didn't know you felt that way."

"We all did." Her brow creased as she glanced at him. "C'mon, don't tell me your keen observational skills failed you back then. You had to be aware."

He thought back, his mind flipping through memories. Yes, he'd been highly successful in college—and since then—but that was the result of his hard work. His talent, which he honed. His skills, which he built and practiced with single-minded determination. That's what got him ahead...

Although. His innate aptitude was not why he earned an editor position on the school's newspaper as a freshman. He hadn't produced any work yet. But a classmate who had been a few years ahead of him at St. Alexander had got him the interview, when they had been reserved for upperclassman at the time. And he never looked back.

It never crossed his mind that Ahmed and Julie were pursuing him. Perhaps because he knew the professional life he wanted would have no space for a committed relationship. He was drawn to stories that required long stints of going undercover with dangerous organizations or being embedded in war-torn territories. His work was meant to bring the corruptly powerful to justice, to create so much evidence that legal enforcement could not ignore it or worse, be bought off. And with that came threats and near misses. Or outright assassinations.

Jamie Lochlainn died while investigating a drug cartel, his body never found. Declan assumed he wound eventually meet the same fate as his biological father. The only exception to his "casual flings only" rule had been Mara, and their sharp turn from friends to lovers had taken him by surprise. Taken both of them by surprise, or so he had thought.

"Is that why you…" No. That couldn't be why she came back with him to his apartment that night, why they fell into bed for one of the most glorious weeks of his life.

Her gaze struck sparks that lit the car's interior. "Are you asking if that is why I slept with you? To get ahead?" The car door next to her opened. The driver's hand extended into her space. She allowed him to help her exit the backseat.

Great. Just great. Awesome start to the evening, Treharne, he admonished himself.

Mara stuck her head back into the car. "For the record, if I had slept with you to get ahead in college, that would have been really, really stupid because it was the week before graduation and there was nothing left to get ahead on. So, thanks for insinuating my mental acuity, as well as my ethics, is suspect." She slammed the door.

Okay. He deserved that. And he had an evening of very sincere apologizing ahead of him. He reached for his door handle when Mara's door opened and she popped her head into the car's interior again. "We're still good for tonight though, right? That's the part I wanted to discuss. We have to be on the same page. Relationship-wise. Or fake relationship-wise, as the case may be. So…are we still dating? For Niels's sake, I mean?"

"Yes," he said, his tone brooking no disagreement. He exited the car and joined her on the sidewalk outside the tall, modern skyscraper that housed the Hansens' penthouse apartment. Mara was wearing flat-heeled shoes, he noticed with a smile. And also a note of regret, because it meant she wouldn't need to cling to him to change her shoes again. "And for the record, I have never questioned your mental acuity. Or your ethics. They have both been always top notch."

Her thin-lipped expression relaxed, and she came to take his proffered arm. "Thanks for that. But we are agreeing to pretend to be…together. So maybe they're a little suspect," she said with a small smile. "Y'know, you never did fill me in on your history with Niels."

She nodded at the security guard, who checked their identification and then led them to a private elevator that would whisk them to the Hansens' residence. Then she turned back to him. "Now would be a good time for the story."

"There's not much to tell." Declan kept his gaze fixed on the digital readout, flashing numbers as the elevator climbed higher. "We were at the same boarding school. I was on scholarship. Niels wasn't. But despite having everything money could buy, Niels didn't like his own possessions. He only wanted the possessions of others."

"And did he take yours?"

A flash of large brown eyes and an always laughing mouth seared across his mind. "What he wanted of mine he couldn't take. So, he hurt someone I was very fond of. Not physically. Emotionally and socially. She was never the same after. And he did it for sport."

Mara's eyes widened. "How terrible. Is she okay now?"

"I don't know. Her family moved away shortly after. She didn't return any of my texts or calls, and she isn't on social media that I can tell." They were almost at the penthouse. "The Hansens have riches and influence and they know how to wield their power effectively and decisively." And he wouldn't let Niels do to Mara what he did to Giulia. The situations were very different—Mara wasn't the daughter of one of the school's housekeepers and thus, she was not more vulnerable to the machinations of a student whose parents were on the board of directors of the institution—but he had no doubt Niels's tactics would be as cruel, if not more so, if he thought Mara was an easy target.

If that meant he and Mara had to pretend to be romantically together, well, he didn't mind the ruse. At all.

He might like it a little too much for comfort.

The elevator dinged and the doors opened directly into the foyer of the penthouse. Mara gasped. Even Declan, who was used to being in the gilded halls of the rich and powerful, had to the admit the foyer was a stunning piece of architectural art, from the honed marble floor to the lapis lazuli and gold mosaic walls and high arched ceiling. She grabbed his arm and whispered in his ear, "I feel like I'm inside a genie bottle."

A young woman in a formfitting black dress came forward to take Mara's coat. "Welcome. The Hansens are delighted you both could attend, Miss Schuyler, Mr. Treharne. If you would follow me, I'll show you to the party."

Mara raised an eyebrow at Declan as they followed the woman through a series of rooms, each more exquisitely decorated than the last. Eventually they reached a large open room with a terrace attached. The glass wall that would normally separate the two had been folded back upon itself so the party could flow indoors and outdoors at will. Declan wondered if he should ask for Mara's coat back, but quickly realized a series of cleverly hidden heaters kept the temperature outside pleasantly mild. Several groupings of tables and chairs had been set up for the guests on the terrace, while the left side of the room was dominated by a built-in bar, sleekly modern with shelves reaching to the ceiling of nothing but top tier alcohol.

On the right side of the room, the wall was severely bare except for one item: the previously unknown piece by Robaire.

Mara left Declan's side and went to stand in front of the painting. Declan had never been an art aficionado and modern art from the first half of the twentieth century left him especially confounded. What was so special about blocks of color or splattered paint? He could grab a canvas and some watercolors and produce the same result. But even he had to admit the Robaire was eye-catching—a six-foot by four-foot canvas that seemed to glow from within. He grabbed a drink from the bar and went to join her. "What do you think?"

"I haven't seen that many paintings by Robaire in person, but this looks on par with his best works," Mara said slowly.

"But of course it is."

Declan turned to see Niels standing behind them. The other man's gaze was fixed on Mara, whose cheeks filled with color.

"So happy to see you again," Niels said to her, stepping forward and positioning himself so his back was turned to Declan.

"Thank you so much for inviting me," she said, leaning forward as Niels greeted her with a kiss on both cheeks, European-style.

Declan failed to hide his eye roll. "Yes, we appreciated the invite," he said, shifting around Niels and then slugging his left arm around Mara while holding his right hand out for a handshake. She was warm and soft, and his hand drifted downward to rest on the curve of her lower back and bring her closer to his side. "We cancelled our five month anniversary dinner so we could attend. Isn't that right, sweetie?"

"Yes," she said, her smile wide. But her heel trod on his toes and he returned his hand to the neutral territory of her shoulders. Good thing she wore flats and not her spike heels tonight.

Niels perfunctorily shook his hand, then turned his

attention back to Mara. "What makes you say this is one of Robaire's best works?"

"Well." Mara shrugged off Declan's arm and moved closer to the painting. "The use of contrast, of light and dark, to draw the observer's eye and ensure we look where he wants us to look. But of course, the areas that he wants us to overlook are where the profound meaning of the work can be found, in the emptiness and loneliness of the negative space. And the use of color—mimicking the observer's emotions as he takes us on this journey—is unparalleled."

Huh? Declan looked at the canvas. He saw nothing but amorphous blobs and blocks.

Niels was delighted. His fleshy lips curved in a smile that was half surprise, half leer. Declan resisted the urge to whisk Mara away from his assessing gaze. "Very good. You do appreciate Robaire."

"Very much. Although, I'm absolutely fascinated by this one. You recently acquired it?"

Niels inclined his head. "In the last few months."

"Interesting, I don't recall him ever using cobalt blue in such a manner. Also, the way he built up the pigment *here*." She indicated with her index finger but, for the life of him, Declan couldn't tell what distinguished the section she pointed out from the section next to it. "Very unusual for him."

Niels regarded the canvas with a frown. "Not so unusual," he said. "In *Woman on Staircase*, he used a similar technique."

"Did he?" Mara squinted at the painting. "Ah, I see what you're saying." She smiled at Niels. "What a find this is! You must have been so excited. I understand this came from the collection of a very private elderly gentlemen in Portugal who recently passed away?"

Niels nodded. "Yes. I was told he befriended Robaire at a time of need and was given several artworks in return."

Mara widened her eyes. "What a great story. Y'know, I recently started as a journalist for LNT and I'm researching a story on Robaire. I would love to interview you or your sister about this painting and the story behind it. I realize it's a big ask—"

Niels smiled tightly. "Too big of an ask, I'm afraid. You understand."

"Of course," Mara said, her smile never faltering. "I hope you understand I had to inquire. I'm so fascinated."

"But of course. Now, may I interest you in a drink on the terrace? There are some other art lovers whose acquaintance you should make. Perhaps they might wish to be interviewed. I would love to introduce you around."

"I would be delighted—" Mara stopped and threw a glance at Declan. "I mean, if that's okay with you, pookie?" She batted her eyelashes at him.

"Go ahead. I'll be enjoying the drinks inside here, where it's warmer." It was true if anyone could be described to have a punchable face, Niels would fit the description. Declan didn't trust him for a nanosecond. But this was Mara's story, and he wasn't going to do anything that would jeopardize her ability to find the information she needed. Especially since his conversation with Bobbi put a fast-ticking clock on his time at LNT. He waved, a cheesy grin on his face, as Niels escorted Mara out to meet the other guests.

His face fell once they were on the terrace and other people blocked Mara from his sight. But this was good, right? Mara was ingratiating herself with the hoped-for source for her story. Sure, Niels said no, but that was only her first time asking him.

Watching her in action, her green eyes flashing and her red locks dancing as she tossed her head and laughed, he had no doubt she would eventually land her story—or any other story she wanted to tell. Before long, she would be an established star at LNT and from there, her career would be firmly in her hands.

And he could go back to doing what he did best: serving the world in his own way by uncovering corruption and injustice.

That was the future he wanted. A future where he was answerable only to his trusted editor and his own conscience. Where, if a compelling lead developed, he could drop everything to run around the world, chasing the information from dawn to dusk and all the hours beyond. If he was incommunicado for twelve days, no one would worry. Well, Bobbi might crease her brow, but she would also trust him to do what he thought needed to be done.

He didn't have to answer to anyone. He didn't bear any responsibilities except telling the truth and making the world a better place He knew some might sneer at his impossible, lofty goals—he'd been a quixotic fool several times—but he'd brought down a CEO who used his power to prey on women and nonbinary individuals. The story he was pursuing involving Alice de la Vigny involved an international consortium of wealthy and powerful people who exploited refugees and desperate families in poverty. His life left no space to be shared.

Although—his gaze caught a flash of navy blue as Mara joined a small conversational group on the terrace, her red hair gleaming in the moonlight as she leaned her head back to laugh—he could see how developing a deeper, more intimate relationship with someone who shared his dreams, concerns and desires had a strong appeal.

He wrenched his gaze away. But not for him. Even though Mara understood his need to pursue stories and would probably dive headfirst into dangerous missions herself—intrepid didn't start to cover her courage—he couldn't ask her, or anyone, to share in the risks when he might not return home one day. He'd been devastated when he lost his mother and she didn't choose to be sick, while he was knowingly risking his life. He would not willingly put anyone else through that pain.

Perhaps Keith had been right to send him away when Declan appeared on this doorstep, all those years ago. No doubt, the loss of Jamie hit him hard, and here came someone claiming to be Jamie's blood, intent on following in Jamie's footsteps. Why put himself through the same loss twice?

His gaze found Mara again. Still, he couldn't deny he wanted her. Never stopped.

The sooner this story was over and she was established as a journalism star—and he could leave LNT and all the painful, conflicted memories being part of the Lochlainn empire stirred up for him—the sooner he could return to his old role and try to forget her all over again.

Six

Mara joined in the laughter, throwing her head back to chuckle loudly just as the man—wearing a suit that had to cost more than six months of her rent—next to her did, although she had no idea if what had been said had been funny or not. Apparently, there was a woman named Bunny and she lost her fur while visiting Gstaad? Or maybe the woman lived in Gstaad and her bunny lost its fur? She didn't know and frankly, she wasn't sure she would understand even if she did know. In-jokes were only funny when one was a member of the in-crowd, and it was clear Mara would not be invited to join.

The cocktail party was turning out to be a bust. While Niels had been overly solicitous when introducing her around to the other guests—a smorgasbord of international socialites, captains of industry, current and retired politicians, and a few stage and screen stars sprinkled in for celebrity glamour—his interest seemed to wane once Declan was out of earshot. Freja was perfectly pleasant when Mara said hello to her, but her attitude clearly indicated Mara was there at Niels's insistence and not hers. Not that Mara blamed her. She and Declan were the only members of the press in attendance, and while the other guests did not shut her out of their conversational circles, neither did they relax their guard. Her attempts to draw various people out and move the conversation beyond small talk, into a discussion of the Robaire and the current art acquisitions being made by the Manhattan art crowd, were politely but firmly shut down.

She wondered if Declan was having better luck. This was his world, with his international upbringing and his Swiss prep school education. He grew up around diplomats and heads of state. He could converse with anyone—like the beautiful Black woman with whom he was currently deep in discussion, their heads so close together they were nearly touching. At first, Mara wondered if the woman had been at college with them, as she looked so familiar. Then she realized, no, he was speaking to Audrey Burt and she looked familiar because Audrey had recently won the Tony for Best Actress in a Musical. Mara was seeing her out of context.

She sighed. Of course, he would attract the attention of one of the most talented artists of their generation. That was Declan. Everyone gravitated to his sun, settled into orbit around his light. He seemed genuinely surprised when Mara mentioned Ahmed and Julie, but there was no way he wasn't aware of his effects on other people.

If only she had remembered that in college. At the time, she thought their friendship was sincere, the attraction that finally boiled over into that week of overwhelming passion mutual. Even now, it was hard to look back and realize how much she'd let herself believe Declan truly cared for her, that he hadn't only been interested in exploring the chemistry between them and then walking away. That she had been so wrong, so off in her reading of the situation.

She would not repeat her mistake.

Besides, she had much bigger fish to fry at the moment. And speaking of… She glanced around the terrace. Odd, she didn't spot Niels. Freja was nearby, speaking with the guest conductor for the Manhattan Symphony and a man Mara recognized from that morning's news program as a bestselling author from Brazil. Freja's calm, cool expression hadn't changed since Mara arrived, never slipping no matter who she talked to, but—Mara squinted—Freja's hands were clenched in tight fists. Rather unusual for someone who otherwise appeared relaxed and in charge.

Interesting. Mara sidled a little closer, pretending to admire the tall trees strung with small twinkling white lights lining the terrace's back wall. She strained to listen but could only hear an exasperated sigh followed by a hissed "Niels" before Freja turned on her heels and vanished deeper into the crowd.

Perhaps she wasn't the only person who had noticed Freja's twin brother was no longer on the terrace.

No use sticking around outside, making social small talk that went nowhere. Finding Niels and pinning him down for an interview went to the top of her list of things to accomplish at the party.

She passed Declan as she entered the penthouse. He didn't even flick a glance in her direction as she passed by. Good. Getting Niels to talk to her might be easier without Declan there, igniting the men's old rivalry. But Niels was not in the main living area, nor the chef's kitchen that would seem well-appointed even by Michelin-starred restaurant standards, nor the exquisite library off the foyer, nor the lavishly decorated dining room that appeared as if a party of twenty-five could be easily accommodated and still have room left over for dancing. She wandered through the rooms, taking mental notes of the other art pieces as she went.

Niels had not been lying. The Hansen twins' collection was indeed impressive. The stuff of which most museums could only dream. But of her host, Mara didn't spot one shining blond hair.

A sweeping staircase off the foyer indicated there was at least one more story to the penthouse, the stairs leading to a mezzanine that overlooked the room below. Mara hesitated, her hand lightly resting on the banister. Did she dare venture upstairs? There was nothing indicating the upper floor was off-limits to guests. But nor were people traipsing up and down the steps. The party was most definitely confined to the great room and the terrace.

The foyer was quiet, so quiet Mara swore she could hear the echo of her own breathing, bounced back by the marble floors and walls. She let her fingers trail along the polished mahogany wood. "Be bold," she heard her favorite journalism professor whisper in her left ear. "You dropped my name when you met the Hansens. Don't embarrass me," she heard Lavinia whisper in her right.

Venturing upstairs might be construed as an invasion of privacy. She turned to go, but glanced one more time at the staircase and the landing above.

Movement caught her eye. A person—dressed in khaki trousers and an oversize, rusty black jacket, their head of bushy gray curls bobbing—walked briskly along the mezzanine and disappeared into an open door. Mara swallowed, her heart pounding in her ears. She couldn't be sure from this distance and angle, but she could have sworn she'd spotted Alan Skacel, the missing art gallery owner.

She took out her phone and scrolled through her screenshots. She knew she had saved a photo of him… there. Yes, that shock of gray hair was distinctive. Not quite Albert Einstein, but close.

She was halfway up the stairs before she was aware she had moved. Oh, well. Score one for being bold. She hoped Lavinia would forgive her if necessary.

The man had disappeared into the second doorway

on the left. Mara entered and found herself in what looked like another library. Only unlike the grand showcase of the room below, this library was human-sized and lived-in. An imposing dark wood pedestal desk dominated the room, papers stacked and sliding in various haphazard piles. Tall bookcases that matched the desk in color and ornateness lined two of the four walls, stuffed with books and photographs and small decorative pieces. Two large wing chairs covered in floral brocade flanked the fireplace on the third wall, and the floor was covered by what Mara recognized from visiting Lavinia's parents as an authentic, antique Aubusson rug. She almost didn't want to walk on it.

Between two of the bookcases on the opposite wall was another door, this one closed. Mara could hear voices. Male voices, muffled by the closed door, so the words were indistinct. Still, if she were in Vegas she'd take the odds that she had found both Niels and the person who resembled Skacel.

She crept closer. Eavesdropping wasn't polite, of course, and she would definitely disgrace Lavinia if she were to be found with her ear pressed to the door, but she sidled up close and listened as hard as she could, nonetheless. But the door was even thicker than it seemed at first—a good solid chunk of wood. The only silver lining was that if she couldn't hear them, speaking at a normal and, at times, louder register, then whoever was on the other side couldn't hear her breaths, which to her ears sounded raspier than an old car with a faulty muffler.

She pulled her hair away from her ear and pressed up against the door. "…onday," she was able to make out. And "…ant my mone…" There was the sound of something hard crashing to the floor—she winced at the noise—and the muffled shouts of two people arguing.

She put her hand on the doorknob and turned, ever so gently, but the knob didn't budge. Locked. Looked like she wasn't getting inside the room where it was happening. The only alternative appeared to be waiting for the two to finish their discussion and approaching them as they exited. Might as well settle in. She sat down on one of the chairs by the fireplace for the duration and hoped no one would miss her presence at the gathering below.

The chair's upholstery was scratchy against the back of her bare legs, the cushions firm—too firm for comfort. The chair was obviously meant for decoration, not for sitting for long periods. She didn't want to drain her phone's battery, so all she had for entertainment was watching the minutes tick by on the grandfather clock in the corner as her legs grew numb. The room was warm and dark and quiet, and her eyelids started to droop—

A silhouetted figure appeared in the arched doorway to the mezzanine.

She jumped, her heart beating in her throat as her brain scrambled for answers as to what she was doing. As the figure advanced into the room, she shrank into the chair. Her heart beat in triple time as the silhouette came closer—

Declan. Of course.

She rose from the chair. "What are you doing here?" she hissed.

"What are you doing?" he countered in a normal voice, and she waved her hands in the universal signal to "lower your voice."

"I'm…" The journalistic ethics on snooping without having probable cause to believe a crime or some other danger was imminent were clear. And she wasn't about to tell him she spotted the missing art dealer when she wasn't sure she had spotted him herself. This was not a good look for her. She glanced around the room, hoping for inspiration. "Looking for an unoccupied bathroom."

He raised an eyebrow. "This does not appear to be one."

"Thank you, Captain Obvious. Now, if you'll excuse me, I really do need to find the ba—"

Muffled voices filled the air. Closer. More distinct. As if the people in the other room were moving toward the door. Mara stared at Declan. He stared back, understanding dawning in his gaze and a smirk started to form on his face. "Right. Bathroom. That's the reason why you're here."

She stepped closer to him, keeping her whisper barely audible. "Niels disappeared from the party. I wanted to pin him down for an interview. But when I went to look for him…" She shook her head. "I know you're going to think I'm seeing things, but I swear I saw Alan Skacel and he went into this room."

"Who?"

"Alan Skacel. The missing art dealer?"

The voices were louder. Whoever was on the other side of the room was right in front of the door.

"And you think Niels and Skacel are in the next room?"

She nodded her head rapidly. "But we should get out of here—"

The doorknob turned. Too late. Mara stared at Declan. "Would you mind?" she asked rapidly.

"Mind?"

"A repeat."

He nodded. "Sure. A repeat of what?"

The door started to open.

"You said yes. Remember that," she whispered against his lips. Then she kissed him.

Now she knew how she must have felt to him, that night at the party. He was still at first, his lips cool and firm, closed against hers.

Then, he wasn't. Not cool or closed, but hot and open, demanding entrance to her mouth which she willingly gave, sinking into his mouth like coming home after a very long, very lonely journey. The heat rose higher, faster than the kiss of the gala, for they had relearned each other, discovered how to coax sighs and clenched fingers and the desire to be closer—ever closer—from each other. They melted into one another as if they could take their bodies and form one, bigger and better than their individual selves.

She forgot where she was. She forgot why she was there. Niels and Skacel and mysterious paintings and dark web money flew out of her head as if they had never fully occupied it. All she knew, all she could feel, was right there, in her arms, under her fingers, his muscles bunching as she deepened the kiss.

His hands tightened at her waist, pulling her closer, spinning her into him, his hard length pressing against her. They bumped against something solid and a corner dug into her hip. The desk? She didn't know and she didn't care. Something fell to the floor with a crash but she paid the noise no heed as his knowing mouth built the flames higher and higher—

The door slammed and voices filled the room, dragging her back from the drug that was Declan's kiss. She stopped, her eyes flying open to meet his gaze, hooded and dark with dangerous lights glimmering far below the surface. "Follow my lead," he whispered against her lips and tucked her right against him before turning them both to face the newcomers.

Or rather, newcomer. Niels stood in the middle of the room, his arms folded across his chest, his eyebrows raised in question or scorn or both. Mara had a hard time reading his expression, both due to the dim light in the room and the fact that her sense still spun as if she had stepped off a merry-go-round set on high speed.

"Niels," Declan acknowledged. "Do you mind? We were busy."

Niels's eyebrows rose even higher. "I see that. But may I remind you this is my office. It is off-limits to guests."

"Can you blame me for looking for a quieter spot?" Declan indicated Mara as if she were a prize he won. She glared back at him. "I mean, look at her."

"My private office," Niels reiterated.

"Which is how I knew it would be unoccupied," Declan replied. "You and business, not much on speaking terms."

Niels smiled. It wasn't a nice smile. "I must ask you to leave," he said, his gaze never leaving Declan's.

Mara felt like she was another objet d'art for all the notice the men took of her. She cleared her throat and pushed herself away from Declan. "I am so sorry. I had no idea this was your personal space," she said to Niels. "I wanted to see the artworks you mentioned, and Declan offered to show me around. Believe me, I had no idea we would be doing…what we were doing…when I first entered the room."

That was the truth. She had no intention of kissing Declan when the evening started. Absolutely none. She enjoyed having a clear head and meant to keep one.

So much for good intentions. They truly were what paved the path to hell. Because now, when she finally found her bed later that night, she was going to do nothing but cloud her brain by reliving the kiss over and over again. Her vibrator hadn't seen so much action in years.

Niels ceased his battle of the stares with Declan and glanced over at Mara. "I know you are blameless, my dear," he said. "I would be happy to show you around. Perhaps I could give you a tour at another date? I must return to the other guests now."

"I would appreciate that. And while I know you don't want to be on camera, perhaps we could have a discussion on the record, for background purposes only. I'm sure I can learn so much from you and your perspective would be so valuable." She gave him her most blinding smile.

Pouring on the full wattage seemed to work. Niels visibly softened. "Let's have the tour first. And then perhaps we can sit down if you are still interested." He ushered her toward the arched doorway, his hand coming very close to her waist. Declan trailed behind her. "I look forward to our next encounter."

"Same here." The three of them descended the stairs, Niels and Mara walking shoulder to shoulder, Declan a few steps behind. At the bottom of the stairs, Niels turned to Mara. "I will leave you both here. You are welcome to stay and enjoy more of the party," he said to her before turning a glare on Declan, "but as your original escort is leaving, if you wish to depart now, I understand."

"He's my ride," she said with a shrug. "And I have terrible luck with cabs and car services at night."

"Then, until I see you again, *à bientôt*." He kissed her on both cheeks again, and then shook Declan's hand for the briefest amount of time possible.

"Good night," she responded, and then she waited until Niels had disappeared into the next room before her shoulders collapsed and she exhaled an enormous sigh of relief. "That was harrowing."

"Yet you got the next invite and maybe even an interview. Let's get going," Declan pushed the button for the elevator, which arrived almost before the button lit up. They maintained their silence until they were seated in the rear seats of their town car, then he asked the driver to put on a classic rock radio station at medium volume.

"Led Zeppelin?" Mara asked. "At this hour?"

Declan kept his voice pitched low, so only Mara could hear him over the music. "I think you're right."

"Right about what?" She was still riding on the high of getting Niels Hansen to agree to talk to her. Sure, on background, but she could get him to go on record.

"About Alan Skacel."

She spun on the leather seat, not caring her skirt rode up as she searched his gaze. "You saw him? In the library?"

He shook his head. "No. Only Niels entered the room." He smiled, a hint of mischief in the closed set of his lips. "Of course, I was a tiny bit preoccupied. I might have missed something. For a second."

Two could play at this game. "Funny, it didn't feel like a tiny bit—"

His smile turned into a self-satisfied smirk.

She narrowed her gaze at him. "It felt like you were a *lot* preoccupied. I, on the other hand, can confirm I heard one step of footsteps enter the library."

She thought. She wasn't sure. Truthfully, an ambulance siren could have gone off beside her and the pulse of her racing heartbeat against her eardrums as he kissed her would have drowned it out. Not that Declan needed to know that.

His deepening smirk told her he didn't believe her. "Regardless. No, I did not see Skacel. But I found this while you and Niels were talking."

He reached into his suit pocket and pulled out a piece of paper which he offered to her. She took it and, using the flashlight on her phone, did her best to comprehend what it said. "This is a bill of sale. For an unspecified painting." She looked up. "So?"

"Read closer."

She reread the document. "To be delivered to…" She looked up at Declan. "Keith Lochlainn. That doesn't make sense. Why would Niels Hansen have a bill of sale for a painting sold to Lochlainn?"

"Keep going."

She scowled at him, then went back to the document. "Curiouser and curiouser. Why does Niels Hansen have a bill of sale to Keith Lochlainn signed by Skacel?"

"Check the date."

She blinked. "This is after Skacel disappeared."

"Don't know about you but seems interesting to me."

"It does, doesn't it? But—" she folded the paper and placed it in her purse. "—it's only interesting. It's not compelling evidence. It doesn't prove that was Skacel at the party tonight. Just that somehow Niels ended up with this document."

"And that somehow they are connected to Keith Lochlainn." He raised his eyebrows at her.

"Then what's the next step? Crash the home of the billionaire mogul who owns LNT and rifle through his art collection? That spells career longevity."

"What if you don't have to crash?"

"You are so buddy-buddy with Keith Lochlainn you can waltz into his home like a long-lost relative at any time?"

A shadow flashed across Declan's expression, so fleeting that if Mara had blinked she would have missed it. "No, I can't walk in," he said. "But we can go to the dedication of the new Jamie Lochlainn wing at the Museum of Contemporary Culture."

"Oh, right. That's the memorial Keith Lochlainn chose when Jamie was declared legally dead. And let me guess. You have an invite." Mara yawned, the adrenaline of the last hour draining and leaving her boneless. "You never did tell me how you got your position at LNT. Is it because you remind them of Jamie when he was alive? You have similar styles as journalists now that I think about it. Similar tastes in stories. You're both drawn to bleeding hearts, 'change the corrupt system' type of subjects."

That dark shadow dimmed Declan's gaze again, lingering perhaps a beat longer. And she wasn't imagining his stillness, his usually kinetic energy tamped down on low. She frowned. "Are you okay?"

He cleared his throat, shaking his head. "Sorry." His voice was rougher than usual. "Got something stuck in my throat. And no, I don't think that's the reason." He coughed, a dry sound that underscored his throat was irritated.

Mara pulled down the bulky armrest between her and Declan and exposed the compartment behind. The cars provided by LNT for their staff and on-air talent were usually stocked with water and breath mints, necessities for attending meetings or conducting interviews. Her eyebrows nearly hit her hairline when she saw what the compartment contained. This car had been supplied for someone who required stronger stuff. She pulled out two airline-sized bottles of whiskey and then folded the armrest back up.

She held up the bottles so Declan could see. "No water, but I found these. And no glasses. I think we're supposed to swig."

He snorted. "Do you know whose car this normally is? George Reynolds."

"No! Really?" Reynolds was LNT's legendary long-running six o'clock news anchor. "Will he mind us drinking his alcohol?"

"He's not going to say anything. Check your contract. No alcohol on LNT property, and that includes the company cars."

"Journalists with no alcohol? That's an oxymoron."

"There was an…incident…a few years ago. Involving Reynolds, by the way. Among others."

"Obviously he learned his lesson. And by obviously I mean he didn't." She unscrewed the top off one bottle and handed it to Declan, then opened the second bottle for herself. "Here's to a successful evening." The straight whiskey left flames behind as it slid down her throat. "Thank you for the repeat. Niels would have caught me in the library and my excuse wouldn't have been anywhere near as convincing without you there."

He smiled. Not the smirk from before, but a real smile. Sincere. Warm. Her heart started to beat a little faster. She told herself the cause was the alcohol. For all that she had just joked about journalists and their reputation for being heavy drinkers, she mostly stuck to beer and wine, and even then that was occasionally. "Happy to help. Good instincts, but then you've always had them. You're amazing, always have been."

Her chest burned, and that wasn't the whiskey. "That's kind of you," she managed to choke out, her gaze fixed on the bare trees lining the sidewalk, counting the minutes until she could get out of a confined space with him and into her small studio apartment, where she could deal with the conflicting, visceral emotions his words raised. "Considering I launched myself at you without really getting your consent. Hope you don't regret saying yes."

"You can kiss me whenever you like, Schuyler."

His words were teasing, but his tone…his tone was raw. Sincere. Authentic. She whipped her head around to catch his gaze and inhaled a deep, shuddering breath.

His expression was still, his eyes dark and unreadable. Not banter, then. She could not tear her gaze away. Her pulse began a syncopated dance, a samba, heady yet hesitant. "Did you mean it?" she whispered into the quiet, broken only by the muffled hum of the car's engine.

"Which part?" he rumbled. "But the answer is yes. All of it."

"The part about how good I am. That you've always thought that."

"You blow me away, Schuyler."

"I do?"

Her hand was next to his on the smooth leather seat. He picked it up in his, his grasp warm and sure. She inhaled at the slide of his skin against hers, the sparks that trailed alongside it.

"My breath, gone," he continued. "From the moment I saw you arguing your point at orientation."

His gaze traced the contours of her face before coming to rest on her lips. Her mouth was suddenly dry and she licked them. The light in his eyes flared, and the desire that had never fully gone dormant since their kiss in the library leapt in answer.

The samba in her veins intensified, the hesitancy gone. She tightened her grip on his fingers as the car turned a corner, swaying in his direction even as he leaned into hers. "I've always been in awe of you," she murmured. "Never could quite believe you were real. I think that's why I hated you at first, so I wouldn't be overwhelmed by awe."

"I never hated you," he said, that hot light now sufficing his entire gaze. "But I never thought—"

The car slowed to a stop, cutting off his words. They must be at her building. She assumed, because she wasn't looking away from him now. "You never thought?"

His smile was slow, sure. Her stomach tensed with

a delicious fluttering of a thousand wings. "That you would agree to come to my apartment that night," he said. "And stay." Her breathing sped up, but she couldn't get enough oxygen into her system. "Mara, I—"

The driver opened her door, cutting off whatever Declan was going to say. She blinked, the rush of cold night air entering their formerly small, contained space acted like a bucket of water thrown on simmering embers. Right. This was Declan being charming again. It didn't mean anything.

She cleared her throat. "This is me. I should go."

She exited the car, the weight of Declan's gaze heavy on her back. She walked toward her building—one step, two steps—aware the closer she got to her apartment, the more things would stay the same, the more they would dance around their past in the hopes of not jeopardizing the present and possibly ruining the future.

But how could there be a future—much less a present—if they never dealt with the past?

She paused. She wasn't looking forward to another bout of sleeplessness, parsing every second of their kiss, examining every minute action or reaction from him for meaning and portents. She'd spent too much of her time since she arrived in New York City going over the same well-worn territory. To the point that her sister-in-law was threatening to make her give her a dollar every time his name came up on their phone calls. "One of us might as well get something valuable out of this," she'd said with a grin in her voice.

Plus, her vibrator wasn't going to cut it. Not tonight.

Turning on her heels, she walked around the rear of the car to Declan's side and tapped on his window. He rolled the glass down, a puzzled frown on his face. "Everything okay?

"The other part. Did you mean it, too?"

His gaze slightly narrowed in question, but he nodded. "I always mean what I say."

"Good. Because I feel like kissing you." She leaned in through the window and kissed him, openmouthed, hard and wanting. He was still, but only for the space of a sigh exhaled against her lips, and then he was open to her, tasting slightly of whiskey and wholly like him, a taste at once intimately familiar and excitingly new as she replaced her memories with the actuality of Declan now, seven years older, seven years more experienced.

With an effort, she broke contact and stepped back far enough so she could catch his gaze. "What were you about to say?"

"When? Got to tell you, my brain is lacking oxygen right now." He grinned and reached for her.

She leaned back, just beyond the reach of this fingertips, no matter how much she wanted to lean into his touch "When the driver opened the door and cut you off. What were you about to say?"

The humor in his eyes fled. His gaze bore into hers, forceful, with sincerity. "I don't have regrets," he said. "Except one. How we ended."

She should be freezing. She was standing on a

Manhattan street in December—the already cold breeze chilled further by the presence of the East River a few blocks away—in nothing but a thin cocktail dress and the barest minimum of wraps, her legs and arms mostly bare to the elements. But she burned, hot and bright and demanding more, demanding to be consumed entirely. "Because we never did end it, did we? Not properly."

"No."

"Right. As things stand now, I'll never be able to concentrate on the story when I'm around you. And this could be a very big story."

His brow creased. "I'm not sure I follow."

"I need to concentrate. You have the connections I need, but whenever we're together we always end up talking about what happened in college—"

"Talking? Interesting way to define—"

"Fine. Kissing," she agreed. "So, we should…clear the air."

"Clear the air. How?" Now both of his eyebrows were raised.

"By finally getting some closure," she said. "Tonight. Now. That is, if you want."

"Schuyler." He smiled, slow and dangerous. She couldn't suppress her shiver. "Are you inviting me to your place to talk?"

She shook her head. "No. I'm inviting you to my place for sex."

Seven

Kissing Mara was something Declan doubted he would ever tire of, not even if he lived to be one hundred and sixty.

Not that he had romanticized their past. They had been painfully young, still kids in so many ways, still not fully launched into the adult world. College had been a cocoon in which to experiment and try on different methods and ways of being. The seven years since graduation had been real in ways that college hadn't been for him: real obstacles, real challenges, real consequences for his actions.

But there had been one way in which school had painfully prepared him for life as a grown up, and that was the lesson that taught him to live by his morals, because the one time he didn't—the one time he decided to let his values slide and accept something that didn't fully belong to him, didn't do enough to make everything right regardless of the circumstances— made him so incredibly ashamed that he couldn't face Mara. Losing her was his penance, one he had been prepared to pay for the rest of this life. Getting her the job at LNT was the least he could do to begin leveling the playing field, only to discover the adult Mara exceeded everything he thought she would be and more. He meant it when he said she blew him away from their first meeting, but she knocked him head over his ass now.

And her last words stole his breath…while other parts of him were coming to hard, almost painful life.

"Sex," he repeated.

Her hands landed on her hips. Her curvy, soft hips to which the silk of her dress clung. He had his reasons for hanging back when he, Mara and Niels descended the stairs. He wasn't ashamed to admit that watching her hips sway as she moved was one of them. "Is that such a terrible offer?" she demanded.

"Terrible? No." He'd wanted to run his hands over that dress all night. Bunch the skirt at her waist, find out if the skin of her inner thigh was still silkier than the fabric. He shifted in his seat. "But have you thought—"

"Have I thought this through? Yes." She nodded. Then she shook her head. "No. Maybe. Look, I know this might make things more awkward. But truthfully, can they get any more awkward? We've been to two events and both times we ended up, well, kissing. And I need you to take me to the dedication of the museum wing next week, and I need a clear head while I'm there. Therefore, logically we should—"

She stopped as he opened his door and unfolded himself to stand next to her. So close that he could see the tiny bumps on her arms raised by the cold night breeze.

Or maybe something else.

The anticipation hanging heavy and sharp between them, the air almost visibly pulsating with static electricity, caused the hairs on his arms to rise as well.

"Didn't mean to interrupt you," he said. "We should what?"

"We should…" She swallowed. "Release the tension. So we can concentrate on our work."

"That's what this is? Tension?"

She moistened her lips, her tongue tracing a sensuous path. He called on his willpower reserves, resisting the demanding urge to replace her tongue with his, to feel those plump, pink lips under his. "Yes," she said. "Something physical we need to get out of our systems. A one and done."

He regarded her. She met his gaze, her chin held high, but he could see the slight wobble in her posture, her hands shaking in tiny quakes.

Growing up, Declan had seen old cartoons where Bugs Bunny or Mickey Mouse or whoever was caught on the horns of a moral dilemma, with an animated angel sitting on one shoulder and whispering "Don't do it!" while an animated devil sat on the other shoulder, telling the hero to go for broke. He never really grasped that visual metaphor until this very minute. Because he should listen to his inner angel. He should tell Mara kindly but firmly that sleeping together wouldn't resolve anything, certainly not the sexual tension that filled every molecule of air between them.

But his inner devil's whispers were seductive, tempting him with the promise of his most reliable fantasy of the last seven years come to life. Mara, naked and warm, her eyes heavy with desire, her legs wrapped around him. His to touch and caress and kiss and stroke until she fell apart in his arms, his name a screamed whisper on her lips.

Maybe she was right. Maybe this pull they exerted on each other would be lessened if they had sex. Maybe the force that kept bringing them together was merely curiosity. The natural response to seeing each other after all these years. It was inevitable sparks would fly.

Especially since the fire never had a chance to extinguish naturally.

"Well?" She raised her chin higher. "Offer is only good for tonight. You can take it," and she swept her arm, indicating herself. "All of it. Or leave it. And I'll find someone else who can get me into the Lochlainn event." She half smiled, half smirked, with a glint of mischief in her gaze that acted on his blood like a match touching gasoline. "Maybe Niels would like to escort me."

She fought dirty. He flicked his inner angel off his shoulder. Besides, he would be leaving LNT as soon as Mara was firmly established—if not sooner. His conversation with Bobbi echoed in his ears. There would be no harm, no foul, no lasting repercussions for either of them this time. They were going into this with eyes open.

And hearts closed.

"One time only, Schuyler," he growled, and closed half the distance between them, the air practically crackling.

Her eyes widened, but she stood her ground. "One time. And we never talk of it again. So you better make it count, Treharne." She closed the remaining distance between them. "Of course, I could always use a new 'worst sex ever' story to amuse my friends. Either way."

He laughed. Sex with Mara had been far from the worst, and they had been much younger then. "Hold that thought," he said, and he stepped away to have a quick word with the driver. When the car sped away, he returned to Mara and pulled her tight against him. She let a soft yelp of surprise escape her, but then relaxed against him, her arms coming up to entwine around his neck, her soft curves short circuiting his ability to think. One thing was clear: whatever he wanted to give, she would willingly take and give back equally, if not more.

"Let's see where we land on the scale of worst to best," he said against her lips, and then he kissed her, hard and hot and openmouthed.

Somehow they made it into her building, Mara fumbling for her keys and turning the lock without ever losing contact, not that his grip on her would let her go very far. Somehow they made it up the four flights of stairs to her fifth-floor walk-up, Declan taking advantage of each landing to press her against the stairwell wall and devour her mouth and her neck, swallowing her gasps, keeping her hands locked in his because she had a very disconcerting and highly welcome tendency to find him, hard and heavy, through the fabric of his suit trousers. They might have remained in the stairwell if one of her neighbors didn't descend the stairs with full trash bags, calling out lewd encouragement as he passed them.

Once inside Mara's apartment, she seemed to gain inhibitions she previously didn't exhibit, even though they were safe from any prying eyes. She pulled her mouth from his and started to make apologies for the size of her studio apartment.

He didn't give a damn. What mattered to him was the bed at the far end of the space—a white cloud piled high with pillows—and a memory long suppressed came flooding back: Mara in her shared dorm room freshman year, her twin bed a smaller version of this one, laughing at something her roommate said with her head thrown back and her cheeks flushed and those glorious red curls contrasting with the bedding.

If he had been able to be honest with himself then, he would have admitted that was when he first fell in love—

Love?

Mara blinked up at him and then followed the line

of his gaze to the bed. "I swear, the bedding is clean. I—okay, not that I thought this would be happening, or may be happening, but Fridays are my day to change my sheets. It's a habit I've gotten into, but if you want to go somewhere else, I'll understand. I know my place probably isn't what you're used to, especially after we just came from the Hansen penthouse—"

He shook his head to clear it, to bring his thoughts back to the here and now and the amazing woman in his arms. "I think," he said, backing her up deeper into her apartment until her legs hit the edge of her bed, "we both need to stop thinking." He kissed her again, his hands finding the curve of her waist, the soft globes of her ass, the elegant line of her spine.

She sighed and swayed into him, slightly stumbling, going limp in his arms as if trusting him to be the only reason why she was still upright. Then she yelped in surprise as he let go and she fell backward onto her bed, her legs bent and her feet on the ground. Before she could recover, he was on his knees, his hands running up the length of her calves, her thighs, persuading her to open for him, his hands finally free to push the silk of her dress up, up, up until she raised her arms and the garment slipped off.

Then it was his turn to gasp, a sharp inhale of breath, at seeing her exposed before him, only the tiniest, sheerest scrap of black lace covering her mound.

Mara raised herself on her elbows, her voice thick

and slurred. "Please don't tear my panties, they cost more than my monthly grocery bill—oh!"

He kissed her inner thigh, once, twice, ten times, sucking and tasting and licking, moving ever higher to the most sensitive area of hers. "I won't," he said, his voice matching hers, and he pushed the scrap of lace to the side. One hand splayed on the warm silk across her belly as he brushed the thumb of his other hand over her stiff nub beneath. She jerked under his palm. A sharply inhaled hiss at his touch.

She was so warm and wet and welcoming, her legs falling more open as he replaced his fingers with his mouth, tracing concentric circles around her sex and then delving into her opening, always paying careful, detailed attention to her clit, testing anew if she preferred featherlight strokes or more pressure. Mara didn't hesitate to let him know if his guesses were correct or wrong, her hand coming down to guide him to her favorite spot, her fingers urging him to faster or slower rhythms.

He became even harder, a feat previously thought impossible, as her hand stroked her clit as he teased her opening, her participation in her own pleasure heightening his. Then her hand fell to the side, her trembling legs beginning to stiffen, and he knew she was close.

He'd missed her. He hadn't realized how much until now—had kept himself too preoccupied, too busy for the last seven years to have space to contemplate what was missing from his life—but now he knew she was etched on his soul on an elemental level, as integral to him as water to drink or fire to keep warm. He slowed his ministrations, wanting the moment to last, wanting this time to never end.

She opened one angry eye. "I'm going to commit bodily damage if you don't go back to what you were doing," she said, her hips bucking against his hands, seeking the pressure she needed.

"I look forward to seeing what damage you can do," he said, and then sucked her into his mouth, laving her clit, tasting anew the sweetness that was Mara and Mara alone.

She screamed his name as she shuddered hard against him, and no sound had ever sounded better to his ears. He stayed where he was, reveling in her scent, her hot wetness, the knowledge he had caused her to fall to pieces, gentling his movements to match her slowing breathing.

When she started to emit tiny, breathy snores, he rose from his position, staring down at her. For the rest of his life, he would carry the impression of a sleeping, sated Mara, her limbs outstretched like a star, her skin pink and flushed, her red hair tousled and tossed. But when he would move away from the bed and leave her to her slumbers, a surprisingly strong grip on his arm stopped him.

"Oh, no, you don't," she said, blinking until the sleepiness disappeared to be replaced by bright mischief. Bright, somewhat evil mischief. She tugged at him until he lay beside her on the bed. Then she rose to her knees and looked down at him. "You're outrageously overdressed," she said. "Shy in your old age?"

"Ha. You know that's not true. Or should I go down on you again?" He rose on his elbows to grin at her.

"Nuh-uh," she said, pushing him back and straddling him before he could react.

There were erotic fantasies, and then there was a nude Mara Schuyler looking down on him, her beautiful rose-tipped breasts within easy reach, and he turned thought to action, reaching with his hands to bring her hard against him.

"Nuh-uh," she said again, and had his hands in hers and over his head before his surprised muscles could react. "Now. I could leave the bed and try to find my restraints, but I'm afraid this—"she rolled her core over the erection straining against his trousers "—might not like being left waiting. Or you could exercise that self-control of yours and grab onto my headboard until I tell you to let go."

"You own restraints?" His mind short-circuited with the images her words conjured.

"It's been seven years, Treharne. I like to keep up with the trends," she husked in his ear, the diamond-solid peaks of her breasts brushing against his shirt fabric. She guided his fingers to the metal bars of her Victorian-inspired bedframe. "You can let go when you want, of course." Mara started to kiss her way from his ear to his jaw, unbuttoning his shirt as she went. Then her mouth was on his throat, his own hard nipples, his belly, her knowing fingers following in her lips' wake to caress and tease until his skin was nothing but aching nerves.

Her hands found the zipper of his fly and pulled

the tab down one metal tooth at time. His hips bucked and she placed her warm hand on his belly, holding him down. The look of pure satisfied power on her face almost sent him over the edge. Finally, his erection was freed and her soft gasp when he was finally bare to her sight made him feel pretty damn powerful, too.

"It's always nice when the reality is better than the memory," she said, her voice thick with an emotion he couldn't identify. Before he could ask her if she was okay, her mouth was on him and he forgot his own name. His universe narrowed to the hot, wet welcome he found, the sensations almost an unbearable pleasure-pain, as she learned him anew with her lips and tongue and gentle scrapes of her teeth.

"Mara," he panted, his eyes screwed shut, his hands gripping her headboard with all his strength, "if you're not careful—"

"I've got you," she said. She gave him one last tug with her mouth and then he heard the rip of a packet, followed by her fingers rolling the condom down his length. Her hand positioned him at her entrance and he opened his eyes so he could watch her sink down on him, her head tossed back to expose her throat, her chest rising and falling rapidly, her eyes wide with surprise and pleasure and something unreadable in their depths as he filled her. "Okay, let go," she breathed, her voice thick, and his hands flew up to hold her, to guide her, as she moved above him and he rose up to meet her.

When he came, he saw stars. And moons. An entire milky way as vast and as awe-inspiring as Mara. And as his vision cleared and his eyes met and tangled with her own passion-sated gaze, he saw home.

Eight

Sunlight tickled Declan's eyelids, the unfamiliar sensation teasing him awake. He normally slept with blackout curtains, a trick he learned when working on stories around the clock, to fool his brain into falling asleep no matter the actual hour, so waking up to anything but dark shadows was disorienting. He blinked…

And then he remembered.

He had to kick his left foot free from the tangle of the sheets. The bed resembled a battlefield in which the two sides reached a most agreeable compromise after several rounds of intense skirmishing to determine who would end up on top. Mara was curled up on her side, facing away from him. The rays streaming through the filmy white curtains turned her hair into a red-gold cloud of tangles. The pale expanse of her shoulders and back presented a strong temptation to trace the knobs of her spine, kissing his way as he discovered and named galaxies of freckles.

He loved her skin in all its variations. The soft smoothness of her inner thighs. The callous on the third finger of her right hand from the wholly unique way she held writing instruments. The slight crinkles beginning to form at the corners of her eyes, a testament to her amazing, mobile expression and constant smile.

She needed her rest. So did he, come to think of it. He always wondered why sex was referred to as "sleeping together" when, in his experience and especially where Mara was concerned, there was very little sleeping involved. But he couldn't resist reaching out to run a finger down her back. She sighed and stirred, and he held himself up on one elbow to watch her eyelashes flutter. Then her eyes firmly closed and her delightful snores—more like rusty squeaks than a log being sawed—filled the air.

He found a pillow on the floor where it had been tossed/kicked/thrown—he didn't remember which—and punched it back into shape, intending to join her in slumber, when a buzzing noise jolted him wide awake.

A phone—set to vibrate instead of ring. Like his. And the noise was coming from the corner of the room, where his pants were currently sprawled after she finally removed them.

He was conditioned to jump when a call came in. A

source, a lead, a tip. If he didn't answer, he might lose out on the story of the century. But it was early Saturday morning, he wasn't on the tail of a story—well, not his story—and he wasn't on staff at the *Globe*. There could be a fire that needed to be put out at LNT, but he had very capable lieutenants and he couldn't think of anyone who would need him on the weekend.

A weekend he was beginning in Mara's bed, and he wasn't exiting his current situation for anyone. Besides, voice mail was invented for exactly this reason. The buzzing stopped and he closed his eyes.

The vibrations started again. Whoever was trying to reach him wasn't giving up easy. He muttered curses under his breath and retrieved his phone. If the caller was an LNT employee, they'd better have a very good reason to call or an ironclad contract if they didn't want to find themselves looking for a new gig. At least the noise didn't disturb Mara. She still slept, her mouth slightly open, an arm now flung over her eyes to block out the sunlight.

He'd never seen her look so delicious.

Then he glanced at the phone screen, at the caller's name, and all thoughts of sleep fled.

Mara's eyes fluttered open. She hadn't slept that hard or this long into the morning since... Since forever. She stretched, her muscles protesting in all sorts of new and rather wonderful ways, and for a second she wondered why—

Declan. She turned her head and the space next to her was empty, although there was evidence someone

had been there recently. The sheets bore a vaguely hu-
man-shaped impression, but more than that, they bore
his scent. She inhaled deeply before raising herself up
on one elbow and scanning her tiny apartment. Nope.
No sign of him. His clothes were no longer tossed to
the furthest walls and he apparently even managed
to find his shoes—she had a vague memory of someone's footwear flying into her kitchenette sink but it
turned out those had been hers.

Oh, well. She tried not to be disappointed. It was
probably for the best he left. They'd only promised
each other one night and while she doubted the vivid
memories created in the last eight hours or so would
ever fade for her, better to not face him in the cold
hard light of day and see regret—or worse, disappointment or pity—in his gaze. Seeing pity might
literally dissolve her into sand.

A key sounded at her front door. She scrambled to
clutch bedsheets to her bare chest, frantically trying
to remember where she had stored her pepper spray,
a gift from her brother when she announced she was
moving to Manhattan. Who could possibly have a
key and use it on a Saturday—

"I have pastries for you and bagels for me," she
heard Declan announce as he entered, her ring of keys
dangling from his left hand. "And coffee." He smiled
when he caught her gaze. "Hope you don't mind. I
borrowed your keys. Didn't want to leave your door
unlocked while you were sleeping."

"I never kick out a person who brings pastries
to my apartment. Even when I originally thought

they were breaking in." She let the sheets fall as she stretched her arms overhead, aware the movement showed off her breasts to their best advantage, and was gratified by his quick inhale of breath. But when she would expect him to approach her—maybe even join her, naked and warm and willing on the bed—he stayed where he was, then moved only to drop the bag and tray of coffee on the small table that pulled double duty as her desk and place to dine. She frowned at him as she reached for the blanket that had fallen to the floor and pulled it tight around her shoulders. The room had taken a chilly turn, and the change in temperature was only partially due to him letting in air from the outside. "You've got something on your mind."

"Do you still take two sugars in your coffee?" He concentrated on opening packets, neatly avoiding her gaze.

"Yes." She accepted the cup he handed her, but put it down on her bedside table, pressing her lips together tightly. It seemed there would be no repeat of last night. And that's what she wanted, right? He'd agreed to her terms. She should appreciate that he was a man of his word. "You can leave, y'know. The breakfast is great, don't get me wrong. But there's no need to do that awkward morning-after dance you do. After all, the sooner you leave, the sooner I can shower, which honestly sounds better than caffeine right now."

He half smiled, half grimaced. "That's not what I'm doing—"

"Maybe someone who doesn't recall you doing a very similar move seven years ago might be fooled, but not me." She tried to fully smile back, but she was pretty sure her expression matched his. "We said one night, we had one night—"

"A great night—" he started.

"Agreed." She cut him off. "Don't worry, last night will not come up when I'm asked to share my 'worst sex ever' stories."

"Wasn't worried, but thanks for the reassurance." He sat down on the other side of the bed. "This isn't seven years ago—"

"I know. I own restraints now. Even if I can't find them." By sheer force of will, her smile did not tremble. "So, we don't need to do this."

"Mara—" he started.

"We banged. It's out of our systems. We can now go about our lives as usual." She made a shooing motion with her hands. "I'll see you on Monday."

He regarded her through narrowed eyes. Then, finally, as if coming to an agreement with himself, he nodded. "If that's what you want."

"We were curious. Now we're not. It's just sex, Treharne. You're still taking me to the Lochlainn event, right?"

He stood up. Was it her imagination or a trick of the light that made his face suddenly seem ghostly pale? "About that. Listen, something—"

"Oh, no. No, you don't." Mara scrambled out of bed and wrapped the blanket around her like a makeshift toga. "You are not getting out of taking me."

"I'm not trying to. But there may not be an event." He walked to the table and opened the bag. "Pastry? I recall you prefer cherry strudel. No matter how cliché."

"Cherry strudel is the one true pastry. The rest are pale pretenders." Still, she wasn't going to be put off by food, even if the bag did come from her favorite local bakery. "What do you mean? Why won't the event take place?"

He opened a small container of cream cheese and began spreading it on a bagel. "Keith Lochlainn is in the hospital."

"Really?" She grabbed her phone and started scrolling through her social media accounts. "There's nothing on my feeds. Did someone at LNT tell you?"

"No, I—yes. Yes. Someone from the Lochlainn Company called."

"Is it serious?"

He shook his head. "A precaution. Or so they told me."

"Glad to hear it." She squinted at him. If she wasn't mistaken, that was the third time he'd put cream cheese on that bagel half. Either he really liked a healthy portion, or he was avoiding looking at her.

Interesting. This was turning into a pattern whenever the Lochlainns were mentioned.

Of course, Keith Lochlainn was the big boss. Declan wasn't one of his direct reports, but it made sense any employee of a Lochlainn business entity would be affected by news of Keith's hospitalization. But why was Declan specifically informed? The news wasn't public yet. Why did he need to know?

On the other hand, he was an executive with the news division, perhaps he needed to be standing by in case the "precaution" took a turn for the worse and some sort of tribute or obituary would need to be aired. But even as the thoughts formed, she rejected them. That was a decision for someone higher up the food chain to make, not him.

Something wasn't adding up. And that something started with the way Declan was currently avoiding her. She sipped her coffee, her brain chasing the puzzle.

"You seem far away," he said, his gaze finally meeting hers.

"I'm wondering why you rate a call from the Lochlainn Company."

"Why wouldn't I rate one?"

"Well, you're *you*, so of course you rate a call as a journalist, but at LNT you're just a producer—"

"Executive producer—"

"Right, but you're not the president of LNT or the executive in charge of news so…why?"

"Why not?" He bit into his bagel.

"I don't know, I…" She started to laugh. "You have cream cheese on your nose."

He rubbed the back of his hand across his nose. The cream cheese spread farther.

"Here, let me." She grabbed one of the thin paper napkins and dabbed at the offending spot. "There." She took a half step back to admire her handiwork, and her heart twinged—a painful pinch. He was so handsome. And he wasn't attractive because of the symmetry of his features or his chiseled bone structure, but because of his soul, for lack of a better word. The light that shone in his eyes when he was excited or interested, the slow smile that she could swear was just for her.

Like the smile he had now. Intimate, warm. Pure sex.

She was very aware she wore nothing but a blanket haphazardly wrapped around her. And the glint in his eyes told her he was very aware of her attire, too. The rush of hot moisture between her legs nearly made her knees buckle.

"Mara," he breathed, and she knew she was being weak, she knew she would regret doing so, but she swayed in his direction, her hands coming to rest on his chest. His firm, warm chest.

"Yes?" she said, her tone matching his.

"You have some cream cheese…" He motioned to the corner of his mouth.

"I do?" She reached up but didn't feel anything.

"Here," he said, and his thumb rubbed ever so softly over her lower lip, his gaze locked on hers. She inhaled sharply at his touch, the aching pressure building in her core—

Wait. She ate a cherry strudel, not a bagel. She smiled at him and leaned back, so that her hand could find the cream cheese container. She used her index finger to take a swipe and then, before he could react, she smeared the cream cheese across his upper lip. "Whoops. Looks like I didn't get all of it."

"You better get on that," he said, his thumb moving to the corner of her mouth, the curve of her jaw.

"Yeah, maybe I should," she said, and then she leaned up and kissed him, her tongue sweeping all evidence away before he pulled her to him and all thought of engaging in more food related pranks fled.

Forget breakfast. She hungered for only one thing and that was Declan. And judging by his hard length pressing against her, he had similar ideas. She tore her mouth from his. "One night. No more. And never to be discussed after."

He let his hands fall. She instantly regretted her words as his grip had been doing more to keep her upright than her own legs. "Right. Sorry, I—"

"But we didn't discuss the fine print."

"You want to discuss fine print?"

"We're not supposed to talk about sex after. So yes, now. To ensure all parties are on the same evidentiary page and all obligations are outlined."

His smile returned. "Wasn't aware you got a legal degree in the last seven years."

"They put me on the consumer affairs beat at the station," she said. "Anyway, 'night' was never defined. One could argue that a night is half a day, which makes it twelve hours long, and since we got back to my place at midnight, that means—"

"We have two and a half hours left." His arms wrapped around her and drew her right for a kiss so hard and deep she forgot her name. He broke off long enough to whisper, "That argument wouldn't stand up in court. But I accept the fine print." His left hand drew patterns on her spine, teasing swoops and swirls that caused her to shiver and laugh.

"What are you doing?"

"Signing my name on the dotted line," he responded, then covered her mouth with his again, his fingers traveling to explore the skin of her hip before cupping her ass and bringing her up hard against the proof he was more than ready to continue their "night."

She was so sensitive, craving him so much that when he slipped a hand between them to whisper over her mound, slipping his index finger inside her for the barest of touches to see if she was as ready as he was, she almost came.

But she didn't want to. She had clawed back two and a half hours more with Declan and she wanted to make them count, not be dissolved in a boneless heap of pleasure for most of the time. And if she only had this time, then she was determined to use it to know him fully, storing up memories like so many hoarded jewels to be taken out and examined long into the future. Memories of him that, no matter where their lives might take them, would belong only to her.

"What was that you were saying about a bath?" he said into her neck, his hands now knowing how to roll and tweak her nipples, how much pressure to apply and when to back off, so that she nearly wept with pleasure.

"There's no way two of us are fitting in my shower," she gasped.

"Tsk-tsk." He clicked his tongue. "Where there's a will, there's a way." Kissing her the entire time, he guided her to her tiny bathroom, with its child-sized tub and handheld shower bracketed to the wall.

"See?" she said. "Let's go back to the bed." She used their time standing to undress him anew until they both stood nude, his skin warm and golden to her flushed and freckled pinkness.

He grinned at her and turned around until they both faced her mirror, which ran the length of the room. "I think we should stay here," he said, stroking her skin as he held her gaze in the mirror. His hand came up to cup her breast before dipping between her legs. His erection pressed against the globes of her ass and she bit her lip as the Mara in the mirror bit hers.

He cupped her mound and the Mara in the mirror jumped, then relaxed into his touch. She started to close her eyes, the better to give herself over to the sensation his fingers created, but he tugged on her hair. "Watch," he said. "Watch yourself come apart." He pressed deeper inside her, finding just the right spot, caressing and retreating and caressing again. "Watch," he said again, his gaze never leaving hers, and she almost cried with how vulnerable she was— open not only to his sight but to her own—and yet how incredibly powerful she felt, watching him watching her in the mirror. He added a second finger and his thumb found her clit, circling and pressing until she couldn't take any more—

"Eyes open," he demanded. But she didn't watch herself. She found his gaze and held it as she flew apart in his arms, allowing another person—allowing him—to see her bared soul for the first time ever.

It wasn't until they were back in her bed, boneless and breathless and falling asleep, that she remembered he never did answer her question about why the Lochlainn Company called him about Keith.

The next time Mara woke up, the clock read one o'clock. Their night was well and truly over.

Declan's side was empty, any warmth he'd left behind long gone. There was a note on his pillow, however. His scrawled handwriting read simply, "See you on Monday."

She crumpled the piece of paper up, and then thought better of her actions and smoothed the note out. This wasn't seven years ago. She'd used her words like a big person and asked him for sex. And he, like an adult, respected the boundaries she set.

No one told her how much being a grown up could hurt.

Nine

Bobbi would not stop calling. Declan sent her latest phone call to voice mail and sat back in his chair in his office at LNT, contemplating his next moves. He didn't know where else to go on a Sunday. He used his apartment mostly for sleeping, showering and changing his clothes. He currently wasn't in the mood to stare at the blank walls he never did get around to decorating. He wasn't a film or television watcher, and his head was too full of Mara, too full of reliving every second he'd spent with her in the last twenty-four hours, to be able to concentrate on reading.

So, work it was. Work was familiar. Work was something within his control.

Leaving Mara's bed was one of the hardest things Declan had ever done, and he included being embedded with a small force that was fighting to liberate their invaded country when the enemy bombarded their position, forcing them to run. Then, he had been fighting for his life. Now he had a feeling he was fighting for something much more important and precious.

But impossible for him to reach. And perhaps, that was the best place for it.

He never tortured himself over things he couldn't obtain. By paying attention solely to what was possible in the present, he avoided remorse over the past and apprehension about the future. His ability to stay in the here and now was, in part, why he was an effective interviewer, keeping his subjects tightly focused on the subject at hand and steering them away from tangents that would derail their conversation.

Until he ran into Cam that fateful day and learned how much he had inadvertently screwed over Mara. Now, his thoughts were occupied more often than not with the past.

With what-might-have-been if he hadn't been so intent on proving Keith Lochlainn wrong, of demonstrating that Keith would be sorry he did not acknowledge Declan was Jamie's biological son. If he hadn't steamrolled his way to the fellowship, failing to ask questions about why the story fell into his lap at that particular time.

And for what? Keith might be dying that very second. Declan destroyed his then relationship with Mara to show up his biological grandfather, only for his grandfather to perhaps pass away without once acknowledging him. The closest he might ever get to being acknowledged as Jamie's son was his position at LNT, a position that came with strings attached and one Declan didn't want for himself in the first place.

But the past was just that. The past. He couldn't go backward, only forward. And dreams…of falling into bed with Mara every night, of sitting across from each other as they composed their stories, of tag teaming heads of state or going into battle zones side by side…were, well, dreams. They weren't reality.

Instead, reality was his phone ringing again. He exhaled before answering. "Yes, Bobbi."

"Do you want these tickets to Paris or what? Speak now or they will forever go to Griff Beachwood."

"Griff— You're not giving the story to Beachwood. This bluff is unworthy of you."

Bobbi sighed through the phone. "We're going to lose the de la Vigny story. *WaPo*, the *Guardian*, *Le Monde*—they're all sniffing. But we're the only ones with the solid lead. And we're the only ones who have you and all your previous work on this story. Or at least, we should have you. You promised if I gave you this leave of absence, you'd come back if the right story surfaced. And this is the right story."

He didn't respond, his gaze staring out of his window and into the office in the building next door. The occupant was doing what she always did at this time of day: concentrating on her computer screen, her fingers flying over her keyboard. Same old, same old. The idea of doing the same thing every workday still made his skin prickle. But then the door to her office opened and another woman appeared, holding the hand of a small child. The office occupant got up from her chair and embraced the newcomer, then knelt and gave the child a hug. Their joy could be felt even where he sat. The child squirmed free and made their way to the window, causing Declan to swiftly swivel his chair so he couldn't be caught observing them.

"Dec? You still there?" Bobbi barked into his ear. "Did you hear me? If you don't hustle your ass into action, we're going to be last in. We'll be scooped by the *Daily Mail.*"

"The *Mail* only cares about the salacious bits. The rest of the story is safe." What was wrong with him? Why wasn't he already on the way to Paris? He lived for this kind of work. Forget blood—this was the substance that kept his heart pumping: running bad actors to ground, exposing their operations and providing so much sunlight they had nowhere else to hide and must face some sort of justice. But—his peripheral vision caught a glimpse of the family in the office across the way preparing to leave together, each woman holding one of the child's hands and swinging the kid between them—maybe one didn't have to live solely for work. Maybe there were other things in the world that could cause his heart to beat as fast.

"Last chance." Bobbi's voice wobbled. And while Declan often forgot she was in her seventies, for the first time she sounded like she would rather be enjoying her retirement than trying to sweet-talk a recalcitrant journalist. "I'd like to be the one to own this story. We've been following it for a long time. You've worked hard on it. But if you can't—"

"If I know Alice at all, she won't talk to the others," he said. "We have some time. I need to stay in New York through the weekend." Bobbi inhaled to speak, and he cut her off. "That's nonnegotiable. Then I'll give my resignation to LNT and arrange to work through my notice period remotely from Paris. In the meantime, I'll share my notes with Beachwood, have him start working on background."

"You better get on that plane," Bobbi said right before she hung up, which Declan knew was her way of saying "thank you."

A week. He bought himself a week to wrap up what he wanted to accomplish at LNT and then turn his duties over to his lieutenants, who, if he were being honest, were doing the bulk of the heavy lifting anyway; he had been lucky and grateful to have been given a team who were all more experienced than he was and who were generous with their time and expert knowledge in putting together the launch schedule for the service. LNT Plus would be in excellent hands and he had no qualms on that front.

With regards to the Lochlainns, however... Leaving early would violate the terms of the challenge handed to him by Keith. Not that Declan was salivating to be included in the old man's will. He didn't need the Lochlainn money.

The one thing he did want was to be acknowledged as Jamie's son, but that had never been part of the LNT offer. Declan had hoped—well, he never really put his hopes into words, not even to himself, but he *supposed*—working for LNT would bring clarity about things he had long wondered about himself. Did he inherit his love of story, and putting puzzle pieces together into a coherent whole, from Jamie? Or his drive to expose and bring down those who would exploit and harm others? Jamie had reported on those same types of stories. But then where did Declan fit in with Keith? Could he have—would he have had—a better relationship with him, considering Jamie had renounced Keith?

If Keith died… Declan rubbed the back of his neck. If Keith died, there went his long-held but never voiced fantasy of bringing reconciliation to the Lochlainn family. Of stepping into the void Jamie left, unable to be Keith's son. Perhaps Declan would claim a true grandson-grandfather relationship.

He never thought he needed a father while growing up. His mother had given him a truly wonderful life, full of amazing experiences and constant exposure to new cultures and ways of thinking. His world had been truly vast.

But when his mother died and he discovered Jamie was his biological father… Well, he supposed it was only natural he wanted to get to know the people whose genes he carried. And wanted them to get to know him.

He picked up a ball made of multicolored rubber bands and began tossing it into the air. He had a mind for investigation. What made a family a family in the first place?

A light came on in the office opposite his and the family hurried back into the room. Apparently the child had forgotten something, for there was much kneeling on the floor and peering under office furniture. Finally, one of the women stood up and raised her arms in victory, a small object in her hand. The other woman picked up the child, who nestled into her shoulder. Their contented happiness was evident even from where Declan sat.

So what if Keith died without acknowledging him, a possibility that now was looming darkly? He didn't need to be a Lochlainn to have a family. He could choose to have a partner, a child, a life outside of work.

His gaze fell on his phone. He picked up the device and swiped to find his list of recent contacts. Mara's name was near the top—

Next to Bobbi's.

He put the phone down. He had commitments he couldn't ignore. Commitments that made the world safer for others. He'd fulfilled his main reason for accepting the challenge to work at LNT: Mara was on the path to career success that should have been hers all along. He had no reason to stay.

He nodded. He would make that plane to Paris.

And there were a million things he had to accomplish before he turned in his resignation. He turned on his computer and opened a new document, resolutely ignoring his phone. Mara made her terms clear. If she wanted to talk, she could call him.

But when he stared at his computer monitor, all he

could see was Mara's gaze holding his in the mirror as he made her come, her need and want for him laid naked and bare before him. Not momentary sexual passion, but her soul, yearning for connction. Yearning for *him*.

As was his for her.

Mara did not see Declan on Monday. Her producer had lined up back-to-back interviews with a gallery owner in SoHo and an art history professor at Columbia for background on Robaire's life and his impact on both the art world and current pop culture. Both interviews were highly informative and full of sound bites that would be very helpful when pulling the edited story together, but both interviews also ran long. By the time Mara returned to the office, Declan had long left for what his assistant vaguely called, "a business thing."

Nor did she see him on Tuesday, Wednesday, Thursday or Friday as their schedules were similarly out of sync. She missed their staff meeting when her subway train broke down. Declan missed their weekly one-on-one check-in when one of the other correspondents angered a senator and Declan was needed to smooth over the relationship. They discussed meeting up at the LNT town hall, a mandatory all-hands gathering of the staff at which the company's goals for next year were presented, but a pipe burst in the apartment next to Mara's and the landlord needed access to her place to check for damage, while Declan had another "pressing engagement come up that couldn't be moved,", according to his assistant. Which meant her first time seeing him would be at the gallery dedication.

He wasn't wholly incommunicado, of course. He texted her several times. About work.

And he called. About work. Maybe the calls would have turned to more personal matters, but they were cut off early because Declan had to take care of a pressing office emergency or Mara was about to sit down and talk to a source.

He didn't mention the hours in her apartment.

But then, neither did she.

Because she was a coward. Because she allowed her to see her deepest depths, but when she next woke up, he was gone. Because she feared that seeing her so nakedly laid bare before him, all pretense that their night was only about sex torn to shreds, had driven him away.

Because she believed being that vulnerable to him would ultimately lead to being hurt and betrayed, and the devastation to her psyche would be even more catastrophic than what happened seven years ago.

By the time Saturday appeared on the calendar, Mara's nerves were strung tight. She threw on her workout clothes and made one of her infrequent trips to the gym, a small, homey space with the bare basics in terms of equipment. The gym didn't have extended hours and that didn't work with her schedule, but she liked the unpretentious atmosphere. It was a place to work out and nothing more.

The speed bag was unoccupied, much to her delight. Hitting something sounded like the perfect match to her mood. She got into her stance, bouncing lightly on the balls of her feet, and settled into a rhythm. Before long, muscle memory took over the repetitive motion and her mind began to wander to the previous Saturday—the exact thing she was hoping to stop by coming to the gym.

Damn it. The whole purpose of sleeping together was to alleviate the tension between them. But that had obviously been a lie. So now, she found herself thinking of him at the most inopportune times, like in the middle of an interview question. The interview would be going swimmingly and then an image of Declan's fingers trailing a path from the underside of her breast to her stomach and beyond would cause her to sputter, her cheeks flushing hot. She'd been able to pass off her sudden lapses in attention as an irritation in her throat requiring a sip of water, which allowed her to regain her composure, but her producer and cameraperson were starting to raise their eyebrows at her when the flashes of memory happened.

Like now.

She hit the bag with more force than she intended.

"Whoa!" Amaranth Thomas, the gym's co-owner and Mara's closest friend in the city, appeared by Mara's side, her dark eyes wide. "Let the bag live to see another day."

"Sorry." Mara stepped away from the speed bag, much to the visible happiness of the young teenager waiting for her to finish her workout. "Lots on my mind."

"Want to talk about it? Or work more of it out?" Amaranth nodded at the boxing ring visible in the next room. "My client just cancelled their training. We can go a few rounds?"

Mara looked at the clock on the gym's wall. She still had many hours to go before she needed to shower and change for the Lochlainn event. "Sure. Give me ten minutes to get ready?"

"Seven," Amaranth responded. "You need as much time as possible in the ring."

"Five," Mara conceded, and ran-walked to the small dressing area where she kept a locker to store her gloves. Hands wrapped, hair pulled back anew, she was ready to go in four minutes.

Amaranth had her blue-tipped locks pulled back in a ponytail—an indication her friend was not going to take pity on her. Mara held up her gloved hands. "Go easy. I have to attend an event tonight."

"Another one? Let me guess—same guy?" Amaranth bobbed on her feet, then threw a straightforward jab that Mara easily slipped. "Is that a problem?"

"Yes to all," Mara said, evading another jab and throwing her own punch. "It's complicated."

"What in life isn't?" Amaranth circled. Mara knew she was looking for chinks in her defense, of which there were many. "Rent is skyrocketing, my kid's best friend is suddenly ghosting him at school and the algorithms are burying this place on review sites. But you pick up and keep up." An intense jab-jab-cross combination had Mara heading toward the ropes.

"I hate to hear Trey is having problems with his

friend," Mara said, somewhat breathless while trying to land her counterattack. "I sympathize. In fact,
the guy in question? He ghosted me for seven years.
Right after I slept with him."

Amaranth's feet stopped moving, but she still
evaded Mara's right and left hook combo. "Okay. This
might be beyond boxing. This might need a drink.
Buy you a smoothie?"

"I thought you'd never ask." Mara climbed out of
the ring, already sore despite the brief bout. She really had to come to the gym more often. Not only
for the physical exercise, but because Amaranth was
one of the few connections she'd made since moving
to New York City. And she was only now realizing
how much she missed having a friend to chat with
in person. Zoom and FaceTime, although godsends
when in person get togethers were impossible, were
not great substitutions for being able to hang out in
three-dimensional space.

Sitting at the juice bar counter over protein shakes,
Mara poured out the entire story of her relationship
with Declan, from their first meeting at college orientation to waking up to a note on her pillow last weekend. Amaranth listened, her calm gaze refusing to
judge until, finally, Mara ran out of words. "What's
tonight?" Amaranth asked. "The event?"

"It's another one of those 'rich people congratulat-
ing themselves on staying rich' things," Mara said.
"The Lochlainn family is dedicating a wing of the
Museum of Contemporary Culture in the name of
Jamie Lochlainn."

"Lochlainn—as in Keith Lochlainn? Isn't he ill?"

Mara nodded. The news hit the media hours after Declan left her apartment. "He was. He's apparently better, so they are going ahead with the dedication, although I'm not sure if he will be there in person."

"And who's Jamie?"

"Keith's son. He disappeared seven years ago and was recently declared legally dead. Jamie was an investigative journalist—a legend, really, despite being relatively young—but his mother was a well-respected artist and Jamie was known as a big supporter of the arts, so I'm assuming that's why Keith chose a museum as a memorial."

"Sounds nice and cultural," Amaranth commented. "So, your problem isn't the event itself."

"Well, sort of." Mara chewed on her smoothie straw. "I'm playing a hunch. And if my hunch is right, this could be a huge story for me. Career-making. But I have no idea if I'm right. Or if the person I need to show up will show up. I'm going off only the flimsiest of evidence, plus my own gut."

"But that's not why you beat up on my poor innocent equipment."

Mara let her head hang forward so her hair, freed from her earlier ponytail, would hide her face. "No."

"So it's the guy."

"It's the guy," she admitted.

"Tell me something." Amaranth leaned her elbows on the counter. "Why does the guy have to be the problem?"

"What do you mean? He's the problem because he's the problem."

"Sure. But why does he have to be?" Amaranth took a contemplative sip. "Seems to me there's really not much of an issue between you two after all."

Mara straightened up. "He ghosted me seven years ago!"

"You told me. But that was a while ago. And he apologized, right?"

"Yes, but—"

"And you've slept with him since, both willing and consenting adults, and from the look on your face it was pretty damn good."

"It was, but—"

"And now you're going to yet another fancy event with him? And he doesn't have to go, right? He's only going because of you?"

"Well, yes, but—"

Amaranth held up a hand. "No buts. Your 'buts' don't work here. Look, I don't know Declan. But in my experience, single men don't get dressed up and go to boring society events with single women just out of some sort of obligation. He wants you. And you want him. So why does this have to be a problem?

Mara sat back on her stool. "He's my boss."

Amaranth opened her mouth, then closed it. "Oh."

"But he told HR we had previously dated, to prevent that from being something someone might try to hold over our heads," Mara rushed to add. "And after the second event, he suggested we sign consensual agreement contracts with HR, in case people thought we were dating." She put her smoothie down. "Huh. Guess he was psychic."

"Or hoping something would happen between the two of you." Amaranth waggled her eyebrows, earning a smirk from Mara. Then Amaranth turned sober. "And are you okay with dating your boss? That's hard because of the power differential. I don't date clients for that reason. Too many things can…go wonky."

Mara puffed air toward her forehead. "We're not dating."

Amaranth raised her eyebrows. "You get dressed up and go out at night, and you've slept together. Is there another definition of dating I'm not familiar with?"

"Maybe the kind of dating where you both agree you are dating?"

Amaranth waved that off. "Technicality. I'll ask again. Why are you making this a problem? You want him, sounds like he wants you, you're squared away with your company—what's the issue? The real one this time."

Mara squeezed her eyes tight. "He might ghost me again."

"Good news—you already know you can survive that one. And you work together. Doubtful it would happen the same way it did before. Next?"

"I don't think… I mean, I…" Mara let her head fall. "I want to win Emmys. I want to win Pulitzers. I want to go on book tours promoting my latest book all about the amazing investigative reporting I did."

Amaranth squinted at her. "Sounds good. What does that have to do with dating him?"

"I don't want to give up my career. Not even for him."

A burst of laughter came from her friend. "What makes you think you have to? Where did that come from?"

"From people I know! Well, people who identify as female. They all met someone, fell in love and gave up their passion to be with the other person."

"I didn't." Amaranth swiveled on her stool and indicated the boxing studio behind them. "I built this place when I was with Trey's dad. Next excuse."

Mara played with the empty straw wrapper. "I'm... afraid."

"Honey, we all are. But it's worth it. Even if it doesn't ultimately work out."

"We...had a moment. An intense moment." Mara shivered at the memory. "But he doesn't do intense. I don't do intense. We haven't really spoken since—"-

"But you'll see him tonight."

"Yes." Mara continued to play with the wrapper.

"At a fancy party with champagne and oysters." Amaranth clicked her tongue. "Still not hearing a problem."

That made Mara chuckle. "Don't know if there will be oysters."

"Then go and get some after. Add some dark chocolate and get your intense on. Problem solved." Amaranth pushed her stool out and slid back. "My next client will be here shortly. You coming to class on Tuesday?"

"I'll do my best to make it."

"Good, because I want to hear all about what happens tonight. The juicy stuff, too." She waggled her eyebrows at Mara and Mara laughed. "See you then."

"You will. And thanks." She stood up to give Amaranth a hug.

"Anytime." Amaranth smiled and then crossed the studio where she met a woman Mara recognized from her previous trips to the gym. She gave them both a wave before returning to her stool and her smoothie.

Was her friend right? Was Mara creating speed bumps in a flat, smooth road? Could she and Declan date—really date? Like lazy Sunday mornings competing to see who could complete the New York Times crossword first, late night discussions over a glass of wine and weekends at her family's farm upstate? Was that what he wanted?

Was that what she wanted?

Gods help her. She was back in love with Declan.

Oh, who was she kidding. She never fully fell out of love with him.

This was awful.

This was wonderful.

This had the potential to either make her the happiest she'd ever been or destroy her.

Ten

Declan arrived at the soon-to-be christened Jamie Lochlainn Gallery at the Museum of Contemporary Culture an hour before the ceremony was supposed to begin. The large, airy space buzzed with noise and bustle as the organizers and their staff ran around making last minute adjustments and ensuring all the details were buttoned down and taken care of. Swag bags were being carefully lined up on tables, tweaks were being made to floral arrangements and a woman with a clipboard and a light meter hurried from spot to spot, speaking with a low but firm voice into her wireless headset, ensuring the art was properly illuminated no matter where one stood. It was an educational glimpse into how much work went on behind the scenes to pull an event like this off and he found himself wishing Mara was with him to share in his observations. But when he received the request to arrive early, he held off asking her to join him and instead arranged to have a car pick her up closer to the ceremony's start time.

Not that he was trying to avoid spending more time with her. On the contrary, the more days that passed where they failed to make a connection, the more the acid in his stomach churned. If this kept up, he'd be looking at his first ulcer before thirty. They needed to talk. And soon. He would be handing in his resignation on Monday, and he didn't want her to be blindsided by the news. He knew he'd made an implicit promise to see her though the art forgery story, but she would be fine. Cliff was an excellent producer, and the piece was shaping up to be the breakout story of LNT's launch week.

In fact, he should have already called her and told her he was leaving. Sent a text. Left a voice mail. But every time he picked up his phone to tell her, he put it back down.

Telling her would make it real. Telling her would mean his time with her was over.

They'd see each other again, no doubt. They would run into each other at award ceremonies and conferences. They might even cover the same stories and find themselves sharing a drink as they discussed sources.

Thinking of that future depressed him. So, he'd hung on to the present as much as he could, doing his best to wrap up his loose ends at LNT while his night with Mara continued to play in his head, capturing more and more of his brain space with each vivid replay.

She was the first thing he thought about when he woke up, and the last image he saw behind his eyelids as he fell asleep. He wanted to know her thoughts: Did she read the front page story in the *Globe* about the latest privacy concerns for social media? What was her reaction to the two-part feature on their rival network ABN about the rising political power of people under the age of twenty? He found himself storing up funny things that happened over the course of the day to share with her later. When he ran into Mads and the author of the novel currently topping the bestseller list while they took a tour around the LNT studio, he broke every rule he had for himself about encountering celebrities and got her to sign an autographed copy for Mara because he knew it was a recent favorite read of hers.

He'd thought he'd have plenty of opportunities to give the book to her, but their paths seemed more divergent than ever, never crossing even in the hallways.

And now he was out of time.

His gaze was caught by the reason why he showed up to the dedication so early and he inclined his head in acknowledgment. Catalina Lochlainn smiled back and, after excusing herself, glided across the polished floor toward him. Hard to believe that in an alternate life, a life where Keith acknowledged he was Jamie's son when Declan reached out to Keith with his evidence, he might have had a relationship with her as his step-grandmother.

"Thank you for coming so early." Catalina's voice was husky, with a hint of her native Castilian accent. Declan knew from his research that she grew up in Madrid and spent several years working in advertising in the Spanish capital before meeting and marrying Keith.

"The invitation was irresistible," he said. "But then, you knew that. How is Keith? Has he settled in well at home after leaving the hospital?"

He kept his tone light and neutral. He'd learned not to expect much information from the Lochlainns. Even with accepting the challenge to program LNT Plus's launch week, he'd been given precious little insight into why Keith had chosen him for the assignment or to what end.

"He is recovering, but he won't be able to be here tonight."

"I hope he gets well soon," he said automatically, tamping the unexpected and unwanted disappointment down. "Anyway, I'm here as you asked. What can I do for you?"

Catalina looked around the space. "I was hoping preparations would be further along so you and I could have a good chat. Unfortunately, I still have much work do. So straight to the point, I want to persuade you to join me on the stage for the dedication in Keith's absence." Declan opened his mouth, but she cut him off with a quick shake of her head. "As someone who is following in Jamie's footsteps as a courageous journalist who fights for justice for those unable to fight. Jamie may be no longer with us, but you are carrying on his work."

Declan worked moisture back into his mouth. "I'm..." he searched for the right words to say. He settled on, "...flattered you would ask. But I don't know if that would be..." He searched again, "...appropriate, perhaps, is the best way to phrase it. It feels like a cheat. You and I know there is another connection. But Keith won't acknowledge it. Instead he plays his games, like his challenge at LNT, but only for a mention in his will." He hesitated. "Once upon a time, I would have jumped at the opportunity to be identified with the Lochlainn family. Even a connection as tenuous as the one you're offering. But I shouldn't need to remind you or Keith of Jamie. My existence should be enough. *I* should be enough."

"I know." Catalina tucked a lock of glossy black hair behind her ear. "You're right. And I am sorry. Keith is... Keith, and he has his reasons for acting the way he is, even though I have argued strenuously he is only hurting you and Anna—"

"Anna?" A hand squeezed his stomach, a most disorienting sensation. "Who is Anna?"

"Right. I've been so preoccupied with the dedication. I'm not thinking straight." Catalina inhaled, and then took his right hand in hers. "We discovered—well, Keith's investigator discovered—Jamie's sperm was used to conceive two children. You, and a daughter named Anna."

Declan blinked. That was the only muscle group

that seemed to be working. The rest of him was frozen, processing Catalina's words. "I have a half-sister," he said slowly. "And you and Keith knew."

Catalina moistened her lips. "Yes. But Keith didn't want either of you to feel as if you had to be in competition with each other. You understand, his father... Well, Archibald insisted on Keith earning his place at the Lochlainn Company, and with Jamie now officially gone, Keith is obsessed with passing on the company to an heir who has also earned it. So, he decided each of you would learn about the family business by being involved with an aspect of it that Jamie loved. Anna was sent to sell Lakes of Wonder, which was Jamie's favorite place growing up, and—"

"And I was sent to LNT. Because Jamie and I are both journalists."

She nodded. "I think Keith was hoping one of you, or both, would fall in love with the business you were sent to learn about. And then he would hand off the entirety of the Lochlainn Company to you or her."

Declan's head was shaking even before she finished speaking. "I'm leaving LNT. I'm announcing my resignation on Monday. And if Keith wanted to know my thoughts about inheriting the entire company, he knew where to find me." He filed away the information about his half-sister to examine for later. He had enough issues to deal with for one night.

"I understand. I told Keith not to do this, but..." She bit her lower lip, and then shrugged. "Back to the matters directly at hand. I still believe having you on stage with me would be meaningful. And appropriate. Keith may have chosen an art gallery to honor Jamie, but we know Jamie's heart laid in his reporting. And even without your connection to Jamie being public, you are still the highest regarded heir to his journalism legacy."

"I'll think about it." He wished Mara was there to discuss Catalina's offer. On the one hand, being part of an event honoring his biological father—and more important, his professional hero—would be meaningful. But on the other, learning Keith was willing to hand over the Lochlainn Company to him or Anna, yet there was still no talk of recognizing his blood tie to Jamie... That hurt. More than he thought would be logically possible.

He could go public about his Lochlainn DNA on his own, of course. Announce to the world he was Jamie's son. He had the paternity tests to prove it; Keith demanded them before Declan started work at LNT.

But he didn't need the world to acknowledge his connection to Jamie.

Just his grandfather.

Which wasn't happening.

Catalina touched him on the arm. "Thank you for considering my offer. I can ask for nothing more, I know." Someone called her name from behind Declan and she waved at them. "That is the head curator. I must go." She handed him her card. "This is my number. Please text me and let me know your decision. Even if the ceremony has already started."

"Wait," he called after her. "The Robaire you're

unveiling as part of the dedication—do you know its provenance?"

Her brow wrinkled. "It came from a collection of a very private Portuguese collector, which is why the painting hasn't been exhibited in public before. It was quite the coup to obtain the piece. I'm told the bidding was quite intense, but Keith was determined to win the artwork for Jamie's gallery. Why do you ask?"

He shrugged. "It's a previously unknown piece and I'm a big fan of the artist."

"That's another thing you have in common with Jamie. Robaire was his favorite artist. Well, after his mother, Diana, of course. I am so sorry she died before she could meet you." She patted his arm lightly. "Please let me know."

"I will." And then Catalina was off in a cloud of subtle perfume that smelled mostly of expense.

So, the Robaire was yet another piece that came from the very private collector. Mara's story definitely had legs.

The frenetic activity that marked his arrival began to die down as the museum staff and the event organizers took their stations and the hour of the event drew close. Declan wandered the space and stopped to look at the various artwork on the wall—including a painting by Diana Lochlainn, his biological grandmother. The canvas was a cacophony of bold, dark strokes interspersed with touches of almost brilliant light. The result was an abstract piece that was wild and passionate, the emotions leaping off the canvas. A placard next to the painting informed him that Diana has created it the year Jamie disappeared, just two years before she died.

He stared at the photo of Diana with a young Jamie, fixed on the wall above the placard. He was glad the public would see this painting for years to come. He would never meet Diana or Jamie, but he felt close to them in this space. And maybe that was enough. Maybe that's all he ever wanted from the Lochlainns—to know them.

He checked his smart watch. Mara should be arriving any minute. Catalina's offer had thrown him off his game. He still hadn't rehearsed what he needed to say to Mara.

How to say goodbye.

Mara ran up the steps of the museum. Thankfully, tonight called for business instead of cocktail attire, so her shoes were sensible flats and her purse remained slipper-free. And she could wear her own clothes instead of formal wear borrowed from Lavinia, which was great because she'd already worn the two dresses her sister-in-law had mailed her. But she still spent far too much time trying to decide what to wear. By the time she left her apartment—the car Declan sent for her idling at the curb far longer than was good for the environment—most of her closet's contents were on the floor as she had tried on and rejected outfit after outfit. She smoothed her hand over the dark gray wool of her trousers and straightened her blazer. The pantsuit she settled on was serviceable if a little drab and utilitarian. But she paired it with her favorite blouse, an emerald green silk that she knew complimented her eyes and made them seem the same rich color. And if the silk was a bit transparent—especially with a black lace bra underneath—well, then she would keep her jacket on. Unless she was alone with Declan.

Her stomach squeezed as butterflies of anticipation danced up and down her nervous system. This was the first time she would see him since their night. Since she realized how deeply she loved him.

Should she tell him? How would he react? What if he looked at her and she saw nothing but rejection? Or pity?

She didn't think she could survive being the object of his pity.

She squeezed her way through the guests, scarcely noticing the stunning architecture nor the artwork on the walls. Normally, being allowed to wander a museum after hours at will, with elegantly prepared hors d'oeuvres and first-class wine hers for the taking, would be her happy place, but she only had eyes for one person and he was nowhere to be found—

There. He was in the corner, by what looked like a Mark Rothko painting. Now her heart took over, pumping erratically. She kept moving, her legs somehow bearing her weight, her brain insisting her knees stay solid and not disgrace her in front of New York's elite. He still hadn't seen her, intent on his conversation, but surely any minute—

"Ms. Schuyler." Niels Hansen appeared her in path, causing her to stop abruptly. He filled her field of vision, cutting off her view of Declan. "So good to see you again."

"H-Hi," she stuttered. "Nice to run into you again I hope you and Freja received the flowers I sent to thank you both for a wonderful evening?"

"The arrangement was lovely, but not as lovely as your company." He bowed over her hand.

Her breath started to come more easily. "That is very kind of you to say. And more than I deserve, well, considering. Again, I am so sorry—"

He pressed her right hand between the two of his. "No, no. There's no need to be sorry. I am well aware you are not the one who owes me their apologies."

"I don't know if it's fair to blame Declan—"

"Blood will tell. It always has with him." Niels waved his hand as if he smelled something unpleasant. "But that is not the reason I wish to talk to you. You've made quite the impression on me, Mara." His silvery gray eyes stared into hers.

She'd been concerned that seeing Declan for the first time since they slept together would be awkward, but whatever she imagined was nothing compared to this moment. "Oh. Thank you. But, um, I *am* with Declan—" At least as far as Niels was concerned. And maybe beyond? She hoped. "So I can't—I mean—"

Too late, she realized the slight shaking of Niels's shoulders meant he was laughing. "No, no, my dear Mara. I mean your questions about my new acquisition. You gave me much food for thought. You see, I was so enticed by the thought of finally adding a Robaire to my collection that I perhaps overlooked concerns about the painting's provenance. I sent the canvas out for analysis. And the results were...not pleasant. Apparently, you were right to suspect the cobalt blue pigment. The chemical report shows that particular pigment came on the market after the period when Robaire was active."

"Oh!" She scrambled for her phone in her purse and held it up. "May I record our conversation? You don't have to go on record if you don't wish."

"I would rather you didn't. Not at the moment. I am speaking with my lawyers. You understand."

"Of course." Mara put her phone down, keeping her expression neutral. "But I hope you will feel comfortable discussing your findings with me in the future."

Niels smiled. "I have asked for more studies. This was only one and I want to be sure the findings were correct. But I must thank you, my dear. You may have saved me and my family millions of dollars."

"Happy to be of service. And if you want to repay me, you know what I'd most like." She waved her phone.

"I'll do you one better," he said. "If the additional tests conclusively prove the Robaire is a forgery, I will appear on camera for your story."

"That's great." She swallowed. Having someone like Niels Hansen—a socially prominent billionaire and internationally renowned art collector—be in her story would be a publicity coup. He rarely granted interviews, so people would tune in just to see him. "I would appreciate that."

"I am in your debt. This would be the least I can do." He bowed over her hand again. "Now, if you will excuse me, I see some acquaintances I must greet. Until later."

"Until then." Mara watched him go, doing her best to keep a tight lid on her emotions. She wanted to jump up and down with excitement, yell her joy to the streets…

Kiss Declan senseless in celebration.

He was where she had last seen him, but now he was alone. Apparently he witnessed her encounter, for he used his chin to indicate Niels's retreating back and then raised his eyebrows at her in question. She nodded back at him, her lips pressed tightly together, but she was sure he'd read the happiness in her gaze when a broad smile broke across his own face. He started to weave his way through the crowd toward her and she did the same, so that they met in the middle of the gallery space. "Hey," he said. He gave her a smile, a lopsided one she'd noticed he saved only for her.

"Hey," she said back. Her gaze drank him in since touching him the way she wanted to would be highly inappropriate in public. Her heart stung with how much she'd missed seeing him in person since last week.

"I purposefully kept my distance," he said. "Didn't think you wanted me around when speaking to Hansen."

"Wise. Since you seem to set Niels off just by breathing."

"It's my talent and my gift," he joked. "So? Seems like you had a productive conversation."

She gave him a brief recap. "I'm still trying to track down Skacel," she concluded. "But if I can get Niels to go on camera…it could be a very solid story."

"Well done."

She basked in his praise. "It is, isn't it? I wasn't sure this story could come together under the time pressure, but I might have a compelling piece for launch week."

"You might."

"Might?" She raised her eyebrows.

"That…decision won't be up to me."

"What do you mean? Of course it's up to you. You're programming the launch." She took a step back so she could search his gaze. What she found wasn't reassuring. She wrapped her arms around herself. "Are you afraid people will think I traded sexual favors for professional advancement?"

"The story is good and your work speaks for itself. You deserve to be included. However…" He ran his left hand through his hair. Because he was Declan, the resulting hair tousle made him appear even more sexy and delectable. "Now is not the time, but we need to talk."

Mara may not have had many serious relationships, but she was well versed enough in dating-speak for the words, "we need to talk" to sends rivers of ice through her veins. "Okay," she said slowly.

His eyes flashed. "Not like that." He reconsidered. "Well, not in that way."

Declan was flustered. And the only other time she'd seen him flustered, he had been apologizing to her. Maybe this wasn't the disaster she was anticipating. "Consider my curiosity piqued."

"Good." His gaze was fixed on a point over her shoulder, and she turned to see what or who had caught his attention. Catalina Lochlainn was looking at him, her elegant eyebrows raised in a question. Declan gave her a rueful smile and a nod, and then turned his attention back to Mara. "I need to go. I've been asked to be part of the dedication ceremony."

"You were? You never mentioned that to me. Not that you owe me a detailed account of your actions, you don't, but—"

"I would've told you. Catalina just asked me earlier this evening."

"She did? Why?"

He smirked at her. "Why not? Are you saying I'm not important enough? I am a journalist, like Jamie. And I do work for LNT."

She rolled her eyes. "Yes, I'm aware you are incredibly important, but when it comes to LNT, you work for a streaming service that hasn't launched yet." Mara glanced around the gallery. "Why not ask the president of LNT? He's by the bar. Or any number of Lochlainn Company executives? I think the entire board of directors is here."

He shrugged. "You'll have to ask Catalina why."

His eyes drifted up and to the left again. She seriously could not believe no one had told him about his tell. Or maybe no one else had gotten close enough to him to notice. The thought made her both warm with pleasure that he had let her in enough to notice and a little sad he apparently hadn't been close enough to anyone else in the last seven years who could have tipped him off. Like she was about to now. "You're doing that thing again, you know."

"What thing?"

"When you're not telling the entire truth. Your eyes slide, like this." She demonstrated.

He frowned. "They do not."

"Yes, they do. I first noticed when we were working on that project sophomore year—the one I had to step in and finish your work on because you were investigating the hack into the engineering school's IT system, but you wanted to keep your activities quiet because you hadn't identified the ringleader yet? You were so obviously leaving pertinent information out of your excuses. And your eyes slid." She demonstrated again.

She'd never seen him look so disgruntled. His grumpy expression caused her heart to squeeze.

That wasn't good. As Amaranth said, she knew she she could get over the overwhelming desire that threatened to capsize her equilibrium whenever he was near. She did before. But this deep-rooted fondness? Wanting to tease away his expression and make him laugh? This was new. And she feared it would be even more painful to weed out.

"I can't believe you never told me."

"Don't worry. Your secret is safe with me." She grinned at him, but her expression faded when he didn't return her smile. "Honest. I promise I won't squeal to your poker buddies."

"No, but we need to—damn it. I have to go. Catalina is signaling. Promise me you won't leave until we have a chance to talk."

She searched his gaze. "Okay. I wasn't planning on leaving immediately anyway. I'd love to talk to Catalina Lochlainn myself about the Robaire acquisition."

"She told me it's another piece from the, quote, private Portuguese collector."

"Oh, the Portuguese collector again. Quite the mystery person with the heretofore unknown treasure trove of art, yet not a single trace of this person can be found. Can you get me an interview with her?"

His expression relaxed. "I can ask."

On impulse, she leaned up to kiss his cheek. They had already cleared their relationship with HR, so she might as well take advantage of the corporate cover. "Break a leg up there."

She wasn't sure what she expected his response to be. Maybe a flirtatious grin, or a shrug to indicate he didn't need her good luck wishes or even perhaps a reciprocal kiss, a chaste one to reflect they were in public.

She did not expect him to cup her face with his hands, his fingers splayed warmly on her cheeks, as his gaze caught and held hers. "We'll talk. Right after this is over."

"I'll be here."

She watched him disappear into the crowd, admiring the way his trousers draped just so to show off his muscular thighs. Then she frowned. Interesting that Catalina Lochlainn had asked him to be up with her on the dais for the ceremony. Yet another inexplicable connection between him and the Lochlainns.

She couldn't shake off the foreboding feeling that the Lochlainn connection was one of the vital missing puzzle pieces of himself that Declan still withheld from her.

Eleven

The dedication ceremony came off flawlessly, despite the absence of Keith Lochlainn who, Mara was sure, had been the main draw for many of the guests. The crowd started to thin out soon after the short ceremony was concluded, people eager to enjoy what was left of their Saturday night.

Mara stayed at the gallery, waiting for Declan to finish making the rounds with Catalina to thank the donors and other guests who were still in attendance. She'd examined every piece on display, read every label tacked on the wall next to the artwork and was on her third tour of the space when she stopped in front of a painting by Diana Lochlainn.

She'd noticed the photograph placed on the wall next to the painting on an earlier round, of course.

The black and white picture depicted Diana Lochlainn in her artist studio, complete with an artist smock and a painter's palette in one hand. But what caught her attention this time was the young boy who leaned against Diana's legs. He was fair-haired and compact in size, his expression intent as he stood in front of his own, smaller easel and canvas. Jamie.

She'd seen photographs and videos of Jamie, of course. What journalism student hadn't? He'd been widely admired for his calm, authoritative yet highly engaging presence on camera as well as his ability to draw out fresh, new insights from even the most jaded interview subjects. Hardened criminals found themselves crying on Jamie's shoulder; heads of state admitted their innermost personal secrets to him.

But she'd seen the older Jamie. The one who had cut himself off from his father when Keith divorced Diana. The man who had weathered several life shocks. This was the first time she'd seen a photo of a young, unguarded Jamie.

And she knew his expression.

She'd seen it in her apartment—on Declan as he propped himself up on one elbow and used his other hand to trace the freckles on her shoulders and chest, making her laugh with how serious he took his task.

She shook her head. No. She had to be imagining things. The last thing she'd consumed was the smoothie with Amaranth. She was dehydrated and needed more water. And her nerves were stretched taut with wanting things she knew she could not want, like Declan.

So clearly, she was seeing him everywhere.

Although... On her way to the bar her gaze sought out Declan, who was standing next to Catalina across the room. Then she turned her head to look back at Diana's and Jamie's photograph, not watching where she was going.

She ran into something hard and solid.

"Oh!" she exclaimed, concentrating on keeping her feet untangled before looking up to offer an apology. But the words died on her lips when she saw who had caused her to almost stumble and fall. "Cam Brower? Is that you?"

"Hey, Mara!" Her former college roommate embraced her with his beefy arms.

"Good to see you! Are you still with the *Inquisitor*?"

He held up his camera with a long lens attached. "You know it."

"I can't believe I ran into you." She grinned at him. "Literally."

"I believe it. You're here with Dec, right? I saw you two talking earlier."

She glanced away, hoping the muted light in the gallery that allowed the paintings to be displayed to their best effect wouldn't also display how red her cheeks must appear. "I'm here for work."

"Work. Right." Cam winked at her. "I saw that photo from the Poets and Artists Ball."

"Photo? What photo?" No one told her a photo existed. There had been nothing in the media.

"The picture was blurry and you mostly saw Declan's back so we didn't run it, but I should've recognized that red hair. That kiss looked hot." Cam grinned. Mara rolled her eyes and opened her mouth to deny being the woman in the photo, but Cam cut her off. "Y'know, Dec said he was going to look you up when we spoke. Glad to see he did."

Look her up? What did that mean? "You spoke to him tonight?"

"Nah. We spoke in…" Cam looked up at the ceiling while he counted on his fingers. "Late September? I interviewed him for the *Inquisitor*."

"Wait, Declan agreed to be interviewed for the *Inquisitor*—never mind. Not important. What did he say about me?" Late September—that was before he showed up at her shoot in Roseville.

"Well, I wouldn't say he agreed. I ran into him at a coffee place and then I wrote down what he said after he left, but you have to grab the fish, right?"

Mara had forgotten talking to Cam was an exercise in going down several verbal rabbit holes that went nowhere fast. "Grab the fish?"

"Y'know…seize the carp."

"Carpe diem," she corrected. "Seize the day—again, not important. What did he say? Exact words. If you can."

Cam shrugged. "I don't recall exactly. We were talking about college and how the IJAW fellowship was the start of his career and I pointed out he stole it from you as it was really your story and then he said he would look you up."

She rubbed her temples. "You said what was my story?"

"The story that won him the fellowship? The campus gynecologist who was abusing female students? That was your story first. I saw your notes on your computer." Cam thumped his chest with his free fist. "I stick up for my friends. You're welcome, Mara."

"What?" She struggled to close her mouth. "No! You have it all wrong. Declan and I were both chasing that story. He scooped me by getting the confirming source on record before I did. I'll admit, it didn't feel good at the time, but he didn't steal anything."

Cam shrugged. "He seemed to feel differently. Anyway, glad to see you two have worked things out and you're together now—" His eyes lit up. "Hey, speaking of scoops, can I have this one? Y'know, you're the mystery woman in the photo? The one Declan Treharne is dating?"

"We're not dating." The last thing she needed was for…whatever was going on between her and Declan…to be splashed across the pages of a tabloid. "I told you. This is work."

"Uh huh. Sure." He winked at her again.

"Listen to me, Cam, and listen hard." She enunciated clearly. "I am not dating Declan and I never will. We were friendly rivals in college and now we're work colleagues. That's it. End of story."

Cam raised his hands as if in surrender. "Fine, if you say so." His gaze drifted over her shoulder. "Hey, Dec. Good to see you again."

Mara froze. "Declan is behind me," she said to Cam through numb lips.

"Yes. I am," Declan said. "Or rather, I was." He appeared at her side. "Good to see you, too, Cam."

Cam raised his camera and took a photo of Mara and Declan before Mara could react. "Got it in one," he said, examining the screen. "Thanks, you two. See you both around." He tipped two fingers to his brow in a salute and then took off.

"We're not—" But Mara's words fell into the empty air. Cam was gone. "We're not," she said helplessly to Declan. "I mean, at least as far as Cam is concerned, we're not. That's none of his business. And definitely not the *Inquisitor*'s business."

"Agreed," he said. "We're not."

Ouch. "Okay, yes, we aren't, but you don't have to agree so quickly," she said, trying to keep the hurt out of her voice.

"I'm agreeing that as far as Cam is concerned, we're not dating. As far as Niels Hansen is concerned, we are. I'm going to start requiring a scorecard, Schuyler." He grinned at her, but there was something missing. A spark of energy, perhaps. She took her first good long look at him since he'd joined her and her heart twinged at how exhausted he seemed.

"Must have been tiring, sitting on the dais," she tried to joke. "You look awful, Treharne."

"Thanks. Can't say the same. You continue to look amazing." He glanced around gallery. Only a few dozen people remained. "I suppose we should get out of here. Oh! Before I forget." He reached into his trouser pocket and pulled out a business card that he handed to her. "Here's Catalina Lochlainn's private cell phone. She's expecting your call about the Robaire."

"Private number? Wow. As always, you work miracles."

She threw her own glance around the gallery. Cam was gone. No one else was near. She cupped Declan's face with her hand and brought his lips down to hers. "Thank you," she whispered against his mouth. "I don't know how I would have gotten this far on this story without you. I'm so glad you asked me to come to LNT."

Then she kissed him. As always, the embers kindled whenever she was in his presence ignited instantaneously when their lips touched. Her bones dissolved and she melted into him, his arms gathering her close. But when she would deepen the kiss, he pulled back and their mouths disengaged. "Mara," he started, her name a warning.

"I know, I know, wait until we're not at a work event," she said. "Sorry. But I'm so happ—"

"Mara. I'm leaving LNT. I'm handing in my resignation on Monday."

She blinked at him. "I'm sorry. My ears must be playing tricks on me. I could swear you said you are resigning from LNT on Monday."

"Because that's what I said." He reached for her hands. She kept them by her sides, out of his reach.

"You are... I don't... Why? Before the launch? Before everything you... I...you worked for." She continued to blink. Maybe if she opened and closed her eyes enough times, she could reset the evening to before his pronouncement. But even if, by some feat of magical thinking, she managed to turn the clock back, she doubted she would ever be rid of the frost that invaded her heart and took hold.

Declan cleared his throat. "I have unfinished business elsewhere. As for LNT…" He shrugged, one-shouldered. "I accomplished what I set out to do."

He didn't intend to tell Mara here, in the museum gallery, with straggling guests passing by as they sought the exits. He planned to take her out for drinks.

Maybe even ask her to come back to his place. If she wanted. One last time, no misunderstandings muddying the next seven years and their eyes open.

Their hearts closed. As was necessary.

Mara was right. They weren't dating. She was pursuing a story and he made a convenient cover. And the sex was good, so no need for two consenting adults to deny themselves. Why not indulge?

That morning in her apartment would be seared on his soul forever, but that was his problem. Not hers.

Mara continued to stare at him, her green gaze searching his for uncomfortable minutes. "You're using weasel words," she said finally. "You're being vague. Talk to me. Why are you leaving LNT now?"

How could he stay, now that he knew what Keith wanted from him was something he couldn't fulfill? Didn't want to fulfill? He had no desire to run the Lochlainn Company.

Knowing that who he was would never be enough to earn Keith's approval and acknowledgement.

In some ways, the knowledge was like losing another parent all over again. Not exactly the same. Not as devastating. Not the howling, visceral pain that accompanied the loss of his mother.

But the conversation with Catalina had caused hope he didn't realize he carried—not much, and buried deep down in his subconscious—and that hope was gone now and he was forced to mourn its absence...

He did one thing right, however. He brought Mara to LNT and set her on the path that should have been hers all along. He took her unresisting hands in his. Her fingers were icy and he regretted, so much, being the cause. But she would thank him one day. He scratched the back of his neck. "I'm leaving for Paris on Monday. So, I'd like to—"

"Monday." She inhaled audibly. "Oh. That is soon."

"There's a story," he said. "An—"

"Important one," she finished for him. Her lips trembled into a semblance of a smile. "Always is, with you."

"A year ago, I was on the trail of Alice de la Vigny, who disappeared. But she's recently been spotted in France. She procures underage women for wealthy men. If I can finally get her to talk, to flip on the men she services—"

Mara's gaze softened. "That is important." She bit her lower lip. "But...the launch."

"The launch is in great shape. Brian, Mads, the

wellness and health series, the morning global politics roundtable—all the heavy lifting is done." He gave her a smile, but even he knew his expression must appear strained. "I'm superfluous."

She didn't return the smile. "And me?" she asked softly. "What about me? Us? Are we superfluous?"

His gaze traced the contours of her face. He knew he didn't need to memorize her features—he would no doubt see her gracing screens big and small for years to come—but this might be his last chance to be this close to her. To watch her green gaze widen and narrow with her thoughts, her eyes truly the window to her expressive soul. To breathe in her scent, warm and lightly floral and all Mara. To zero in on his favorite freckles—the constellations that frosted the apples of her cheeks whenever she smiled.

"You're going to be a star," he said. "I've spoken to the president of LNT. Not just streaming, but the entire operation. She's seen rough cuts of your work and is very impressed."

Mara didn't react. Her gaze continued to hold his.

"Did you hear what I said? You're on track to obtain everything we talked about in college. Everything that should have been yours after graduation."

"I heard," she said slowly. "I heard that you didn't answer my question. And I was doing fine before coming to LNT. I was happy at WRZT."

"I know, but—" he gestured at the art gallery around them, at the Robaire—or supposed Robaire—painting hanging in the place of honor "—

you could've been doing more. You are doing more. You deserve to do more."

"Covering local news is important—"

He scratched the back of his neck. "I didn't say it wasn't, just that I knew you had dreams to cover stories that mattered—"

"Local news matters. It matters a lot—"

"Of course it does. But I know you. We discussed many times what you dreamed of doing. And you never mentioned covering pumpkin pie contests." Why was she fighting him on this?

Declan was good at regulating his emotions. A childhood spent navigating the world with a single mother, who was also a skilled diplomat, taught him not to take offense at matters that were often cultural misunderstandings. And four years of boarding school with callous and cruel rich scions like Niels Hansen gave him much practice at keeping his cool and biding his time. But the last week—the hours with Mara in her apartment, planning his imminent trip to Paris to plunge back into the chase for Alice, his presence at a memorial to the man whose donated sperm gave him life, Catalina's kind insistence he sit on the dais with her but her firm regret that Keith had no interest in meeting him—had chipped away at his equilibrium until he was grasping at tatters.

"Then why—"

"Because I know you, Mara. You were the one who first uncovered the gynecologist scandal at the university. You were the one who found Jane Doe and spoke to her about going on record. That story changed the school. Laws were passed to ensure young women wouldn't be put in such vulnerable positions across the country. That's what kind of journalist you are. Those are the stories you should be covering—"

She was shaking her head so hard, her red locks bounced off her shoulders. "I didn't do that. You did that. That was your story. You scooped me, fair and square. I know it's been several years, but—"

"I got an anonymous tip about the gynecologist. I always thought the tip had been left by one of the victims. But now… I think I know who gave it to me." She couldn't hold his gaze. He may have a tell, but her entire expression gave her away. "You should have won the fellowship. Not me."

She tried to laugh off his suggestion. "Is this because Cam said something to you? I know you two had coffee a few weeks before you showed up in Roseville—" Then the color drained from her face. "Wait. Is this why you tracked me down and asked me to come to LNT? Because Cam Brower, of all people, said you stole from me?"

"He didn't say 'stole' in so many words—"

"Listen to me, Declan." She took a deep breath. "Yes, Jane Doe was my source first. Yes, I did a lot of the research that the 'anonymous tip'—" she made quotes in the air with her fingers "—left for you. But I couldn't complete the story. Some of the women he hurt were my friends. And so I chose to be their confidante, to hold their confessions private. The story wasn't mine—it was theirs. Bringing the gynecologist's abuse to light required another writer, someone who could be objective and detached. And I was happy when your story came out. I cheered when it led to his dismissal and charges were brought against him."

"You didn't congratulate me—y'know what, never mind, it's a petty grudge to hold on to."

"You had just broken up with me! I wasn't exactly in a congratulatory mood."

"I thought…it doesn't matter."

"Did I want the fellowship? Did the story I submit pale in comparison to bringing down a predatory abuser in a position of trust at the university? Yes." She stepped closer to him. "But the story was yours." She poked him in the chest with her right index finger. "You wrote it." She poked him again. "You won. But me?" She poked herself in the chest. "Apparently, I have to be given opportunities out of pity, not because I earned them."

What the…? "You can't seriously think I brought you to LNT because I felt bad for you."

"Not any less than I think last weekend was a pity fuck." Her gaze widened. "Oh, God. It was, wasn't it? I mean, I propositioned you. At least you seemed to enjoy it, like last time. But now you're leaving. Like last time."

He grasped her shoulders. She stilled at his touch. "My leaving has nothing to do with you. Nothing. You would be the only reason I would stay."

Her chest rose and fell several times, and then she relaxed in his grip. "So why don't you? Stay, I mean."

He let his hands fall. "I told you. Alice. I can get her to talk."

"And no one else can? You're the only one who can report the story, or you don't want anyone else to get the story?" Her gaze sharpened. "Why did you come to LNT, if chasing Alice was so important?"

"I told you. She disappeared."

"If there's one thing you excel at, it's perseverance. Why do you think I tipped you off about the gynecologist? Because I knew you wouldn't let the university administration or donors hoping to head off bad publicity stop you."

He'd forgotten this about Mara: the way she could peel him like an onion, remove his protective layers. He did his best to keep them in place. "She was thought to be dead. And I was offered the LNT position."

"Right. LNT." Her gaze slid to a point over his shoulder. When he followed her gaze, he discovered she was looking at the painting by Diana Lochlainn. He frowned. "You never did tell me why LNT hired you."

"Pretty sure I did."

She shook her head. "No. You always managed to evade giving me a straight answer. Care to give me one now?"

He wanted to. He could tell Mara the entire story: How his mother wanted a child and decided to use an anonymous sperm donor. How he put two and two together and came up with Jamie Lochlainn as that sperm donor.

How Keith Lochlainn rejected him. And now, was using LNT for some sort of esoteric test of familial worthiness that Declan knew he was failing.

He opened his mouth. "Come with me. To Paris. Work on the story with me."

He wasn't sure where the invitation came from. He wasn't embarking on a sightseeing trip. He would be going into an unknown situation—he was certain that Alice wasn't dangerous, but she associated with people who had no qualms making problems disappear, and journalists fell into that category—and he didn't know how long he would need to stay in Paris. And if Alice decided to bolt, like she did last time, he would need to follow her.

But he couldn't leave things with Mara like this. Not with this artificial mask covering her features, with hurt that was still visible beneath. Not with her believing he only brought her to LNT to assuage his conscience. Yes, he might have driven to Roseville because he wanted to make things right, but as soon as he saw her…

As soon as he saw her, he realized how much he once cared for her. And still did. Would always.

He would make the situation right. He just needed time. "I can get you a ticket, arrange for time off—"

She looked at him with sorrow in her gaze. Sorrow for him, he realized. "I can't go to Paris. You know that."

"I know. You're in the middle of the art forgery story. But when you're done—"

She was shaking her head before he could finish.

"I can't go because you break my heart. You don't mean to, but you do." For the first time that evening, moisture shimmered in her gaze. "That morning in my apartment... If there's a piece of me you want, it's already yours. But it destroys me, knowing that you won't give me even a little piece of you." She leaned up and kissed him on the cheek. "Go save the world, superhero. Find Alice and stop the trafficking."

His world was slipping away from him. He tried to gather and hold what he could, but it was like trying to keep a sandcastle intact at high tides. "I'll call you."

She smiled sadly. "Don't make promises you can't keep, Treharne." Then she was gone.

Declan stayed in the gallery until the security personnel kicked him out. Going to Paris was the right decision. There was nothing for him at the Lochlainn Company, just the machinations of an old man who wanted an heir, but only on his own terms. While lives would be saved if Alice told the world what she knew.

Then why did he feel as if his own world stopped spinning once Mara left?

Twelve

Two months later

LNT Plus was a bustling hive of activity. For once, the floors that contained its studios and offices weren't considered the hinterlands of the Lochlainn Company's empire. They were, instead, the epicenter of the multinational media conglomerate's universe. Rumor had it that there was more at stake than bragging rights to having the most popular streaming service in the cutthroat world of broadcast news; the whispers were that Keith Lochlainn himself had some sort of personal stake in the venture's success or failure and that the future of the entire company was somehow riding on how well LNT Plus performed.

Mara sat in a chair in the hair and makeup room,

with one ear listening as the people dusting her face with powder and smoothing her hair so that no errant curl would appear on camera gossiped about her coworkers and the avalanche of positive press that had descended upon them once the opening lineup of stories for the launch had been announced. As she predicted, Mara did indeed land a prominent spot on the lineup. The head of LNT herself had personally congratulated her on the art forgery story and for bringing "culture, intrigue and wealthy people getting ripped off—the trifecta of attracting a broad viewership" to the service. In fact, she was so pleased with the story, she gave Mara a live segment for a follow-up interview with Niels Hansen, who had finally agreed to speak on camera about his counterfeit Robaire painting.

Her other ear was attuned to her phone. Niels was expected at the studio any moment, and security promised to call her as soon as his car pulled up to the building. She twisted her hands in her lap. Not that she was nervous—she had plenty of experience appearing live on camera, and she was relishing the adrenaline of knowing there were no second takes and she only had one opportunity to nail her interview—but for the first time since that evening at the gallery, she had space and time available for her mind to wander. She'd kept herself occupied nearly around the clock since his departure, nailing down the specifics, filling any holes and polishing her script and her delivery until they couldn't be perfected further. She'd worked on three more stories that were in contention for future slots. Her office was far more familiar to her than her apartment, and she hadn't joined Amaranth's boxing classes in forever. She hoped her friend would take pity on her whenever they got into the ring next, because Mara doubted she could throw a decent jab currently.

She'd been the first to raise her hand for a new assignment and the last to ask for time off, and while she told herself she was working her butt off to prove all the naysayers and gossip peddlers wrong about her, to demonstrate that she was at LNT Plus due to her own merits, she knew the real reason.

The more things she gave her brain to work on, the less she would obsess over Declan. Who did call her when he reached Paris, but had been radio silent the last few weeks. Not that she was counting the days. And not that his current silence wasn't to be expected. She knew his pursuit of Alice was at a critical juncture, and he had far more important things to do than to check in with her. Still…

"Any word?"

Mara startled. She caught the eye of Jack, the makeup artist, in the mirror. "I'm sorry?"

Jack nodded at the phone clutched in Mara's hand. "From your guest. We're ready for him." He dabbed at Mara's forehead, and then stepped back with a smile. "You're done."

Mara slipped from the chair. "Thank you. All looks great, as usual. And no. We're still waiting."

A production assistant bustled into the room. "Turn on the television." She pointed to the set in the corner, which was currently showing a Mexican telenovela. Everyone was addicted to the daily dose of drama, including Mara.

Jack frowned. "But we're waiting to see if Gabriel will recognize Yolanda after her makeover."

The production assistant grabbed the remote and changed the channel to NCN, LNT's main rival. Mara raised an eyebrow but leaned over the counter to examine a lock of hair that would not lie flat despite the best efforts of the hair stylist.

"—hanks for joining us on News Channel Network," said the host of NCN's morning show in her soothing, low tones.

"Thank you for having me," said a voice Mara knew well. She straightened, her hair forgotten, and joined the others in the makeup room, staring at the television.

Niels Hansen was on the screen. He didn't have a gleaming blond hair out of place, Mara noted. He sat in a chair across from the NCN host, his suit perfectly tailored, the perfect picture of sophistication and elegance.

"Isn't he supposed to be here?" Jack stage-whispered to Mara. "Do you think he got the networks mixed up?"

"Not funny," Mara said back, not bothering to keep her voice low.

On screen, Niels addressed the camera. "It has come to my attention that there has been a concerted effort to discredit several major new art discoveries by claiming they are forgeries. This group is even targeting me and my sister, casting aspersions on our reputation as art collectors. I am convinced this is an attack on our honor by those who wish to do irreparable harm to the international art community—"

"But to what end?" asked the NCN host. "Who would derive benefit from such a campaign? What reasons do they have?"

Niels leaned forward, the perfect picture of wounded innocence. "There are many reasons for such a nefarious scheme. To cause confusion in the market and to artificially manipulate art prices being main among them. An original Robaire painting is worth millions. But if its authenticity is questioned, then the price would plunge, leaving the owner with an investment that is worth less than the picture frame that contains it."

"Some of those frames are rather costly," said the host with a small laugh.

Niels did not appreciate her attempt at a joke. "This isn't a laughing matter. This is a blatant attempt by a small group to financially destroy their rivals."

The host frowned. "That is quite the accusation. Do you know who this group is?"

Niels smiled. It wasn't a very pleasant one. "Ask yourself who commissioned the story and whose company provides the platform to spread it, and you have your answer."

The makeup room erupted into loud buzzing. "Okay," Mara said. "We've seen enough. Turn off the channel." Her own pocket started to vibrate and she pulled out her phone. The caller was exactly who she expected to be calling her. "Yes, ma'am," she answered. "I'll come to the set right away."

Mara kept her head down as she made calls and then entered notes on her phone, her muscle memory allowing her to navigate the hallway to where it opened into the studio—a large, cavernous space that was split into realms: the dark shadows where the production crew lived, gathered around the playback monitors known as video village, and the well-lit set decorated in bright blue and metallic gold, the signature colors of the parent network LNT. Two modern easy chairs in shades of burnt orange were set up facing each other, while the tall backdrop was a high-definition video screen that would change scenes as Mara and her guest spoke.

"Hi. I know that sounded like a hit piece on the Lochlainn Company. And obviously, Hansen won't be joining us for the live segment, but I have—"

"Mara. It's good to see you."

Her gaze jerked up. That voice didn't sound like her producer. That voice sounded like…

Declan.

Oh, he looks good, her heart whispered. His hair was longer, shaggy even, and in desperate need of a haircut. His skin was tanned and his dark blond hair sported the kind of highlights that only came from exposure to the sun. He hadn't shaved in at least a week, judging by the growth of his beard, and while his eyes drooped at the corners, indicating exhaustion, his smile was brighter than ever before.

She wanted to hug him and kiss him hello—okay,

kiss him into oblivion for being there and in one piece and no longer the bane of her worry if she were being honest—but the set was bustling with people, from crew members to several LNT executives she rarely saw outside their offices.

"Hey, Declan. You look tired. Did you just get in?" She didn't know what else to say. What she wanted to say would probably get her fired, if that wasn't already the purpose of the executives descending on the set.

"You look amazing. As always." He grinned at her.

"Yes, yes, we all look great." Nan Greenwald, the president of LNT, approached them, several of her lieutenants by her side. Mara swallowed. She'd only met Nan once, and that had been a brief handshake at the launch party. Declan came to stand beside Mara, his nearness as comforting as it was distracting. What was he doing here?

"Is everything set?" Nan continued. She turned to the director. "I want everything perfect, understand?"

"Perfect for what?" Mara asked.

"For the live interview." Nan looked at Mara as if she had grown a second head.

"Right," Mara said slowly. "Well, I do have a backup ready." She checked her phone. "He'll be here in five minutes—"

Nan shot Mara another puzzled stare. "He's already here."

"What?"

Declan cleared his throat. "Hi."

Mara whirled to face him. "I'm not interviewing you."

"You can't have dead air. Niels isn't coming—"

"Obviously—"

"And you need a story big enough to distract from his accusations. So, here I am."

Mara started to laugh. "Look, superhero, I appreciate you swooping in out of the blue to save the day, yet again—and how did you know Niels would pull this stunt, anyway?—but I've got it under control."

"The interview has been promoted for weeks. As soon as I heard Niels was your guest, I knew you needed a backup—"

"But you didn't bother to tell me—

"Because I wasn't sure if I would be able to pull this off." He shrugged, his grin slightly sheepish. Damn it, the expression made him seem even more appealing. Now that she had had some time to adjust to the fact that he was there, next to her, in person, her heart decided to react by beating in triple time.

"Pull what off? Flying in from Paris?"

"He means me," said a gruff male voice from the shadows on the edges of the studio. And then Keith Lochlainn came into view, leaning heavily on a cane.

Mara had never met the legendary mogul, but she had seen plenty of photos and watched many a video. Now the presence of Nan on the set made sense. "Is it weird I have an impulse to curtsy?" she whispered to Declan.

"I heard that," Keith said. "Go right ahead." Then he turned to Declan. "Redhead. Nice."

"She's more than nice. She's good," Declan said. "Ready to be miked up?"

"Time out." Mara made a "T" sign with her hands. "What the hell is going on?"

"I'm going to give you the scoop of the century. I'm—"

"A Lochlainn," Mara said. "I figured it out the night of the gallery dedication. And having Mr. Lochlainn here—" she bobbed, if not a curtsy, then a short bow "—confirms it." She glanced at her phone. There was still thirty minutes to go before she was supposed to go on air. She pointed at Declan. "You. Me. Private conversation. Now." She looked at Keith and Nan. "If you two will excuse us."

Keith shrugged while Nan waved them off. Mara left the set, pulling Declan down the hallway to her small dressing room. She waited until the door was firmly shut behind them before turning on him. "What the hell, Declan!"

"Hello to you, too, Mara."

"What do you think you're doing?" A new thought hit her. "And what about the Alice story? How could you leave that? Now?"

"Griff Beachwood has secured Alice's cooperation. His story should run in the *Globe*'s next Sunday magazine."

"Griff— But that's your story! You've worked so hard—"

Declan closed half the distance between them. She swallowed her words, her synapses, as always, scrambled by his nearness. She had missed him so much. Her gaze traced his face, his broad shoulders, his narrow hips and powerful thighs. How could one human look so amazing? She licked her lips, hoping to work moisture back into her mouth.

"And Griff will do an excellent job with it. I realized, sitting in the South of France—"

"Oh, poor baby," Mara tried to joke, hoping to leaven the tension that always sprung to life whenever they were alone together, her nipples already contracting to points of need. "What a terrible assignment…" Her words trailed off as he closed the distance again. Now he was within easy reach. All she had do was lift her hand and she could reassure herself he really was there, with her, and not just a very realistic waking dream.

"As I was saying," he said, and then his hand did touch her, his fingers finding hers and squeezing, "I was sitting at a café, alone, discussing with Bobbi which stories to submit for consideration for various prizes, when I realized—the only person whose opinion really mattered was you. Always has been."

"Me?" There must be something wrong with the ventilation system in her dressing room. She could scarcely breathe. "Always? But that week in college… and then you walked away…"

"I don't know if you remember, but I did a story on Jamie Lochlainn for the alumni magazine. After talking to some of his buddies, and putting a few hunches together, I was pretty sure Jamie Lochlainn was the anonymous donor my mother used to conceive me.

That week coincided with Keith telling me to get lost when I brought him my evidence."

"Oh, Declan. I'm so sorry." She reached for his other hand with her free one and brought the distance between them to scant inches.

"I was hurt. Ashamed. The fellowship promised a way to prove myself worthy to him. I took it and never looked back. I didn't want to look back. Can you forgive me for walking out on the best thing that ever happened to me? Because it's you, Mara. Always has been. Always will be."

It wasn't possible for birds to be singing in her windowless dressing room. But she heard them. She smelled roses, too. And felt fresh summer breezes. Or maybe that was Declan, bringing the joy and hopefulness of a bright spring day with him. "You were forgiven the first minute you showed up in Roseville." She dropped his hands, but only so she could entwine her arms around his neck. "Thank you for telling me about Jamie. Are you and Keith reconciled now?"

He rested his forehead against hers. "I've spent my adult life chasing Keith's approval. It wasn't until I refused to jump through his hoops and told him he was going to acknowledge me as Jamie's son, live on air, that I earned a modicum of respect."

"You confronted Keith for me?" She pulled back enough so she could catch and hold Declan's gaze. "Thank you."

"I love you," he said simply. "I offer you one psyche, a bit battered and bruised, but all yours. If you want it."

The entirety of the sun filled her heart, hot and glowing and all encompassing. "I'll always want you. All of you. Then, now, forever. I love you so much."

But when Declan would kiss her, she pulled back, regret making her eyes wide as she pulled out her buzzing phone. "I have to be on the set in ten minutes."

"Right. That means I do, too."

She shook her head. "Actually, no, you don't. Because my backup guest is ready to go." She turned her phone around so Declan could see the messages on her phone.

"Skacel? You found Alan Skacel?"

"Found him, and he's more than willing to go on record that the forgery ring was being run by Niels. We thought he might pull something like this, to not only throw suspicion off himself but to also target you. Alan was waiting at a coffee shop around the corner in case I needed him as a special guest when Niels was scheduled to be my guest. Now he will spill all the details and then it will be up to the authorities."

Declan was shaking his head. "You're very sexy when you talk about nailing a story. Did you know that?"

She looked at her phone again. "Seven minutes until I need to go live. So that gives you five minutes to show me how sexy I am."

"How about the rest of our lives?" he said against her lips.

"Challenge accepted," she replied, and she kissed him.

Epilogue

One year later

Keith Lochlainn was dying.

But not today. And not this year.

Not for the foreseeable future, in fact.

He read the medical report for the fourteenth time that day. During his recent sojourn in the hospital, a doctor that was new to Keith's care reexamined his charts and ordered a new battery of tests. It turned out that what his old—and now fired—doctor thought had signaled the beginning of the end for Keith's life was something the new—and now hired—personal physician had developed a procedure to fix. Keith wasn't clear on the details, but he didn't need to be. All that mattered was that he felt better than he had in the last seven years—ever since Jamie died.

And while he gave his new doctor full credit for his clean medical bill of health, Keith suspected the true cause of his renewed good health was sitting around the Thanksgiving table with him.

To his left sat his granddaughter Anna, beautiful and golden-haired. She was laughing at something her husband, Ian, said, her smile as wide and as open as her heart. Of course, Keith still couldn't believe he was now related to a Blackburn, after decades of trying to squash the upstart rival family. He even believed he had been on the opposite side of the table from young Ian himself, and of course came out the winner. He always did.

Still, Ian appeared to make Anna very happy, even if Anna decided to forego her Lochlainn inheritance in order to run the Lakes of Wonder theme park with her husband. Keith couldn't be too angry that Anna had eschewed his offer to be a key part of the Lochlainn Company, however. Lakes of Wonder had been very special to Jamie—so special, that Keith could barely stand to hear the park's name mentioned once Jamie cut himself off from Keith. So having Anna run the theme park—with photographs of Jamie decorating not only the executive board rooms but also the private apartment in Lakes of Wonder's iconic Lighthouse, which was now available for very special guests such as children suffering from chronic illnesses to stay in—felt…right…to Keith.

Seated on the other side of Ian was Mara, Keith's newest grandchild-in-law. She and Declan were in New York City as a pit stop between covering the meeting of the G6 in Europe to observing what promised to be a contentious election in South Asia. Mara's sharp wit and ability to keep Declan and all of them, for that matter, on their toes was appreciated by Keith. He'd always had a weakness for redheads, anyway.

And there was Declan. Keith didn't do regrets. If he did, he wouldn't be able to get out of bed in the morning with the thought of the years he lost with Jamie. *You always think you have time to reconcile, to explain, to make up for things said and done*, Keith thought, *until you don't.* If he dwelled on everything he lost when Jamie died, the gulf between still death, Keith would be catatonic. So he kept moving and never looked back.

But if he did do regrets…then, next to Jamie, his treatment of Declan would be up there. He supposed Declan reminded him too much of his lost son—from his dark blond hair to his choice of profession—and so even though he knew Declan was in the right about Jamie being his birth father all those years ago, he pushed him away. Slammed the door right in that face with the determined expression that was a carbon copy of Jamie's and wiped the encounter out of his heart.

Keith was too late to be a father—a real father—to Jamie.

But he finally learned it wasn't too late to be a grandfather to Declan and Anna.

Even if neither of his grandchildren wanted anything to do with his pride and joy, the Lochlainn

Company. The future of his company after he was gone still rested heavily on Keith's shoulders.

"Everything alright?" asked Catalina. "Here. Chef made this special for you." She placed a plate of plain white turkey and steamed brussels sprouts in front of him. Everyone else around the table dug into plates piled high with mashed potatoes swimming in butter, brussels sprouts roasted with bacon and turkey with all the trimmings, from cranberry orange relish to decadent stuffing.

"Bah," Keith said, pushing a sprout around with his fork. Then he looked over at Catalina and gave her a smile. A rusty one, no doubt, but sincere. "Never better."

Catalina arched an eyebrow and picked up her fork. "Good to hear. I have to admit, family dinners are more congenial since you stopped badgering Anna and Declan about joining you at the Lochlainn Company."

"They don't want to be involved. I respect that."

Catalina blinked at him, then smiled. "That's very mature of you, Keith. Good on you."

"Bah," he said again, but there was no heat in it. Even he had to admit it was nice to have peace at the dinner table.

He took a bite of turkey. It wasn't half bad. The bird was juicy and flavorful. He didn't miss the stuffing after all. If eating like his doctors ordered would help him live another twenty or thirty years, then this was how he would eat.

After all, if he wasn't mistaken, Anna was pregnant. She refused wine with dinner and she and Ian kept sneaking glances at each other as if they had a secret they were bursting to tell but couldn't just yet. Mara was drinking champagne like there was no tomorrow—she might as well drink his good stuff since he wasn't able to—but Keith was confident in his ability to talk her into giving him great-grandchildren, too.

Before long, there would be new heirs to the Lochlainn dynasty. And he knew just the way to determine which heir should inherit his empire.

* * * * *

MATCHED BY MISTAKE & THE RANCHER MEETS HIS MATCH

MATCHED BY MISTAKE
Texas Cattleman's Club: Diamonds & Dating Apps
by Katherine Garbera

A very public dating app snafu has matched Jericho Winters with Maggie Del Rio! The high-profile rivals agree to a date to keep the PR positive. But when fake kisses lead to real desire, they must choose between burying the family feud...or destroying each other for good.

THE RANCHER MEETS HIS MATCH
Texas Cattleman's Club: Diamonds & Dating Apps
by J. Margot Critch

How in hell did Misha Law's dating app match Trey Winters's brother with a family rival? The alpha tech entrepreneur demands answers and—after one look at the beautiful programmer—so much more...

FROM HIGHRISE TO HIGH COUNTRY & BAD BOY GONE GOOD

FROM HIGHRISE TO HIGH COUNTRY
High Country Hawkes • by Barbara Dunlop

Professor Ruby Monaco would never compromise her academic integrity. But her intense attraction to wealthy rancher Austin Hawkes means they're *both* playing with fire. Can she succeed at her job assignment without exposing the Hawkes family secrets?

BAD BOY GONE GOOD
Hartmann Heirs • by Katie Frey

Bad boy August Quaid is determined to rebuild his future in Montana and become worthy of his best friend's little sister. But when the Hartmann family insists on a different match for "little" Evie, everything goes up in flames!

JUST A FEW FAKE KISSES... & THE TRUE LOVE EXPERIMENT

JUST A FEW FAKE KISSES...
Hana Trio • by Jayci Lee

Virtuoso violinist Anthony Larsen needs a scandal fix—pronto. Entering into a fake relationship with the alluring Chloe Han might save his image, but she is *much* too tempting for his sanity. Too bad resisting the fiery attraction between them is virtually impossible!

THE TRUE LOVE EXPERIMENT
by Anne Marsh

Billionaire scientist Nash Masterson has the perfect proposal for his best friend, Wren Wilson. He'll be her fake date to her ex-boyfriend's wedding if she buys him at an upcoming bachelor auction. It's a no-stress win-win...until a heated kiss disrupts their platonic friendship and upends everything.

You can find more information on upcoming Harlequin titles, free excerpts and more at Harlequin.com.

HARLEQUIN
PLUS

Try the best multimedia subscription service for romance readers like you!

Read, Watch and Play.

Experience the easiest way to get the romance content you crave.

Start your **FREE TRIAL** at
<u>www.harlequinplus.com/freetrial</u>.